"McKenna opens her Desert Dogs series on the perfect note, presenting readers with a story that is sizzling, intelligent, and completely absorbing . . . and her well-executed badlands setting reflects her biker gang perfectly: gritty, rugged, dangerous, but noble and utterly captivating. . . . Without a doubt, this is a series to watch."　　　　　　　　—*Romantic Times* (4½ stars)

"McKenna ratchets up sexual chemistry and danger in equal measure, and tension stays high to the end. Readers will eagerly turn pages to learn the outcome of both the mystery and the romance."　　　　　　　　—*Publishers Weekly*

"Like a smooth shot of whiskey after a dry desert ride, *Lay It Down* quenched my thirst for wicked-hot romance. Cara McKenna knows how to write sexy-as-hell bad boys."
　　　　—*New York Times* bestselling author Jaci Burton

Hard Time

"A lovely, heartfelt romance. . . . The letters, the sweetness, the tender eroticism made this book a recommended read for me."
　　　　　　　　—Dear Author (recommended read)

"McKenna has crafted an intense, at times dark, heated romance."　　　　　　　　—*RT Book Reviews* (4½ stars)

"It's different and sexy, and I love that Cara McKenna explores protagonists that . . . have more real, grittier lives."
　　　　　　　　—Smexy Books

"*Hard Time* has gripping, emotional sections paired with some serious sexy times. . . . Fans of McKenna will be happy with her latest offering."　　　　　　　　—Fiction Vixen

continued . . .

ALSO BY CARA McKENNA

The Desert Dogs Series
Lay It Down

Other Novels
Hard Time
Unbound
After Hours

GIVE IT ALL

A DESERT DOGS NOVEL

Cara McKenna

A SIGNET ECLIPSE BOOK

SIGNET ECLIPSE
Published by the Penguin Group
Penguin Group (USA) LLC, 375 Hudson Street,
New York, New York 10014

USA | Canada | UK | Ireland |Australia | New Zealand | India | South Africa | China
penguin.com
A Penguin Random House Company

First published by Signet Eclipse, an imprint of New American Library,
a division of Penguin Group (USA) LLC

First Printing, February 2015

Copyright © Cara McKenna, 2015

SIGNET ECLIPSE and logo are trademarks of Penguin Group (USA) LLC.

ISBN 978-0-451-47127-7

Printed in the United States of America
10 9 8 7 6 5 4 3 2 1

Biggest thanks to my editor, Christina, who worked as hard on this book as I did. And to Claire, who gave it the final polish. And with love to Tamsen, and to my agent, Laura, and to the readers who waited so patiently for Duncan's dismantling. Enjoy.

Chapter 1

Agent Ramon Flores eyed his suspect through the glass.

An average sort of man. Average height, a touch heavy, mouse-brown hair in need of a cut. His clothes were filthy, but that came as no surprise. He was sunburned to boot, scalp flaking where his hair was thinning, and the past weeks he'd spent as a fugitive had aged him—he looked sixty, not the forty-seven Flores knew him to be.

And Flores knew a lot about David Peter Levins. He'd memorized the man's file in the month since he was assigned to finding the guy. Levins had a wife and two grown sons in Mesquite, and twenty-four years' experience in construction. He'd been a foreman for a big commercial operation—Virgin River Contracting. And it seemed he'd thrown it all away in a fit of greed.

"He's ready to spill," said Dan Jaskowski, Flores's colleague. "Some of these guys just aren't built for the fugitive lifestyle."

"He cracked enough to turn himself in," Flores said. "No doubt he's got some interesting shit knocking on the backs of his teeth, just dying to get let out."

"Like whether he and Tremblay acted alone."

Flores nodded. "And whether he had anything to do with Tremblay getting offed in the county jail."

"Whole town's gonna be curious to hear some answers, once his surrender makes the news," Jaskowski said.

"I'm curious myself." Flores grabbed his recorder and his fat file labeled LEVINS, DAVID P. and headed for the door. *Let him fold.* Let him break, and let Flores get back home to Spring Valley in time for his daughter's sixth birthday party in two weeks. Combination pony and mermaid theme. Highly anticipated.

Levins was stooped in his hard plastic seat before the metal table, wilted by exhaustion, but he sat up straight at the click of the lock. Flores closed them in together, in this little cube of cinder block intimacy.

"David," he said, and sat. He switched the recorder on. "I'm Agent Flores. Everybody's been looking for you, son." He tacked the diminutive on just to keep the guy on edge. No matter that Levins was eight years his senior. "Me especially. Can't figure out if I'm disappointed I didn't catch you myself, or relieved you finally decided to give us all some closure. You ready to talk?"

"Do I get my sentence lessened? Because I turned myself in?"

"That all depends on what comes next," Flores said. "On how cooperative you decide to be. Because three people are dead. A fine deputy—Alex Dunn—and your accomplice, Chuck Tremblay. And this mysterious body we've heard about but not actually been able to get our hands on."

"Tremblay handled the bones. I got no idea what he did with 'em."

"How convenient for you. And how about Tremblay's bones? You got anything to do with his unfortunate end?"

Levins shook his head violently. "No, no way. I was in Texas when I heard. But I know who did it—his creditors."

"Creditors?"

"He had gambling debts. Huge ones—a hundred grand, at least. I dunno who with, but some real rough characters. Mob types down in Vegas, if I had to guess."

Flores hid his surprise. He'd heard nothing about that, though it had a ring of truth to it. Tremblay had been an alcoholic—fifteen years sober, but one self-destructive compulsion often got swapped for another. He made a casual note, one that would prompt an intense investigation and probably ruin somebody's weekend.

"That's why he needed my bribes," Levins continued.

"Bribes in exchange for what?"

"For overlooking some corners I had to cut, with the work."

"Now, why would you be cutting corners, David?"

"'Cause all the foremen get big bonuses for hitting these crazy deadlines that the Virgin River bosses laid out for us. Shit they promised the casino developers to score the contract in the first place. Only way I could've hit those was to cut corners. And I couldn't cut corners unless I had somebody in the department willing to rush and fudge my permits."

"Why'd you approach Tremblay? Seems awful ambitious, going straight to the sheriff of Brush County."

"I didn't—Tremblay approached *me*. I was sweating over this blasting permit I needed, like, yesterday. They sent Dunn over, but no way was he signing anything without going through every goddamn check box. So I went straight to Tremblay. I was desperate, and I kind of knew him from other issues with the construction. I knew he was really pro-casino, and thought maybe he'd respect my worries about the deadlines. He told me, if he helped me out, would I maybe help him out? Slip him a percentage of my bonus? As a 'show of appreciation,' I think he called it."

"And you said yes."

Levins nodded, looking . . . sad. "I did. I had to."

"Had to?"

The man shrugged. "Looking back, it sounds so trivial . . . But I got two kids, one in college and one about to start. My wife's out of work. I needed the money. It was harmless shortcuts I was trying to take, just red-tape, bureaucratic shit. Nothing that would hurt anybody."

"But now it has—Dunn, for one. Your old partner in crime, the sheriff. And who else, David? Whose bones did that migrant worker find on your site?"

"I dunno. I really don't. Just a heap of charred shit, in a shallow grave. Some drug runner, Tremblay figured."

"So you covered it up?"

"Yeah. We did. The way we saw it, if we obeyed the law, then construction gets halted. We lose our slice of the bonuses, hundred men lose a few weeks' pay while guys like you investigate it. We find out in the end it *was* just some shit-bag narcotics mule, probably some illegal—"

Flores raised his eyebrows at that, and Levins blanched.

"Some undocumented migrant," he said, backtracking. "Some criminal, not worth risking all that money, and all those workers' paydays, to do right by."

"That's an awful lot to assume about some pile of bones, David. And there's some folks who don't believe you actually found bones. They think maybe those bones were still inside that man or woman or child's body, and that you maybe burned them up yourself. Forensics thinks that's real likely, matter of fact."

Levins went pale beneath his sunburn. "No, it was bones. Just bones. Animals had started digging them up. I've never killed nobody in my life. Not Dunn—that was all Tremblay's plan. Not Tremblay, neither. I was in Texas, like I said, too scared to risk coming back here. And not those bones. I never killed *no one* in my entire life. I wanted the money, that's all. Wanted the best for my family."

"Maybe you did. But that doesn't change the fact that now there's three human beings—with families of their own, I'd wager—dead. And what I need, and what you have to bargain with, is answers." He consulted his notes. "These creditors of the sheriff. Now, why would they do that? Have the man murdered? Surely that's no way to collect on his tab."

"So he wouldn't disclose who they were, I guess. When he went to trial. Their outfit didn't sound too legal."

Flores made another note, faking boredom, so Levins would stay eager to be of use. "These answers are all very convenient, David. You sure nobody else from Virgin River was in on your little arrangement with Tremblay?"

"Nobody I know of."

"So there's *nobody* else? Nobody with blood on their hands, aside from you and the late former sheriff?"

Levins swallowed, eye contact wavering.

"Tell me."

"There is one other guy who knew about it all. Who got his slice, just like Tremblay."

"Tell me who."

Levins licked his sunburned lips. "Not from VRC, or the sheriff's department."

Flores leaned in, leveled the diminished man with his stare. "Tell me, son."

Chapter 2

I've got to stop sleeping with Miah.

Raina shifted under the covers, feeling him all around her. His arm locked to her waist, the warm length of his sleeping body pressed along her back and legs. His bed beneath her, his scent in the pillow under her cheek.

She was surrounded by old smells. Familiar ones. Though strangely, until a few weeks ago, she'd never actually been in Miah's bed. They'd been lovers for a few short, blazing months, two summers back, but the man was claustrophobic. They'd come to know each other's bodies on blankets under the wide-open northeastern Nevada sky, on the grass, and in the bed of his truck ... Closest she'd ever come to laying him indoors had been the cab of that F-150. She still remembered every moment. The radio had been playing. "Life in a Northern Town" had come on, and goose bumps had broken out all over her skin, Miah's fingers on her clit and his mouth on her neck as she'd come.

This is different, she reminded herself.

Jeremiah Church's long, strong body was dressed in a tee and shorts, and Raina still wore her jeans and tank and bra.

This sleeping together was strictly literal.

But it really had to stop.

They'd lost a childhood friend six weeks ago—Alex Dunn, a sheriff's deputy. Raina hadn't slept properly since the day she accepted that Alex's death hadn't been the drunk-driving accident everyone had believed it was. The same day, Sheriff Tremblay had been called out and incriminated himself. She'd shut Benji's late that night—three a.m., probably—and even after that, she and Miah had sat together on the bar's front stoop, nursing a whiskey between them. Miah had been too drunk to drive home, and too upset besides.

They'd fallen silent. It should have felt cold. It got down to the forties at night in Fortuity, even now at the close of summer. But Raina hadn't registered the temperature, couldn't even remember the minutes or hours passing, with the two of them just sitting there.

After a long time she'd said, "Well." No other thoughts had come, no lament about the state of their town or the tragedy surrounding their friend.

Miah had said even less. Not a single word. Instead he'd gotten to his feet and taken her hand. He'd led her through the bar to the back stairs, up to the second floor to her apartment. Through the kitchen and den and into her room, where the dawn light was just beginning to slip through the front windows and swallow the aura of the neon sign flickering outside.

He'd thrown the covers wide and she'd taken his lead when he pushed off his boots. Whatever he'd needed, she'd have given. Any persuasion of sex that might have offered an escape for the both of them. But all he'd done was draw her onto the mattress and held her. Spooned her. Fully dressed. No words, no sex or kissing, just the jerky sound of his uneven breathing against her neck, and his strong arms clinging as though she were the only thing keeping him from drowning.

The same thing, the night after. And the night after that. Then they'd switched to meeting at Three C, Miah's family's cattle ranch, as his work demanded that he get back to his usual routines. And her new routine became driving over there once the bar was closed. She'd find him waiting on the front porch, and he'd lead her inside. Sometimes he held her, sometimes the other way around. Sometimes they lay on their backs, fingers laced on the sheets between them.

It was weird, and probably not especially healthy, and no doubt confusing. But so was everything about their lives just now. She was thirty-two and he was a couple of years older, but all the recent uncertainty had them feeling lost as teenagers.

She took a deep breath, ribs expanding and pressing her into Miah's warmth. Everything was so fucked right now, fucked and shapeless, the mysteries far from solved. But their two bodies were solid, amid the chaos—something to hold on to.

This fraught spooning was what Miah needed, and Raina had gotten herself accustomed to offering far less to men, the past few years. It felt nice, being what a man needed beyond the mechanical release of sex, for a change. And this particular man deserved good. Which was more than she could say for most of the ones she'd known. Or fucked.

But she really *had* to stop sleeping with him. Last night, he'd whispered to her as they were drifting off, about how she was the only thing that let him sleep. His lips had moved against her neck as he'd said it, and heat had trickled through her. Something in those words or the caress of his mouth had her thinking, *Sooner or later, this need is going to turn carnal.* He was going to want more from her—the things she'd taken away when she broke his heart, two summers ago. The things she was promising now, frankly, by coming back every night. Things she wanted, too, in her body . . . but not any place deep enough to make it okay. Because he wanted far more than Raina had in her to give.

As another dawn rose, staining the sky dark aqua through the skylight above them, Raina's thoughts turned to another man. The near stranger who'd helped her friends find some truth in the shadows obscuring Alex's murder. A man who presented like an entitled prick, but whose reckless actions had been those of a reluctant hero.

The stranger was tall, also. But where Miah smelled of the ranch—of leather and sweat and earth—the other man smelled of civility. Linen and soap, and a hint of cologne that didn't cloy, merely flirted. A man whose jaw was as smooth as Miah's neglected one was now bearded. Whose eyes were clear gray to Miah's near-black ones; his hair light brown and styled, versus Miah's overgrown black waves. His voice cultured and British and velvet-dark to Miah's down-home, plain-speaking one. Their accents, their hands, their shoes, their jobs—everything opposed. The Churches were well off—they came from old railroad money on Miah's father's side, and were rarities in that they still managed their ranch; most owners were rich absentees. Though you'd never guess Miah was wealthy, to look at him. He dressed like the ranch hands he oversaw, whereas that other man oozed privilege from every pore. Everything about the two of them was mismatched, but for the way they roused Raina. In that, they were perfect equals.

As the sky grew lighter, her instincts urged her, *Go.* Miah would be waking soon to start his long workday. She always slipped out before he rose, worried he'd try to kiss her good-

bye. Worried one kiss would be all it took for them to tear aside
this flimsy barrier and find themselves clawing at each other's
clothes, hungry hands moving over familiar skin. And tempting
as the sex was, it wasn't fair. Because he was a good man, and it
meant far more to him than it did to her. He was rare, that way.
Sex was an expression of his feelings for a woman.

For Raina, sex was merely the scratching of an itch. And
that itch was all she felt, for men. All she *wanted* to feel for
them. It made her think of that other man, one too cold to ever
get truly close to. A beautiful shell, too glossy-smooth for the
creeping vines of attachment to take hold. Safe. The man at her
back? Dangerous.

For long minutes she willed herself to wake Miah, to get her
balls together and rip off this Band-Aid, quit leading the man
on. But the morning air was cold, his body and the covers so
warm. And she was so goddamn tired from not having slept
properly in what felt like forever.

But it had to happen.

Miah's arm was draped along her side, his exhalations hot
and lazy on the back of her neck. She touched his wrist, stroking softly until he stirred.

"Hey," he murmured, then yawned into her hair.

"I want to talk to you, before you have to start work."

"Talk away."

She took a deep breath. "These past few weeks have been
awful."

"Yeah."

"But this has been nice. Us, I mean." She could sense his
hopes rising, and realized her wording had been cruel in its
kindness. "But it has to stop. It's been simple, but it won't stay
that way."

He rolled her over, and suddenly she was losing her footing
in this talk, that handsome face like a punch to rearrange her
priorities. Even after a few hours' sleep, his breath was sweet.
"What do you mean?"

"You and me, pretending like we can just spend night after
night in the same bed together, and not take things too far."

He smiled faintly. "Would that really be so awful?"

Reckless, tempting logic. But she knew better than to trust
it. "Not at first, no."

"We both know what we're missing, Raina." His hand
closed around her wrist, and her breathing grew shallow as she

let him lead her slowly, so slowly, between their bodies, then cup her palm to the front of his shorts. She swallowed, head swimming.

Too true. I know exactly what I'm missing. She could feel precisely that, stiff and hot against her hand. If any other man on the planet tried that shit with her—took her hand and showed her where to put it—she'd have torn him a second asshole. But she trusted Miah implicitly, far more than she trusted herself. She indulged him for a single, incendiary stroke, then gently escaped his grip.

"I won't lie," she said softly. "I do miss that. I *want* that, or my body does. But you need things I can't give you. And you deserve those things."

"You mean love."

Intimidated by the eye contact, she drew closer to speak below his ear. "Love, for keeps, whatever you want to call it. Dating, marriage, kids, forever—all that stuff any other girl on earth would die to give you. The most I'm willing to offer you is sex, and I know that's not enough." And that was the cruelest part, because she knew how good they were. She wanted him so bad right now her body was begging her mouth to promise him anything, just to feel him inside her again.

He sighed, the noise thin with annoyance, steaming against her temple. "You think I can't be selfish, too? Can't make this just about sex?"

"I know you can't. Not with me, anyhow."

"Wow. Think that highly of yourself, do you?"

She pulled back to meet those dark eyes. "I'm not blind. I see how you look at me. And I felt what I did to you, when we were together—both the good and the bad." The wonder of their chemistry, then the aching, dogging grief that tailed the both of them well after she'd broken things off. She kicked away the covers and left the bed. "You're the most eligible man in Fortuity, cowboy. You should have moved on ages ago."

"You're not that easy to replace."

"Well, try harder. Because this is never going to end with you and me and a farmhouse full of brown-eyed babies, Miah."

As she pulled on her socks, he asked, "It's him, isn't it? Welch."

She sought his gaze, held it. "No, it's not."

"Don't lie to me. People in this town talk, and I've heard from plenty of them, asking me how I feel about the way my ex has been flirting with the developers' corporate mercenary. The public face of the casino that's brought nothing to this town so far except death."

"Those murders have nothing to do with Duncan Welch — he risked his job to help us."

"Doesn't change how people think of him, though. And his personality's not doing him any favors. He keeps strutting around town the way he does, he'll wind up with worse than the broken tooth Tremblay gave him. You'd be a fool to get yourself associated with all that."

"Welch means far less to me than you do, so trust me — my ending things between us, it's nothing to do with him. It's about me, and you know it. It always has been. We had the only break-up in history where the 'it's not you, it's me' bit was true."

"I've seen the way you two talk, in the bar." Miah sat up. His black hair was rumpled, his arms tan against his dark gray tee. So handsome she had to turn away.

"And he can no doubt see the way you and I look at each other," she said. "But Welch is nothing to me beyond a customer and a curiosity. But you — you've been my friend since we were kids. You're my ex." She chanced a quick glance. "The past few weeks we've been each other's therapy. But I'm stopping it, because deep down I know I'm using you, and as good as it's felt up until now . . . it's starting to feel shitty."

Miah seemed to hold in a reply.

"I hope you're using me, too," she added, and stepped into her boots, their leather cold and stiff. "Though I'm afraid I know you better than that." He gave too willingly to possibly know how to exploit anybody.

He swung his legs over the edge of the bed, planting his elbows on his thighs. "Guess we're going back to bartender and patron again, then."

She took the elastic off her wrist and snapped it around a sloppy bun. "Bartender and patron — and hopefully friends, for both our sakes. And for the sake of the club."

Before this summer, the Desert Dogs had been nothing more than the name they'd called their bygone gang of childhood friends. Back then, they'd spend long summer days hiding from the baking sun in the auto shop, dicking around on motorcycles, thinking high school would go on forever. They were in their thirties now, and life had lost its simplicity. Miah was married to his job, and Raina was tethered to her dad's bar. Their friend Casey had disappeared to chase after shady money for close to ten years, earning himself a criminal record in the process, and not returning until a few weeks earlier. His older brother, Vince, had done time as well, for recreational felonies. Alex was *dead*. And the mysteries shrouding Fortuity seemed unlikely to lift any time soon, so the four of them—Vince, Casey, Miah, and Raina—had resolved to come together again, but with a purpose now. To protect their town from threats unknown, while the law was preoccupied with the more obvious ones.

Miah didn't reply, looking more weary than annoyed. She sighed and stepped close; touched his dark hair, laid a kiss on the top of his head. "You always were too good for me, Miah."

"Says who?"

"Everyone but you, I imagine."

He caught her wrist, holding it until she met his eyes. "Whatever you are to me," he said, "it counts for a lot. I ever hear about you going with some man who has the nerve to say that to you—that you're not good enough for him or for anybody else—I'll have more than words for him."

She smiled sadly as he let her go. "I know you would. And I know I'm a fool for running from what you've got to offer. Again."

His lips thinned to a tired smirk. "You always were good at running."

She nodded, throat tight and hurting. "Watch me go." She checked for her keys, grabbed her helmet off Miah's dresser. As her fingers closed around the door's cool knob, she heard words at her back, nearly too soft to make out.

"You know I will."

The old farmhouse was quiet save for the muted sounds of Miah's mom in the kitchen. She'd be starting the coffee, probably making pancakes or eggs and bacon or some other perfect, wholesome breakfast, fit for her hardworking husband and son. Some meal Raina never would have made as well, had she ever let herself get deep enough with Miah to wind up a cattleman's wife. A Mrs. Church. She wasn't built for that shit. For the softer sorts of nurturing. She'd been birthed by some flighty facsimile of jailbait, raised by a bachelor bar owner who'd needed as much caretaking as he'd offered. She had zero qualifications to be the woman Miah had coming to him . . . and zero interest in earning them. She slipped out the back, skirting the far side of the house like a coward, in no mood to run into the warm and lovely woman who'd never, ever be her mother-in-law.

Her little Honda growled to life between her legs in the cold dawn air, and as she exited the ranch's big front lot, the grinding of rubber on gravel felt like the only noise in the world.

The wind bit, waking her quicker than coffee ever could. The closer she drew to downtown and home, the heavier the guilt grew.

Any sane girl who wanted something real, something good, would've taken what Miah had offered two years ago. Stayed with a man whose body roused hers and whose nature promised stability. She'd have fallen past lust and into love with him, got married maybe, had a kid or two, settled down for a life of relentless reliability. Raina had been given the chance to pick a guy worthy of acting as her anchor, and then what? Resent him for taking away her freedom? Or, worse—lose him, maybe, as she'd lost her dad? Care enough to cling, then lose him to an accident or another woman or a midlife crisis or who knew what? Miah was steady, but he was still a man.

"I can make you happy," he'd told her once, back when they were lovers. "Why won't you just *let* me?"

She hadn't answered him. Hadn't been honest and simply said, "I don't want a man who'll make me happy. I want to feel relief when things end, not grief. Why would anyone choose grief?"

Regrets were ugly, but they scattered like ashes soon enough.

It was attachment you had to look out for. Affection. Love. There was a certain line, where emotions were concerned, past which experiences ripened to memories, and it couldn't be passed over lightly.

Love had bones to it. Solid, rattling things bent on cluttering you up long after the soft parts melted into the ether. You had to carry those bones around with you. Make room for them, dust them, trip over them.

She parked behind the bar and headed for the back door.

Sex and moments of easy companionship were enough—just don't let those bones grow in. Keep it soft and shapeless with no skeleton, no means to follow you when the time comes to walk away.

Raina stepped across the very threshold where she'd been

left as a baby, and into a thousand dusty memories of her dad. She shut the door behind her, feeling interred.

Good God, what was she doing here? She should have sold this place and moved on three years ago, after he'd died, quit surrounding herself with nostalgia for the only man she'd ever truly loved, and given these wounds a chance to finally heal.

There was still time. A flashy new bar and grill was coming to town in the next year, ahead of the casino, and only a block west of Benji's, on Station Street. The outsiders would be tearing down the derelict old tack shop and building from scratch. They had big money, and big plans, and undoubtedly stood a better chance at attracting the future gaming tourists than Raina would. They'd serve food, with a side of clean, friendly, faux-rustic charm. That basically left Raina cornering the Friday night fistfight market, with not nearly enough profits coming in to fund the overhaul she'd need to put in a kitchen, hire more staff, and undertake the renovation necessary to stay competitive.

And why bother? This place had been her dad's project, not hers. He'd opened it just before she showed up, and with Raina's mom MIA, he'd struggled to nurture his child and his business in tandem. This bar had been her home her entire life . . . but now it was her burden, a constant reminder of how badly she missed her father. A reminder, too, that she was still cleaning up after him, still keeping his dreams afloat, and her own on hold. It was a haunted place, its heartbeat silenced. She could sell it, and handily. Developers would be scrambling to buy up commercial real estate as the Eclipse's grand opening drew closer.

She could find a new place to call home. A new town. A new life. It wasn't too late . . . Was it?

Maybe this is your home now, a voice in her head whispered. *The boneyard itself.*

Can't you hear the clattering, girl?

Chapter 3

Duncan Welch eyed the vodka and tonic sitting before him on the bar. His second of the night, and the sun had only just dipped behind the mountains to the west and dunked the town in premature dusk.

A troubling development, one that had arrived right along with his recent professional worries.

For all intents and purposes, Duncan was on probation. He worked for Sunnyside Industries, the development company that was designing and eventually running the Eclipse, the casino slated to open in two years, here in Fortuity. He was Sunnyside's legal counsel, and more to the point, their fixer. Up until six weeks ago, he'd been a model worker. Up until he'd met Vince Grossier, king of the local roughnecks, a man on a mission to prove that his friend had been murdered. Duncan had been drawn in to run interference between Grossier and the people at Virgin River Contracting, but then circumstances had grown complicated. He'd exploited his position to uncover information that led to very real suspicions of criminal activity on the part of VRC. Sunnyside couldn't in good conscience fire him, not when his trespass had resulted in the exposure of a murder cover-up. But they weren't pleased. And Duncan had never been in this position before—never given an employer cause to chastise him. Having his reputation damaged made him deeply uneasy . . . had him wondering if the careful façade he'd built around himself these past twenty years might be showing cracks.

He took a deep drink.

At least he'd cut down on the Klonopin, in recent weeks. One vice was human; two was a crutch.

He eyed his bartender. Make that three vices.

Raina Harper. So not Duncan's style, yet he'd grown all but infatuated with her. He was tall, and so was she—perhaps five foot eight—though their similarities ended there. She was dark—wavy dark hair, dark eyes, tan skin. Black tee or tank, always, and black lace tattooed over one shoulder, like a veil that had slipped from her face and caught there. Long legs in tight jeans and cowboy boots. She was probably thirty-one or -two to Duncan's thirty-eight, yet in some ways she made him feel hopelessly childish. She'd probably shot a gun, ridden her share of horses, taken dares, placed bets, crashed a car, fucked more people than Duncan ever would, and with far more abandon.

She made him want things he'd never given much thought to. Noisy, messy sex; nails raking his back. Instincts he didn't trust any more than he trusted his newfound two-drink minimum.

He shifted on his stool, trousers feeling tight.

Raina was the owner of this charming-cum-rabid establishment, Benji's Saloon, currently Fortuity's sole watering hole. An old wooden whale of a place, its thick rafters ribbing the high ceiling, a dozen world-weary Jonahs gathered around the jukebox in the so-called old-timers' corner, swapping tales from the bygone golden days. They'd be off soon, replaced by the next generation—noisy, lively packs of ranch workers who drank, and presumably mated, with the boundless, indiscriminate enthusiasm of youth.

Raina's monopoly on the town's nightlife would change when the casino was up and running ... provided it ever got finished. Construction had been halted for a month now while the feds investigated Virgin River for widespread corruption. With progress frozen, Duncan didn't have nearly enough to occupy him. And the idleness chafed at him like a cilice.

He watched Raina chatting with patrons at the other end of the bar.

Another woman was working—Abilene. A girl, really. She was plump and short and angelic, the perfect foil to her employer. She came over as Duncan set his empty tumbler on the wood.

"Another?"

He smiled. "I'll wait." He let his eyes drift to Raina's profile. "Not that I find anything lacking in your bartending skills."

Abilene smiled back. "I don't blame you. Those ones she mixes you must be, like, two-thirds vodka."

"Perhaps she thinks the tonic is a garnish."

Abilene was called away by another customer, and Duncan went back to studying the unlikely object of his fixation. The two of them made about as much sense as Duncan made in this bar, with its gritty floors, dusty rancher clientele, and everflowing river of watery domestic beer. Then again, none of the things that transfixed Duncan had ever made much sense to him. Perhaps Raina was simply par for the course.

Plus, he doubted anything was ever going to happen between them. He was merely an amusement to her—an obnoxious, entitled outsider who tipped like an overzealous ATM, fit only for toying with.

Which was perfect, really, as Duncan quite enjoyed the sensation.

Abilene passed by her boss, saying something to Raina that Duncan couldn't hear. But he could guess, as the woman turned and headed straight for him.

Slender fingers circled his empty glass, but she didn't take it away just yet. "Another?"

"Please."

"Two's usually your limit. Do I need to stage an intervention?" She was teasing—hers was a bar where men proudly boasted of downing a dozen shots just to celebrate the close of a workweek.

"I'm afraid all the recent inactivity doesn't suit me," Duncan returned.

"Poor baby. I'd kill for a night off. Don't think I've had one in three years. But even if I got one, I'd probably spend it tattooing."

Ah yes, her side gig. Duncan rankled inside his expensive suit jacket to imagine her hands inching over strange men's naked skin.

"At least you're still getting paid," she said. "Want to feel bad for somebody, save your sorrows for the dozens of construction guys who're twiddling their thumbs for nothing, waiting to find out if they'll ever get to go back to work at all."

She mixed his drink and he tipped her outrageously, then watched as she gathered the empties scattered around the counter. The vodka was working, now. He felt warm and loose, urges and emotions slipping out from under the cap he kept on his vulnerabilities, to flurry about in his blood. To make him hungry. The vodka, or the lust? In either case, he ought not to trust the way he'd recently begun gravitating toward both. Yet here he was. Night after night.

Raina had an ex, one she was still close with. Or at least Duncan thought Jeremiah Church was her ex ... the way the man looked at Duncan sometimes, he had to wonder if there was still something simmering there. Though apparently not anything strong enough to keep Raina from flirting with Duncan, the virtual friction between them so intense it was a wonder their clothes didn't catch fire. The question marks surrounding her and Church had gone from poking him to clawing at him as of late, however. The hazards of an idle brain. He was itchy for answers, wanted them even more than he wanted to maintain the flimsy illusion that he couldn't care less who warmed her sheets.

He made it ten minutes—half his drink and three laps of Raina around the bar—before he blurted, "So, you and Jeremiah Church."

She batted her lashes, posture changing utterly. She cocked her hip and chin, subtle as a cat hunkering down to stalk a mouse hole. He could just about see her tail twitching. "Yes?" she asked sweetly.

"What exactly happened between you two that he gives me a look most men would reserve for their mother's ax murderer?"

She shrugged, graceful collarbone flashing beneath two layers of black lace—the straps of her top and the ink decorating her skin. "Guess my side effects include withdrawal or something."

"You turn a tame man feral."

She busied herself stacking nearby empties. "Don't all women?"

Not the ones I'm used to. "You dumped him, I take it?"

She smirked. "I like you drunk, Duncan. Makes me suspect you might even be half human, under all that smooth, icy snakeskin."

A snake, am I? How terribly Edenic. Though Raina had clearly bitten into that apple ages ago, savored every scrap of its flesh, and spat the seeds at her jilted lovers' feet.

It didn't matter that he'd helped her and her friends get to the truth surrounding the death of Alex Dunn. Or that Duncan had gotten pistol-whipped in the process—by the sheriff, right before Tremblay attempted to escape. That had been a month ago. Duncan's broken tooth had been fixed and the stitches removed from his lip, and once again he was back to being a suspect outsider in Fortuity. He'd earned the cursory nod of greeting from Vince Grossier, but that didn't change the fact that he was the face of the company that was bringing a massive resort casino to their sleepy town. He was gifted with dirty looks daily by any number of distrustful Fortuitans, and he knew what people called him. The names ran the gamut from *faggot* to *cop killer*. The former didn't bother him, but the latter stung. He'd risked a lot to expose Alex Dunn's actual murderer, but to some of these locals, his mere affiliation with the casino made him complicit. Guilt by association. He was probably taking a risk even drinking here, but if there was one thing Duncan Welch didn't abide, it was intimidation. Especially when it tried to come between a man and his vices.

Duncan's image didn't do him any favors, either. He was corporate. He was overdressed; he was a British expat; he was wealthy. He was cold and clean and calculating. He was wrong here, in every possible way. Wrong for Raina Harper's bed, as wrong as her ex was right. And yet *ex* was the operative word, wasn't it?

He sipped his dwindling drink and the alcohol spurred him to tell her, "I don't think your ex is over you."

"That's his problem, not mine."

"And you accuse me of being cold."

She grabbed some bills left by another customer and organized the register as she spoke. "Maybe we're not so different, then, Duncan. In any case, I'm perfectly happy on my own."

"Handsome, rugged cowboys need not apply?"

She smiled, the gesture indulgent. "If I didn't know better, I'd think you're jealous."

"Simply curious."

"Well, I don't need a man, handsome or otherwise. Not for more than a night or two. I'm already everything a woman wants to be—a mother to everyone who spills their drunken souls all over this wood," she said, stroking the bar in front of him. "A sister to my closest friends. A lover when it suits me."

"A corruptor," he added, lifting his glass.

"That also suits me."

"I can appreciate your desire for impermanence."

She smirked at that. "I'm sure you can. I bet you're counting down the days until the casino's built and you get to book it the fuck out of Fortuity, move on to the next job."

"Indeed. Though it'd be unfortunate if the construction's stalled indefinitely and I have to leave two years sooner than planned, with nothing to show for it. Just a load of unfilled foundations drilled into your foothills."

He anticipated her reply, something to the tune of glee at the idea of the casino never arriving to take over her hometown. But she surprised him, frowning thoughtfully. "You know, it seems like an odd match for a man like you—working on the Eclipse. Luxury resort or not, gambling seems too seedy to be your style."

"I'll stoop to most any adjective you can think of, if the pay is good. I'm not bothered what my bosses are planning." He sipped his drink. "Casino, water park, megachurch—it's all the same to me. I came here only to do my job, and to do it well. My commitments are about as personal as a whore's."

She smiled. "A high-class one, no doubt . . . Shame my town hasn't treated you too gentle, so far."

Duncan's tongue went instinctively to the smooth resin that now composed half of his left front tooth as Raina was called away to attend to other customers. He watched her at it.

Her assumptions about him offered some comfort. It seemed he still appeared to be in control, above it all. In truth, his life was feeling anything but certain. And it went far beyond all this boredom, as everyone waited for Virgin River to get the green light to recommence construction.

He tongued his imposter tooth again, feeling a kinship with it. The both of them were imitations. Passing for perfect but underneath . . . broken.

Raina was starting to think the evening was never going to pick up and that she'd have to send Abilene home, when a dozen regulars came through the door—a pack of young women and the ranch hands that followed them like lemmings. The lot of them tipped like shit, but they brought some much-needed energy on a quiet Thursday night like this. The jukebox made a U-turn, lazy country giving way to pop and dance music, the bass throb of foreplay.

Raina watched them, her own hips swaying softly behind the bar, body restless. She'd been trying to ignore Duncan's presence, but her body felt hard-wired to his. Like opposite poles, the two of them attracted. And the closer she let herself drift to him, the hotter she crackled, the harder the pull.

Then it came on—her song of the moment. She didn't even know who sang it, but the beat was infectious, relentless, the tone of it pure red wine, making a woman's blood pump hot and thick.

The opening notes drifted from the speakers like phero-mones, and Raina knew her cue, as though this had been or-dained. No patrons waiting on refills, everyone's glasses looking refreshed, Abilene on top of the stock. The frayed tether that had lashed her back together with Miah finally cut. She skirted the bar and strode right over to where Duncan was scanning the glowing screen of his phone. He'd shed his jacket, crisp sleeves rolled up to display the elegant muscles of his forearms. She plucked the cell from his fingers. His face cocked up, gray eyes flashing cold as steel, then softening as he regis-tered it was her, not some drunken local looking to start some-thing.

Raina smiled to know he thought her less dangerous than her male counterparts.

"You dance, Duncan?" she asked.

"No," he said evenly, taking back his phone. "I do not."

"Perfect time to learn, then." She took that smooth, mani-cured hand and led him to the space before the jukebox like a dog, wedging them between the younger bodies. He came will-ingly enough, though she suspected that it was merely some aversion to scene-making. Or perhaps the vodka's doing. Ei-ther way, she turned, boxing herself into his space, bringing their thighs tight. Not much choice, in this crowd.

A man led a waltz with his hands, but Raina led the dance with her hips. She glanced up, expecting discomfort on that flawless face, but if anything, her partner looked blasé. He moved a little more, a little more, answering her cues with min-imal finesse, but also zero embarrassment. A snake indeed. She'd bet his blood ran cold as Dead Creek. She knew Miah's would be coursing like lava if he were here, watching this.

I'm not his property.

But she *was* his friend—a friend she'd shared strange but definite benefits with, and she knew she had the power to hurt him. Badly. Yet it was hard to parse lust and guilt at the same time and deny that the latter was an aphrodisiac in itself.

She studied Duncan. Watched him change, ever so slightly. His lids looked heavier and his lips were parted. She saw him swallow, and in that tiny gesture she caught a crack forming, a glimpse of his humanity shining through.

Or if not humanity, heterosexuality.

She turned with the beat and moved against him, butt to crotch—Fortuity's official mating dance.

Finally, a hot palm at her waist. Then another, and a brush of his thigh against hers. Moment by moment, the heat of his body grew as he sealed them closer together. His hips against her ass, moving subtly, then bolder. The boy had rhythm. Who knew?

He had more than rhythm, actually, to judge by the hard excitement rubbing against her. And his breathing had grown audible, exhalations hot at her temple. She felt the same heat wave settling around her body, but she'd be damned if she let him know it. One thing she craved more than sex just now was a chance to have the upper hand on the man who so clouded her instincts.

She smiled over her shoulder and found his gaze foggy.

"Dancing tells a woman everything she needs to know about how a man'll be in bed," she informed him.

"I can't imagine what dancing with me is telling you." That buttery voice had changed, just like his breathing. Lower, darker. Distracted.

She grinned, unseen. "Tells me you're a quick study."

"I was always an excellent student." More flippant words, but his tone said she had him. That she could *have* him, if she wanted. "You mix a very strong drink," he said. "If I didn't know better I'd think you wanted me to forget myself."

"Just your snooty manners," she countered, dropping low for a moment, sliding back up. "What are you like in bed?"

His entire frame stiffened for a beat, and he seemed to catch himself, gathering his misplaced control like a dropped jacket. "It's amazing how little of your business that is."

Funny how his annoyance seemed to rouse her as another man's excitement might. "Judging by your perpetually shiny shoes," she said, "I bet you keep a box of wet wipes on the bedside table and shower the second it's over."

After a pause, "That's a theory."

"Or," she drawled, grinding low against him, "maybe you're a real freak in bed. Maybe that's how you cut loose, when the stress of being so collected and perfect gets old. Maybe you're into some real kinky shit." To spank, or be spanked? "You like girls, Duncan?"

He answered with his hand, spinning her around. Long, graceful fingers hooked into her belt loops, drawing their middles together. Still rock hard, against her mound now. Eyes burning down at hers. She reeled, her lead in this exchange lost in a heartbeat.

"What do you think?" he breathed, his cock giving its answer with every veiled stroke, every motion of his hips.

"I think I may have underestimated certain parts of you."

"Are you trying to seduce me, Ms. Harper?"

"Trying's not really my style. A girl doesn't like to look too eager."

"Well," he said, "I've already sacrificed a tooth to help you and your little hoodlum friends. It strikes me as greedy that you seem to want my honor as well."

She laughed. "I'll have you tattooed within the week."

His smile was slow and dry as summer. "I'd sooner consent to most any other thing you could think of."

"Would you, then? I'll give the options some thought."

His face came close. So close she discovered there was stubble on that seemingly flawless jaw, and felt his nose graze her cheek.

That velvet voice turned to moss, lush and earthy in her ear. "Your intentions intrigue me."

Her intentions . . . In truth, she hadn't intended to seduce him at all—just to wind him up, rattle him. Scandalize this man she'd taken for an uptight prude. And in further truth, she couldn't say which of them was doing the seducing anymore.

"This is all just dancing," she lied. "Shame on you, Duncan, for making it into something sordid." She let her hand drift up, fingers seeking his hair. Soft as his skin and voice. Soft as the lips whispering along her temple.

"Shame on me," he agreed, and his own hand drifted— warm and sultry, fingers spread to snake up her waist, over her ribs, stopping just shy of her breast. "Mean old coldhearted corporate bastard, come to rape your innocent little hardworking town."

"Fortuity's far from innocent," she said, letting her hips underline that fact.

"And its residents are far from subtle," he breathed. And

suddenly he was gone, hand falling from her waist, body drawn back by a step, then another. He gave her a look—a zing. *Nice try,* that sharp smile said, while his mouth said, "Thanks for the lesson, Ms. Harper." He smoothed his tie from his collar to the V of his vest and they both wandered from the gyrating crowd. "Consider me educated."

"I'll consider you warm-blooded."

Another smirk. "The alcohol must have ignited me."

"I got you dancing," she mused. "You asked about my ex."

"And?"

"So much humanity, all of a sudden. This all because you're underworked? You only taking my bait because you're bored?"

"Does it matter? Business or biology—neither's personal."

"You sure know how to make a girl feel special, Duncan Welch." Though she shared that philosophy herself.

"Apologies. But if you'll excuse me, I have a date with my motel room and a box of wet wipes."

Snarky little fucker. "You're a real piece of work, aren't you, Duncan?"

He met her eyes with those pale ones. "I've been told I'm a real piece of something. I leave it to the individual to fill in the blank."

She came close, pretending to fuss with his tie but tugging the knot loose, shifting it all cockeyed. He corrected it the second she took her hands back, the act looking more reflexive than petulant.

She smiled sweetly. "I bet you jack off with your pinkie stuck up in the air, don't you?"

His smirking lips twitched, faint and quick as a flea sneezing. "Picture it however you like."

"Good night, Duncan."

He offered a smarmy bow. "Ms. Harper."

She gave a little curtsy, glaring at his back as he exited. She couldn't tell if she wanted simply to fuck with that man's head or straight-up fuck him. In either case, she'd pay good money to hear him beg for mercy.

Chapter 4

Duncan was hungover.

He couldn't remember the last time he'd been properly hungover. Overindulgence was *not* his style. He'd walked back to the Gold Nugget Motor Lodge with a sway in his step, the five or six shots' worth of liquor in those drinks like a bender to a normally temperate man. To a man who craved self-discipline. He'd escaped, slipping out of range of a cat's batting paws before he could find out what Raina might want out of him. Would that have ended with Duncan's body wound in her sheets, or did her pleasure come merely from her ability to wind him up? She had far too much control over him. And control was a commodity Duncan treasured above all others.

So rather than follow the flirtation to its natural conclusion, he'd headed to the motel, popped a couple of Ambiens and more than a couple of ibuprofens, and woken up with a brass band playing in his skull, and chores beckoning. Always chores.

The bathroom fan whirred all around him, and the world was speckled laminate and smooth white acrylic. His knees hurt, the towel-thin bath mat and his lounge pants doing nothing to protect them from the biting tile. But he wasn't bowed before the toilet, sick from the vodka. No, he was sick in a far different, and deeply familiar, way.

His shoulder ached, and his lower back, and he felt high from the bleach. But that was good, surely. Meant the stuff was doing its job.

He scrubbed at the plastic tub. Plastic—worst. Porcelain would be so much easier to disinfect. Plastic never felt clean enough to trust. Never.

Degrading though these chores were, the calm was coming to him now. The fumes and the ritual were subsuming him, quieting his brain, banishing the panic and the pulsing headache.

He could hear his bygone foster mother's voice in his head—that soft, cultured accent offering the only kind words he'd known in the first half of his life. *Look at that! You cleaned that all by yourself? What did I do to deserve such a good helper?* To deserve *him.* Insane, those words had seemed—insane and wondrous as a choir of angels after ten years of being called a burden at every turn. Thirteen measly months he'd gotten with his silver-haired savior. Then she'd been taken away, her kind voice and eyes hollowed out by a stroke that had scared Duncan worse than any slap or threat issued by his harsher guardians. She was gone as quickly as she'd appeared, and Duncan had been dropped neck-deep back into the shit of the foster system. Just over a year, she'd given him. One good year, and a fondness for Wagner, and this compulsion to clean when he felt uncertain.

He scrubbed harder, so hard that it roused the perennial ache in his right elbow, cartilage whining. *Repetitive strain injury,* a doctor would tell him. *Whatever you're doing, knock it off.* Same as a doctor would tell a masochist to quit with the self-flagellation and those raw red stripes would clear right up.

Yes, because that's going to happen. He might as well give up breathing while he was at it.

The bucket was just about empty, the scrubber sponge shedding blue flecks. He braced his rubber-gloved hands on the ledge of the tub and shakily made it to his feet, joints wailing. He turned on the shower to rinse his handiwork.

Clean. Pretty damn clean. The tub was shining. The sink, too, the mirror spotless, and the grout between the mint green backsplash tiles whiter than it had been since the Carter administration, surely. No surface neglected, no room for oversight. The plastic would never be perfect, but by anyone's standards, no trace of this tub's former sins had been spared. He felt marginally cleaner himself.

Satisfied, he snapped the gloves from his hands and draped them over the rim of the empty bucket. He washed his hands once, twice, three times, rinsed the sink. He flipped off the light but left the fan on to suck at the fumes.

He eased the bathroom door open a couple of inches, peering out and finding his roommate predictably planted at the threshold.

"Keep out, Astrid. Bad enough your daddy's disinfected half his brain cells. Let's keep one of us lucid." With a gentle push of his foot, the tabby gave up her post, rising to stretch and saunter toward the bed.

Duncan shut the bathroom door at his back and gulped two lungs' worth of comparably fresh air.

He wandered to the edge of the bed and switched on the television, greeted by the regional news. His shaving bag was behind him and he fished out an orange bottle and swallowed a Klonopin dry. Astrid leaped onto the covers and he stroked her back, her spine rising in reply. Poor beast, stuck with these four walls and the parking lot for a view. She had to be missing their Southern California skyline as much as he was. Still, the motel beat any other housing option at the moment—better than some grubby little room for rent, or a trailer such as the Virgin River foremen stayed in. He'd also negotiated an insanely generous bonus for this job, spearheading Sunnyside's first big out-of-state project. A bonus, and a promise to be kept close to home for his next assignment. Time would tell if it proved a worthy trade beyond the figures on a page.

"Two years," he murmured, taking in little more than flashing colors and garbled words as commercials assaulted the screen. He flopped backward and Astrid took it as an invitation to sit on his belly.

Two years until the project was done. Allegedly—this current delay might merely be the first of many. Even after the casino was running, who knew how long until Duncan's service was deemed complete? The Eclipse's PR demands would merely evolve after the ribbon was cut by that walking Napoleon complex known as Mayor Dooley. At least by then Duncan would be set up in one of the luxury apartments slated for construction on the east face of Lights Out. And for all of its *many* faults, Fortuity did boast one hell of a sunrise.

Shit, though. He'd be in his forties by the time his contract was fulfilled.

Time passes quickly for the industrious, he reminded himself.

With the bleach smell fading, the calm wouldn't linger, but the ritual performed him, not the other way around. *Do as it says or have a panic attack.* Not really a choice, in Duncan's estimation. Normally the demands of his job kept him too busy to indulge the urges more than once or twice a week — he went through the motions of his role each day, cleaning up the messes left by progress. It kept his brain too distracted to push him around. Kept his mortgage paid and his cat fed.

Kept his mind off Raina Harper ... and his right hand off his cock when he inevitably failed at the former. Christ, when would this standstill be *done*, already —

A startling *thump, thump, thump, thump* at the door had him sitting up so suddenly Astrid tumbled hissing to the floor.

He hastily zipped the prescription bottle in his bag and lamented his relative state of undress. He smoothed his hair as he went, a perverted bit of him hoping against hope it'd be Raina. Though what good would that be, when the incriminating state and scent of the bathroom precluded him from inviting her in?

He needn't have worried — the peephole offered a bespectacled tan face and buzz-cut hair, a dark suit.

He undid the chain and opened the door. "Can I help you?"

"Duncan Welch?"

"Yes." The morning air was cold on his naked arms and feet, the rising sun piercing his pickled brain through his eyes.

"Going to need you to put on some pants and come with me," said the man.

Duncan frowned. "And who are you, exactly?"

The man pulled a wallet from his back pocket — not a wallet, a badge. He flipped it open. Fed. "Agent Flores."

Duncan blinked, cold misgiving creeping across his bare skin like spreading frost. "What's this about? The Virgin River investigation?"

"Just change out of your pajamas and come with me." He nodded to a silver SUV parked beside the Mercedes.

Duncan's eyes narrowed. "You do realize I've been more than cooperative in these matters for the past month, don't you? I can't say I appreciate being addressed like a suspect."

Flores looked grim. "I'm sure you can't. But you may want to get used to it."

Not ten minutes later, they pulled into the Brush County Sheriff's Department, half a mile down Railroad Avenue. As Flores parked, Duncan tongued his tooth again, eyeing the spot on the asphalt where he'd fallen to his knees, cupping his bleeding mouth. No good ever came of this place, he decided.

His guts were churning, and from far more than the hangover now. Flores had refused to discuss anything on the way, and the uncertainty was torture—physical torture, wringing his insides with vicious fists. They exited the vehicle, the sun already baking here at the edge of the desert, its glare sharpening Duncan's headache. He felt naked, dressed in jeans and a T-shirt, probably still smelling of bleach. No time to shower or fix his hair or put on proper clothes. He felt as though his skin had been stripped away, exposed to his very nerves.

You've nothing to worry about. He'd already been punished by Sunnyside for the one thing he'd actually done wrong. And if this matter had to do with that bit of trespassing . . . surely that was no concern of the feds. As they strode for the BCSD's entrance, Duncan faked the confidence he was entitled to.

The young assistant looked up from her computer screen as they entered, but Flores led Duncan down a short hall and into a windowless room. Two mismatched chairs, one table. An interrogation room.

"What, no handcuffs?" he asked, shooting Flores the tiniest taste of the contempt boiling in his body. "No orange jumpsuit? I feel unloved."

Flores didn't reply until he'd set a tape recorder on the table and depressed its red button. "You're a suspect, not a criminal."

"A suspect for what crime, precisely? Up until this morning I was a valued and cooperative witness."

"Have a seat, Mr. Welch." Flores waved to one of the chairs, a hard plastic utilitarian number, sitting himself on the far more dignified, upholstered one.

Duncan sat, clasping his hands in his lap to hide their shaking. "Tell me what on earth this is about."

"This," Flores said, lacing his fingers atop the wood, "is about money. You like money, don't you, Duncan? Nice car I saw in front of your room. S-class, isn't it? What'd that put you back? Ninety grand? Ninety-five? And nice clothes, I'm told. Nice state-of-the-art, luxury high-rise condo, back in San Diego."

Duncan frowned, lost. Another loathsome sensation. "I make a decent salary. Surely that's not an arrestable offense."

"No. But accepting bribes is."

The blood drained from Duncan's head, seeming to rush into his heart to force thick, strangling beats. "Excuse me?"

"Specifically, accepting bribes from a suspect in a murder and conspiracy investigation."

"What are you talking about?"

"We've been informed by a key party that you accepted bribes from Virgin River foreman David Levins in exchange for not reporting shoddy construction practices to your bosses."

"What?" Being found guilty of such a crime could get a person permanently disbarred—and to Duncan, a man whose profession was everything he'd worked for, everything that defined him, the possibility felt tantamount to execution. "Who said this?"

"I'm not at liberty to say."

Duncan paused, body rocked with every roaring heartbeat. *Wait.* "Levins. Has Levins been caught?"

"Does that make you nervous?" Flores asked, leaning forward.

"No," Duncan said, livid. "No, it does not. Because I've never exchanged a thing with that man aside from pleasantries and paperwork." Still, the thought calmed him some. "Is he the one who's accused me? If so, it's a criminal's word against mine, and I've done nothing wrong that hasn't already come to light. And why on *earth* would I have participated in the investigation that implicated him, if he was privy to my own complicity?"

"We've wondered the same things," Flores said smoothly.

"As you should. There's no case to be made here. Probably just a desperate man's ploy to distract everyone from the real scandal, the real crimes. Or retribution, for my involvement. Do what your job demands, but we both know these accusations are going nowhere."

"Do we know that?" Flores asked, eyebrows rising dryly.

Duncan sighed, annoyed and tired and insulted. And hung the fuck over. Mustering courtesy took a superhuman effort. "I appreciate that you have protocol, and motions to go through, but come on. You know as surely as I do, there's no evidence against me."

Flores tapped a pen against a yellow legal pad. "I'm afraid that's not entirely true."

Duncan's head went eerily quiet. "Excuse me?"

"A worker's come forward. A laborer with Virgin River, who claims he saw you accepting money from Levins."

Duncan gaped, feeling struck. "That's preposterous. Money? What, a big stack of bright green bills? A fat envelope with *Bribes for Duncan* written on it?"

"Calm down, Mr. Welch."

Duncan realized he'd leaned forward in his seat. His chest hurt, and his underarms were prickling with sweat. He needed to be careful, before he gave himself an attack. "When was this meant to have happened? My accepting bribes?"

"We'll get into details soon enough. Just wanted to let you know how everything's shaping up. I take it you're not changing your position based on this development?"

"You can't honestly believe this is a credible witness. Levins could have arranged it all before he turned himself in. Paid this person off, or intimidated him—"

"It's not my job to believe anybody. That's what judges and juries are for. Just consider yourself in the loop."

"I'm free to go, as it were?"

"Free to go? That's all relative. Free to leave Fortuity? Not any time soon, except under special circumstances."

"For Christ's sake."

"Free to escape my company? Not yet. I need to take a look inside your motel room."

"What?" Duncan felt more naked than he'd have guessed, imagining strangers poking around in his borrowed space, smelling the evidence of his compulsions, upsetting his cat. They wouldn't find anything incriminating, surely, but suspicious . . . ? Some aspects of his daily routine did defy logic.

"Search warrant should be waiting at the front desk by now," Flores said calmly. "I just want to take a quick look around. If you have nothing to hide, you have nothing to worry about. I'll drive you back to your premises. Then you'll be asked to wait outside. Any property seized as a result of this search will be made known to you—"

"I know how a warranted search works."

Flores smiled. "Do you, then?"

Duncan rolled his eyes furiously, not in any mood for banter. "This is fucking ridiculous. All of it."

Flores's eyebrows rose. "Then you've got nothing to fucking worry about, I imagine. Be thankful you haven't been accused of anything violent or deemed a flight risk—no need to detain you."

"I should hope not." He sighed his disgust. "Haven't you got more pressing matters than this to occupy yourselves?"

"Sure. But until the team gets a viable lead on those bones, looks like I'm stuck ruining your day, Duncan."

Bones. Christ, that word. Everything had begun to go wrong with that one little syllable, spoken by Deputy Dunn, obsessed over by Vince Grossier. Now those bones had drawn Duncan into their miserable orbit.

"Perhaps your team ought to try a little harder," Duncan said. "Those bones will prove me innocent as surely as they'll prove Levins guilty." Forensics would supply the victim's identity, likely motives, and lead the investigation to the truth—and away from Duncan.

Ignoring that, Flores got to his feet and beckoned Duncan to do the same. "We've been in touch with your employers, of course."

All the misplaced blood was suddenly rushing in Duncan's ears, leaving his face hot. That was *all* he needed, when he was already on informal probation. He pulled himself together. "Of course. This wretched morning wouldn't be complete if you hadn't."

"You'll probably need to negotiate some time off. We'll be chatting again soon, maybe often."

Time off. He'd be lucky if Sunnyside didn't sack him. Christ, then what would he do? Who would he even *be*, with that blemish on his otherwise perfect professional record? And God forbid these accusations make the news—exonerated or not, he'd be a pariah for the rest of his career, to say nothing of what the angrier locals would want to do to him . . . Duncan got dirty looks simply for being associated with the development. If people believed him complicit with the men who'd murdered a well-liked deputy, he'd be attracting more than just glares.

"How long am I trapped in this town, precisely?"

"Hard to say," Flores said, drawing car keys from his pocket. "Search shouldn't take too long. Once you let us in, feel free to go find yourself some breakfast."

Duncan would take a walk, at any rate. He needed the air, the sun, the ground under his feet. Proof the world was still solid, that he still existed.

They headed out to the front room, where Flores was met

by a slim young black woman dressed in BCSD khaki, curls pulled back in a voluminous ponytail.

"This is Deputy Ritchey," Flores told Duncan. "She'll be assisting me in the search." To Ritchey he simply said, "This is Welch."

She offered a curt nod, then held out an envelope to Flores.

He opened it and glanced at the paper inside. "Would you like to view the warrant?" he asked Duncan.

He read it. It granted Flores permission to search his motel room and his car for suspicious amounts of money. Annoying, as it meant they could basically tear his room apart, but at least they couldn't seize his phone or laptop—he suspected he'd be needing them in the coming days.

"Understood?" Flores asked, taking the paper back.

"It's neither here nor there. I've nothing to hide," Duncan lied. He'd very much like to hide all traces of his mental issues, for his pride more than anything—under this warrant, Duncan's meds and cleaning supplies and any other oddities were none of Flores's concern. Still, they probably wouldn't help matters.

They headed outside, where the deputy climbed into a beige cruiser. The sun was far too bright and cheerful, Duncan decided.

"I have a cat in my room," he told Flores. "Upset her and I'll be very cross."

Flores unlocked his car. "A cat?"

"Yes, a cat. She's been specially trained to digest human skeletal remains and I've secreted thousands of dollars inside her."

Flores's smile dropped. "Don't get cute with me, Welch. I'd prefer not to form any biased opinions about you." They climbed into the car and buckled up, not speaking until the three of them were at Duncan's door.

"I'm coming in to put my cat into her carrier," he said to Flores and Ritchey as he unlocked his room. "She's not good with strangers."

Flores nodded to tell him to go ahead.

"She'll be less likely to panic and lacerate me if you let me go in alone."

Flores shook his head, no surprise.

"Fine." Duncan preceded the others, and managed to wrangle Astrid into her carrier with Deputy Ritchey's help, both of them suffering the consequences. He offered her his stiff thanks, then turned to Flores. "Please be sure to lock up behind you, and leave the cat where she is. My car keys are in the desk drawer—do lock that as well. I'll be at the diner for the next hour. I imagine you've already got my mobile number?"

"I do." Flores fished in a pocket and handed Duncan a business card. "And now you've got mine. Don't leave town without contacting me first."

Duncan's eyes narrowed. "Why not just clamp an ankle tracker on me?"

"Don't tempt me. Take care of yourself, Duncan. We'll chat real soon."

"I'll count the moments."

Flores rolled his eyes and turned his attention to the room.

As Duncan exited and aimed himself downtown, he felt his very identity being peeled from his being, falling in tattered strips like a ruined costume, like flayed skin. The sensation was so painful all he could think of was how to stop it. How to stop feeling, to go numb.

All in good time. He needed to call his bosses first, to know if he still had a job. A scrap of anything definitive that he could cling to, to keep him suspended above this pit of steaming shit.

The sunshine was hot on his hair, too bright in his eyes. He walked a block down Railroad Ave and took out his phone, cued up his boss's number. His thumb wavered above the CALL button. One push, and he'd find out if he still had a job—still had a purpose, an identity, any roots at all still linking him to the ground, to his sanity. And his sanity had never been completely under control.

He hit the power button, and the screen darkened. He pocketed the phone neatly, then strode to the nearest stand of scrubby trees and was sick.

Chapter 5

Benji's was bustling—Raina's favorite kind of Friday night, when it felt as though half the town were in attendance. Felt like an impromptu Desert Dogs club meeting as well—minus Miah.

Both Grossier brothers were loitering at the bar, always the picture of contrast. Vince was older, taller, more thickly muscled behind his dark tee, with black hair, and black ink on his neck and arms, hazel eyes. His little brother wasn't quite so big, overall—not quite six feet—and fair, with coppery, overgrown hair and a red beard any Viking would be proud of. They both wore old jeans and boots, but Casey was sporting one of his usual plaid button-ups. On Vince's other side was his girlfriend, Kim, who looked like the Portlandian she was, dressed in stylish, casual clothes and trendy glasses, dark blond hair in a ponytail.

Casey, as was his wont of late, was tracking Abilene with his eyes, and hitting on her in his ham-fisted fashion whenever she passed by.

Abilene deflected the attention with a weary charm, excusing herself for a bathroom break. She took a lot of those, and Raina could guess why. The girl also winced whenever she got too close to the olives in the garnish bin, and had once dry-heaved at the smell of Kahlua. All these intimate tells were lost on a dolt like Casey, but Raina was going to need to have a little chat with her employee, to the tune of *So . . . when exactly are you due?* It was hard to guess. Abilene was a naturally round sort of girl. She could probably keep that secret right up to the third trimester.

"Goddamn," Casey said, thwarted. "Someday she's gotta say yes."

Vince shot Raina a look, expression dry. Oh-ho. So he knew what she did? Made sense—he was the one who'd advised Abilene to get work at Benji's to begin with. Raina grimaced to say, *Train wreck waiting to happen.* Vince raised his bottle in agreement.

"She's not interested," Raina told Casey. It was a lie, though. Body language said Abilene was as crushed out on Casey as he was on her, but of course the girl had enough problems without hitching her wagon to a flighty con man.

"I'm gettin' really mixed signals from that woman," he said, and sipped his bourbon.

"Girl," Raina corrected. "You've got ten years on her, easy." Abilene's Texas license said she was twenty-four, but Raina knew a fake when she saw one. Abilene's alleged birthday had also come and gone a couple of weeks back, and when Raina had asked her if she was doing something special that night, Abilene's expression hadn't suggested it'd been anything other than a Wednesday. Raina suspected that pregnancy was merely the largest of her employee's secrets.

Casey's blue eyes suddenly grew wide, and he turned to Vince. "Maybe she's a virgin or something. Maybe that's why she's acting all hard to get."

Raina bit her tongue.

Vince smirked. "Oh, I doubt she's a virgin."

Casey froze, then glared. "Wait, what? You fucked her? When?"

Raina laughed, and Kim covered her face, surely to stifle her laughter, not her horror.

Vince glared at his brother. "Of course I didn't."

"Are you sure? You seem pretty certain. Plus, you've fucked most of the girls in—"

"Shut. Up."

Kim looked about ready to hyperventilate, clutching her middle.

"Just trust me," Vince said to his brother. "The girl's not as innocent as she looks."

"How do you know?"

"None of your goddamn business. Ask her yourself."

Casey asked Raina instead. "You're with her a lot—she ever go home with anybody?"

Raina shook her head. "I think you're onto something. Definitely sounds like a case of persistent virginity."

Casey looked intimidated, but intrigued. His eyes narrowed with curiosity when Abilene reappeared.

"We better make a move," Vince said, draining his bottle. "We're on Mom-watching duty." His and Casey's mother was mentally ill, and they split the caregiving duties with their neighbor, Nita. Vince settled the tab and headed for the bathroom while Kim got serious about finishing her beer.

Abilene collected the empty and asked Casey, "You sticking around for another?"

"Yeah, sure." He leaned on the bar while she poured him a fresh bourbon on the rocks. "You ever gonna say yes when I ask you out?"

Her smile was both flirtatious and cagey. "I've got a lot going on just now."

"One date—that's all I'm asking."

"Take no for an answer, Case," Raina said.

"But she hasn't told me no yet," he said, gaze on Abilene. "Trust me, I've been paying attention."

"Maybe someday," Abilene allowed, taking the five he handed her.

You know, someday, Raina mused, smiling. *Like maybe two years from now, when the girl's done breast-feeding and in half a mood for entertaining male demands.*

Then Casey the dumb-ass stepped aside, and Casey the scam artist took his place. He leaned on the bar. "I know why you keep saying no," he said to Abilene quietly.

Raina groaned. "Don't, Casey."

"Oh?" Abilene asked him.

Casey nodded. "My brother told me."

Abilene's hands went to her middle in horror and she glanced around, presumably looking for Vince so she could tear him a new one. "That asshole." Raina didn't think she'd heard the girl swear before now. Abilene tacked on a hasty "No offense, Kim."

Kim smiled. "That shoe occasionally fits."

"Jeez, what a shit. He promised he wouldn't tell anyone."

Casey held up his glass. "That's my brother for you. Can't be trusted."

Raina kept her mouth shut and crossed her arms, preparing for a show.

"Well," Abilene said slowly, "what do you think about it?"

"I'm . . . I want to know how *you* feel about it, I guess," Casey said. A decent bluff, Raina had to admit.

Abilene thought a moment. "I'm not sure. I mean, I do *like* you. I'd like to go out with you, sometime."

"Me, too. Perfect."

"If that's not too weird, I mean."

"Why would I think it's weird?"

Abilene shrugged. "I dunno. Some guys would. I just figure if a girl was pregnant by some other man, most of them—"

Casey's eyes widened. "Wait—you're pregnant?"

Kim grimaced as if a car wreck were about to go down, then hopped off her stool to intercept Vince as he returned from the men's room. She steered him to the exit, and Vince offered a perplexed parting wave over his shoulder.

Abilene stared at Casey. "Yeah, I'm pregnant. What the heck did you think we were talking about?"

Casey blinked. "Fuck, I don't know. But not that."

She planted her hands on her hips and glared. "Your brother didn't tell you shit, did he?"

"No, but—"

"I'd advise you to shut up now, Case," Raina said.

Abilene's angelic face was murderous. "Good to know which Grossier's got the balls to tell me the truth."

"I'll just finish this and get going." He took a long swallow of his drink, neck and ears pink.

Abilene eyed Raina, looking nervous.

She waved the girl's worry aside. "I guessed weeks ago. You're welcome to keep working as long as you like. Though we'll probably want to switch you to afternoons soon."

Her shoulders dropped in obvious relief.

A group of ranch hands came in, and Raina nodded to tell Abilene to tend to them—get her and Casey separated for a few minutes.

"Fuck me," Casey said, staring at the drink in his hand.

"Next time, take our advice, maybe."

He shook his head. "Jesus . . ."

Raina was poised to tease him, but then the door swung in, admitting the man she'd managed to keep her mind off for a good fifteen minutes, thanks to Casey's romantic implosion. Duncan.

He strode for the bar, eyebrows set in a tight line. Uncharacteristically dressed—a heather gray T-shirt and jeans. It was Saturday, but that didn't matter—seeing Duncan Welch wearing anything less than two-thirds of a three-piece suit made Raina feel as if she were staring at the man buck naked.

She met him at the corner of the counter, tossing a coaster on the wood. "Good evening, Duncan's doppelgänger. You drink V and T like your evil twin?"

"Double." He didn't meet her eyes, and she couldn't help noticing how his fingers trembled as he fished bills from his wallet.

"You okay?"

He swallowed, eyes on his shaking hands. "Not particularly, no."

A touch worried, she mixed his drink in record time. As he brought it to his lips, she could see the liquid juddering like a stormy lake.

She was stymied. Though they'd been briefly tangled in a load of drama together, and flirted as if they were aiming to catch fire, she had no clue how to relate to him just now. *Concern* wasn't something she was much good at, and she suspected *rattled* wasn't a state Duncan Welch wanted anyone to witness him in. Yet here he was.

"What's wrong?" she asked.

The glass clacked as he set it shakily on the bar. "Personal matters."

A deep male voice from near the jukebox cut her off, bellowing, "Turn the TV up! *Turn the TV up!*"

The flat-screen was mounted on the short wall that ran around the drop ceiling above the bar, and with the exception of Broncos games, it was normally muted. Raina couldn't see the screen, but she grabbed the remote from under the register and tossed it to the shouting man. Somebody jerked the plug on the jukebox, the neon lights going dark.

The stern voice of a news anchor rose to the TV's max volume.

"—in custody after being apprehended in a motel outside Kerrville, Texas. He's a prime suspect in the murder of disgraced former Brush County Sheriff Charles Tremblay—"

"Oh fuck." Raina jogged around the counter to stand with the others. "They got Levins?"

One customer confirmed just as another shushed her. She'd

have taken issue with the latter, but the news was too important.

"—foreman is also a suspect in two other high-profile cases linked to the future Eclipse Casino in Fortuity. One involves human remains allegedly exhumed during the initial construction, as well as the death of Brush County Deputy Alex Dunn. It's been speculated that Charles Tremblay and David Levins may have conspired to kill Dunn, to prevent news of the remains from becoming public, and endangering the progress of the casino. Virgin River Contracting is under federal investigation for widespread corruption, and it seems perhaps Sunnyside Industries might be joining them—unconfirmed reports say an employee of the developers is being questioned regarding bribery allegations."

"Fucking corporate bottom feeders," someone grumbled, echoed by another man's "Like they don't get paid enough already."

"For the latest bulletins on David Levins's arrest, stay tuned to KBCN, Brush County's number-one news station."

Several people clapped, and one man said, "Run like a deer, get caught by the wolves."

His neighbor said, "Casino ain't even fucking built yet and already this town's going to hell."

"We was already halfway there," her friend countered.

A beer bottle came down with an angry thud. "Fortuity ain't much, but it's ours. I got half a mind to drive these goddamn vultures out by force."

"Fucking right," chorused another man.

Raina's blood cooled, her thoughts turning to Duncan. No chance it was him who'd taken bribes—she'd never met a man with a bigger hard-on for rules in her life. But it wasn't going to help his standing among the locals if Sunnyside got tarred with the same brush as VRC.

Raina stared at the screen, commercials flashing. "Fucking hell."

"Well put."

She turned at the words, finding Duncan standing beside her, drink in hand, eyes on the TV.

The jukebox stayed dark, the TV volume turned down a few notches and all but drowned out by the dozens of conversations now buzzing throughout the bar. People slowly gravitated to their tables and stools, and Raina got back to work. Duncan and Casey settled again on their seats.

"Well," she said, filling a pitcher. "I didn't see that coming. You sure this is where you want to be tonight?" she asked Duncan. The natives were even more restless than usual, and unless he boasted some secret karate prowess, she didn't give him great odds in a bar fight.

He didn't reply, but Casey was animated—and probably relieved to be talking about something other than his massive foot-in-mouth episode with Abilene. "'Bout fucking time they found him."

"No kidding," she said. "I figured he must've made it to Mexico by now."

"He turned himself in." Duncan's tone was flat, expression blank. And his glass was empty, clattering softly against the wood in his jittery grip. His eyes were dark, pupils large and eerie. She'd seen him like this once before, and gleaned that it indicated a nasty combo of liquor and whatever prescription meds he'd mentioned taking.

"Dunc—"

He slipped, nearly falling sideways off the stool, catching himself with an elbow on the bar.

"Jesus." Raina bent over the counter and grabbed him under one armpit, every pound of him feeling limp. "Casey, help me."

Casey hurried over, shoving an arm under each of Duncan's from behind. "Whoa, dude."

Raina knew what had to be done, much as she preferred to fix things herself.

"Abilene, call nine-one-one."

Chapter 6

"No," Duncan cut in as Abilene headed for the phone. His voice was hollow and odd, but some clarity had returned.

"Do it," Raina told Abilene.

"Don't," Duncan countered, and managed to stand up straight.

Casey let him go and stepped back a pace. "What the fuck you on?"

"Nothing fatal. I'm just having a bit of a reaction," Duncan said, eyes unfocused, words reedy and far off.

"A reaction of what and what?" Casey asked.

"Pills and alcohol and a rather potent anxiety attack."

"Good God, get him upstairs," Raina told Casey. She pulled her apartment keys from her pocket and Casey caught them.

She gave the bar a quick scan, filled an order, but found most folks preoccupied with the news. To Abilene she said, "Think I'm going to need you to fly solo for a bit."

"Oh. Um, okay."

"I'll get Casey to help out. He worked here when he was your age." Raina tossed her bar towel aside and rounded the counter. "Anybody tries to rob us," she said to Abilene, "there's a loaded shotgun between the cooler and the cupboards."

She jogged up the back stairwell and heard Casey swearing through the open apartment door. She hurried through the kitchen and found him easing Duncan onto the center couch cushion in her dark den. By the light slipping in from the kitchen, the man looked woozy, but conscious. His lids were heavy, those normally blade-sharp eyes dull.

Casey waved a hand in front of his face.

"Yes, yes. I see you."

"What the fuck'd you take?" Casey repeated.

"It's prescription."

"You better not OD in Raina's apartment, man. That's so fucking rude."

"I took two Klonopins," Duncan said. "Or maybe three."

"And two shots," Raina said. "What's Klonopin do?"

Casey flipped on the side table lamp, illuminating his frown. "When I did time, my cell mate took that shit to keep from going psycho."

Duncan seemed to will himself lucid enough to glare at Casey. "I take it for panic attacks. And anxiety."

"Doesn't seem to be working."

Raina felt her perceptions about Duncan bang a U-turn, with his normally dominant character trait—cool control—suddenly gone.

"Were you shaking from the pills when you came in," Raina asked, "or the anxiety?"

"The latter," Duncan said. "Or both." He leaned forward to plant his elbows on his knees and rub his face. Inappropriate though it probably was, Raina got distracted, watching his arms. She'd never seen him in a T-shirt, never seen his bare skin past the elbow. *Nice.* Inappropriate, but yes, very nice.

"What are you so anxious about?" she asked.

Not meeting their eyes, he said, "I've been sacked."

Raina blinked. "Whoa."

Casey did a double take. "Sunnyside fired you?"

"I've been on probation since we got Tremblay arrested," Duncan said, long fingers tangling in his messy sandy brown hair. He had more stubble on his jaw than Raina had imagined him capable of growing. The man was coming apart at the seams.

"That's shitty," Casey said.

Duncan sat up straight, still avoiding their eyes. "That was only fair, considering the way I exploited my position."

"But now you're fired, for real?" Raina asked.

Duncan took a deep breath. "David Levins told the feds I was accepting bribes from him, in exchange for not reporting shoddy construction practices."

"Jesus. That was you?"

"It was an accusation."

"Is it true?" Casey asked.

Duncan leveled him with a stare like smoldering coals—a

blaze, subdued. "Of course it isn't. I've never broken the law in my life, not until I met your brother and the rest of you lot. I don't need to, besides. Sunnyside paid me too well for money to have ever been a temptation."

"Way you dress and that car you drive," Casey said, "not sure if people will believe that."

"Yes, thank you. So I've been told."

"Half the town already thinks you're a dick. Hope they don't upgrade you to something worse."

Raina said, "Shut up, Case." Though she shared his concern.

"Just saying. It's bad enough everybody's been calling him Mr. Peanut."

Duncan stiffened, frowning. "Mr. Peanut?"

"Because you're, like, one monocle shy of a dandy," Casey said.

"Mr. *Peanut*, really . . . He's not even British."

"Isn't he?"

"You're not helping, Casey," Raina cut in. To Duncan she said, "The feds won't have any proof."

"Not any credible proof, no . . . Though apparently a witness has come forward who claims to have seen me accepting money from Levins. My motel room and car were searched this morning, though they won't have found anything."

"A witness? Shit. You could fight it, though. Sunnyside would have to give you your job back."

"Yes, I could fight it." But his posture and his voice said he didn't have the fuel, just now. "Though I'd prefer a time machine, so I could go back and keep far away from the lot of you."

The comment stung Raina deeper than she wanted to admit. "We might not have proven Alex was murdered, without you."

"Forgive me if I'm finding it hard to give a shit about your dead friend at the moment."

"Hey—" Casey was poised to take issue, but Raina grabbed his arm and stilled him.

"He's freaked-out and basically high. Let him be an asshole."

"That was a real fucked-up thing to say," Casey spat at Duncan, fists clamped to his sides. "Our friend was *murdered*. All you lost was a fucking job."

Raina corralled him toward the kitchen. "Go help Abilene

behind the bar. And don't go telling anyone about any of this."
Surely Duncan wouldn't have spilled half of what he had if
he'd been in his right mind.

"You're welcome," Casey muttered, and headed for the
door. "Exactly what I wanted to do on my Friday night . . ."

Raina crouched and put a hand on Duncan's knee. It
seemed like the kind of thing a nurturing woman would do.

His lips were a hard line, eyebrows drawn and angry, but
when he spoke, he sounded cooler. "Apologies. I shouldn't
have denigrated your friend's death."

"You have any clue of the kind of nasty shit I hear, surrounded by drunk people every night? Save your apology for
Casey."

Duncan sank back on the couch, glaring up at the ceiling.

"Can I make you some tea or something? I've got black,
and some kind of mint."

"I don't need nursemaiding."

"Funny, seeing as how you needed hauling up the stairs just
now."

He stared at her, gray eyes softening by a degree in the
lamplight. "Fine. Tea would be lovely. Black, please."

"How do you take it?"

"Milk and honey."

"No honey. Sugar?"

"One. Thank you."

She headed to the next room and turned the burner on under the kettle. "Have you eaten much today?"

"Just some toast, around ten. And that didn't stay down, I'm
afraid."

"Well, Jesus. Three pills and a stiff drink on no food? And
that horrible slap in the face? No wonder you're a shaky,
douchey mess. Come in here."

He joined her after a moment, pulling out a chair at her
small table. Raina looked through the fridge. "I've got . . . not
a lot. Leftover spaghetti. Or I could make turkey sandwiches."
She turned to find him studying her, with something like uncertainty or surrender on his face, the anger gone.

"A sandwich would be nice," he said tightly.

"Mustard or mayo?"

"Just dry."

"Easy enough." She got them started, and filled a mug with

water when the kettle squealed. She set sandwiches on the table, then Duncan's tea. "Milk and one sugar."

"Thank you."

She laughed to herself. "This is so weird."

He blew on his steaming cup. "My breakdown?"

"No. My acting like a hostess."

He cracked a little smile at that. "Not the happy-homemaker type, I take it."

"Whatever gave me away?"

He glanced around the kitchen. "Looks homey enough to me."

Raina shrugged. "Hasn't really changed since I was a kid."

They ate in silence for a minute, and she watched Duncan's eyebrows rise as he studied the writing on the mug. *A Giant Cup of Suck My Dick.*

"My dad's," she said. "I forget sometimes what it even says."

"He must have been quite . . . colorful."

"When he got diagnosed . . . his doctor said something like 'Mr. Harper, you have stage-four lung cancer.' We were sitting in the guy's office, and my dad just shot out of his chair and told the doctor, 'Well, you can suck my dick.'"

Duncan's shoulders hitched with a silent laugh, expression officially softening. "He chose to take the denial and anger steps two at a time, it sounds like."

"It became kind of a thing. Us and my dad's buddies telling cancer to suck our dicks, when we got too sad or angry or frustrated about it. I forget who got him that mug, but it was his favorite."

"I'll be careful with it, then. And what about your mother?"

Raina shrugged. "I never met my mom. I mean, I did, obviously. Briefly. But she dumped me on my dad's doorstep when I was a couple days old."

"And he was actually your father?"

She nodded. "Yeah. I mean, he remembered my mom. They met when she was about twenty and he was in his late forties."

Duncan's eyes widened.

"Yeah, I know. I don't think much logic went into it. She was this mysterious Mexican girl who blew through town, made a middle-aged bachelor feel ten feet tall. Blew back out the next week. Fast-forward nine months—instant fatherhood."

"And you haven't heard from her since?"

"No. I used to wonder if she'd ever come looking for me, but after thirty-two years, I've quit holding my breath."

"Have you considered trying to find her yourself?"

She shook her head, smiling. "I'm hard-wired to harbor grudges, not longing."

Duncan held her stare. "I believe that."

They ate their sandwiches, and Raina put the plates in the sink and puttered around while Duncan drank his tea. "You seem way calmer, now," she said.

"I suppose I am. Now I merely feel drunk."

"Well, as I said—I like you drunk, Duncan."

"I operate best under chemical influence," he said faintly. He looked up and held her gaze. "I didn't mean what I said, about regretting having helped you all."

She smirked as she sat. "You did. But I don't really blame you. You've got no loyalty to us." And now he was in hot water over it all. And if Duncan was telling the truth—if he hadn't taken bribes, and the accusation and witness were false . . . "Why were you so sure that Levins turned himself in?"

"I'm not *certain* he surrendered—it's merely a hunch. He's behind the fabrication of this alleged witness, of that I have no doubt, and he wouldn't have bothered to arrange that if he hadn't known he'd soon be in custody. I think he set it all up so he'd have something to trade the feds, in the hopes of a lighter sentence. With the bonus of ruining my life, as I helped ruin his."

She nodded, head filling up with worries. Filling up with thoughts of Alex. Like her friend, Duncan was tangled up in the plot that had claimed three lives already—one good man, one bad one, and one as yet unknown.

She glanced over to find Duncan studying her, a curious look on his handsome face. "What?"

"Do people really call me Mr. Peanut?"

She smiled, though the fear still nagged. "It's not so bad. He's a sharp dresser."

"And an anthropomorphic nut."

"I'm sure they just couldn't remember the Monopoly man's name."

"Uncle Pennybags," Duncan murmured, sinking back wearily in his chair.

They'll be calling you worse things, she thought with a

shiver, *if it gets out that you were the one accused of taking bribes.*

Duncan stretched his neck and said, "You can return to work. I won't be long—I just need to get ahold of myself, and then I'll go. I promise not to steal anything."

"Oh yeah, because I was totally worried about you making off with my ancient beige computer and my two-hundred-pound tube TV. You just chill out awhile. I'll join you. Casey and Abilene have the bar covered. You want to watch something?"

He looked stymied, and Raina stood. She smacked his back. "Up you get." She ushered him to the den with a hand between his shoulder blades.

She switched on the television and handed him the remote. "You pick—there's only five channels. If you want to avoid news bulletins about Levins, stick with channel four—that's all telenovelas and weird Mexican Jesus shit, twenty-four-seven. I'll make more tea. Take your shoes off, get comfortable. Hug a pillow. Cry your guts out."

He sat and Raina headed back to the kitchen.

Duncan Welch, framed . . . if she believed him, which she did. Framed and fired. And pretty fucked-up. Duncan Welch, on her couch. Why was it so unmistakably charming to see this man in tatters? To see everything that made him *Duncan Welch* ripped away. He'd never seemed like more of a stranger. And she'd never felt quite so . . . tender toward him.

But she had to worry, beyond this moment of weakness, beyond the nasty legal mess Duncan might have ahead of him . . . It was likely that others had been complicit in Alex's death, in Tremblay's, in the unknown fate of those bones. And it spelled danger for Duncan, alone in that motel room. She pulled out her phone as the kettle heated and sent a text to Vince, Casey, and Miah.

Calling a meeting tomorrow at noon.

They owed Duncan, for the risks he'd taken—and that he was paying for now, if Levins's accusations were payback for his role in August's drama. They owed him protection. And it might take all four of them to convince Duncan to accept it.

All three of us, she corrected herself. Vince would be on

board, and Casey would, too, with enough arm twisting; his emotions had no attention span, and his anger would burn off by morning. Miah, however . . . he'd be a tough sell. He'd have to call on every last ounce of fairness in his being to muster sympathy for Duncan.

She gave it some thought, then texted Vince. And bring Kim.

Kind of a ploy, but Kim had been in Duncan's position. She'd seen and heard things she shouldn't have, things that could've gotten her locked in Tremblay's and Levins's sights. Miah had found room for her at the farmhouse. It'd be hypocritical of him to deny that Duncan deserved the same rallying efforts, with Kim standing there. Both were outsiders who'd gotten wrapped up in the Desert Dogs' problems, through no fault of their own. If they really were a club now, they'd look out for Duncan.

She carried the steaming kettle and a pot holder out to the living room and set them on the coffee table, then went back for the tea bags, sugar box, and milk carton. Duncan refreshed his cup, and Raina propped her feet on the table. Unsurprisingly, he didn't follow suit. But his legs were crossed, and he'd taken off his shoes. His socks were charcoal gray, his feet long and elegant beneath that soft-looking weave, arches strong. It seemed so bizarre, to realize this man had feet. With delicate veins, and well-groomed toenails, surely. Too . . . human.

She gave him a pointed up-and-down, smiling, and he met her eyes. "Yes?"

"You look weird, just in a T-shirt and socks. Like you're naked."

"You look strange, out from behind that bar."

"You've seen me away from there before. When we went after Tremblay."

"Indeed. I saw you on the back of Jeremiah Church's motorcycle that day."

She paused. "How'd that make you feel?"

"You sound like my therapist." But he seemed to consider it. "I can't recall how I felt. I got distracted when your charming town's head of law enforcement struck me in the teeth with his gun."

"Fair enough."

He held her stare. "I do remember you kneeling beside me, wiping the blood off my face with the hem of your shirt."

She smiled. "That's why I wear black."

He sipped his tea.

"You shouldn't stay at the Nugget anymore. You should crash with one of us, if you're sticking around Fortuity."

"If? As though I have a choice. The feds wouldn't be impressed if I skipped town just now. Though trust me—there's no place I'd rather be farther from."

"Good."

"But I don't need protecting, as adorable as your concern is."

"How come you came into the bar, so worked up?" she asked, changing tacks. "Doesn't seem like you, inviting an audience to your mental breakdown or whatever."

He didn't reply, his brow furrowing as though he shared her surprise. He could've grabbed a bottle of vodka from one of the two liquor stores up the street, suffered his identity crisis in the privacy of his room. Why Benji's? On a busy Friday night? She didn't dare presume it had anything to do with her, with whatever twisted little bond they had. Maybe he'd simply known, deep down, that he'd wind up taking things too far, between the pills and the alcohol, and wanted witnesses. Seemed likely. Self-preservation was this man's style, more than cry-for-help. She supposed that meant she was giving him what he needed, just now . . . though a silly part of her was disappointed to think it wasn't personal, his coming to her when he was freaked-out.

"Maybe," she said, baiting, "it was because of what happened when Tremblay pistol-whipped you. Maybe that's why you came to the bar tonight, instead of holing up in your room. Because you knew I'd mop you up."

"You read far more humanity into my motives than I dare give myself credit for."

Liar. He was achingly human, she knew that now, beyond a doubt. But she let the *why* of it slide. Duncan had been put to enough screws for the time being. "Can I ask you something?"

"You may."

"You really only took a couple of your pills, right? That wasn't like a . . . you know. An *attempt* or anything?"

Those eyes were all at once wide and awake. "What, a suicide attempt? Dear God, no. How insufferably melodramatic."

"Okay, good. I know some people's identities are tied up in their jobs, is all. And, no offense, you seem like one of them."

"People aren't everything they appear," Duncan said mildly,

his attention moving to the screen, to some laugh-tracked sit-com.

She considered that, knowing he was right. About himself, surely. She'd never have imagined he was a man capable of a panic attack, before tonight. He'd seemed so ... contained. She thought of Vince, too, and how he advertised as something far harder and more self-serving than he really was. Did his brother have hidden depths? she wondered. Doubtful. For a man whose erstwhile job demanded pure guile, Casey Grossier was a hopelessly open book. Abilene had some shadows to her, though.

As for Raina herself, she liked to think that what you saw was what you got. Same as Miah. There were simple people, and tricky people. And Duncan was growing trickier by the minute.

"Have you ever been married?" she asked.

He met her eyes. "No. Not even close."

"Huh."

"Why? Do I seem like the marrying kind?"

"No, but you seem like the divorcing kind somehow."

His lips twitched. "I suppose that's fair. I'm exceedingly difficult to date."

"Oh yeah?"

"I possess a winning combination of impossibly high standards and stunted empathy."

"At least you know it, I guess."

"Arrogance without self-awareness is unbearably gauche. No one's cataloged my faults as studiously as I have. I wonder sometimes what I'm paying my therapist for."

She laughed. "You're so weird. Weird and fancy. Easily the fanciest man who's ever sat on that couch. What are your parents like? Crazy-posh?"

His smile faded at that. "No comment."

"Fine. I'll let it go, only because you've spent enough time getting interrogated for one day."

"Appreciated. As is this," he added, and held up his cup.

She shrugged. "Bringing people drinks is kind of my bag."

He turned to meet her eyes. "Just say, 'You're welcome.'"

"You're welcome."

Apropos of nothing—or perhaps apropos of the chemical crisis—he asked, "Why'd you end it with Church?"

She shrugged, hiding her surprise. Surprise at the sudden

change of topic, and undeniable pleasure that he cared. "He wanted to make a decent woman of me."

"The cad."

She looked to the TV, fighting an urge to open up to him. She'd gotten deeper inside Duncan's head than she'd ever guessed she might, and the imbalance it created felt cumbersome. After a long pause, she told him, "I don't like feeling like I'm being taken care of by anyone." With her father, she'd been both the child and parent, and as much as she'd loved him, she'd never felt entirely secure in his care. Never entirely trusted him. Not because he'd been mean, but because he'd been weak—flighty at the best of times, and straight-up useless when he drank. About as reliable as a teenage boy. Good intentions, poor results. "I'd much rather be needed than do the needing," she concluded.

"Ah."

She sought his gaze. "You want to analyze me?"

He didn't reply.

"Feel free. Seems only fair."

"Go on, then."

She toyed with her tea bag's string. "I loved my dad. I cared for him well before he was sick, and nursed him when he was. I relied on him and nobody else, when I was little, for better or worse. Confided in him. Lost him. Most of the things a woman feels for a man, I used up on him. My tank's empty, for all the love that matters." She met his gaze. "Any needs I have left over, any decent, convenient, good-looking man is welcome to satisfy. But my heart's spent. And Miah wanted my heart."

Duncan's reply was quiet and a touch earnest. "That's rather tragic."

"Nah. Tragic's giving everything you have to one man, then getting it handed back all banged up and smelling of another woman's perfume."

Duncan looked back to the television. They drank their tea, watching the crap flashing by on the screen, not talking. She wondered if he felt as naked as she did, finding the two of them on this new level together. Not friends, but something above their usual bartender-and-customer flirtation. Kind of scary, kind of pleasant. Definitely doomed to flee once Duncan sobered up and the sun rose to fade the memory of this talk.

And when he did leave, the fear would take his place—fear that the next time Raina watched him go, it could be the last time she saw him alive. Mutinous locals would be dangerous enough on their own if his accusation went public, but Duncan was on Levins's bad side as well, and who knew if that shit still had coconspirators on the outside?

Raina had lost Alex only two months ago. They'd grown apart in recent years, as his drinking had begun corroding him, a habit snowballing into an addiction she'd known all too well, as the daughter of a functioning alcoholic. It had felt too familiar, too scary. And too fraught, when her role as Alex's friend had become overshadowed by her role as his bartender, the distance growing each time she'd had to cut him off and send him home. It had only made losing him harder. Though she had no idea what she ought to have done differently, she couldn't help feeling she'd failed him. As she'd watched his casket being lowered, all she'd thought was *I'm sorry. I'm sorry.*

Duncan Welch might mean far less to her than Alex had meant, but she couldn't bear the thought of suffering all that regret again. Of feeling as though she hadn't done enough, when she'd had the chance.

Eventually she stood and juggled the empty mug and kettle and pot holder. Her guest would probably want to go back to the motel now. The idea made her queasy, but he'd be tough to convince to stay, for the night. But she could be tougher.

"More tea?" she asked.

No reply, and she looked to his face for the first time in twenty minutes. He was asleep. Tilted gently to one side, eyes shut, lips parted. He looked . . . peaceful. As loose as she'd ever seen him, and she had to smile.

She grabbed the old afghan off the back of the rocker. She held her breath as she lowered the heavy thing over Duncan from the shoulders to the shins. Tucking it along his sides, she was struck by how soft his skin was, and how hard his biceps were. His hair was uncharacteristically messy, and she smoothed it off his temple. Also soft. Three crisp lines creased his forehead, etched by a million dry eyebrow raises. He had little lines beside his eyes, too, and at the corners of his mouth. She wanted to touch his dignified nose, his pale eyebrows, his perfect ears and neat brown lashes, his near-blond stubble. He . . . he fascinated her. She wished she could lay her body against his without waking him. Spoon him as she had done Miah for these past few weeks, see how much warmer or colder or harder or sweeter he'd feel.

Psycho. She stood up straight, backed off. Took the sugar and milk to the kitchen and poured a glass of water. She left the glass on the table before Duncan and switched off the television. Behind the muffled din of the bar, she heard his breathing. Faint and steady.

She flipped off the light, studied his face a final time in the glow of the moonlight. She wondered if she'd see that face again in the morning, or if he'd sneak out in the dead of night. She knew now, she couldn't guess.

She didn't know this man at all.

Chapter 7

Duncan woke from the heat—from a beam of hot sunshine baking one side of his face. He opened his eyes, recognizing nothing at first. Nothing aside from the smell of toast; a faintly burned scent, echoing the disturbing dream he'd been tangled in. Charred black bones, just out of his reach.

"Good morning, star-shine."

He turned, finding Raina leaning along the frame of her kitchen door, and it all came back to him. He'd fallen asleep, slumped on her couch. A cold wave washed through him, chased by the heat of humiliation. He couldn't think of anyone he'd less rather have been so weak in front of.

She'd draped a blanket over him; it pooled in his lap as he sat up straight. He faked nonchalance even as the burn of embarrassment warmed his throat and ears. "Good morning. I didn't expire in the night, then?"

She shook her head. She was wearing . . . not a lot. A tank top, as usual, but her jeans had been replaced with quite-short shorts. Soft little cotton things with a taunting drawstring, barely more modest than panties. Her wavy hair was bundled up in a messy knot, giving Duncan a fine view of the part of her he found most alluring of all—her neck. That shifted the heat, embarrassment giving way to darker sensations, if not completely.

"You want coffee or tea?" she asked. "Or a shower?"

"No, no." He had to get back to his motel room. Even jobless, he still had *some* responsibilities. Astrid would be wanting breakfast. "Thank you."

"I'm meeting with the Grossiers and Miah today, at noon.

I'm going to tell them you'll be needing our help while you ride out this legal drama. We owe you that much."

He frowned. "I have plenty of money, thank you."

"Not money. Protection."

He shivered, blaming it on the desert's morning chill. "That strikes me as unnecessary."

"Don't care what it strikes you as," she said, rubbing her bare calf with her heel. "There's no guarantee that the corruption ended with Levins and Tremblay. And after what happened to the sheriff, and to Alex, we can't take any chances. Plus, Kim helped us, and we made sure she stayed safe. Same applies to you."

"I don't require protection." He had done so, once upon a time as a child, but hadn't been offered the luxury then. Without it he'd suffered kicks and slaps and cigarette burns, but lived to tell. Well, not to *tell*—to suppress, mainly. But in any case, he didn't need anyone's protection. "I appreciate your concern, as well as your logic. But no. I'm not some helpless victim in need of a safe house." Not anymore. Not ever again.

"Like I said, I don't care what you think you need. Just know it's being arranged. Sure you don't want anything to drink? Or some toast?"

He stood, folding the blanket. "I'm perfectly fine." As if she'd buy that, when he'd been steered bodily into her home, intoxicated and shaking. It shamed him to remember, with a clear head. She was the last person in this town he'd ever have wanted to see him in that state.

So why did I go to the bar in the first place? Indeed. Straight to her. He stuffed the thought down.

He found his shoes and sat on the coffee table to lace them. He longed for his oxfords, for a suit and tie, for his car. For the trappings of the man he'd worked so hard to become, whom he'd lost yesterday when his job was taken from him. He was like a screen, the position a projection he relied on to give him his identity. Without it, would the clothes even be enough? Or would everyone see him for the flimsy, blank expanse of nothing he was?

"I'll let you know what we decide," Raina said.

He met her dark eyes, letting his irritation drown out the distress. "I thought Vince Grossier was pushy, but you're giving him competition." It was obnoxious and patronizing, and strangely, it made him want to pin her against the doorframe and remind her which of them was the more aggressive sex.

Her stare was steady. "If pissing you off and pushing you around means I don't wake to the news that someone shut you up, the way they silenced Alex and Tremblay, in that crummy little motel room . . . Then yeah, I don't have any issue with that."

"Being pushed around requires consent," he said, checking his pockets for his wallet and keys. "And rest assured, I won't be tendering any. Thanks very much for the tea and sympathy, Ms. Harper." He brushed past her into the kitchen.

"If you're going to be stubborn, somebody could stay with you, instead. Unfortunately it'd probably be Casey. He's the only one of us with time on their hands."

"No one's helping me. No one ever has before, and I'm perfectly comfortable with that." And he was showing far too much emotion. He steadied his voice and met her eyes with his hand on the doorknob, recalling what she'd said last night. "If you want to be what a man needs, Ms. Harper, we both know there's another one waiting, more than willing to volunteer."

Her smile was sharp and dry. "We'll resume this conversation later, Mr. Welch."

Raina was first to the spot. She dug out her keys to open the left-hand bay door and hauled it up, sunshine spilling into the old auto garage, glinting off the carcass of a touring bike Vince had liberated from the junkyard. She'd lugged a case of beer up the street from Benji's, and she stocked the fridge. Miah would need a couple of early ones, if he was going to be convinced to open up Three C to yet another endangered outsider. And God knew what Duncan would take, to be convinced to accept the help. He'd gone from an accessible, sedated mess last night to his old impenetrable self this morning. She'd been stupid to think something had truly changed, just because of the things they'd said, the new sides of him he'd let her see. Dumb, when she knew a drunk's promises could never be trusted, and he'd been wasted, as surely as he'd been vulnerable.

She sighed. "One step at a time." She'd talked her dad into going to the doctor, four years ago, a seemingly impossible feat accomplished by threatening to sell his record collection. She could handle Duncan, provided she figured out his leverage.

The rumble of a motorcycle grew in the distance—no, two

of them, she saw, as the Grossiers rolled into the lot, Kim on the back of Vince's old R80.

Once the engines were muted she called, "Afternoon, kids."

"Hey," Kim said, first to reach her.

Vince offered a slap on her arm, and Casey cut to the chase. "What's this shit all about?" Apparently his foul mood from the night before had followed him to bed. Though whether it was Duncan's slight or an awkward night spent skirting Abilene behind the bar, who could say?

"Let's wait for Miah." Raina handed him a beer, which shut him up like a pacifier stuffed in a toddler's face. If only Duncan would prove so simple a creature.

"This about Welch?" Vince asked, just as Miah's Triumph came growling down Station Street. He caught the bottle Raina tossed him, but didn't open it. He wasn't as easily distracted as his brother, and plainly he'd been tipped off about Duncan's little breakdown. Kim declined a beer.

Miah parked and strode in, greeting everyone and meeting Raina's eyes last.

"Beer?"

"Nah. I'm only on a break. Too much to do today. This about Levins?"

"Kind of." She opened a bottle for herself and hopped up onto the worktable. "But Vince called it—it's mainly about Welch." It felt funny calling him that. He'd come to feel like plain old Duncan to her, since last night. Since she'd seen him in his socks.

Miah crossed his arms, gaze jumping irritably to the street. The claustrophobe was annoyed, and eager to escape back outside.

"What about that dick?" Casey asked. "What happened last night? You sober him up?"

Miah was suddenly all eyes and ears, eyebrows drawn.

"I did," Raina said. "It wasn't anything self-destructive, I don't think. Not really. He just went off the rails." She glanced between Miah and Vince and Kim. "You guys missed it, but he showed up all doped out on his prescription meds. Sunnyside fired him yesterday. Levins accused him of taking bribes, in exchange for ignoring corner-cutting."

"Damn," Kim said.

"You sure it's not true?" Miah asked. "What's to say he *wasn't* taking bribes?"

Vince's expression darkened. "That was Tremblay's scene. Why the fuck would Welch have risked his own job to help me, fucked up a lucrative arrangement with Levins, then put himself on the man's bad side by spilling what he knew to the feds?"

"It gets a little more complicated," Raina said. "A witness came forward, corroborating what Levins said. A construction worker for VRC, it sounds like. That's about all Welch knows."

Vince shook his head. "This is starting to stink of some major planning."

Raina nodded. "Duncan's innocent," she said, catching the familiarity of the name too late, relieved she wasn't one to blush. "I believe that. It makes no sense as anything aside from a distraction, on Levins's part. And payback, because yeah, Welch *did* help you, Vince, and Levins got busted. Duncan'll get his job back, eventually. He can afford a good lawyer, if it comes to that."

"So what's the issue?" Casey asked.

"The issue is that we don't know if Levins set this shit with the witness up on his own or not. And who, if anyone, might've conspired with him to have Tremblay offed, and how loyal they still are to him. We'd be fools to assume Levins is harmless, just because he's locked up."

"To say nothing of how angry people are about anything to do with the developers," Kim added. "If Duncan's name gets out before he's acquitted, Levins might be the least of his problems."

Raina nodded. "Duncan's stuck in town until the feds decide they're done with him. That could be weeks, and the Nugget's about as secure as an outhouse. We offered Kim a safe place to hide out, when she needed one." She said it to the group, but looked at Miah.

His posture stiffened.

"Three C's the obvious choice," she went on. "People coming and going, tons of witnesses who all know each other, should anyone suspicious come poking around. A local address, to keep the feds happy."

Miah shook his head. "I don't want that man in my house. It's his company's fault we've got property vultures trying to buy us out at every fucking turn."

"Kim worked for Sunnyside when she first got here," Raina said.

"As a freelancer," he cut back. "Taking photos. No agenda.

It's in Welch's job description to shut troublesome locals up, keep the casino's wheels greased. In a year or two *your dad's bar* is going to be gone, bought out or run out, because of men like him."

And because of me, maybe. She didn't think she could spend the rest of her life going through the motions of a dead man's dreams, no matter how much she'd loved her father. "Duncan doesn't work for them anymore. They *fired* him."

"And if they hadn't, he'd still be marching around, shooting us all those snobby looks he reserves for every last person whose town he's planning to wreck. So no. No fucking way. Maybe he's not the enemy, strictly speaking, but come on—he's complicit. And he's a jackass."

"Jackass or not, we owe him," Vince said.

"Then you house the shithead," Miah shot back, knowing, as they all did, that the Grossiers had absolutely zero room to do so at the moment.

"Fine," Raina said, locking her arms across her chest. "*I'll* put him up. My place isn't anywhere near as secure as Three C, but it beats the four of us taking turns playing bodyguard at the motel."

Miah's black eyes widened at that, burning hot. "Fine." He just about spat the word.

"Agreed," Vince said, and though she wasn't a member, Kim nodded as well.

Raina looked to Casey.

"Like I give a shit."

"I'll take that as a 'yea.' Okay, settled. I'm on Welch-protection duty."

"You got ammo?" Vince asked.

"Unless bullets expire, tons." She'd fired that .22 exactly twice since Vince gave it to her, six years ago—harmless sky shots to scare off coyotes, both times.

Miah was frowning again, probably reconsidering his stance, now imagining Raina was inviting trouble to set its sights on her home. But even if he suddenly changed his tune and offered up the ranch, she was married to this plan. It appealed to her desire for control. She had that in common with Duncan, it would seem.

"Any other business?" she asked, looking at everyone. All heads shook, so she grabbed a socket wrench and thumped the worktop. "Adjourned. Drink up."

Casey circled Vince's work-in-progress. "Feel like dicking around?" he asked his brother.

"Give me a few—I need to drop Kim back home."

Kim rolled her eyes. "I've got a shoot to prep for—somebody's wedding announcement photos." Her expression said it wasn't her first choice of subject matter.

"I've been meaning to ask you," Raina said, "if you'd ever be interested in a different sort of portrait photography."

Casey looked up from what he was doing. "Nudie shots?"

"Shut the fuck up, Case."

"Tasteful ones, obviously."

She ignored him, turning back to Kim. "My own portfolio's pretty sad, photography-wise. I'd love to have some of my tattooing clients over to Benji's some night, the ones with the work I'm most proud of. Would you ever do that? Photograph a load of roughnecks, in the bar?"

Kim's eyes lit up. "That'd be awesome. And I could shoot you—a portrait to use on your Web site."

She laughed. "My what, now?"

Kim's gears were obviously turning. "I could do that for you, too—you can get a template site for pretty cheap. I'd help you upload and organize everything."

"You say this like my clients are especially Web savvy."

But Vince looked intrigued as well. "You should. If and when the Eclipse comes along, we're gonna get a load of bikers coming through. You could be the go-to artist around here. A real destination. You're good enough for it."

She hopped down from the table. "On that much, we agree."

"You could make enough to hire more staff for Benji's, retire your towel. Get to bed before four a.m. for a change."

Indeed. She could retire more than her towel—she could shut the bar for good, find her fresh start elsewhere, use the money from selling up to open a little studio someplace. Maybe Kim was onto something.

"Come by the bar some night soon," she said. "We'll talk estimates."

Kim was plainly framing shots in her head already, eyes bright. "Deal."

"C'mon," Vince said. "Better get you home." To Casey he added, "Back in twenty."

"Cool." Casey began organizing tools, and Vince and Kim cruised away. Raina expected Miah to follow suit, but instead he shot her a look she knew well. One that said, *Outside.* Once upon a time, that had meant, *Meet me out back so we can kiss until our lips chap.* Not so much anymore. Raina grabbed her beer and followed him into the forecourt.

She took a drink and held his stare. "Lay it on me," she said.

"I'm only gonna say it once—be careful. And be selfish. This guy's safety really worth putting your own at risk?"

"Vince said it himself. We owe him."

"Where does this end?"

"I dunno, Miah. I'll let you know when I get there."

He shook his head, gaze on the ground between them, and ran a hand through his black hair. It was getting really long, nearly brushing his shoulders. Looked good on him, too.

Raina sighed. "We both know you won't change my mind."

"Yeah," he said. "Yeah, I know that all too well."

Christ, were they ever going to be able to talk to each other just as friends? Everything was so heavy now, draped in this cumbersome ex-lovers' shroud.

"Did you two . . ." He trailed off.

"No. We haven't done anything." She didn't even bother telling him it was none of his business.

"Not yet," Miah prompted.

False hope would be a cruel gift to offer this man, so she nodded. "Yeah, not yet."

His jaw clenched, if only for a breath.

"You—"

He cut her off. "How the fuck does it feel like we've got so much history between us, after two months of fucking, two years ago?"

She shrugged. "I dunno. Maybe because we grew up together. Maybe because we're so exactly perfect in one way, but so exactly impossible, in another."

"Is he right for you?"

Raina laughed, feeling sad. "No, of course not."

"Then why bother? Why bother sleeping with him, if it's not going to lead anyplace?"

"You'd never ask Vince this same question, about any of the girls he ever hooked up with."

"Because Vince isn't my ex-girlfriend."

"No, because Vince isn't a girl, period. And like Vince, I don't need to see a future in the eyes of every person I take to bed. Nice if I respect the guy, but some nights, that's just not one of the needs I'm looking to meet. I'm not supposed to admit that, though, because it's *unattractive.* I approach sex like a man, I'm a slut. You—you approach sex like a woman, wanting affection and connection, and a chance at something permanent. You're a saintly fucking cowboy unicorn. You win a spot on *The Bachelor*, and I get a big red skank badge on my sash."

"Don't make this about feminism."

"Then don't *you* act like you get a say in what I do with my body. I never promised a thing to anybody. And I'll fuck who I want, maybe somebody you can't fucking *stand*, and your feelings about it will be your problem."

"I know all that."

"Good. Then I won't need to say it again."

His eyebrows were a hard line. "No, you won't."

She softened her tone, feeling heard for a change. "I know this sucks, and it probably will for a while. But here's the deal—I get with somebody, I don't rub your face in it. You have hard feelings about it, you try your damnedest not to let me see it. That's what I'd do for you. You fall in love tomorrow, I'll smile and act like my heart's not a little bit broken."

He blinked.

"Don't look surprised. Just because I can't stay with you doesn't mean a part of me doesn't want to *be* with you. And just because something didn't end in wedding bells doesn't mean it wasn't worthwhile." Some people wanted to think that, but as it negated Raina's entire romantic and sexual history, she refused to bend over and take it. "But to all that other stuff—deal?"

A single, tight nod. "Deal."

For a long moment they stared at each other. When Miah finally turned to walk to his bike and strap on his helmet, she headed back inside, feeling some closure, finally.

Casey shot her a look, one that told her he'd watched the entire exchange. "I guess—"

"Shut the fuck up, Case."

Chapter 8

Raina climbed into her dad's truck back at the bar and aimed herself toward the mountains.

My truck, she reminded herself. She couldn't seem to get rid of the thing, and it was high time she quit thinking of it as his. His truck, his bar, his apartment. She couldn't say why she was so cagey about attaching herself to those things . . . as though she hadn't grown up in that bar and that apartment. As if she hadn't been borrowing this truck since she turned seventeen.

But if they're mine, what's still his? And if things quit being his . . . would she stop remembering him at all? Was that maybe a good thing, even? It'd make selling the bar easier . . . or at least *less* impossible.

She found Duncan's motel room easily, thanks to the shiny black Mercedes sedan parked in front of it. She frowned as she slammed the truck's door, spotting something strange—fluorescent orange words, spray-painted in crude capitals across both driver's-side doors.

CONFESS OR PAY THE PRICE, JACKAL.

"Fuck." Well, she sure as shit wasn't overreacting, then. Duncan's name must have made the news, in relation to the bribery charges. Nothing about Duncan Welch said "trust-worthy" to the average Fortuitan, and clearly the charges were as damning as a conviction. Great. The way rumors flew around here, Duncan could be complicit in Alex's murder by sundown.

He couldn't know about this yet—if he did, he'd surely have had his precious car in for detailing an hour later. Apparently she got the honor of breaking the bad news.

She stepped up onto the walkway and knocked on the door labeled 4.

Duncan answered after half a minute, cracking the door a few inches, enough to frame his handsome face. All those intimate little lines she'd studied while he slept . . . They felt like hers somehow.

"Ms. Harper."

"Afternoon." Raina felt her eyebrows rise at a strange, strong aroma. Bleach? It flashed her back to a mystery Vince had once asked her to solve, before Duncan had proven himself an ally—to find out why Kim had seen him carrying cleaning supplies into his motel room. At the time it had sounded suspicious, especially coupled with Kim saying she'd seen him talking to someone before slipping inside the door. Perhaps she'd wind up with answers to that old riddle after all.

Then she heard something that only deepened her confusion. An unmistakable meow.

Duncan asked, "How may I help you?"

"Is there a cat in there?"

"Yes, there is."

"Why?"

"I don't know," he said. "Because dogs are filthy?"

"Right . . . Look, I hate to break this to you, but your car's been vandalized."

His eyes grew wide. In a breath he was exiting, pulling the door shut behind him, sweeping past Raina to circle the Merc. "Bloody fucking shit."

She held in a little snort of a laugh. She'd never heard him swear quite so Britishly. She wondered if he got more English, the angrier he was. And he was wearing yellow rubber gloves, which raised her eyebrows. Aside from those, he was underdressed, barefoot in charcoal lounge pants, a nicely fitted navy T-shirt stretched taut between his shoulder blades. She'd bet the tee cost as much as her good leather jacket had. She eyed his feet with distraction. Long and smooth and pedicured, odd against the tired asphalt. Handsome things, just as she'd suspected.

Duncan shook his head, looking dazed. "Fucking rednecks."

"Hey, now," she said, not especially offended. A lot of her neighbors and patrons did indeed fit that bill. "You should take it to Elko," she offered. "Fortuity's mechanics can keep just about anything running forever, but I wouldn't trust them with that paint job."

He stood with an aggravated sigh, snapping the gloves from

his hands with a striking—and strikingly erotic—authority. "I suppose I can spare the time. If I'm ever allowed to leave town, that is."

"You seem kinda calm, for a man who just got a death threat."

"It's not my first." He glared at the paint. "Merely the most expensive."

"Aren't you worried?"

He shot her a leveling look and walked back to the door. "I can handle myself, Ms. Harper, though your concern is charming." He didn't look especially charmed. And if his idea of handling himself was to get fucked-up on vodka and pills again, she'd arrived just in time.

"Can I come in?" She asked partly to take her attention off the way his shirt fell, outlining a hard set of abs. "To talk?"

He paused—a long, long pause, eyes seeking the door. "No."

At once, her gut plummeted. Because why did men keep women from seeing the insides of their motel rooms?

"You got a chick in there?" she teased, letting her tone hide the nauseated pang the idea gave her.

"Now, that would be highly efficient of me, wouldn't it?"

She smiled. "You seem like a highly efficient man." And with the thought fully processed, it did seem a touch ridiculous. But he was hiding something, that was clear. "Are there kinky sex props strewn all over your bed?"

"If you have business with me, Ms. Harper, we can conduct it here." He nodded to the walkway under his feet.

"What's with that?" she asked, stalling, nodding to the yellow rubber in his fist.

"That's nothing."

She bit her lip and lied. "I hate to add insult to injury, but there's more paint, across the back."

His eyes grew round, and when Duncan strode forward to inspect the made-up offense, Raina opened his door, slipped inside, and engaged the chain lock.

The room was dim, curtains drawn. A tabby sat on the queen-sized bed, and it watched as Raina followed her nose, chasing that odd, strong smell. She heard Duncan's shout from outside, then the sound of the door opening.

"Let me in this instant."

"Just a sec." The fumes led her to the bathroom, and when she pushed the door in, it hit.

Definitely bleach. An olfactory wall of it. "Jesus," she muttered to herself. "What have you been doing in here?" She buried her face in the crook of her arm.

"Don't think I won't have you charged," Duncan shouted.

Not finding anything scandalous, she headed back through the room, meeting Duncan's eyes through the gap in the door.

"What the hell are you playing at?"

"You get extra British when you're angry."

"Tell me."

"I just wanted to know why it smells like bleach in here." And to check for stray conquests and whips and so forth.

"Let me in my room or I'll call the police."

"Say please."

His head cocked. "Fuck you."

She nearly giggled at that, giddy to have roused such crassness in this man. She shut the door and undid the chain. He was inside a moment later, the anger draining from him. He was gathering his self-control, shrugging back into that invisible suit of civility. He glanced around the room, expression mellowing. She'd bet Duncan was stingy with his anger, gifting it only when someone absolutely deserved it. She wondered what she'd do next to earn the honor.

"You know," he said mildly, "I've had fantasies about you turning up unexpected in my room. But it never looked like this."

She shot him a look, feeling surprised and a bit warm to hear one of them finally admit it—that this attraction went beyond some chiding game. Or perhaps he was just using that little flirtatious ploy to steal the power back from her.

"It never smelled like this in *my* fantasies." She turned her attention to his outfit. "And you're underdressed."

"I'm cleaning."

"So I saw. Why? I can see you being dissatisfied with the job housekeeping does, but to do the work yourself . . . ?"

Duncan walked to the bathroom and Raina followed. He flipped on the light and fan, illuminating gleaming plastic and porcelain and grout, a red bucket on the floor by the wall, blue sponge perched on the tub's ledge. His arm brushed hers as he leaned to toss the gloves over the bucket's rim.

"Seriously," she said, "what's the deal? Why bother?"

"I have my reasons."

Confusion sent wild images flashing across her imagination—of Duncan cleaning blood off a hacksaw or something, disinfecting evidence, complicit all along. "What reasons?"

"A trillion invisible offenses, ones that no one but I would ever waste half a breath worrying about." He edged past her to rinse his hands in the sink, drying them primly and refolding the hand towel.

Raina turned and wandered back into the main room with suspicions nagging. The cat shot off across the bed as she neared. She pulled open the top dresser drawer—crisp shirts, folded with military precision in flush rows, gradating from white to cream to pale gray to charcoal. Ditto his pants in the drawer below. Perhaps a dozen pairs of identical shorts, tidily rolled beside as many pairs of socks. Gleaming shoes stood at attention by the wall beside a pair of stylish sneakers, arranged so neatly they could've been occupied by invisible soldiers. Duncan had followed, and he watched, saying nothing. There was a slick laptop charging, its brushed aluminum corner nested perfectly with that of the desktop. Phone set precisely parallel.

What the frigging frack?

She stared at him. "You OCD or something?"

He swallowed. "Yes. I am. Are you really so surprised?"

She considered it. Maybe twenty-four hours ago, before she'd seen him shaking in the bar, yes, she'd have been surprised. But after last night?

"I dunno," she said. "You seem so in control. Isn't OCD all about being powerless?"

His expression was impossible to interpret. "Power is nothing if not mercurial."

"You don't seem like a germophobe." Fussy sometimes, but he'd watched her make his sandwich and eaten it without any obvious distress. Then again, he'd been medicated.

"I'm not offended by germs so much as I am imperfection."

"How often do you need to do that kind of stuff?" she asked.

He considered it. "With some things I have to arrange them every day, before I can leave the room. Make the bed just so, set the toiletries in their correct places, organize the items on my desk. Quite a thorough going-over with a lint brush," he added, glancing at his cat.

His cat—the reason Kim had seen him crack his door open,

the party he'd spoken to before entering? Not awaiting a roommate's permission to enter, but making sure his *pet* didn't escape.

"What about scouring your bathroom?" she asked.

"As often as my brain demands it. When I'm busy, perhaps two or three times a week."

"And now that you're idle?"

He frowned. "Twice a day, lately."

"Jesus. That sounds exhausting."

A dry smile. "Exhausting, degrading, tiresome. Anyone you see who looks the picture of control ... It's all a costume. Underneath you'll always find a naked, trembling fraud. Trust me."

She stared at him, long and hard. His hair was messier than usual, feet surely dirty from the parking lot, manicured hands likely still stinking of rubber ... but his clothes were immaculate, despite the casual getup. He was a wreck, dressing daily to pass for a successful, commanding professional. And just now, he was failing.

"Do you even realize how strong the fumes are, in there? It's a wonder you haven't passed out and cracked your skull on the bathtub."

"There's no wonder in any of it, merely dysfunction."

She studied Duncan's unearthly face, like the perfect façade of a fancy house ... but behind the drawn curtains, junk stacked up to the ceiling. "This what you take the pills for?"

"This, and the panic and anxiety attacks. Though they do little to help now."

"You are one steaming hot mess, aren't you?"

"If only my therapist offered such candid assessments. Incidentally, I'd be grateful if you kept this to yourself."

I'll bet you would.

"Man, I had you pegged way wrong." Mr. Perfect, a cold, calculating corporate sniper. In reality, a slave to a set of compulsions Raina knew about from books and television and movies but couldn't begin to truly understand. He needed saving, in more ways than she'd ever guessed. And she had to admit, as a woman who resented feeling dependent upon anyone, a busted-up man held a certain appeal. She'd far prefer to be needed than beholden herself. Spelled *doomed* for any kind of serious relationship, but it was a drill she knew well, thanks to her dad, a role she could fill in her sleep.

"Pack your shit, Duncan. You're coming home with me."

That sad smile sharpened and he leaned against the door-frame. Even a touch slumped, the man was tall. Luxurious. He was too many things that shouldn't fit together, yet here he was, standing before her, smirking.

"Because you suspect I'm in danger?" he asked. "Or because of what you've just seen?"

"Both. Though I came because I think you're vulnerable, here on your own, and that little valentine written on your car confirms it. Who knows who's behind those charges? But add those to an angry mob, and you'll realize it's true. You need help."

"And so you're graciously volunteering to associate yourself with public enemy number one?"

"I'm not afraid of anybody. Plus, nobody fucks with the owner of the town's only bar. So get packed and let's go."

"I don't care to be told what my decisions are, Ms. Harper. In fact, there are few sensations I resent more."

"You're preaching to the choir. But consider the benefits, at least. You get access to a kitchen, a washer and dryer, all the vodka you can drink—provided you don't pair it with pills. Your cat can shed all it wants, in whatever room it likes. It can claw my boots to shit and I won't even complain. Make yourselves at home. In fact, feel free to clean my bathroom."

His eyes narrowed at the joke.

She huffed, frustrated. This must be what it felt like, arguing with herself. Poor Miah.

"Come on. You have to admit, it's safer than staying here."

"If I wanted a bodyguard, I'd have the feds put me in protective custody. But I don't. I'm not going anywhere."

"Look, I get it. All I want is some assurance I won't switch on the news some morning and see that you've been lynched by a load of drunk locals. Or that you've pled guilty, and know it's because somebody threatened you or your loved ones. Because I know you're innocent."

"I don't have any loved ones," he said stiffly.

"Your cat, then—whatever. Or, who knows? To hear you've been shot or something. Or trapped in your burning motel room. I wouldn't put anything past the people who offed Tremblay in his cell. Or my own neighbors, come to that."

"If they were smart," Duncan said, crossing his arms over his chest, "they'd fake an overdose."

A chill washed through her. "That's not funny."

"It wasn't meant to be."

"Just . . . just *stay* with me."

"You're trying very hard to avoid saying please, aren't you?"

She sighed, exasperated. "Fine. *Please.*"

"Please what?"

Christ Almighty, he knew how to tease. "*Please* come stay with me. Just pretend it's a really shitty-ass bed-and-breakfast. Even that has to beat this dump."

He shook his head.

She huffed. "You made me plead, and the answer's still no?"

He smiled and she wanted to slap him. Handily, she had an even lower blow to deal.

"I'll tell people about your OCD."

The smile faded.

"That you're crazy, and that you've come into Benji's on multiple occasions to drink on top of your medication. Think that'll help your case, Duncan? Think I'd make a good character witness?"

His eyes narrowed. "You were trying to help me a moment ago."

"I want you safe. But I'd prefer you professionally ruined and alive to stubborn and dead."

"I think you're being sensationalist."

"And I think you're being naive. Come stay with me or I tell everyone you're a fucking nutcase."

After a pause, "Like a bed-and-breakfast, you say?"

She held her breath, nodding.

He was clearly pissed but forcing self-control. It was pretty hot.

"I'd have to pay you by the night, then," he said tightly.

She shrugged. "Like I'd try to stop you."

Duncan took a deep breath, glancing around as though taking an inventory.

"Deal?"

"This isn't a deal. This is me, submitting in the face of your threats. Thanks very much for not scrawling them across my car."

"So, deal?"

"Deal," he finally muttered, but didn't offer his hand. And with that, he strode to the closet and returned with a suitcase.

She made a face. "Wow. That was slightly easier than I'd expected."

A mirthless little huff. "Easy? You extorted me."

"I twisted your arm."

"Semantics, Ms. Harper." He unlatched the case and propped it open on the bed. "You ought to consider a career in law."

"Just a bit of persistence. That's how I got Vince and Miah and those guys to let me hang out with them when we were kids."

Leaving Duncan to pack his perfect designer clothes into his perfect designer suitcase, she headed to the bathroom to gather his fancy toiletries, putting them in the leather shaving bag she found on the counter. She was probably organizing them all wrong. Maybe he'd have to take everything out and do it over. No matter. Just like Duncan, she only wanted to be doing, just now.

She stole a sniff of his cologne, wishing she could dab it between her breasts and smell him there all day. Silly impulse. Anyway, she'd have the real thing sleeping in the next room, soon enough. And if there was one tried-and-true antidote to attraction, it was cohabitation. She'd get this man back in perspective in no time. She had zero doubt that he'd make an infuriating houseguest.

"Why did you *want* to hang out with them so badly?" Duncan asked when she left the bathroom. "The Desert Dogs or whatever you called yourselves."

She shrugged. "They were always covered in dirt, and shouting. And laughing. Always getting in trouble and going on adventures. It looked like way more fun than Barbies to me. You'd have hated it. We broke a lot of laws and got our clothes all ripped and filthy."

He smiled, she thought, though it was hard to tell with his face cast down, attention on the task of arranging his bag.

"Here's your toiletries," she said. "I probably packed them all wrong. I won't be offended if you redo it."

He tossed the shaving bag into his suitcase without inspection.

"Give me something to do," she said.

"Astrid's bowls are in the corner."

"Astrid? Who calls their cat Astrid?"

"I do. She's named for Astrid Varnay."

"I have no idea who that is."

"I didn't expect you would. She was a singer."

Raina gathered the cat's brushed steel water and food

bowls. "Wish my dishes were half this posh. She probably gets Fancy Feast, huh?"

Duncan's nostrils flared with a little laugh. He nodded to the dresser. "Bottom drawer."

Raina stooped and pulled it open, finding cat food cans. "'One hundred percent certified organic minced chicken liver,'" she read. "'Immune support. Grain-free. Cage-free. *Gluten*-free'? Oh my God, you're obnoxious."

He chuckled at that, stacking folded shirts on the bed. It was perhaps the first true laugh she'd heard from him. She wanted to make him do that again. And again, and again.

"How much do you pay for this crap, per can?"

"I'd rather not say."

"I wouldn't mind being your cat, Duncan," she said as she carried the bowls to the bathroom. "Sounds like a good gig. Unless you bleach the poor thing, that is."

"Perish the thought."

He probably protected the animal from all the fumes, probably had a special feline respirator for it. Meanwhile he was poisoning himself with that stuff, to say nothing of the pills and liquor he downed in the name of mental health.

"You're a weird, weird man," she said under her breath, rinsing the dishes.

Half an hour later, they pulled up behind Benji's. Raina took Duncan's many suit bags and the bucket and cleaning supplies, while he hefted his luggage and the cat in its carrier. The Merc's trunk shut neatly with a tap of his foot beneath the bumper.

"I bet Vince could help you with the paint," she said. "Not a perfect job, but better than nothing."

"I'll look into that."

Duncan had changed and smoothed his hair, looking a bit more like his public self, in jeans that fit too well to cost less than two hundred bucks. He looked like . . . well, like weekend Duncan. Not broken Duncan. She imagined telling the other Desert Dogs everything she now knew about him, and felt an immediate wave of revulsion. Guilt. Maybe that threat had been a bluff, all along. She wanted everyone to keep believing in the costume, as he'd called it—keep believing that he was two-dimensional, cold, and unhurtable. Perfect. Not human, not cracked and threatening to break wide-open.

Raina held the apartment door for Duncan as he passed by.

"You can put your stuff wherever for now—in here, or the living room. I need to strip my dad's bed and make space in the dresser and closet." She grabbed a fistful of trash bags from under the sink.

And after three years' procrastination, it was the only way this particular chore ever could have happened—in a rush of necessity. No time to sip whiskey and listen to the man's records and pore over every worn handkerchief and nostalgic smell. She'd grab his clothes from those drawers, shove all but the most sentimental items into bags, and drop them off at Goodwill before she had a chance to question any of it.

"I'll pay you in advance," Duncan said, following her into her dad's old room. He was fishing through his wallet. He handed her six fifties.

"This for the week?"

"We'll call it a hundred a night."

"Jeez. Well, like I said—I won't stop you." She folded the bills and slid them into her back pocket. A thought crossed her mind, slipped through her lips. "Can I say something tacky?"

"I'd expect nothing less."

"If you and I wind up fucking, you don't get to pay me rent anymore."

His eyebrows rose. "Because you'd feel like a whore?"

She smiled sweetly. "No. Because I'd feel greedy, taking your money on top of your innocence."

His lips twitched, eyes narrowed in a way that made Raina's belly all warm and tight. "You're not coy, Ms. Harper."

"You're not wrong."

"I rarely am."

She turned back to the room. "This could take a while. Would you grab me a beer out of the fridge?"

"Sure."

He delivered it and then looked around. "I could help, if you told me how."

She considered it. "I dunno. I've been putting this off for ages—going through my dad's things. And not to demean our little bonding session last night, but there's no fucking way I'm gonna cry in front of you."

"I'll attend to some work, then." Building his defense case, he had to mean.

"You going to represent yourself in court? If it goes that far, that is."

He nodded.

Probably a good idea. Surely he was dying for a purpose. The strategizing might hold him over until he could reclaim his job.

"I think you'll do just fine, Duncan."

"You say that as though you hadn't just threatened to destroy me yourself. And as if you know me."

"Don't I, though? As well as anyone, aside from your cat and your therapist? What about your parents?"

The light left his eyes, clear gray going flat as concrete, same as last night. "I'll leave you to it."

And he left her there, alone and surrounded by a mountain of her dad's things. Her throat stung, aching to call out terrifying words. True ones. *Come back. I was wrong. I do need help.* But she'd seen what losing one's identity had done to Duncan, and she wasn't brave enough to bring the same on herself. She didn't need help. Help always had price tags dangling off it, ones labeled *Self-respect* or *Independence*, or ones that meant that you owed somebody something. Like love, only worse, since you didn't get sex out of the bargain.

"Fuck that." She strode to her dad's dresser and yanked the top drawer open, and invited the ghosts to do their worst.

Chapter 9

"This all of it?" Flores asked Jaskowski as he sifted through the papers. They were standing on either side of a dinner table in the late ex-Sheriff Charles Tremblay's kitchen, yellow legal-pad pages fanned out between them.

"That's all of it."

"Where'd you guys find this?" Flores asked. The team had been busy through the night.

"Manila envelope, tucked under the silverware tray."

Sure as shit wasn't the bones Flores had been hoping the team would find, but that would've been too easy, wouldn't it? And there was plenty they could still uncover here—clues to suggest further conspirators, hopefully. Clues to suggest the identity of those elusive bones. Clues to who had actually committed Alex Dunn's murder—Tremblay or Levins or someone else entirely. The house had been gone over from top to bottom before, and more than once, but Flores was growing more desperate each day they went without a real break. And though these pages might not be the bones, they weren't nothing.

"We sent scans to a handwriting guy," Jask said. "These papers, plus the pad Tremblay kept beside the phone. It's a strong match."

"No names mentioned, I take it." But these couple of dozen pages of quasi-legible notes sure did seem to corroborate what Levins had spilled—that Tremblay had owed somebody, and big. The figures noted here took leaps from month to month, occasional payments doing nothing to stanch the money hemorrhage.

He whistled, reaching the final page. "Hundred and sixty grand. Fuck of an interest rate."

Jaskowski nodded. "Kind of debt folks wind up paying back with broken fingers."

"This means Levins isn't *completely* full of shit."

"Not completely."

Flores frowned. "This could spell bad news for Welch. I had my money on Levins's claims being bull, but if the gambling debts are real, and that witness is legit . . ."

"You think he did it?"

"Fuck if I know anymore. I think he likes money, for sure. But I also think he makes plenty of the shit for himself, legitimately, and that he's the kind of guy whose personality just begs people to resent him. Especially guys like David Levins. To them, Welch looks like some entitled asshole whose mommy and daddy rocked him in a gold-plated cradle."

"And is he?"

Flores shook his head. "Orphan, best I can tell. Got no record of who his parents might've been. And he grew up in a part of London that sounds more like the projects than Buckingham Palace."

"Huh."

"He's either self-made or a complete fucking scammer. Though all his pedigrees seem to check out."

Jaskowski smiled. "You think he's innocent."

"I did . . . Only a clinical-grade narcissist would talk to me the way he did in questioning. Either he *was* entitled to feel like he got slapped in the face, or he *felt* entitled to it. So I'm not so sure. I think he's guilty of being a cocky prick, and of keeping some shady company, which isn't doing him any favors. But I didn't think he took bribes, no. I thought somebody must have sore feelings toward him, for sticking his nose where it didn't belong."

"Somebody must have real sore feelings toward that Grossier thug, then. Tremblay and Levins wouldn't have gotten busted if not for him."

"Yeah, but who's gonna fuck with Grossier?" Flores asked. "Welch is the easy target, if somebody's feeling bitter—he's the outsider. Punish him for getting involved, cause a distraction while the real bad guys cover some tracks . . . But now I might need to rethink Welch, in light of Levins's claims not being a hundred percent fabricated." Funny aspect of the job, being forced to second-guess your best tool—your instincts. And he'd begun to feel as if something wasn't quite right about Welch, ever since he searched his hotel room. There *was* something unwholesome about a guy that clean and organized. Something about him stank faintly . . . not unlike that bleach-reeking bathroom.

"So, can we agree I'm your hero," Jaskowski asked, "for finding these papers?"

Flores rolled his eyes. "Find us some fucking bones and get me home by next weekend. Then we'll talk."

"What if I sweeten the deal?" Jaskowski reached into his jacket pocket and drew out a plastic bag with a chunky flip phone in it.

Flores blinked. "What's that?"

"Found it wedged in a little space next to the underside of the kitchen sink. No account—it's a disposable."

Pay-as-you-go phone? Now they were talking. "You get call logs off it?"

Jaskowski nodded. "All unlisted, every single one, incoming and outgoing. No voice mails. He was careful. All except one time."

"Oh?"

Jaskowski headed for the counter, fetching a stapled stack of papers. "Text message," he said, flipping through the pages. "To the cell phone of David Levins."

"Excellent. And?"

Jaskowski cleared his throat. "August fifteenth, eight seventeen a.m. 'If a guy named Welch comes by, just give him whatever he asks for. Keep him sweet.'"

Flores felt the floor shift beneath him. "Well, shit."

"Doesn't look great for your little expat orphan buddy."

"No, no, it doesn't." Fuck if he hadn't called that one wrong.

"Not enough to arrest, but plenty for a subpoena to get his phone records and seize his computer," Jaskowski offered.

"I'll put in the request, then give him a couple days," Flores said. "Call him in, waste his time, turn a couple screws. Get him frazzled, give him a chance to scramble and maybe dig himself into a deeper hole." Goddamn, he'd really wanted that asshole to be innocent, too. Thank fuck they hadn't started a pool.

"So now I'm your hero?" Jaskowski asked.

Flores rubbed his sweaty forehead, beat and energized and angry and giddy—everything this job made him feel. Every kind of hungry. "Yeah, you're my hero, Jask. Now quit jerking off and find out what happened to those goddamn bones."

Duncan jumped in the easy chair—his music was suddenly gone, headphones lifted from his ears. He craned his neck to find Raina behind him, smiling. She'd been in and out between the guest room and the kitchen countless times in the past hour or two, but Duncan had taken little notice, caught up in research for his defense.

Raina put the phones to her ears, blinking. "Opera?"

He took them back. "Often."

"Classical, I could see. Opera seems a bit . . . dramatic."

"To each his own." He hit PAUSE on his phone.

"Wait. Is your cat named for an *opera* singer?"

"I got her not long after Astrid Varnay died. I'm averse to sentimentality, but not immune."

"Good God, you're weird. But listen—I'm starving and short on groceries. You want to grab a late lunch across the street?"

Not a bad idea, his stomach suggested. He glanced around, finding Astrid on the windowsill behind the couch, looking lean and alert, but somewhat settled. "I would."

As they headed down the stairs a few minutes later, he said, "I'm assuming Abilene is holding down the fort."

"Yeah. I'll join her around seven. Afternoons are easy. Boring. All the same old men, drinking the same old beers, listening to the same old fifty songs they've been playing since my dad opened the place."

"Predictability has its merits."

"It's painful some days, but it's also the reason I read five books a week. I bet you read a lot," she added as they crossed Station Street.

"Not as much as I'd like to claim."

"No?"

He shook his head. "Reading requires a quiet mind, which isn't something I possess. It takes an exceedingly riveting story to keep my compulsions in the periphery. Though I enjoy audiobooks."

"Of course you do," she said with a smile. "You can read and clean at the same time."

Duncan held the diner's door open for her. As they slid into opposite sides of a booth, he said, "Don't mistake a disorder for a hobby, Ms. Harper. I don't strictly enjoy cleaning. I merely enjoy it more than the sensation of panic that occurs if I *don't* clean."

The older waitress took Duncan's request for a hot water and Raina's coffee.

"What happens," Raina asked, "if you *don't* clean?"

"In reality? A panic attack. In my head . . . I don't know. It seems as though there is no *if*. As though whatever will happen is too horrible to comprehend. Either way, it feels like a matter of life and death."

"Jesus."

The waitress dropped off their drinks and they placed their orders. Thankfully Duncan had made a regular of himself here, so the woman wasn't too put out when he inquired after just about every ingredient that went into the chicken club, eschewing the mayonnaise and requesting spinach in place of iceberg lettuce. He tipped waitresses as generously as he did bartenders, so she accepted the revisions cheerfully enough, then left them be.

Raina watched as he slid a shiny gold envelope from his back pocket. "You bring your own tea bags?"

"Are you truly surprised?"

"Not really. But if you ever pull that shit in Benji's—show up with your own organic lime wedges—I'll bar you."

He smiled, attention on the bobbing bag. "I'm certain you would. How's your father's room coming along?"

She rolled her eyes.

"My offer of help still stands."

"So does my stubborn refusal."

"Theme of the day. I asked Vince about a paint job, by the way."

"Any luck?"

"He said to bring it by the garage tomorrow. I'm not expecting a miracle, but anything is better th—"

Duncan's heart stopped as the diner's door jingled, admitting two men. Flores. His companion was taller, with a big belly, also wearing a generic suit—surely a colleague. Christ, why did they make Duncan feel so *suspicious*? He wasn't doing a thing wrong. Drinking tea. Chatting with a . . . with an acquaintance. Waiting for a sandwich. How had he gone from entitled to paranoid in the span of two days?

"What's wrong?" Raina asked, and she turned in her seat to

see who'd entered. She looked back to Duncan. "Are they from Sunnyside?"

He shook his head. "The one with the glasses is the agent who brought me in."

She frowned, eyes narrowing at the men. "Was he a jerk to you?"

"A touch snide. But nothing out of a film—no blinding lightbulbs or hands slamming down on tables."

"He's got to know you're innocent. You taking bribes from Levins is ridiculous."

"How about we drop it?" he asked as their food was delivered. "I'd like to spend a few minutes *not* thinking about my predicament, if that's all right."

"Fine."

They ate quickly and split the bill. Duncan cursed his heart for beating hard as they made their way to the exit, the agents seated at the counter eating matching burgers. He focused his attention on Raina's backside, but the distraction fell apart at the sound of her voice.

She stopped behind the two men. "You Flores?" she demanded.

The man swiveled on his stool and caught sight of Duncan, offered a little nod as he swallowed a bite of burger. He looked to Raina. "I am. Who's asking?"

"I just want you to know," she said quietly, "that if you think Duncan took bribes, you ought to get your badge revoked for having the mental capacity of a turd."

The other fed snorted, and Duncan ground his teeth. "Christ."

Flores's eyebrows rose above his glasses. "I don't discuss ongoing cases with the public. Though your opinion regarding my likeness to a turd has been noted."

"If you ever come across the street," Raina said smoothly, "I'll see to it personally that your drink gets spit in."

Flores smiled. "You asking for a visit from the health inspector, Miss . . . ?"

"Ms. Harper," Duncan said, and steered Raina toward the door. "Excuse us."

"I think you're a prick," Raina tossed over her shoulder at Flores. "Just so you know."

Duncan cast Flores a mortified look. "She's very passionate," he said grimly.

"Bet she is," said Flores's partner, smirking.

"See you soon, Welch," Flores called.

Out in the lot, Duncan glared at Raina. "Oh, *thanks* very much for that."

"You're welcome."

They crossed the street. He worked hard to hang on to his annoyance, but it was like wet tissue paper trying to pass for a tarp—a flimsy attempt, not hiding what lay beneath. And beneath was undeniable pleasure. And wonder.

She stood up for me. With vulgarity, doing him precisely zero favors, but no matter, because no one had *ever* stood up for Duncan before, not for any reason. It made him feel too many things. Patronized, yet delighted. He hoped she couldn't tell.

Once back in the apartment, they resumed their respective projects, but by four, Duncan was at a standstill. Without knowing the nature of that so-called witness and his or her claims, there could be no strategizing about it.

He stood and stretched, and with his headphones off he heard music coming from the soon-to-be guest room. He walked to the threshold. The space was chaos—half-filled boxes and garbage bags all over, every drawer open, books and records and shoe boxes stacked into a dozen towers. The music was coming from a dated turntable perched on the dresser, the record an old blues album.

Raina was humming along.

He ought to be angrier with her, for the way she'd managed to bring him here, and for that gaffe in the diner. He ought to be furious, and anxious as well—she could threaten to play the OCD card anytime she wanted something more from him, tonight or tomorrow or next week. He resented being manipulated. Yet if anything, he rather admired the ploy. And perhaps he could play nice until he stumbled upon a secret of hers and landed them in a stalemate. A truce, two equally sharp knives held with perfect parity at each other's throats.

Good luck. The shameless are exceedingly difficult to blackmail.

She had her back to him, and a heap of notebooks beside her on the bed. She was slumped, her rounded posture and the bundle of waves gathered at the top of her head making her seem like a teenager. She wasn't crying, he didn't think, just lost in the open book in her lap.

He knocked softly on the doorframe and she turned. Her smile was odd, sort of sleepy, as he imagined she might look if he woke her, first thing in the morning. Not that he'd imagined such a thing ... white sheets against her bare skin, the sharper edges worn off her cutting words by the doziness. No, he definitely hadn't imagined any of that.

"You want to see what my dad looked like?" she asked.

"Sure." He came around to sit beside her. The book in her lap was a photo album.

"That's him," she said, tapping an old snapshot. The man in the picture was bartending, wearing a huge, showy grin as he poured liquor in a long stream into a glass. He sported a shaggy eighties haircut and a Sonny Bono mustache. Not a handsome man, but Benji Harper seemed warm and welcoming. Fun.

"He looks very friendly."

"He was. He was never angry. Well, never aside from when he watched football."

Astrid pushed against Duncan's shin and he stooped to pick her up. "You two don't look much alike. Do you have any photos of your mother?"

"I don't, no. I'm not sure if he did, either, though I've got plenty of boxes still to dig through." She seemed to say it mainly to the cat, and gave its neck a rub before examining the collar's tags. "Tell me these aren't, like, custom-engraved platinum from Tiffany."

He smirked. "Sterling. And not Tiffany, no." Though no less pretentious.

"And I bet she was a pedigreed, pampered kitten whose mother, like, won the cat equivalent of Westminster or something," Raina went on, petting her.

"Hardly." Duncan circled Astrid's left ear with his thumb and forefinger, showcasing its clipped tip. "She spent her formative months stray, and I got her from a shelter ... She likes you," he added with surprise. "And she doesn't normally like anyone."

"Animals dig me." The cat purred its approval of Raina's attention. "I have assertive energy. That's what Miah told me, anyhow."

"Astrid clawed my last girlfriend's neck and ruined her handbag."

"Maybe Astrid knew something you didn't. Also, that's strange—you having a girlfriend," Raina clarified, still spoiling the cat. "That seems way too normal somehow. What do you do, on dates?"

He shrugged. "Dinner. Drinks."

"Movies?"

"Not usually. I don't like movie theaters."

"Too dirty?"

"I just don't see the appeal. Why on earth would I want to pay twelve dollars to sit in a dark room with sticky floors, watching a film I may hate, all the while listening to strangers chatting and ... and chewing?"

She laughed. "Fair points. I only ever went for the making out."

Duncan caught a faint whiff of alcohol on her breath, and looked to the dresser, finding an open bottle of whiskey there. "Are you drunk?"

"Buzzed."

"What time have you got to start working? Seven?"

"Yup."

Well, that gave her three hours to sober up, he supposed. Duncan was far from the poster boy for temperance, but going to work intoxicated was unacceptable. "I'll make you some coffee."

"No, thanks."

He set Astrid on the floor and stood. "I wasn't offering, merely informing you."

"Very forceful, Mr. Welch. Are you one of those well-dressed, domineering, kinky millionaires I've heard about? Shall I get the handcuffs?"

"A gag wouldn't go astray." He headed for the kitchen. "And I'm not a millionaire," he called back. Not in terms of liquidity, anyhow.

Raina came to stand in the threshold, crossed arms making a distraction of her breasts. "Cold," she said as Duncan rooted through the cupboards, looking for coffee. "Colder. Wait—warmer."

He touched a drawer by the sink.

"Colder."

Back toward the stove.

"Warm. Warmer."

He opened a cabinet.

"Hot. Like, scorching hot."

"Ah." He grabbed the canister and the little mesh one-cup

filter sitting on top of it. He got the kettle heating and selected her a mug, one boasting a cheesy watercolor image of mesas with *Phoenix* under it in rainbow script. Thinking she needed it strong, he packed the filter nearly to the top.

"Milk and sugar?"

She shook her head. "Black."

"Have a seat," he said, pointing to the table.

Her cheeks grew round. Whether she was amused by his pushiness or holding in a snide comment, he couldn't guess. He didn't care, besides—he was too struck by how lovely she looked, smiling and sedate.

Raina sat and Duncan leaned against the counter, waiting for the kettle. "So, what's driven you to day-drinking?"

The smile was gone in an instant, snuffed like a candle. "Nothing. Or maybe everything." She freed her wild hair and gathered it in her hands, twisting it up, letting it fall. Her shoulders rose and dropped. "I dunno. It's a lot. A whole big room full of too many memories. And not just memories. Things I've never seen. Sides of him I never met. I'm sure he got rid of anything he really didn't want me seeing . . . but little things."

"Like?"

"Photos of him from ages before I was born, with people I don't know. Road maps for northern California, from when he was in his twenties. All this proof that he must've had a thousand stories I never got to hear."

The kettle whistled, and as Duncan poured steaming water through the grounds he asked, "What was he like, as a father?"

A quiet, fond laugh. "He was sort of terrible, in some ways. Not, like, a terrible father. Just clueless. He had two brothers, no sisters, and apparently my grandma was kind of a hard-ass—not the nurturing type. So he had, like, zero clue how to relate to a girl."

"Ah."

"But we had fun. It's not like I was some pink sparkle ballerina princess . . ." Another sweet, soft laugh. "He was famous around town for accidentally leaving me places, at first. Like leaving the stroller parked outside Wasco's while he went in to buy cigarettes, then forgetting I was there until he'd walked halfway home. But I mean, you could get away with that, back then. In Fortuity, anyhow. I'm sure if this was some civilized suburb, I'd have gotten swept away by CPS. He sometimes walked a fine line between 'flaky' and 'negligent.'"

Duncan let the filter drain, then carried the mug to the table. "Well, you turned out the better for it, I'd say. Autonomous. Self-sufficient."

"Hardhearted commitment-phobe," she corrected with a smile.

"Better than doormat."

She lifted the mug. "Hear, hear."

"Let me help you with the rest of the cleaning," he said firmly.

"I dunno."

"I'll be a terrible bully, keep you moving too quickly to have time to think very hard about any of it." *You've bossed me around enough. Let me boss you back.* He'd felt so out of control the past two days; he'd take a hit of that security wherever it might be found.

"Maybe."

He smiled dryly. "Again—not a request."

She held his gaze, a smile playing at the very edges of her lips. "Fine."

"And no more alcohol. It pairs dangerously well with the sloppier emotions, and quite terribly with work."

"Agreed. But I have rules, too."

"Shoot."

"If I come across, like, some Father's Day card I made him in second grade that he's kept, and I start crying, you pretend you can't tell."

He nodded. "All right. Anything else?"

"Just . . . Just don't be nice or anything. Don't change how you and I are with each other, just because I seem emotional or whatever."

He felt a funny shiver to hear her encapsulate them like that. *You and I.* As though they were a unit somehow. That the two of them linked together created something altogether new.

"You treated *me* differently," he said. "Last night."

She frowned. "I just made you tea and a sandwich."

"And now I've made you coffee."

"Just don't treat me gently. Just because I might cry doesn't mean I'm delicate or want to be hugged or whatever. Pet your cat backward and her reaction'll show you roughly how well I handle other people's sympathy."

"Noted." He stood. "And rest assured, I don't hug."

"Good."

"So let's get to work."

Duncan led the way into her father's room. "We'll need a system. What's the plan—things to keep, things to donate, things to bin?"

"Yeah."

"Everything worth keeping—more or less than what would fit on the bed?"

She considered it. "I guess that might be a good way to keep it under control."

"Good. Anything on the bed, we keep. Anything on this side of the bed," he said, gesturing toward the far wall, "is rubbish. Everything on this side, we find homes for." He grabbed a black trash bag from a nearby box. "Let's do his clothes. Anything for charity, give it to me." He whipped the bag open and held it at the ready.

Raina went to the closet and began stripping shirts and sweaters from their hangers with an admirable efficiency. "Donate. Donate," she said, dropping things into Duncan's waiting bag. "Hmm, too mothy." She tossed a holey sweater toward the door. As she went, she said, "If you see anything that's your style . . ."

He laughed. "Cheers."

"I bet all this stuff, every last thing, back when it was all new, wouldn't be worth as much as even one of your suits."

"Probably not."

She smirked. "I Googled your cologne. It costs five hundred twenty-five dollars."

He shrugged. "It lasts for years. I don't think a few dollars a week is such a steep fee, in exchange for smelling nice." Did she like how he smelled? he had to wonder. Did she *hate* it? If she did, he'd pour the couple of hundred dollars' worth left in the bottle straight down the nearest drain.

"So, how much *do* your suits cost?" she asked. "Help me put your priorities in perspective."

"You don't want to know."

"I wouldn't have asked if I didn't. How much? Like that really dark, espresso brown one. I've seen the pants and vest, and there's bound to be a jacket."

"Of course."

"And I'm sure it's some crazy posh wool from, like, endangered Italian yaks. And lined with silk from the last worm of its kind. How much?"

"With tailoring? Probably close to three thousand."

She shook her head, though she looked more amazed than disgusted, he thought. "Jesus. That's literally more than I've ever spent on any one thing. Including vehicles and bar supplies and tattooing equipment. Anything. What do you get for three grand, aside from the suit itself?"

"What do you mean?"

"Something about it must get you hard." She dropped a load of musty flannel into the bag, their knuckles brushing. "Is it because you want everyone in the room to know you can afford it, and they can't?"

"Perhaps that's a part of it . . . Though I genuinely like nice things. I get pleasure from owning and wearing nice clothes." Clothes made to fit only him, never so much as tried on by another person. The fetish objects of an angry boy who'd resented every last scrap of ill-fitting, castoff clothing he'd been handed.

"I bet I don't want to know how much your car cost," Raina said.

"Likely not."

"How would you feel," she asked, tugging the last sweater from its hanger, "if you had to just put on a crummy old T-shirt and jeans and white sneakers, climb into some beat-up car, and cruise around for a day? Would that, like, kill you?"

"It might give me a panic attack," he said, knotting the overstuffed bag, "but no, it wouldn't kill me." He'd lived the equivalent for the first half of his life.

"Why would it be so awful? What do you care what people think about you?"

"Can't a man simply be vain?"

"Not simply, no."

Touché. But she needn't be made privy to the *why* of it all. Like her, he resented sympathy. She needn't know about the boy he'd once been, the one who'd been treated like this dead man's possessions—eyeballed in the name of deciding *keep* versus *discard*. He'd only once been deemed worthy of keeping, but that hadn't lasted. His childhood had made him feel not unlike the trash bound for the tip, or at the very least a burden, like the donations. Left behind and unwanted, yet demanding that someone take pity and give him a home. The detritus of charity.

"Well, I suppose I don't know why I care," he said. "Only that I do."

"It was a hollow threat, anyhow, offering you my dad's stuff. I don't need to see his old clothes anyplace except in photos. I'll be dropping all this stuff off in the next county. Don't want to see some local walk into Benji's wearing any of it. I've got enough ghosts in my life at the moment."

He considered that, thinking of Alex Dunn. The man at the heart of Duncan's own problems. He'd been having trouble sleeping lately, and often found himself thinking about those alleged bones, the ones everybody was so swept up in finding. Bones indeed. They were the skeleton strung through the center of everything that had gone terribly wrong lately, but without them, the shape of the greater whole was indiscernible. Duncan hadn't thought much of the mystery before, but now that he'd been dragged into it, he'd begun finding himself preoccupied, guessing like everyone else where those bones might be. Who they might've belonged to. Who might be missing that person . . .

Perhaps those bones belonged to someone like Duncan. Someone easily misplaced, with no one caring enough to come looking for him. Disposable people. Not worth missing.

He eyed Raina, thinking how she'd cared enough to threaten him, to *force* him to let her look after him. The thought brought a taut, painful sting to his jaw and throat, and he pushed it away.

Raina went through the drawers next, and they quickly filled another bag with donations. Every now and then she'd pause to smell a sweater or shirt and smile to herself.

"Is this easier, with two?" he asked.

She nodded. "Yeah."

He smiled at the silence that ensued. "You're welcome."

Raina rolled her eyes. If they hadn't been standing in a room scattered with her dead father's things, he'd have been sorely tempted to push her down onto that bed. If ever there was going to be a right time for the two of them to collide, it was now. With Duncan spread open by everything she now knew about him — and had exploited — and Raina exposed by these tasks . . . Given how stubborn they both were about admitting their feelings, it was now or never.

Fear had Duncan almost hoping, however, that it would be

never. She knew him too deeply already, had too much power. To welcome her to see that most uncivilized side of him . . . Too much. He wasn't sure he could survive being known so thoroughly by any one person. It'd feel too much like handing her a knife, inviting her to slit him wide open and handle his most vulnerable organs.

"I'll keep all the photos," she said, hefting the albums. "I'll move them to the den and look at them later. Same as his journals or whatever these are." She added three battered old notebooks to the pile, their spiral bindings squished and misshapen.

"What can I do?" Duncan asked.

"Um . . . You can clean, I guess. It's pretty dusty in here. If you strip the bed, I'll get the laundry started."

He followed her out of the room, heading to the kitchen when she stopped to move the albums into a bookshelf. She'd left his bucket and gloves on the floor by the door, and he filled the former with hot water and found rags beneath the sink.

He stripped the bed and remade it with spare sheets Raina gave him, old, pilled flannel with an awful pattern of autumn leaves, but he was too weary of his own judgments to care. He turned his energies to the cleaning.

The room was dusty, but with every swipe of damp cotton, and every stripe of clean wall or wood they revealed, he felt the calm coming on. All the aggression he'd been feeling toward Raina—anger and attraction alike—dulled under the influence of the act.

He cleaned for what felt like half an hour, but as always, the act altered time. When he next checked his phone, he realized he'd been working for three times that long. His fingers were wrinkled, grime packed under his nails. He had aches and pains he hadn't registered, and his eyes stung from the dust. He stood from where he'd been wiping down the baseboards, and surveyed the progress.

Better.

Not perfect, but a great improvement. He had to thank his compulsions at moments like this. Cheaper and more productive than the pills, and just as mood-altering.

He'd tackle the bathroom next, he decided, eager to poke through Raina's cabinets—a more subtle version of the snooping she'd undertaken when she barged into his motel room this morning. Fair was fair. She'd seen inside him, against his will.

She owed him a few secrets of her own. And when she went down to babysit the bar, he'd most definitely be stealing a good long snoop through her bedroom.

But as he carried the bucket and rags into the den, the sight of her banished that righteousness. She was curled at the corner of the couch, the window behind her making her hair burn bright auburn at the edges. One of her dad's notebooks was on her thighs, and her brow was furrowed, gaze scanning rapidly.

Peering into the shadows of one's bathroom was one thing. Reading a dead loved one's journal was quite another beast. Duncan knew that for a fact.

The moment it had become clear that his kind foster mother's stroke was going to send Duncan away, he stole her bedside diary. He had it locked in his wall safe in San Diego, though he hadn't read it in years. He didn't need to—he'd memorized every fact he could glean about her from those two hundred twenty-nine handwritten pages. Turned her assessments of him into commandments, striving to embody the things she'd praised. *Hardworking. Smart. So eager for a job. I daresay he's going to go places, this one, if he takes enough pride in himself. So preoccupied with order and fairness . . . With a thicker skin and a respectable accent, he could make a fine lawyer someday.*

She'd seen something in him. Mapped out a path for him to follow with her words, a recipe that might make people like him, as she'd liked him. She'd *wanted* him. He'd done just as she'd prescribed. Thickened his skin, refined his accent, taken pride in himself. She'd been right—he had gone places. He was as alone as he'd been as a child, but he liked to imagine she'd be impressed with him nonetheless.

What had Raina's father hoped for her, he had to wonder, and was it spelled out on the pages she held?

"What have you got there?"

Her eyes kept scanning, taking in line after line after line before she finally replied, "It's a journal. Sort of."

"Personal?"

"Yes. And no. Business plans, for the bar."

That place had a business plan? He moved to sit by her, approaching slowly and giving her plenty of time to tell him to fuck off.

"May I see?" he asked, scooting closer.

After a minute, she brought her feet to the floor and rested the book on their touching thighs. Duncan fought to smother the fire that contact roused, focusing on the page.

There were drawings, as well as lists and notes. Business plan? No. More a journal of the man's hopes and dreams. He'd sketched floor plans in a steady, elegant hand, making Duncan wonder if Raina had inherited her artistic side from him . . . and curious for the first time to see some of her tattoo work.

"Looks about right," Duncan said, meaning the floor plan. Same horseshoe layout of the bar, and the pool table and juke-box were right where her dad had meant them to be.

Raina turned a page, and the spread had several magazine and catalog scraps taped to it. The furniture and fixtures pictured were outdated, but handsome. Far nicer than what Benji's currently boasted. He pointed to an image of finely lathed spindles that created a lattice around the top of a bar, stained a dark, lustrous brown. "Those are quite nice."

"And this," she said, their fingers nearly touching as she tapped another photo. It pictured recessed shelving, backlit to illuminate rows of liquor bottles. "Kind of eighties, but I like the general idea."

"Indeed."

"There's pages of this. Pictures he liked, budgets he'd sketched out for stuff—mostly stuff I've never seen downstairs."

"A wish list?"

She shook her head. "Plans. To-do lists, but they're all dated in the months before I got dumped on his doorstep. Look, here's when it happened—December third. I was born December first, we're pretty sure." She turned to the dated page, to a single entry, on a single line.

December 3. Going to need to rethink the mahogany.

He glanced up to find her smiling faintly, then looked back to the page. December fourth's entry was a far different sort of list, in a far messier, more frantic hand.

Things we need: crib, car seat, diapers!!! stroller, formula, powder? lotion? birth certificate?? Must talk to Janine.

"Who's Janine?" he asked.

"Janine Wasco. She and her husband own the drugstore—though it's only her now. I can just see my dad running in there with me, like, wrapped in a tablecloth or stuck in a picnic basket or something, asking her what he needed to keep me alive. She has five kids—she'd have set him straight."

"The poor bastard. I can only imagine what a demanding little terror you must have been."

She elbowed him for that. "Anyhow, that's where all the interior decorating clippings end. Look." She turned a page, then another, another, each looking much the same—primitive spreadsheets of projected bills and income.

"He wanted so much more than he ever accomplished downstairs. He'd planned to put a kitchen in the back. I never knew that. He even made notes about what the menu would look like. Curlicues and all."

Duncan tried to gauge her expression, but her sadness was a flat, unreadable expanse. He angled for clues to how she felt about it all, offering, "I doubt he's ever regretted trading his dreams of a fine dining establishment for fatherhood and a slightly more colorful bar."

"He never made me think Benji's wasn't exactly what he'd wanted it to be . . . But to see it all here, in ink on paper. Everything he'd imagined, and how little of it he actually got to realize."

"Change is coming," Duncan said gently, just as Astrid leaped onto the next cushion to assert herself into the scene. "Property scouts will be here soon. There's no reason to think perhaps you couldn't partner with one of them, find some middle ground between their business model and maybe achieving a few of your father's original goals."

She shook her head. "You know what those people are going to want to open. Chain steak houses, with fake Wild West memorabilia hanging off every blank inch of wall. I'm no businesswoman—not really. They'll steamroll me. Turn this place into whatever they want. Downstairs might be rough, but he did it all with his own hands."

Duncan nodded, having imagined the same fate for the bar himself. He'd only offered the lie to make her feel better.

Raina closed the notebook with a sigh. "Well. That sobered me up. How's the bedroom coming?"

Duncan smiled as he stroked his cat, thinking they sounded like an old married couple. "Considerably less dusty."

"Not sure what you're paying me a hundred bucks a night for," she said, rubbing her face, "when you have to clean your own room before it's habitable."

"Perhaps the first night could be gratis." Perhaps they could all be gratis, if her little remark about not wanting his money anymore, should they start fucking, had been more than an idle come-on. Best to get his mind off the question, though. "Where do you do your tattooing?"

She nodded toward the kitchen. "Room through there. You want to see?"

Did he want to see the space in which she drew indelible images across strange men's naked skin? "No, thank you."

"I keep it locked—my equipment's the most expensive thing I own. But anytime you want a tour . . . or an estimate." She raised her eyebrows hopefully.

Duncan smirked and stood. "I'll check on the laundry. And you're probably due downstairs." The sun was nearing the mountains, and it'd be dark soon. With the dusk came the more demanding patrons, and that peak was going to steal Duncan's company, along with the daylight. He wouldn't be going down himself, this evening. Not after nearly falling on his face in front of all those yahoos the night before. Not with his name so freshly linked to the bribery allegations. Those things wouldn't keep him away for long, but not tonight.

"I'd better make a phone call," he said, heading for the easy chair where he'd left his laptop and cell. He found Flores's card in his dossier and entered the digits.

"Flores."

"It's Duncan Welch."

"Ah. Welch. I was just thinking about you."

"How flattering."

"Not calling to apologize for your lady friend, I hope? I've been called way worse, you know."

"I'm merely calling to let you know my premises have changed."

"What?"

"Don't panic. I've not gone far. I'm staying with my . . . acquaintance," he revised, his eyes meeting Raina's dark ones across the room for the hottest instant. To call her a friend would've been a familiarity too far. "In the apartment above Benji's Saloon, on Station Street."

"That dump, huh?"

Duncan felt heat flash up the back of his neck.

"Doesn't seem your style."

Duncan cooled himself. "Despite the surety your little folder might suggest that you possess, you don't know me, Mr. Flores. Not remotely."

"Why the move?"

"Concerned parties have suggested, perhaps with some prudence, that I might be wise to stay with a friend during this investigation. Seeing as how I'm not a favorite with the locals, and now I've been tarred by these ridiculous charges—"

"I get it. Let's save our discussion of the case for a future meeting, shall we?"

"Just keeping you apprised."

"Speaking of meetings, we need to have another one. Tomorrow. Eight thirty, at the sheriff's department."

"Oh dear, I hope I shan't miss Mass."

"You and me both," Flores said, his eye roll audible. "I just want to go over a few things with you."

"Fine."

A pause, a tiny huff of a laugh. "Raina Harper, huh?"

"Excuse me?"

Papers shuffled behind Flores's voice. "Raina Catherine Harper. Owner of Benji's Saloon. Your greatest defender, also your roommate now?"

"She may be."

"She may also be friends with some of the locals who've admitted to getting themselves involved in a certain little homegrown investigation against Charles Tremblay. I'm sure you know all that."

"I'm sure I do."

"I'm sure you can appreciate that it'll look odd to some people, you fraternizing further with casino opponents—ones who've arguably impeded justice, and trespassed on—"

"Ones who've outed two potential murderers, who'd been poised to get away with their crimes, if not for those meddling kids."

Raina laughed, then quit eavesdropping and disappeared into the kitchen.

"Yes," Duncan continued, "I'm sure I can appreciate it. I trespassed with them, you'll recall. That fraternization should be no bombshell."

"Listen, Duncan."

He sighed, the familiarity shtick so fucking maddening. "Yes, Ramon?"

An equally annoyed sigh answered him. "You want to convince everyone you're one of the good kids, don't go sitting yourself at the back of the bus with the troublemakers. With saloon owners and parolees."

"Your concern has been noted," Duncan said. "As, I trust, has been my new address."

Another sigh. "Yeah. Fine."

"Good night, then, Agent Flores."

"Counselor Welch."

They hung up.

Raina returned, leaning against the wall just inside the door with her arms crossed, a funny look on her face.

Duncan polished his phone's screen on the hem of his tee. "Yes?"

"They tell you I'm a bad influence?"

"Not you specifically," he fibbed.

She smirked. "You're a terrible liar. He tell you not to stay here?"

"Not precisely."

"You tell him what happened to your car?"

"No. I've lost enough freedom already—I'm not getting locked away in a safe house just because some yokel can afford a can of spray paint."

"Why am I not surprised?"

He smiled. "Because you'd do precisely the same thing, in my position."

Her eyes narrowed, the look telling him he was right. And that perhaps they weren't that different, after all.

The room felt very still. Very stifling, all at once, that phone call having let the stress of everything intrude on what had been a strangely pleasant, strangely *human* afternoon.

He eyed his roommate, and allowed himself the luxury of imagining all the inappropriate things he'd like to do with her. Things he might just let himself give in to, with a little chemical lubrication.

"Does Casey Grossier work for you now?" he asked.

"Not officially. Why?"

Duncan turned a thought around for a moment before giving it voice. "I think you ought to call him, and tell him he's bartending again tonight."

She held his stare. "Oh? Why's that?"

"Because you and I need to get drunk."

The flicker of a smile. "Do we, then?"

He nodded once, definitively. "We do. No pills, I promise. Just you and me, and a bottle of something, and your father's old records and photo albums."

"You and me and a bottle," she echoed. "That sounds like an invitation for trouble."

He smiled. "Oh, I'm already in trouble. This would merely be a spot of fun."

She checked the clock on the DVD player and seemed to consider it, finally nodding. "Okay, sure. If Casey's free, you're on. It's a date."

A rather reckless, messy, fucked-up sort of date, Duncan thought. One they were weeks overdue to embark on together.

He smiled. "So call that motherfucker."

Chapter 10

"Motherfucker." Casey glared at his phone when Raina ended the call.

Vince looked over from the couch, where he and Kim were gathered around the coffee table, playing cards with Vince and Casey's addled mother.

"I've just been informed I'm working again," Casey said. "Like, right now."

"At the bar?" Kim asked.

"Yeah. Funny how I don't remember filling out any W-2s."

Vince smiled. "Few days ago you might've jumped at the chance."

"Yeah, well, a few days ago that girl wasn't pregnant, far as I knew." And with a felon's baby. A felon, Vince had told Casey, who didn't yet know he was a father-to-be. And who'd been put away for smuggling firearms, and earned himself the kind of respect inside that only violence afforded. A charismatic, manipulative type, Vince had said, with a cold demeanor that hid a hot temper. Nasty combo. And this guy was likely to be getting paroled in the next six months. Now, that was *baggage*. That was a whole fucking carousel of the shit.

"Can't play hearts with only three," their mother said absently.

Casey pocketed his phone. "Apparently this is club business." He said it mainly to Vince—their mom wasn't really listening.

"Club shit? How so?"

"Raina's looking after Welch or whatever."

Vince smirked. "Sure she is."

Casey zipped his hoodie and checked for his wallet. "If I'm

stuck slinging drinks because she's upstairs getting laid, don't put it past me to skim from the till."

"You didn't put up much of a fight," Kim said savvily.

Casey couldn't hide the blush warming his face if he tried; faintest touch of embarrassment—or arousal, for that matter—and his ears and neck and cheeks went red as beets. "It's not all bad. Chicks love bartenders. Plus, if Raina owes me, maybe I can get a free tattoo for my troubles."

And fine, Kim had him pegged about right. He missed flirting with Abilene. That last night, when Casey had put his foot in it, it'd been pretty awkward, sure. But the girl had mellowed some by the end of the night, everybody distracted by the news about Levins. She'd even smiled at him when she'd climbed into her car after they locked up, and she never looked prettier than when she smiled. Besides, what Casey felt for her . . . He hadn't felt this way about a girl since he'd been a teenager. Goofy, simple crush. He'd wanted to fuck her, no doubt, but with that off the table for self-preservation reasons, the other stuff still felt good. Kinda sweet, in the midst of all the complicated shit going on in Fortuity. So yeah, flirt with the girl, go home, beat off. No harm in that.

No harm, he thought, starting up his bike, provided he didn't flirt *too* hard. Sweat broke out under his arms to imagine somebody telling her baby's unwitting gunrunner father they'd been cozy while the guy was incarcerated, and that Casey had known about the kid before the dad had. Christ, maybe this wasn't simple at all.

He headed downtown, deciding he'd better just take the concerned, brotherly route with Abilene. Seemed like an option less likely to get him shot in the knee.

The lot was half-full when he arrived, the night already shaping up to be a busy one. He glanced up at the lit windows of Raina's apartment but spotted no incriminating silhouette of her and Duncan getting freaky. Still, what did she expect Casey to believe they were up to?

He parked out back and entered through the rear—she'd given keys to everybody in the club a few weeks ago. The bar was noisy when he strolled in, Abilene shouting out a party's ready order before starting on the next.

"What needs pouring?" he asked from behind her.

She cast him a skeptical glance. "You again?"

"Raina didn't say? She's still playing nurse upstairs, apparently. So yeah, me again. You okay with that?"

"Makes no difference to me." She handed a pitcher to a customer and started another, not meeting his eyes. "I need four shots of Jack."

He poured them, made change, and turned to the next expectant face.

There'd been a bit of a logjam, but after ten minutes things calmed down. Already hot, Casey unzipped his jacket and stuffed it into a cubby under the register. Abilene tossed him a towel, then set her own on the bar. "I'll be right back."

"Where you going?"

"I'm six months pregnant. Where do you think I'm going, every ten minutes?"

"I have no clue."

She rolled her eyes. "I'm going to snort coke off a hooker's tits," she said, heading for the back.

Casey just stared for a moment. She'd never talked like that before. She looked about sixteen, so the effect was sort of hilarious. "Hormones much?"

"Fuck off, Casey."

"Definitely hormones. Oh—wait. Peeing!" he called after her retreating back. "You're peeing, right? See, I know some stuff about pregnant women."

"Tell the whole bar," she shot over her shoulder before disappearing.

Casey filled a couple more orders and she returned, little wisps of her long dark hair plastered to her temples.

"You look hot," he said. "Like, sweaty, I mean."

"Wow. Thanks."

"I mean, you look overheated. Yet still attractive. You need a break?"

"I'm fine," she said, not sounding fine at all.

"You're not going into labor, are you?"

She paused, sighing her exhaustion. "Not for a couple months. I'm just sweaty. And tired. And my body's going insane, because there's a tiny human moving my organs around."

"Raina should keep you on afternoons."

She glared at him. "I'm *fine*. And I make a hundred bucks more on nights, so don't go telling her to take them away from me."

"You can have my tips," he offered. "I'm not even supposed to be here. I don't even work here, officially." *Officially*, Casey didn't work anywhere.

"Just . . . just leave me alone, Casey. Just fill orders, and I'll quit being such a bitch, and we'll get through tonight, and everything will be fine."

He frowned. "You're, like, legit pissed at me, aren't you?"

She turned away to gather empties, and he tailed her.

"Why? I'm not saying you shouldn't be—I fuck shit up *all* the time. I just don't always realize it. But if you tell me what I fucked up, I'll try to fix it."

She laughed, a sad, small noise. "There's nothing to fix. And you didn't fuck anything up. You said it yourself—it's just hormones."

He tried to let it go. Tried to just handle orders and make change, get lost in the familiar, jerky rhythm of this place. Didn't do much good, though.

Casey hated simmering conflicts. It was the reason he always moved on, whenever he messed shit up. He sucked at cleanup. Still, it bugged him how this acquaintance had gone from fun to painful so goddamn quickly. Maybe he'd been naive, thinking their flirtation had been the one simple thing left to enjoy in this complicated town. That *she'd* been simple—an open book. Come to think of it . . . he really didn't know jack about her, did he?

"What's your last name?" he asked during a lull.

She shot him a distrustful look. "Why?"

"Just seems weird I don't know it, that's all. Mine's Grossier."

"Everyone knows what your last name is."

"Because my brother's, like, the king of the local dicks, you mean."

She smirked. "Kind of."

"So, what's yours?"

"Price."

"Okay. And when's your birthday?"

She chewed her lip.

"Mine's April fifth," he said. "I'm thirty-three. How old are you?"

"Twenty-four."

"And your birthday?"

She looked real wary at that, making Casey doubt the age she'd told him.

"Whatever, never mind. It's cool." A customer caught his eye, a clean-cut Hispanic guy with glasses. "What'll it be?"

"I don't suppose Raina Harper's working tonight?" The man's voice reeked of law enforcement.

Casey shook his head, crossed his arms. "She's off. You want a drink?"

He scanned the bottles lined up on the highest shelf. "Amstel."

"Watching your figure?"

"How much?"

"Four bucks."

They swapped a beer for bills and the guy disappeared into the crush. Casey turned his attention back to Abilene, who was loading the washer. "Just figured I ought to know some shit about you. Since we're basically coworkers and everything."

"You know stuff about me," she said, glancing at her middle.

"I mean, just boring stuff. Favorite color. Favorite band. Favorite food."

Her lips twitched, and before heading out into the greater barroom to collect empties, she said, "Barbecued brisket."

Casey smiled, watching her go. He restocked the coolers and the ice, and when she returned he thought he could chance teasing her, sensing she'd thawed some. But he was way wrong. The second he said, "I knew I'd defrost you, sooner or later," the claws popped back out.

She turned quickly, ponytail whipping around, blue eyes bright and angry. "Defrost me?"

He crumpled the empty ice bag, staring into a pair of glaciers. "Um, yeah. I was just teasing. Did I just—"

Her hands shook as she went to rub her eyes. "God, why's everything all . . . *fucked-up*?"

"Fucked-up? You mean because I fucked them up, or . . . ?"

She shook her head, smoothed her hair. "The baby's fucking everything up." She clutched her middle, looking chastised. "It's not her fault. But she is."

"She? It's a girl?"

"Shut up, Casey, please. I'm trying to have a breakdown."

"You and Welch. Maybe if you head upstairs, Raina will fuck you into better mental health."

Finally, a smile. Casey broke out in one of his own. "Hey, now, look at that! You don't hate me after all."

She pursed her lips. "I never said I did."

"You've been way different, since last night."

"Of course I have. Everything *is* different. The baby's making everything—every last part of my life—totally fucked and weird and stressful and . . ." She trailed off, breaths coming quick and frantic.

"Hey, sit down. Chill. Of course the baby's fucking everything up. That's what babies do. Haven't you ever watched *Maury*?"

She wiped at her welling eyes, and Casey angled his body to keep most of the patrons' views blocked, to give her a little privacy.

"It's not even here yet," she sniffed, "and already I can't cope with anything. How awful is it going to be after it's born?"

"You got family in town?"

"No."

"Where's your parents?"

"My mama's back home in Texas. But we don't talk. I hardly talk with any of my family."

"Texas, huh? You from Abilene, Abilene?"

"No," she said simply.

"Well, I was living in Lubbock the past couple years."

"Doing what?"

"Oh, things. Anyhow," he said, nodding to her belly, "a kid's a pretty powerful trump card against moms. You might be surprised how quick bridges get mended when grandparenthood's at stake. Old people fucking love that shit."

She cracked another little smile at that.

From behind them, somebody shouted, "Pitcher."

Casey ignored him. "You'll get through this. You know how many dumb-asses give birth without ever even realizing they're pregnant? You're *smart*. And hardworking. You'll be fine—"

"Pitcher!"

Casey turned to glare at the guy. "Would you hold your fucking horses?"

"Would you do your fucking job?"

Casey cocked his head. "You feel like comforting the poor girl? She's fucking pregnant. She's got hormones and shit, making her crazy." He circled a finger beside his ear. "Two fucking minutes, okay?"

The guy glared but wandered back into the crowd.

Casey turned to Abilene, finding a hand plastered over her eyes in mortification.

"Oh, come on," he said. "Everyone's gonna find out soon enough. Rip the bandage off."

"Someone'll tell Raina her bartender was crying. I'll probably get fired, and there's only, like, two jobs I'm even qualified for in this whole stupid town."

"She won't fire you. You have no idea the shit that woman pulls when she's on the clock herself."

She smiled weakly, and after a pause, she gave him a little shove on the shoulder. "You really thought I was a virgin?"

"I dunno. Seemed likely, the way you were avoiding saying yes to me and everything."

"You think your charms are that irresistible, huh?"

"No, I think my charms are about as smooth and subtle as a cinder block. I couldn't figure out how you kept managing to ignore them."

"Go fill some orders," she said. "I'll use the bathroom and be out in a minute."

"I'm giving you all my tips," he said firmly. "You need 'em more than I do." Casey actually had a pretty healthy chunk of change to his name at the moment. He got a funny rush, imagining doing what his brother sometimes did—helping out people who needed it. Helping Abilene, if she'd let him. God knew he didn't need the money himself, especially now that he wasn't paying rent.

Abilene shook her head. "I don't want your tips."

"You're getting them anyhow. Like a special bonus, for putting up with me."

She smiled. "We'll fight about this later."

She headed for the back, and Casey's heart felt all warm at those words. Fight about it later. As a couple would do—bicker over doing each other favors.

He caught himself, and quickly conjured the imaginary mug shot he'd assigned her ex. He had no clue what James Ware really looked like, but his brain had composed a hulking brute with ink on his shaved, scarred head, and fists like cantaloupes.

Yeah, knock that shit off, thinking like she's anything more than your coworker. And giving her money? Yeah, right. Only thing a violent con must hate worse than not being told about his unborn kid was hearing that some shiftless scam artist had been paying for the girl's upkeep.

Casey focused on the orders, focused on his job. Not on responsibilities and urges that were a million percent not his business. Focused on keeping his nose out of other people's drama, and keeping all his bones unbroken.

Chapter 11

"Important decision time." Raina stood beside Duncan before her open cabinet, a wide variety of spirits lined up. "You've got your own personal bartender for the night. What are we drinking?"

"What did your father drink?"

Oh dear, was this going to be some kind of overdue-mourning sad sacks' party? "Middle-shelf whiskey."

"That'll do, then." He shut the cabinet and headed to the guest room, where Raina had left the bottle in question atop her dad's dresser. *Her* dresser. Or perhaps Duncan's dresser, if only temporarily.

"TV?" she asked when they met in the den.

He shook his head. "Music."

"No opera."

"Perish the thought. Fetch us two glasses."

He left the bottle on the coffee table and came back with the turntable. Raina cast it a nervous glance and set tumblers beside the bottle.

"I'll let you pick the album." He took a seat on the couch. Astrid immediately claimed his lap, then meowed irritably when he crowded her, leaning forward to fill the glasses.

Raina cued up a John Denver LP. She joined her tenants after changing into soft cotton lounge shorts, officially off duty for the evening.

"Cheers," Duncan said, and they tapped tumblers.

After a taste, she asked, "Which one of us is all this drinking for, anyhow? The grieving daughter or the man on the brink of professional ruin?"

He shrugged and took a sip, wincing as he set the glass

primly back on the wood. And not just who—she wanted to know what the ultimate aim of all this was. For one or both of them to sob or laugh their guts out? For Duncan to get Raina drunk enough to share some dirty laundry he could use to counterextort her and get his freedom back? Good luck to him—small-towners knew better than to bother getting attached to their secrets. Raina had precisely two that she preferred to keep quiet, and no way in hell she was sharing either with Duncan, wasted or not.

Though, thinking about it, Raina suspected there was a very good chance this vice-fest was just a means for them to wind up surrendering to a different kind of debauchery. One that had been growling at both of them for weeks, demanding indulgence.

"Tonight," Duncan said, taking another sip, "is merely about two wrecks getting drunk enough to find their troubles amusing—instead of depressing—for an evening."

She nodded. "Cheers, then." The whiskey was already working, reigniting her faded buzz. She curled into the corner of the couch and propped her feet on Duncan's thigh. It might've been a flirtatious move, except she wasn't sure how distasteful he found feet. He seemed unbothered, casting her toes a curious, passing glance, before returning his attention to the purring cat.

"Sooo," Raina sighed, the liquor making her feel warm and slow and lazy; easy, just like John Denver's voice, crooning about country roads. "I want to know things about you."

"Such as?"

She swirled her drink and sat up a little straighter. "I dunno, everything. I mean, two days ago I thought you were one thing. Now I know you have OCD, and a cat. And you like opera. And you won't talk about your parents." He stiffened in an instant, and she waved her hand. "Don't worry. I won't bother asking. But man . . . What do I want to know? Everything. Like . . . how old were you when you got laid for the first time?"

"Will you be answering all of these questions yourself?"

She smiled. "Will you be admitting you want to hear my answers?"

He nodded.

"Okay, then."

"Okay, then," Duncan agreed. "I lost my virginity when I was seventeen."

"OCD doesn't keep you from getting your rocks off, then?"

His smile was slow and wicked. "Sex is one of a very few things in this world that I prefer dirty, Ms. Harper."

His words flushed her, and she held her own smile back, licking her lip. "Call me Raina."

He shook his head.

"Too personal?" she asked. "Too close to acknowledging that maybe we're friends?"

"I believe you owe me an answer to your own question."

"Fine. I was fifteen."

His eyebrows rose a fraction.

She laughed. "There's not much to do in Fortuity. Most of us start fucking just to pass the time before we can get our drivers' licenses."

"Who was it?" he asked. "Anyone I know?"

"Anyone you know, meaning what? Miah? Or one of the Grossiers? No. A boy I went to high school with. He moved away ages ago to work on an oil field."

"And how was it?"

She frowned thoughtfully. "It was . . . efficient."

He laughed—the second of those rich, thrilling chuckles she'd been gifted. Christ, she'd pay five bucks a pop to keep hearing that noise.

"He got better," she offered.

"Did you love him?"

"No, probably not. But when you're fifteen, lust will pass for it."

"What about Miah?" he asked.

She nodded. "Yeah, I loved Miah. I still love Miah."

"But you're not with him."

"And you're sneaking way too many questions in, Mr. Prosecutor. Who was *your* first?"

"A woman from my apartment block."

"A woman?"

He shrugged. "She seemed like a woman, anyway. Older than me, but not scandalously so. Maybe twenty."

"How very statutory."

"She was a clerk at the liquor store across the street. She seemed very . . . *dangerous*."

"And *dangerous* is your type? I find that surprising."

"My life hasn't always looked as it does now."

She sipped her drink and waited, feeling as if she was on the cusp of something interesting and not wanting to scare it away. When he didn't go on, she prompted, "How so?"

He spoke to the cat, stroking its rising back. "I wasn't raised posh. I grew up in East London, which isn't what you'd call genteel." He met Raina's eyes. "Though I wouldn't say my grooming and manners are a lie—I worked very hard for them. But I wasn't born into my inflated sense of entitlement. I earned it."

"Huh. So your parents aren't Lord and Lady Welch of Snobbington-upon-Thames?"

He shook his head. "Unless I've been greatly deceived, no."

"When did you decide to better yourself, or however you think about it?"

"When I was young—ten or so. I threw myself into my schoolwork. Then when I was accepted to Cambridge, I put the next phase of the plan into motion. Refined my accent, began investing in my appearance."

She smiled. "Very calculating. Very you."

"I thought of it as a reinvention, not a deception." He smiled back.

"And when did you come to the States?"

"For law school, when I was twenty-one."

"That seems young."

"I finished both secondary school and university early. I saw little attraction in lingering in England any longer than I needed to."

"And you're a U.S. citizen?"

"I have been for twelve years, yes."

"Why California?"

He shrugged. "The weather, primarily. The ocean."

The distance from your past, Raina mused, wondering if she had it right. "Do you miss England?"

"Not for a moment."

"Why not?" she asked.

"It's clammy, and gloomy, and terrifically classist."

"You seem pretty classist."

"I am. But that doesn't mean I want to surround myself with a load of miseries like me."

She smiled. "And that's not your real accent?"

"I've been speaking this way since university. I'd say it's mine."

"But what did your old one sound like? Tell me you're a Cockney, please."

He sipped his drink. "No comment."

"You get more British when you're angry, or wasted. Do you sound like a cabbie when you're, like, about to come or something?"

"Good God, you're crude."

Raina threw her head back and laughed, officially drunk. She sighed giddily, grinning at him. "Yes, yes, I am. But apparently that can be overcome. You want to be my Henry Higgins? Train this wayward bar owner to pass for royalty? Dress me up all frilly and respectable?"

He didn't reply right away, sipping and looking pensive.

"What?"

He spoke to the cat again. "There was a time when . . . There was a time when I did want that. To dress you."

Her eyebrows rose. "What in? An evening gown? A leather catsuit and nipple clamps?"

"Something classic." He eyed her thoughtfully, assessing. "A sheath, perhaps. Knee-length. Black, maybe lace. Tame that hair. Tone down the eye makeup."

"You want to give me a makeover?"

"Wanted to, yes." He drained his glass. "But I've since grown accustomed to you, to paraphrase a certain professor of phonetics. Tattoos and bra straps and all."

She sat up straight, bracing her elbow on the back of the couch. "You wanted to *Pretty Woman* me."

"They were passing impulses."

"Yeah, they better be. I should be insulted . . . except that sounds exhausting just now, so I don't think I'll bother."

"Good. I appreciate the pardon."

She studied him. "Did you ever get around to taking off my fancy new clothes, in these daydreams of yours?"

He studied her right back, then leaned forward to refill his glass. Raina held hers out and he topped it off as well. "Would you like the honest answer to that question?"

"Yes."

He cleared this throat. "No, I didn't take your fancy new clothes off, in my fantasies."

Disappointment cooled her like a cloud. "Oh."

Duncan smiled. "I fucked you on a barstool, with the dress pushed up around your hips." He sipped his whiskey while lust snaked the length of Raina's body like a sizzling fuse. She wouldn't have expected such a reaction, given the image, but overthinking things wasn't her bag.

"Did you, then?"

He nodded, a glimmer of that very un-Duncanish grin still curling one side of his lips.

"I guess you didn't bother putting panties on me, then."

"They'd only leave a line."

"I bet you watch, like, the classiest porn there is. Does *Masterpiece Theatre* make skin flicks?"

His smile was tight, demure. "I don't watch pornography."

She snorted.

He took a drink. "You don't believe me?"

"Well, you're a human, A. And B, you're a male human. That makes it a two hundred percent probability."

"Well, I don't."

"What do you jerk off to, then? Do you have a better imagination than I'd guessed?"

"I'm touched you bothered guessing."

She squinted at him. "No, really. You must use *something*."

For a split second's pause, she could read his thoughts: *What do* you *use?* But he simply said, "I don't masturbate."

She didn't even laugh. "Bull. *Shit*, you don't."

"Very, very rarely."

"Do your meds make you not care, or . . . ?" Oh shit, did his meds make him impotent?

"I suppress those urges."

Thank fuck for that.

"The energy's better spent on practical pursuits," he added.

It sounded nuts, yet she'd never once suspected this man would waste said precious energy on lying. "Good God, when's the last time you came?"

"I'm not a nun, Ms. Harper. But weeks, easily."

Weeks. How many? *Since before you met me?* Christ, she wanted to imagine she'd inspired him to give in to those needs.

"Better you than me," she said with a shrug. "I bet I'd make it three days before I murdered somebody."

He didn't reply, silence reigning for half a minute. And with every second that ticked by, Raina's body seemed to warm by a degree.

"Something's going to happen," she said slowly, narrowing her eyes at his mouth. A handsome set of lips, wide, with a deep and dignified bow in the upper one. On the lower one he had a scar, from Tremblay's pistol-whipping. Usually it was a smudge of lighter skin, but now it was dark. Those lips, normally the subtlest pink, flushed . . . From the sting of the liquor? Or a spike in this stoic man's pulse?

"Happen?" he prompted, too innocently.

"Something's going to happen between us. Something biblical. Tonight."

Pale eyes regarded her calmly above the rim of his glass. "Such as?"

She shrugged. "Fucking."

"You make it sound like a storm we ought to prepare for."

"Time will tell."

He took a drink. "Shall we simply commence said fucking at an appointed time, or would you like to progress via the usual protocol?"

"Protocol?"

"Kissing. Petting."

She snorted. "Petting?"

"Groping, fondling, friendly game of grab-ass," he clarified, and Raina laughed. "Hit a few bases before you rush me headlong across home plate? Before I become just another notch in your lipstick case?"

"I don't wear lipstick."

"I'm glad." He smiled, attention dropping from her eyes to her mouth. "Unless that means you don't plan to remember me at all."

She bit the inside of her lip, the gesture purely reflexive. "You want to kiss?"

He took another drink, Adam's apple working; then his gaze rose to meet hers. "I believe I do."

Raina took his glass, setting it with hers on the table, and the cat hissed its offense as she tossed it toward the far cushion. Duncan grabbed her ankles, hauled her legs across his lap. They leaned in as one and then paused, mouths mere inches apart. Those calculating eyes took her in, just as hers did the same . . . Those little lines she'd grown so enamored of—proof that this man felt things. And his stubble, evidence that his perfect image was a fleeting, demanding illusion. She touched his jaw, the near-blond bristles soft and rough at once.

Suddenly the kiss could wait. She was touching him. Touching him in a way she'd never imagined he might let her—in a tender, curious way she'd never guessed she'd offer.

He touched her in turn, pushing her hair back, tracing her ear with smooth, cool fingertips. He touched her like a man examining a finely cut gem—with fascination, as she'd never been touched or admired before. But she wanted so much more than this clinical approval.

She put her lips to his, surprised at their warmth. Surprised at how they parted, and how they knew at once how to flirt with hers. He pressed his thumb to her cheek and cocked his head, wasting no time in the shallow end. Deeper, hungrier. His tongue stroked hers and the room was burning, this cold-blooded man searing her skin, drawing her breath short.

He kissed the way he dressed. Sumptuously, confidently. *Expensively* somehow. Yet the deeper they took it, the more tenuous his control seemed to become. His fingers were in her hair, cradling at first, now nearly gripping. She heard his breathing turn shallow and strained between ravenous tastes— needy little gasps. Hot as fuck. What she'd give to hear him moan against her throat—

"Get on my lap," he said, and his cultured, velvet voice had edges.

Yes, sir. When she straddled his legs, those elegant hands got impolite, tugging her close. Close enough to feel him against the crease of her thigh and hip, stiff and stifled. His mouth was burning, hands cool as they slipped under her tank to palm her waist. Did he feel as she did, as though a floodgate had opened? As if a fence had been torn down and they were finally allowed to do as they'd been imagining for weeks, for a month or more, letting their palms and fingers roam over the skin each felt entitled to? As if the wanting had made it mutually, rightfully theirs?

She stroked his shoulders and upper arms, struck again by the hardness there. Those perfectly cut clothes hid shapes she'd never bothered imagining—sharp triceps, and the firm swells of strong shoulders.

Too many surprises packed into one man. She focused on the one thing she'd accurately predicted about this moment— that their chemistry was bat-shit-crazy hot.

She needed his erection. Needed him to reach down and adjust himself, so she could flex her hips and tease them both into hysterics. Needed him to undo his belt and frame his cock in his open fly. She needed it so bad she'd lose her ever-loving mind if he didn't give it to her.

Yet he didn't. He merely kissed her, deep and dirty, his palms growing warmer as he coaxed her motions and kneaded her hips. She imagined these same caresses, only with all their clothes gone, her on top. With nothing between them but the thinnest skin of latex. She grew light-headed, breaking them apart to steal a gulp of air and cool her head.

Letting him see what he did to her, she swallowed and blew out a delirious breath.

He smiled.

"You don't taste like Duncan," she said.

"And what should I taste like?"

"Like Absolut and tonic. No ice. Lemon or lime, my choice."

"You always choose lime."

Indeed. "You taste like . . . poor-judgment Duncan."

"You taste precisely as I'd guessed."

She glanced to the far cushion; the cat had run off.

"Lie down," she said, and moved off his lap. Duncan reclined. She planted her knees on either side of his hips and studied him. She'd fantasized about each and every button she'd undo on his crisp dress shirt, each and every inch of pale skin she'd uncover as she went. This wasn't what she'd pictured, but his body looked beautiful under the gray tee.

"What's your shirt made of?" It was far too soft to be plain old cotton, and clung far too nicely to his contours.

"It's a merino blend. Outrageously overpriced."

"Of course it is." She ran her hands up his middle, his hem rising to reveal a trail of golden brown hair leading to his navel. Another thing she'd not imagined. She'd pictured him smooth. Hair seemed somehow uncivilized . . . but she liked it. His fingers were restless, cradling her ribs, thumbs tracing the cups of her bra. Her nipples tightened in anticipation, but he was in no apparent hurry. She didn't blame him. They'd been waiting an eternity for this—why rush? Instead she surveyed his abdomen with curious, grazing touches, then his chest. Not bulky, but come on—did Fortuity have a gym no one had told her about?

He cradled her head, drawing her down to kiss him. As she settled on her forearms, her breasts glanced over his chest. Duncan drew her wild hair back, holding it as their mouths danced and flirted and made the dirtiest wordless promises to each other.

She tucked her hands beneath him to feel the restless muscles of his back flexing. She freed her lips. "How the fuck'd you get this body?"

Between kisses he whispered, "Pilates," and Raina was too horny to care if it was a joke, or to roll her eyes at the Duncanness of it, or to do any other thing except taste his mouth and imagine what he must look like naked.

"Get on top of me."

They wrestled around until the cushions were under her, Duncan's hips spreading her thighs. She wrapped her legs around his waist, willing their clothes to vaporize. No such luck.

"What you said before," he murmured, thrusting faintly now, excitement stroking hers. "If we should find ourselves in bed together."

"That's not what I said. I said if we wind up fucking."

"I was paraphrasing."

"And I hadn't pictured a bed."

Finally he smiled. "What you said. About us fucking."

"Yes?"

"Why?" His body went still above hers, and he sounded a touch incredulous. "Why would you want that, from me? Knowing how I am?"

She shrugged against the cushion. Had *none* of his lovers known about his compulsions? A live-in girlfriend would've noticed, surely . . . provided he'd ever had one. But no matter.

"You think any of the men I've been with *haven't* been crazy, in some way or other? You're still gorgeous. We still have this *thing* between us, same as always. I'm not looking to marry you, so what more would I need?" And in all honestly, if anything, she wanted him worse. The more she knew about him, the less she understood him, and the more he fascinated her. She wanted to know how he fucked, because she couldn't for the life of her guess.

"What are you like in bed?"

He smiled again. "What do you think I'm like?"

"I have zero fucking clue. That's why I'm asking."

"I'm . . . vigorous."

A little laugh escaped her lips. A word choice as silly as it was incendiary. "I'd like to see that."

"Perhaps some night you will."

"Per-*haps*."

With an impressive show of strength, he sat up, scooting the both of them back so he was upright, Raina once again in his lap. His kisses intensified, tongue sweeping deep, hands possessive as he cradled her head. Every second, they burned brighter and hotter. With every fidgeting motion of their overheated bodies, their collective breath grew more shallow and gasping. She needed his excitement, against her. In her hand. Anywhere. Raina slid her palm down his chest and belly, fingers finding the cool metal of his buckle.

"No," he said softly, and plucked her hand away.

"No?"

"Not . . . not yet." He swallowed. "I like to be the one doing."

Ah, the control freak. Of course. Didn't stop the curiosity from eating her alive, though.

He stroked her bare thighs, and she stole a glance, memorizing his skin against hers. Manicured fingers traced the hems, then slipped underneath, teasing her hips, surely feeling the lace trim of her underwear. She moved in time with those stroking fingertips, in tiny undulations that put spurs to the excitement already humming in her clit. The room went fuzzy when he reached back, palming her ass through her shorts, squeezing softly, short nails dragging against cotton. They weren't even kissing anymore, merely breathing together with their noses touching, Duncan's chin rasping hers.

She was aching for him—physically hurting—and wet. From kissing, and yes, petting. Nothing more. He hadn't touched her between her legs, not even her breasts.

"Take this too far," she murmured, nearly begging.

He did. The edge of his hand rubbed her through her shorts, stroking that entire crazy nerve-rich zone, along the cleft of her ass and all the way around, fingertips glancing her clit. The pleasure drew taut, a grasping fist.

"That," she panted. "Do that."

He changed, swapping cool control for something greedier. Needier.

"Christ," he muttered, his hand working quicker. "You couldn't wear a skirt, could you?"

Not for years. She arched her back, and Duncan eased his thighs wider, forcing hers to do the same. His mouth was hungry at her throat, breath scalding. She threaded her fingers through that soft hair, lost to the maddening friction he was giving.

"How long have you wanted this?" he murmured, lips teasing her damp skin.

"Wanted what?"

"My hands on your body."

She shivered. "Since maybe the third time you showed up at my bar. When I first saw some cracks forming in all that ice you keep stacked up around you."

His breath steamed her neck, teeth rasping softly. "I've split straight down the middle now. You must be positively overwrought."

"You talk like a robot butler," she said, stroking his hard chest and arms. "Why the fuck does that get me so wet?"

His free hand slid up between them, cupping her breast, and she decided the why of it was moot. "Let's go to my bed."

He spoke against her throat, a single, neat syllable sweetened with unmistakable cruelty. "No."

"I'm going to die if I don't get you inside me."

"What a shame," he murmured. "You're so young."

"You want me to beg, don't you?"

"I want you to come," he corrected, fingers stroking deep and quick, his other thumb toying with her nipple. And she could do just as he wanted—she could come, just from this. She was smelling him now, his skin and his hair, a hint of sweat and that goddamn glorious cologne. Worth every fucking penny.

"I don't need any man, ever," she said, practically moaning against his temple, "but I need you. Inside me. Tonight. Right now."

"That's terribly flattering, Ms. Harper."

Christ, that nickname. "If we don't fuck, I'm going to murder you."

"That would be ironic, given the entire purpose of my stay."

"Shut up, Duncan."

"Come, Ms. Harper."

And she was—she was already there, her sex hurting, taunted and teased and hounded by this wanting. All she could think about was how badly she wanted his body, surging in and out of hers. At the image, pleasure crested to a hard, angry edge, surrender inevitable.

"Fuck."

"Good." Those fingers kept stroking, stroking. "Let me hear."

Her arms wrapped around him as the orgasm peaked, her fingers grasping at his hair. The release was quick, searing—a combustion, not a crashing wave. She growled his name, hips riding his caresses, still begging for his cock. As she stilled, so did his hands, until his palms slid along her sides to settle at her waist. Mild gray eyes studied her face, his fascination quiet, almost wondrous.

"Jesus," she mumbled, drawing her hair off her sweaty neck. A calm came over her muscles—everywhere but between her legs, where the pleasure still ticked, pulse slowing as she came down.

He smiled, and the way his eyes crinkled just about unwound her heart.

She did something she normally wouldn't do at such a moment with a new guy, during an impulsive encounter—she kissed him. Slow, and nearly tender. *And is this really so impulsive?* Ditching her shift, getting drunk, yes, those were a touch reckless. But being here, with this man? Practically predestined.

She pulled away and licked her lip, studying his face. Possibly the best-looking man she'd ever been with . . . though Duncan and Miah looked so unlike each other, she really couldn't say. But the most *lavish* man she'd ever been with, no contest.

"Yes?" he asked when her study became scrutiny.

"Just looking at you. How old are you?"

"Thirty-eight."

She couldn't say if that was older or younger than she'd expected, but now that she knew, the number felt exactly right.

"I daresay you're quite a bit younger."

"By six years. Casey and I graduated together."

A faint smile. "I trust your wayward upbringing leaves us on par." He'd cooled, she realized. Not cooled to her—cooled his lust. Nothing save for the pulse winking at his throat gave away how eager he had to be for his turn.

She moved against him, brushing his still-hard excitement with her mound. "You've been patient."

"That implies I haven't already gotten exactly what I wanted."

She blinked. "How so? Did I not spot the camera? Was this all a ploy to score a sex tape, something to counter my little extortion offensive and win you your freedom back?"

"No ploy. Merely pleasure."

"Mine, anyhow. But the night's still young . . ." She ran her palms over his chest, drinking in hard flesh through the softest fabric. "Tell me what I can do for you."

"Nothing," he murmured. "Not this time."

What a tease this man was. She'd complain, claim he was torturing her, but it was more twisted than that. He was in charge, the bossy one in bed, it would seem . . . yet she was the one who'd just come. Duncan hadn't so much as gotten his cock stroked through his jeans.

"You sure?" she said, mouth at his throat, hand sliding down the hot planes of his chest and belly. "You must be hurting—"

He caught her wrist as her fingers found his belt buckle. "Of course I am."

"I could fix that for you."

His smile was cold and cutting, and infuriatingly sexy. "No."

All at once, she wanted to see him come ten times worse than she'd needed to get there herself. Needed that mouth open and moaning, those eyes shut tight with concentration or disbelief. Maybe that manicured hand stroking, forearm flexing. "You could fix it yourself," she teased, "and let me watch."

His smile softened and, oddest of all gestures, he planted a patronizing kiss on the tip of her nose. "There's nothing I crave more than control just now. Not even relief."

His grip had loosened, and she slid her palm gruffly between his thighs, cupping the stiff length of him through the fine denim. His jeans fit perfectly, practically tailored, surely binding him up against the brink of madness now. But in a blink his fingers were wrapped around hers, holding them still.

"There's *nothing* you crave more?" she asked.

"Nothing."

"Not even a nice, tight, slow hand on your dick?"

He swallowed, eyes shutting for a breath. "Nothing." His voice was thick and incriminating.

"Or a nice, warm mouth, maybe?"

He fanned his long fingers over the back of her hand,

squeezing it to his excitement for just a moment before stilling it again. "Nothing."

She was burning up herself, so bad it was as if she'd never come at all. "Maybe there's something *I* crave, then. Maybe you could let me help you out, just as a favor."

"You've watched me fall apart in enough ways, these past few days."

"So let me see this, too." She wanted to see *everything*. Wanted to watch him give in to his basest, most animal nature, see that gorgeous face pained, hear that velvet voice reduced to pleas and moans, and taste the evidence of his humanity on her tongue.

He moved her hand to his waist, the taut flesh there rising and falling with racing breaths. "You've gotten enough of me."

More than you're used to showing to a woman? A few scraps of his mysterious childhood, the knowledge that his cultured façade was just that—a façade. A fabrication, albeit one he owned as truly as he did his own skin. More, perhaps, than he'd ever let anyone know of him before? Goddamn, why did that idea get her so hot?

He shifted her to the side, standing with the quickest, most dignified adjustment of his cock behind those binding jeans.

"Off to fix what I've done to you?" she asked, lounging back against the couch's arm.

"No, I'm not." He gathered their glasses. "I could use the discomfort, frankly. It's a welcome distraction."

"Well, I hope maybe I'll be there when you finally crack under all the pressure."

The driest little smirk, and he didn't meet her eyes. "Of course. Because you haven't seen enough of my helplessness already."

"No, not even close."

And that was it, wasn't it? She'd gotten inside him, just a little, the way they'd talked tonight. Exposed him, if only in glimpses. So he'd stolen the upper hand right back from her, dictating the terms and dynamic of the sex.

Tricky motherfucker.

He'd disappeared into the kitchen, and when he passed by with a glass of water in hand, his erection was still evident. "I'll see you in the morning."

"You'll see me inside ten minutes, in your imagination. Doing things I'd happily do to you for real, right now."

He paused, turning in the threshold of the guest room. "Do you need another orgasm, Ms. Harper? Would that help you sleep, and shut that maddening mouth of yours?"

She bit her lip. "Maybe you'd prefer my mouth if—"

"Good night," he said, sounding torn between amusement and exasperation. "Thanks for the suffering." The door shut.

She smiled. "Anytime."

Chapter 12

Duncan woke up in discomfort, but for a change it wasn't to do with alcohol or pills. Instead it was an aching urgency between his legs ... an ache he didn't think he'd felt this badly ever, or at least not since adolescence. And all because of the woman probably still sleeping soundly—and satisfied—in the next room.

He sat up and checked his phone, shocked to find it was pushing eight. Astrid was dozing in her favorite spot, the V-shaped nest of covers between his shins.

"Why didn't you tell me how late it had gotten?" He had that godforsaken meeting with Flores this morning, and not even an hour to get there.

In the bathroom, he stole a glimpse in Raina's scandal-free medicine cabinet before stripping and turning on the shower. She wasn't a terrible housekeeper, though he had noted the bra hanging from the doorknob, and the tub wasn't without a haze of soap residue and the odd long, dark hair plastered to the tile. His compulsions nagged at him, itching to dictate, but thankfully Duncan cowed to punctuality as well as order, and he didn't have the time just now. He could hear his therapist remarking what an excellent invitation this was to practice a little self-guided exposure therapy, standing here in this not-perfect bathroom. It was about as comfortable as wearing a suit made of thumbtacks, but he focused on the things he approved of. Good water pressure. A refreshing minimum of products cluttering the caddy hooked over the showerhead. *The massaging showerhead*, he noted, then promptly stopped himself from wondering with too much interest about how she might employ it. For whatever willful reason, he wasn't indulging his lust on this one. He could use the fuel—might help him keep his edge through this morning's meeting. Where confidence and certainty wavered, the carnal frustration prickling through his veins could help him pass for indignant.

Plus, if a release was in the cards for Duncan, Raina would be there for it, he resolved as he uncapped his shampoo. He'd needed the control last night, but if they fooled around again, it'd be a different matter—

"Knock, knock." Her muffled voice came through the door, followed by the click of the knob.

"I'm terribly indecent."

"That's fine. That's what showers are for."

He waited for something brash, for the curtain to be whipped aside, or her face appearing at its edge, but nothing.

"You eat eggs?"

He eased the curtain open enough to meet her eyes. "Eggs?"

"I can make them really good scrambled, or not quite as good over easy. But no soft-boiled and definitely nothing where I have to take the yolks out."

"No, thank you. Tea will suffice."

Raina's gaze seemed to make an inventory of his wet hair, or dripping chin and hand, or however much of his chest she could see. "Suit yourself. Got all the toiletries you need? Fifty-dollar conditioner and whatnot?"

"Plenty."

She smiled. She was wearing the same clothes as last night, and Duncan wanted to bury his face in her cleavage and breathe in her sweat.

"Are you waiting for an invitation?" he prompted.

She shook her head. "You just look good, with your hair and eyelashes all wet."

"And you never look nicer than when I'm making you come."

Oh, that dirty smirk. "I'll see you for caffeine." And she left him be.

Duncan finished up and dried off, shaved, tended to his hair, then shut himself back in the guest room. He dressed to the nines; no way he was sitting down opposite Flores looking anything less than his best, not ever again. As he prepared, he eyed the few piles of Benji Harper's things still cluttering the corners of the room, and wondered what this place had been like when it was still Raina and her father. Had they joked a lot?

Likely. Watched television together? Cooked meals for each other? What must it feel like, to be close enough to a parent to care for him that way? Did it feel good enough to offset the pain she must have suffered when he'd passed?

When he found Raina, she was pouring steaming water into two mugs—one with a coffee filter, one with a tea bag. Her eyebrows rose at his ensemble. "Wow, all gussied up. You going to court?"

"It's not a trial—it's an investigation. But yes, I'm going to the sheriff's department to meet with Flores. There's no evidence. There's no way I'll be charged with anything." He realized a beat too late, she'd not asked if he was nervous, so that little show of confidence must have been for himself.

She stepped closer to take in his clothes—quite possibly his favorite suit. Darkest gray pants and vest, cream shirt, black tie. She smoothed his damp, combed hair, the contact familiar and . . . and *crackling.* "You look like you again."

"I feel like me again." By which he now realized only meant he felt like a fraud . . . though it wasn't without its comforts. Still, this woman knew better now. He couldn't say why, but the more he felt she knew him, the more aggression he harbored toward her. Like a cornered animal. In dark, reflexive moments, he wanted to lash out at her. Not in violence, though. Not with his fists or words. In darker, baser ways. Animal indeed.

She set the milk carton on the table. "Oh—guess what."

"What?"

She went to the sink, pulling out the trash can from the cabinet and angling it to show Duncan a tiny gray corpse. "Your cat got a mouse!"

He frowned. "How disgusting."

"How useful," she corrected, shutting the cupboard.

"Thank goodness she's had all her shots." He stirred sugar into his cup.

"Gold star for Astrid. Apparently a posh name and organic cat food weren't enough to take the cold-blooded killer out of her. And you're both earning your keep now."

He drank his tea quickly, standing, and checked his phone's clock. "Thank you for this," he said, leaving the mug in the sink. "I'll be back by lunch, I imagine—I have an errand to run after the meeting."

"Cool. I should have the last of my dad's stuff sorted out by then."

He fetched his leather dossier and a pad and pen, more as a shield than anything else. He was likely going to spend the morning getting interrogated, but at least he'd stride in looking too good for this ridiculous charade. "Enjoy your morning," he told his bartender-extortionist-landlady-body-guard.

"Break a leg."

Downstairs, a raucous din greeted Duncan as he opened the door to the back lot. A gang of crows were camped out on top of the Dumpster, cawing madly, black as death.

"A murder indeed," Duncan said, checking that the door was locked. He eyed the malcontents as he walked to the Merc; then his heart stopped, along with his feet. Another half dozen of the bastards were standing atop his car, shiny black feathers against shiny black lacquer. And that wasn't all. White.

"You shat on my car?" he asked them. "Are you fucking kidding me?" He waved his arms wildly until they dispersed. Amid the crowing he heard a squeak from above, and looked up as Raina stuck her head out the window.

"Oh, jeez. They've never done that to my truck."

He didn't have words, just gestured at the vehicle, dumbstruck.

"It looks way worse from up here."

"Oh, cheers. Thanks very much."

She smiled—bit her lip as though she hadn't meant to let him see it.

"You laugh and I'll throttle you."

Another stifled grin. "It's just a car. We can wash it this afternoon."

"Just a car? Have you *met* me?"

"What's a little bird shit, compared to the graffiti? Don't be late, Duncan."

He shook his head, found his keys, and unlocked the driver's side. "I hate this town," he informed her.

"I'm pretty sure it hates you right back."

"I'll see you in a couple hours, darling."

She laughed. "Bye."

He drove around the building, wipers and washer fluid doing little to clear the offenses on the windshield aside from smearing them into chalky rainbows. She was right, of course— the spray paint was far more mortifying, and it was only a fierce streak of pride that let him drive through town sporting that message—a fuck-you to whatever ignorant hillbilly had presumed he could be intimidated.

Though he'd be calling on Vince Grossier at the garage the second this meeting was dealt with, and seeing about a temporary fix. Duncan was as vain as he was stubborn.

Intellectually he knew his attachment to presentation was a manifestation of his mental illness, but that didn't lessen how naked he felt, driving through town with his car looking so ... neglected. Few things rankled him as badly as a lack of care being paid to things. Surely most saw it as showing off, as him wanting to shout, "Look at me, I'm rich and I'm better than you!" It was far sadder than all that, he'd realized. Obsessive safeguarding to keep his fingers gripping the edge of the cliff, clinging desperately to his self-image, the one he'd spent the past twenty years meticulously cultivating. He'd suffered too many pointing fingers, too many taunts and whispers making a mocking inventory of his awful charity clothes, his ugly shoes, his laughably uncool school bag, whatever horrid haircut he'd most recently been subjected to. Now, driving through town with his car defaced and beshatted, his precious veneer vandalized ... He doubted many people had ever looked at him and felt anything particularly warm, but he vastly preferred to inspire contempt over ridicule.

Or worst of all, pity.

He opened the center console and swallowed a Klonopin. And if he hadn't had this meeting to tend to, yes, he'd be wishing he had a shot of vodka handy to amplify it.

Mercifully the town was quiet—the heathens still had a few hours to sleep off their hangovers before church, and nothing would be open yet. Nothing aside from the door to Ramon Flores's borrowed office, it seemed. Duncan nodded tightly to the BCSD's front desk girl, then headed down a hallway he was getting far too familiar with. He knocked.

"Come in."

Flores hit RECORD before even looking up. He was dressed down this morning, in gray chinos and a black polo. Duncan felt about two inches taller striding in this time, dressed to kill. Figuratively.

"Welch, hello. Have a seat."

"No rest for the wicked, I take it? What could be so pressing that you just had to speak to me first thing on a Sunday morning?"

"In my line of work, there are no weekends. Coffee?"

Duncan smiled wanly. "You do love to keep me guessing whether this assignment is as much of a joke to you as it is to me."

"Also no jokes in my line of work. Just offering you a coffee."

"No, thank you."

"Good choice," Flores said, and took a sip from his own cup. "It's pretty disgusting."

"Shall we dive right in?"

Flores crossed his legs, leaning back. "This is probably no surprise, but the bureau's going to need to audit you."

Duncan sighed. No, it wasn't a surprise. But Christ, it'd be a headache. "That's fine by me. I have impeccable records. Such an intrusion would only serve me." He'd never so much as written off a paper clip unless it got attached directly to a legal form. Rules had been his Jesus, for years now. Until he'd come to Fortuity, that is. Since crossing into this town, he'd grown a touch lax, as though criminality traveled through the air just like that relentless red dust. Though he never got sloppy when it came to accounting.

Flores made some notes.

"Anything else?" Duncan asked. "I'm more than happy to get you in touch with my accountant. We could've had this little chat over the phone, incidentally." Of course the man knew that. The beck-and-call act was surely a means to get Duncan feeling annoyed, agitated, jerked around, to trick him into giving something away. Charming.

More notes, and Flores didn't look up, trying Duncan's patience. He rubbed his forehead, unable to hide his angst.

"One other thing," Flores said slowly, and finally met his eyes. "Raina Harper."

"What about her?"

"No chance she's got anything to hide, in her books?"

He frowned. "What, you think she's been laundering these supposed bribes for me? We met six weeks ago. When was I meant to have begun collecting these gratuities, precisely?"

"I'm being thorough, that's all."

"Ms. Harper's accounting is none of my business."

"No? I heard from a few locals that you once furnished her with a large amount of cash."

Duncan sank back, feeling slapped. "What? When?"

Flores flipped to a page in his pad. "Circa August fourteenth."

Duncan thought, frowning deeper. "The night of Casey Grossier's homecoming party? I donated approximately four hundred dollars from Sunnyside's public relations budget to open the bar. It was fully reported, a charm offensive to take the edge off the locals' skepticism toward the casino. PR was the bulk of my job."

"Four hundred bucks? Not exactly putting the 'petty' in petty cash."

Duncan made his expression dry. "You underestimate Sunnyside's resources, I promise you. And it's all on their books. Leave Raina Harper alone." God knew what state her finances were in, or indeed if she might have something worth hiding, unrelated to this case. She wasn't the embodiment of professionalism, and the bar was a prime entity in which Vince Grossier might want to obscure some of his own shady earnings. "She has enough to deal with, without adding you to the mix," he said.

The man made some more notes.

"I also gave her three hundred dollars cash yesterday, for rent," Duncan added.

"Rent," Flores muttered, scribbling. He took so long at it Duncan could only assume he was being toyed with.

"I don't know what you're trying to do here," Duncan said, "but don't punish me for cooperating. And don't punish Raina Harper for having such poor judgment as to keep my company." He paused, telling his body to cool, his breath to slow. His anger to subside. He glanced at his cuffs, and the creases running down his thighs, reminding himself, *This is me.* Cool, together, in control. "Don't you have more important things to investigate, Agent Flores? Like the whereabouts of human remains, perhaps?"

Flores smiled. "Sadly for me, that's not my assignment. My digging revolves around David Levins's dirty laundry, and sadly for *you*, you're in that pile."

"This is all such bullshit," Duncan sighed, knowing he was giving his emotions away but feeling too much to keep it all inside without risking an attack. "And since you've cost me my job and threatened my very professional viability, I've half a mind to go and find those miserable bones myself—give you all something actually deserving of all this squandered energy.

The longer this ridiculous investigation shuffles along, the more time I spend trapped in this town, surrounded by angry, uninformed idiots who believe me complicit."

Flores glanced up at that. "Have you been harassed?"

Duncan froze, realizing what the truth could very well invite. He didn't relish the animosity he might encounter around town, but if he felt this upended and powerless now, he wasn't about to discover what outright isolation in protective custody would do to his mental health.

"Not harassed, no." *Threatened.* "I just want this resolved, same as everyone else. And I won't stoop to the cliché of reminding you my tax dollars pay your salary."

"I'm sure you won't." Flores smiled. "I think we both know I'm not the bad guy here."

"Then why do I want—" Duncan stopped, reminding himself he was being recorded, and that sharing his desire to strangle a federal agent would be a terrifically foolish slip of his judgment. "Are you done with me?"

"For now, yes."

Duncan gave Flores his personal accountant's contact information and filled out some forms, and was dismissed. It wasn't until he stepped out into the BCSD's front lot that he registered precisely how *angry* he was. It was the powerlessness, of course. The sensation of being bullied and jerked around.

His hands shook around the steering wheel as he drove down Railroad Ave. He took a left on Station and pulled up in front of the drugstore. A gang of surly-looking teenagers parted as he strode for the entrance, their chatter going quiet at whatever evidence of Duncan's emotions was emblazoned across his face.

One, eyeing his clothes, had the balls to singsong a quiet "Faggot" as Duncan passed.

The comment didn't offend him, but the situation flashed him sharply back to his childhood. Thirty-eight years old, and still getting mocked by a gang of nascent thugs. He was grown now, but the rage inside him had been fermenting for decades. Duncan turned on his heel and jabbed the kid square in the chest, sending him back a pace, and looming to underline precisely how many inches he had on the brat.

"Fuck yourself, you redneck little shit."

The teenager went still, eyes widening, but Duncan heard

their voices rising again as he disappeared inside. He didn't care. He strode down the center aisle and grabbed a bottle of Advil, marched to the counter, and paid in cash. Back outside, no retaliation awaited him; the teenagers had disappeared. But when he got to his car, he stopped dead in his tracks. His hood ornament was gone, the neat little silver Mercedes emblem snapped clean off. He could've had his own face slashed and felt precisely this violated. Duncan stared at the wound, the world blazing bloodred.

He cocked his chin skyward and bellowed, "Fuck this town!"

Chapter 13

Duncan climbed behind the wheel of his vandalized, shit-splattered, amputated car and drove back to the bar chewing three Advils. Fuck the paint job. It could wait. He slammed his door and rang the bell beside the rear entrance, listening to distant steps until Raina appeared.

"Better find you some keys. How did it—"

"Get upstairs."

Her eyebrows rose, gaze dropping to the rattling bottle in his hand, and Duncan brushed past and marched up the steps ahead of her.

"Did it not go well?"

"We're not talking about it," he called over his shoulder. They weren't talking, period. No more thinking, no more of anything rational. There was no logic to be had in this town, no respect, no fairness. No measure of any of the things Duncan valued, just sloppy human impulse.

And he could stoop to that right about now.

Raina followed him into the kitchen and shut the door. Duncan eyed her, his gaze surely flinging sparks. She'd showered; her hair was wet, face bare, and she'd dressed in jeans and a black T-shirt, boots on her feet as though she'd planned to go out. He'd be ruining those plans now. Moving on pure instinct, he found his fingers in her damp hair, tasted coffee on her lips. Felt her gasp at the ferocity of his mouth, and felt eager fingers digging into his back. Felt twenty fucking feet tall. Felt *right*, slipping into this aggressive, reckless man's skin.

She said, "You taste weird."

"It's Advil." And that ended that discussion.

Duncan didn't fuck before the third date, as a rule. But the rules didn't apply here. They hadn't had a single date, and neither seemed as though they desired to change that. Yet she'd watched him come apart this week . . . watched him lose his job and identity and, in moments, his very sanity. She'd bypassed nudity and seen straight *through* him.

So fuck rules. Fuck dates. Fuck the fact that they made absolutely no sense together, because for once, sex wasn't an audition to Duncan. Before now, it had been another test to pass, to see if he and whatever woman he'd started dating were compatible enough to carry on toward something serious. He and Raina were compatible in precisely this one way, and infatuation was the flimsiest twig to hang a relationship on. They'd never be anything real, but this . . . this was inevitable. This was nature. And this was the first time Duncan had ever pursued what he suspected his soon-to-be lover was an expert at: sex for the sake of sex. Not as a means to predict the viability of a coupling. Just *fucking*, because each person's craving for the other was so strong it drove them both mad. So strong it felt he'd need to break something if he didn't get to feel his cock inside her.

There was anger in him as well—toward his circumstances, but toward her, too. Anger to feel so known, and exposed. He wanted to take it out on her in the crudest ways. She had to taste it in his spit, feel the heat of his need pulsing from his skin.

Between deep strokes of his tongue, she asked, "This finally happening?"

He turned her by the waist, pushed her up against the kitchen wall. Her knee rose to hug his hip and he gave what the gesture asked for—the hard crush of his excitement against hers. "This is happening."

He cupped the back of her head and ground their bodies together so hard he felt the wallpaper grating his knuckles. The next moment he grabbed her ass in both hands and hauled her up. When her legs locked around his waist, he carried her to the kitchen table. A pepper grinder toppled and rolled to the floor; papers crinkled. Raina was working at his buttons as he yanked her tee up, and she raised her arms and let him peel her bare. Her bra was sheer plum lace, perfection against her tan skin. They got his vest and shirt open together and he stripped them as though they were aflame. He was dying to feel the air and sun on his skin, dying for her eyes on him. Her hands on him. Everything. He did nothing in half measures, so he let this exposure, this *surrender*, strip him bare.

Her boots were next. He tugged each free and let them hit the floor. "Christ," he muttered. "You really can't just wear a bloody skirt, can you?"

"Work for it, Duncan."

He jerked at her belt, and once it was open, she lay back and he peeled those jeans down her long legs, slow. Everything slow, suddenly. Her panties didn't match her bra. Not at all. A black-and-white polka-dot thong. No matter. He stripped that little scrap of cotton as well, and went still, studying her. So still he felt his heartbeat swaying his body. He could see nearly all of her.

"Get your bra off."

She did, now naked before him on her cluttered table. A feast. He memorized everything. All the contrasts: her tan lines; her dark nipples; the black, soft hair between her legs; the flushed pink of her sex. As he ran his hand down her shoulder and arm, he committed that contrast to memory as well—pale against tan, a man's groomed hand brushing over a wild woman's tattoo. She leaned in close, fingers seeking his belt. Duncan shut his eyes, savoring the tug-and-give as she freed the buckle. Last night he'd needed control, but he was beyond that now. He needed violence—that intimate melee called sex.

She had to see him already, the hard outline of his cock through the fine wool. The heel of her hand brushed his erection as she worked at the clasps, then the zipper. He moaned when the restriction eased, sucked a harsh breath as she pushed his pants low on his hips. He tucked his thumbs under his waistband and exposed himself. "Stroke me."

She braced one arm behind her and clasped his aching flesh in her warm hand. His eyes squeezed tight as a noise of pain and relief fled his lips. He'd been burning for this since last night on the couch, *hurting* for it, needing it so badly the plea-sure rivaled torture. Her pulls were long and hungry, making him feel bigger than he ever had felt. "Yes."

He let himself watch, not caring if it was tacky. His cock looked thick in her fist, flushed dark and gleaming at the crown, obscene in the bright daylight. Thrilling. "Good." Her sex was blocked by the motions, just a tempting, dark shadow beyond her pumping fist.

She murmured, "You're more than I expected." And the

statement excited him more than he'd have guessed. Too many men viewed endowment as a personal achievement, but Duncan valued only what could be earned. It was a compliment fit for a more primitive, simple man than he, and yet the praise had him panting.

"What else have you been expecting?" he asked.

"That I'd be the rough one. But I don't trust any of my assumptions about you anymore."

He smiled. "As you shouldn't."

"My jeans," she said, releasing him. "Back pocket."

His brain was foggy and slow, and she waved at the floor, at her pants. He stooped, cock screaming from neglect as he found her wallet. The leather was still warm from her body, and he didn't have to look hard to find what she wanted—the condom, and each of its predecessors, had branded a circle into the hide. He fished it out, held it up. "You realize that as storage systems go, a wallet—"

"It's fucking fine. Put it on."

Point taken. He opened the packet, slid cool latex down his pounding flesh. He grabbed her by the waist and pulled her forward, right to the edge of the table.

"Slow," she said.

"You're bossy," Duncan murmured, and brought his head to her swollen lips. "You know that?"

"Just you wait." But she was breathless, attention nailed right where his was, at his hurting, hard excitement sinking into her.

He moaned. "Fuck."

No sooner had he slid deep than her hands were tugging at his hips. He eased out slowly, rapt at the sight. She held his face, pressed their foreheads together, and they watched.

She whispered, "Faster."

"In good time." For now he wanted only to savor every second of this, of his cock gliding in and out, again and again. She was everything he'd been panting for—lush and hot and slick, a dozen testimonies to the truth that she wanted him as badly as he wanted her. He had worries, gnawing, gnashing ones, but just now, locked in this bright, hot moment with this woman, he couldn't recall what they might be. There was nothing beyond their two bodies, two voices, two pairs of greedy eyes.

She stroked his belly and chest, making a study of the shapes his obsessive diet and exercise routine had built. No great bulk, but no excess, either. Every aspect of his person had been molded around a philosophy of efficiency and performance, until so very recently. Everything about him—his clothes, his body, his grooming, his possessions—spoke of the balance between discipline and luxury. Everything one could see, that is. Everything outside his broken mind, his private rituals, his pathetic memories.

He took her deep and slow with exaggerated rolls of his hips, savoring the contrasts—cool air against his fevered body, her darker coloring meeting his pale skin and the lighter hair that framed his cock.

"Jesus," she murmured, gaze hungry. "You are fucking hot."

The words sizzled like a brand, and had him granting her request, hips racing.

She pushed his shirt from his shoulders, eyes darting.

He was inside her warm body, smelling her excitement, hearing her hot exhalations at his throat, fucking her in her kitchen. But he wanted more. Wanted to be in her bed, on her covers. Wanted the memory of this burned there, so hot she'd never climb between those sheets without thinking of him.

He grabbed her ass and hauled her against him, her strong legs wrapping tight around his waist once more. He walked them awkwardly, hurriedly to her room, clutching his trousers to his thigh with one hand. Once she fell back against the covers, he left her warmth long enough to strip his shirt and kick away his pants and shorts. She was grabbing at him before he even got his knees spread between her legs, tugging at his arms and shoulders and the back of his neck. She wanted him with such an open, nearly *brutal* physicality it sent a shock of pleasure through his body. *Wanted* was a loaded sensation to Duncan. An unmet need so fierce he'd long ago quit allowing himself to register it, preferring the numbness of living without to the sting of the yearning.

Everything she roused in him . . . everything hot, and aggressive, and out of control . . . everything he worked so hard never to let himself feel. It wanted out. And with his armor rusted to red powder, he had no choice but to obey. Had to give his cock what it was screaming for, and to hell with his tiresome persona.

He grasped her wrist. Blood pounded through him, his cock aching. He grabbed her other wrist and forced her hands up above her head. His hips sped, and hers seemed to fight them, wrists twisting in his grip, everything about the sex suddenly darker, rougher, raw—

She jerked her arm, hard, and struck him square in the eye with her elbow.

Duncan shouted. He froze. He clapped his palm to his eye and gaped at her with the other. "What the fuck?"

"Don't *ever* hold me down."

His heart and cock and injury were all throbbing, pulsing. "You could have bloody told me 'Stop.'"

"Just don't do it again."

"I won't, if that's the result. Christ." He let his hand drop, blinked to make sure he could still see. He started to leave the bed, but she grabbed him by the shoulders.

"I didn't say to stop fucking me."

"I read between the lines."

"Keep going."

And too hard and hurting to overthink it all, he gave her what she wanted. What he wanted as well—rough, fast thrusts, his forearms tucked up tight against her ribs to mimic that feeling of restraint he'd so utterly buggered up a moment ago. He gave her all the aggression he craved as the pleasure built, let his hips punish and pin her as his hands weren't allowed to. His needs would change, the closer he got to the edge, but for now, all he wanted was to own her.

She stroked his shoulders, his back, his ass. Curious fingertips found the pit just to the left of his spine, circling the deep scar.

Cooled by the contact, he said, "Turn over."

She fumbled onto her hands and knees, and he sank back in, deep. His grip on her hips was tight, probably too tight, but her moans didn't protest. He took her hard, reveling in the control he felt. He told her with his body which of them was older, stronger, bigger, male. He gathered her long hair in his fist and urged her head to turn. Urged her gaze to watch him, to remember this the way he was doomed to. Indelibly. For the rest of his life.

"Look at me."

She did, lips parted, wordless. Awe in those dark eyes. He told her with this sex, *You're mine.* True perhaps for these fleeting minutes alone, but no matter how long it might last, yes, she was his. The woman who'd brought this hounding hunger to his body, and the only one who could cure him of it. But not before he heard those sounds again—the moans and gasps that had heated his throat as his hand had teased her until she quaked in his lap. He reached around, finding her curls, then the hard, swollen tip of her clit. She bucked, flooding him with smug satisfaction.

"Fuck, you feel good," she said.

He took her deeper, quicker, stroking her in tight little circles. Her body was perfection, tattoos and all. A gorgeous hourglass, with muscles forming twin ridges along her spine, softer flesh at her hips echoing his thrusts. Strong. Feminine. Nothing like the willowy ideal he'd sketched for himself so long ago. Wild and crass. Shameless. How he'd ever go back to those civilized, icy women, when his life once again looked as it should . . .

Should. What was happening now wasn't what he *should* do, but funny how fucking incredible it felt.

"Don't stop," she said, the words halting from his impact.

His grip dented the delicious swell of her hip, fingers teasing as though he'd been pleasing her for ages this way. He couldn't help feeling there was a *rightness* at work. And for once, fuck the control. There was nothing he wanted more than her eyes.

"On your back."

"No. I'm close."

He pulled out and slapped her hip, cock aching in the cool, dry air. "On your back."

She groaned, pissed, but flipped over all the same. He sank deep with her nails digging into his arms.

"Touch yourself," he said.

She slipped her hand low, fingertips on her clit, gaze on his cock.

"Look at me," he murmured.

"I am."

He propped himself on one arm, freeing a hand to tilt her chin up, locking their eyes. She hugged him tight with her legs, drawing him deep, matching his thrusts with her own motions. Duncan tucked his arms along her ribs again, lost in the friction, the heat, those eyes on his.

"I want to watch you," she said. "Sit back."

"We can't both be giving the orders."

"Yes, we fucking can. Sit back."

And though he'd never expected to enjoy taking direction,

the way her gaze took him in as he sat back to kneel upright between her thighs . . . Christ, this felt too good. He'd never wanted admiration this badly before, to see that heat in her eyes as she watched him. Pure desire, and one that went beyond his possessions or his packaging, his hard-earned pedigrees. He felt the same. He wanted her—wanted this person who was so precisely wrong for him.

"My God," she murmured, riveted. "You can fuck."

"You sound surprised."

"A girl doesn't want to assume."

He owned her hard, stealing a glimpse at her fingers, teasing her clit. This view might be what she craved, but Duncan wanted leverage. He leaned in and grabbed the headboard, the position letting him take her with long, rolling thrusts. The fire in her gaze told him she approved. Approval didn't drive Duncan quite the way control did, but coming from this perpetually unimpressed woman, it warmed him like a fire.

He felt the wood of her bed under his palms, her covers under his knees, her tight, hungry body gripping his cock. No doubt he wasn't the first man to feel these things, wouldn't be the last, either, but he'd make it his mission to be the hardest one to forget.

"Is this everything you guessed?" he asked, panting. "Us?"

"Way dirtier."

The best you've had?

She stroked his belly and ribs with her free hand. "You hide a lot of secrets behind all that tailoring."

Strip me bare, he thought. *Take me apart. See me as no one else ever has, then tell me good-bye.* He couldn't live this way; couldn't be with a woman and show this much, give this much . . . but for one blazing morning?

"Watch me," he said again. And when her gaze dropped to his driving cock, he didn't protest. Whatever she wanted from him, that was what he'd be.

She changed beneath him. Her legs hugged him tighter, clenching in short bursts, and her arms locked up, fingers stroking her clit furiously. Her lips parted, eyebrows drawing tight in the disbelief of cresting pleasure.

"Do it," he said, hips racing.

"Fuck, Duncan."

He flushed to hear that—his name. Like a secret, the way it

wrapped him up in her. "Good," he said, and shut his eyes, savoring.

"Yeah," she murmured. "Don't stop."

Not for anything. And a breath later, he felt it. Her entire body stiffened and stilled. He drove deep and held there to feel the fluttering spasms. Intoxicating. Everything came into sharp relief in those sweet seconds: the scent of sex and latex, the hush of her breathing, the feel of the sweat slicking his back and chest, the sun warming his hair and his face. Around his hips, her legs loosened their hold, her body going soft atop the messy covers.

He let the headboard go, bracing on his forearms. Pushing the damp hair from her forehead, he studied her brown eyes, half-hidden by dozy lids. "That what you needed?"

She nodded, smiling. "You have no idea how bad."

"Trust me, I do." He'd gotten her off scarcely twelve hours ago, but Duncan nearly never masturbated, and that denial coupled with this blazing attraction had him strung taut as a crossbow. His cock was ticking inside her, that pulse feeling like rage, he was so frustrated.

She urged him to move, coaxing his hips with damp palms. The second that friction resumed, he was close. So close. But he could fuck this way for an hour and not get there. He was beyond the motions—he needed more. Needed the only thing that had ever let him get there . . .

She stroked his hair, kissed his neck. "You gonna come for me this time, Duncan?"

He could only moan, her words reducing him to a graceless, frantic mess. Yes, he was going to come. Provided he could give the one order that would allow it.

He swallowed, and the dogging need to come drove to him articulate the desires that pride always precluded, outside the abandon of sex. "Hold me," he murmured.

After a pause, the hands admiring his arms and hips circled him, one palm on his back, the other cupping his neck. The sensation washed over him like a wave—a thrilling, terrifying force he could only bow before.

"Say my name."

He'd whispered it, and she replied in kind. "Duncan."

He moaned, the sound joining the weight of her arms and the heat of her body, rousing every last inch of him, so many more places than just his pounding cock. In his mind, in his blood.

She said it again, and again he flushed. His hips lost their grace and he felt the pressure building, the control cracking. Felt fire gathering into a searing ball in his belly.

"Duncan."

She said it as though she wanted him here, this way, doing precisely these things with her ... She said it as though she wanted him, period. And though the knowledge shamed him, made him feel pathetic and needy and so fucking *predictable*, this was what got him off. Feeling wanted. And welcome. Valued.

You're such a joke. But he couldn't care, not now. Joke or not, these sensations made him come like a goddamn force of nature. Lamest fucking fetish ever, but effective.

He moaned, the pleasure sharpening, deepening. She stroked his hair and spoke his name, the sound affecting him as truly as caressing hands. His body was helpless now, taking orders from his cock. The surrender, for once, was welcome.

"Come on," she whispered. "Come on, baby."

Baby. Fuck, even that name—all wrong. Yet here he was, panting into her hair from it. Her palms slid to his ass, urging his racing thrusts. "Come on, Duncan."

It hit him like a tornado, sucking the air from his lungs, stealing gravity and time and leaving the earth miles below them. It suspended him in a rush of blinding, quenching pleasure, reality reduced to the heat of her, the smell of her. The inevitability of her. That all-wrong rightness. He felt his body falling in the wake of the sensation, and her arms seemed to materialize around his shoulders, her lips against his jaw.

He sat back on his heels, reeling. He took her in as he stripped the condom, and she didn't look as he'd suspected she would in this moment. A touch smug, yes, but flushed and sleepy as well. Softer than he'd have guessed. Placid. Beautiful.

Duncan ditched the rubber and lay down beside her, welcoming the dry desert air to cool his sweat. Their wrists touched, and Raina spread her toes along the top of his foot playfully, bobbing it up and down. Nothing demanded to be said. Nothing demanded to be done aside from this wallowing. The panic would come in time, along with the questions.

Will this happen again? Should it? Perhaps it would be best to leave it as it was, so much better than expected, and avoid risking . . . what? The realization that this time had been a fluke, a trick of the anticipation, and that no encore could ever match it, perhaps.

But no, even Duncan wasn't that deluded.

Risk attachment. That sensation Duncan both feared and craved above all others, that force Raina resented. They could fall madly in love this very hour, yet it wouldn't change the fact that their lives would never converge along the same track — not for keeps. He hated her world as surely as she'd hate his. She couldn't keep him here in this dirty patch of endangered America, and no sooner could he host her like a pampered cat in clean, urban luxury. Sunnyside could give him his job back and the casino could keep him tethered to Fortuity for another two years, but two years was *nothing* at his age. Time accelerated after thirty-five. Two years was a breath. End it now, end it later — it all boiled down to good-bye, farewell, to a parting full of angst or sadness or apathy or relief. A parting, unavoidably. As unavoidable as this collision.

Through a yawn, she said, "That was fucking perfection."

He took her hand, gave it a squeeze. *Perfection.* The thing he strived for at the expense of his own mental health. Perfection, with this all-wrong woman, in this all-wrong place, at this all-wrong moment of his unraveling life.

And with absolute certainty, he said, "Yes, it was."

Chapter 14

If Duncan had expected to find lasting peace in the wake of that sex, he'd been sorely mistaken.

For a time, relief had suffused him, effective as a sedative. He'd fallen asleep beside Raina even, but perhaps twenty minutes later, his eyes had popped open, and in a breath the worries were back, swarming his mind like ants and leaving him itchy as the afternoon arrived. Raina left to run errands, and practically the second he heard her truck drive away, he was on his knees in her bathroom, chasing the calm.

For two hours Duncan scoured, scrubbed, polished, rinsed, until every last square inch of porcelain and glass gleamed bright enough to blind.

With the impulse surrendered to, Duncan felt calmer by a degree. He sat on the couch and tried to entice Astrid to visit, but she could always smell the panic on him—she never wanted a thing to do with him in the moments that preceded a cleaning bout or an anxiety attack.

"Fair-weather friend," he said to her retreating tail.

Christ, he needed a job. A purpose.

He wandered around the apartment. Puttered. Fretted. He went downstairs and rummaged in Raina's supply closet until he found a can of spray paint, and did a laughably inadequate job of covering over the bright orange letters on the Merc's doors. The paint looked pathetic, matte near-black against glossy jet lacquer, but with each coat, the message began to fade. And as it did, a different word rose in Duncan's mind.

Bones.

Like Vince Grossier before him, Duncan was growing fixated on those five letters. They followed him back upstairs, and in

moments that afternoon—waiting for the kettle, smelling some
bit of food blackening under the burner—he was flashed back
to August, to the foothills, to the night when Vince's suspicions
and Duncan's snooping had led them and Casey to a disused
mine entrance, not far from one of the construction sites. A
starry sky overhead, and the terrible smell of charred flesh in
the air. The smell that had promised those things Vince had
been so fixated on.

Bones. They hadn't found them, merely the evidence of
their fate. And what they saw told them that the bones were
black, not white. They'd been broiled fleshless in a metal barrel
and then buried, and ultimately uncovered by a worker. Then
Alex Dunn had been called to the scene, but Tremblay had
arranged for his untimely demise before the truth could get
out. Now those elusive bones were gone, deposited who knew
where. Or destroyed—pulverized, or dissolved in some chemical or other.

Yet it wasn't the fate of those things that dogged Duncan so
much as the identity of the victim. Who had he been? Why and
how had he died? Before or after he'd been curled inside that
barrel, and set alight like so much rubbish? What had he seen
that had demanded so *thorough* a silencing?

All everyone needed for some answers were those bones.
There'd be dental records, missing persons databases, an ID
made, some closure, a motive to pinpoint a perpetrator. If
someone could only find those fucking things, maybe everyone
could get back to their regularly scheduled lives. He nearly
wished that task were his, grim and daunting as it was. Clearly
the feds weren't having any luck, and if anyone in this town
could use the focus of an impossible assignment, it was Duncan.

A foolish impulse, of course. Duncan was smart, but his
powers of logic and deduction were limited to the legal realm;
he had no business playing detective in the dusty desert.

*Neither did Vince Grossier. Yet if he hadn't, everyone would
still believe Alex Dunn had gotten himself killed driving drunk,
and his murderer would still be the sheriff of this county. And
how is an ex-con quarry laborer more qualified to meddle than
I am?*

Shut up, brain. The mere urge was madness.

*Stick with what you're good at. Your exoneration lies in
books, not in the badlands.*

But that evening, the mad urges got the better of him. Raina was working, and restless from sitting about, flipping through the same pages of notes he'd made in his defense again and again, Duncan climbed into his car and went for a drive. An hours-long drive, without ever leaving Fortuity, a loop that took him out to the fences of the Three C cattle ranch, along the foothills, past the quarry, snaking back through the residential areas before turning down Station Street. He eyed the horizon, dark now, delineated only by the light of a half-moon, searching his undernurtured intuition for some tingle—some tell. Some sign that might whisper, *Here we are. Come and find us. Come and dig us up.* But nothing, of course. And no way to get to the places where Tremblay or some other actor would've been most likely to bury those bones, if they did indeed still reside in Fortuity.

Then on Duncan's fourth trip around town, something did finally call to him.

One of the two big bay doors of the erstwhile Eastside Auto garage was up, the building lit brightly and spilling rock music. Duncan spotted Vince Grossier's bike parked outside, then the man himself, carrying some tool from the workbench to the center of the space, where another bike was propped.

The man who'd arguably ruined Duncan's life. Through no real fault of his own, of course, but if not for Vince, Duncan would still have his job, progress would still be humming along, and he'd never have even heard of the wretched bones that were robbing him of his focus. He turned into the lot, knowing in a flash what he wanted. What he *needed*.

Vince squinted at the Merc until Duncan killed the headlights and revealed himself. The man's expression changed, from alert to amused, as Duncan strode into the garage.

"Mr. Grossier."

"Welch. Nice shiner."

Duncan frowned, and stooped to examine his face in the bike's mirror. Sure enough, Raina's elbow had left a nasty purple bruise blossoming between his lid and brow bone. He'd been too consumed by cleaning the bathroom mirror to even register his own reflection.

"Not getting into fistfights, I hope," Vince said. "Though if you were, I could go for a good scrap." He seemed to size Duncan up, looking intrigued.

"It was . . . It doesn't matter."

"I was expecting you while it was still light out. 'Fraid I can't do your paint job now. Maybe tomorrow afternoon."

"It's no longer urgent; I've found a temporary fix."

"Well, sorry if you wasted the trip. You want a beer?" Vince asked, stooping to pick up a bottle of his own and tilting it to his lips.

"No, thank you." Duncan cut to the chase. "I didn't actually come here about the paint."

"No?"

"I think . . . I think I'd like a motorcycle. Something that can go off-road."

Vince stared at him, long and hard. "You been abusing your prescription again?"

"Not today. I've just been prioritizing."

"Fair enough. A bike, huh?" Vince glanced at the wheelless, seatless, barless one he was tinkering with. "You a brand whore for Mercedes? 'Cause if not, this old Toaster Tank's a beauty under all the dirt, with no buyer yet." The silly nickname was self-explanatory, thanks to the bike's chrome gas tank. "R-series, '73," Vince went on. "Seven-fifty cc, only a hundred thirty thousand miles. Just needs a few transplants. You and me, Welch—twinsies." True—that'd make two of them on black BMWs, yet so woefully mismatched in every other way.

"I'm not choosy," Duncan said. "Whatever can handle the terrain. I'll pay most anything you ask." And likely sell it back to him for a song. No chance he'd actually grow attached to the thing, once its purpose had been fulfilled—or Duncan's fixation exhausted.

"Hope you're not in a hurry," Vince said. "I got wall-to-wall shit to handle this week. I just snuck over here while Kim's talking portfolio stuff with Raina. I can't get her finished till Saturday."

"Damn."

"You feel like knocking the club a little surcharge for the rush job, and I could get Casey onto it."

Duncan's face must have revealed his skepticism.

Vince laughed. "My brother's only a dumb-ass when it comes to people. He's real handy with mechanical shit."

"Just tell me how much."

"Will you tell *me* what you need it for, first?"

Duncan wasn't comfortable himself with this little mission's utter lack of reason. And not comfortable at all with the anxiety he suspected was spurring this obsession. He had feds toying with him, Levins trying to ruin him, rednecks hungry for his blood. On top of all that, to admit he was now fool enough to be chasing after the thing an entire team of investigators had yet to find . . . ? Let Vince think he was fucked, fine — but not an idiot, to boot.

"I'd prefer not to," he said. "Is there a surcharge for secrecy?"

"Nah, I'm just curious. It's not exactly your brand, is all. But let's say four grand for the bike — that's parts and labor, with an I-owe-you-big discount. I'm pretty sure I've got all the shit it needs on hand . . . Make it five even and Casey'll have it for you by tomorrow afternoon."

Duncan stuck his hand out. "Deal."

Vince stripped off his work glove and they shook. "Case can give you a lesson riding it, too."

"I'm sure I'll be fine."

The man smiled, the gesture always oddly boyish, not matching the rest of his macho packaging. "And I'm sure you've never ridden at all, let alone off-road. I lost you your job and half a tooth — let me at least spare you a broken leg."

Duncan submitted. He could endure Casey Grossier's company for a couple of hours to do this properly. Though his desire to do things properly — lawfully, logically — had waned of late.

"Get yourself some boots," Vince said. "No need to drop a bomb for actual riding boots — just something sturdy that'll cover your ankles. Jeans are good. And we've got spare helmets lying around."

"Jacket?" He had a leather one, but it wasn't designed for a ride any more than Duncan was.

Vince shrugged. "Preferable, but you'll probably live without it. You won't be going too fast, so you're way more likely to tip over and crush a leg than you are to go flaying yourself on the asphalt."

"How reassuring."

"Gloves are nice," Vince went on, "but if you don't want to destroy those schmancy driving ones you've got, you'll get by without them, too. With a few blisters."

"Noted."

"Tomorrow. Three o'clock. That'll give you maybe four hours before Lights Out steals the sunshine," Vince said, meaning the high peak to the west that cast Fortuity in an early twilight each evening.

Duncan nodded.

"Raina give you that black eye?" Vince asked.

"No comment."

That smile again. "You earn it?"

"Not especially."

Vince laughed. "Good fucking luck with her. She'll bang you up way worse than the bike ever could, if you get on her bad side."

"I'll keep a helmet handy."

Vince turned back to his project and Duncan headed out after casting his future motorcycle a final curious glance.

The bar looked busy as he pulled around to park in back, and he considered a drink. Raina would be busy chatting with Kim between filling orders, and he didn't much feel like sharing her attention. His body warmed as he slammed the car door, remembering everything that had happened that morning. Those burning eyes on his body and face. Those greedy hands stroking, tugging, kneading, urging.

It'd probably never be that good again between them. After all the anticipation, the teasing, the torture . . . Surely anything they did with each other from this point on would pale in comparison. As he slammed the Merc's door and fished out the keys she'd given him, he realized they'd be wise to avoid any further encounters. It had been perfect as it was—dirty and rough and raw—and it would be a shame to taint it by attempting to stage a repeat. Yes, they ought to leave well enough alone.

Though he had to wonder if he'd have it in him to resist her, if Raina decided she wasn't done with him yet.

Raina looked at the number Kim had jotted on a pad, an estimate for the photo shoot they were hoping to set up. "That seems fair. That's per hour?"

Kim nodded, sipping her beer. "I'd guess four hours, six tops. Depending on whether people show up when they're supposed to, and how many there are."

"Any added fees, for touch-ups or whatever?"

"Yeah, but that's the brunt of the damage. You want to talk about the Web site stuff?"

"Not yet. One overdue stab at professionalism at a time."

Above Raina's head, the empty beer bottles lined up on the ledge rattled, always a tell that the rear door had just opened and shut. She pictured Duncan from that morning, for the thousandth time. Very distracting, those memories. She waited to see if he might come through the rear door, maybe gift her with a fine view of that gorgeous face under the low lights, a nice look at those elegant—and talented—fingers wrapped around a tumbler. But no. A moment later, the muted sounds of his steps moved to the kitchen above.

She finished mixing two gin and tonics and found Abilene handling the rest of the customers. She turned back to where Kim was camped out, making notes and doodles in a pad at the bar.

"It'll be tricky, getting everyone here on one night," Raina said.

Kim smiled. "I live ten minutes away. We can do it over multiple nights."

"Won't that be a pain in the ass, you having to set up lights and stuff over and over?"

Kim shook her head. "Only one light, I think. We'll mainly work with what the bar's got. It'll look more authentic that way."

"Kinda dim." She caught herself as she said it, realizing she was doing something she rarely did—second-guessing herself. Maybe even trying to talk herself out of the plan. If she was honest, the entire idea intimidated her. Getting her portfolio together, assembling her clients this way . . . it'd make everything feel real. And she'd be admitting to everyone, herself included, that she wanted this. A lot. That she cared about it, and that if it went nowhere, she'd be disappointed. It was so much easier to tell yourself you were happy as you were.

"Trust me," Kim said, "it'll be badass."

Raina nodded, and quit fighting it. "That's probably the look I should shoot for. Vince seems to think the biker set's my primary market. I'm surprised he hasn't gotten you on one yet," she added. "A bike."

"He talks about it, but it's nerve-racking enough just riding behind him. I'll stick with my hatchback. As for the shoot, we've got a hundred amazing sets and props going on in here. Pool table, jukebox, the front stoop with the bikes in the background, the bar itself . . ."

Raina nodded, torn between pride and guilt and confusion.

This bar. Her dad's baby, and her livelihood the past few years. Her claim to local somebody-hood. A place she longed to escape from more and more lately, but also the only home she'd known. A softer woman than Raina might have been swayed by those journals, and gotten busy rethinking her intentions to sell out and move on—a more selfless woman.

But even so, she could imagine what her dad would say to her, if he was here.

I had my dream, and sure, you showed up and messed it up some. Now you go chase yours, and if you're lucky, the right man or maybe a child will show up someday and mess it up right back.

She picked up her glass of ginger ale and tapped Kim's beer with it. "Here's hoping you can help turn my seedy little hobby into something lucrative."

The rest of the shift passed slowly, and she sent Abilene home early. By midnight she gave up hope that Duncan might grace her with his presence, and instead hoped maybe she'd go upstairs and find him awake. And in the mood.

She cashed out at two, locked the doors, and put the stools on the tables. Her pulse spiked as she hiked up the back steps, but she found the apartment dark. She walked to the den, but there wasn't even a sliver of light glowing beneath the guest room door.

She pouted. "Damn."

"Damn what?"

She yelped—not a noise she normally ever made—and scrambled to switch on the lamp. Duncan was stretched out on the couch in a tee and lounge pants, looking bleary. Astrid vacated her spot on his belly, heading for the kitchen.

Raina rubbed her racing heart. "Jesus, you scared me. Good thing I didn't sit on you."

Duncan sat up. "Why did you say 'damn' just now?"

"I thought you'd gone to bed, and I'd kinda been hoping to get laid."

He smiled at that, eyebrows telling her he found the statement both tacky and charming. "Is that all I am to you? A live-in booty call?"

"Don't ever use that term again—there's something very wrong about you saying it. And no, you're more than that. Yes, you're a great fuck, but you also clean, and—"

"I'm your maid, then?"

She nodded. "You're my sex maid."

He looked deeply offended, then shrugged. "I believe I'll focus on the bit where you called me a great fuck."

She pursed her lips. "So. You up for it?"

He looked her up and down, pretending to deliberate. "I could be enticed, I suppose, though I can't say I appreciate being propositioned—"

"Great, see you in five. I need to brush my teeth." She headed for the bathroom. As she capped the toothpaste she called, "So, what did you get up to all evening? Aside from cleaning my bathroom?" That had been an interesting development to come home to that afternoon. She doubted the fixtures had been this shiny when they left the factory.

Duncan appeared at the threshold. "It was an odd night."

She raised her eyebrows, mouth full of froth.

"I wound up driving around town for a quite a long time," he said. "I saw Vince was at the garage, so I stopped—"

A crash sounded from the kitchen—a crash and a clatter, then a hiss and the sound of Astrid booking it through the apartment.

"That was glass," Duncan said, heading for the commotion.

Raina spat, wondering how an eight-pound cat had managed to break something so vigorously. She wiped her mouth and followed, hearing Duncan's "Fuck" just as she reached the kitchen.

He'd turned on the light, and there was glass everywhere, the window over the sink smashed.

"You're barefoot," she said to Duncan. "Stay there." Her boots crunched over shards, and she found the projectile in the sink—a yellow brick, with a lined notebook page snapped around it with a rubber band. She stood on tiptoe to peer out the window. The motion-sensor light had come on, but she saw nothing in the back lot—no one sprinting or speeding down the street in either direction.

"Run to the front and see if anybody's fleeing," she told Duncan, and he did.

Before she touched anything, she pulled out her phone and took a few pictures. She picked up the brick, blowing the glass flecks from it and then carrying it to the den.

"Nothing," Duncan said, coming out of her bedroom. "No people, no vehicles. What does it say?" he asked, sitting next to her on the couch.

She unfolded and smoothed the page. The writing was familiar—those jagged capitals from the message scrawled on Duncan's car, only in Sharpie this time, not paint.

EVERYONE KNOWS WHAT YOU DONE. CONFESS AND MAKE IT EASY ON YOURSELF. OR ELSE WE MAKE IT HARD ON YOU.

The penmanship was so self-conscious and awkward she had to wonder if the person had done this left-handed, to disguise his or her handwriting.

Duncan said nothing, just leaned forward to plant his elbows on his thighs and rub his face.

"Assholes," Raina muttered, reading the note again. "Wrecking my plans to get laid."

Duncan sat up straight, looking slapped. "This isn't funny. Someone threw a brick through your window."

"Rumors spread fast—didn't take them long to hear you were staying here."

"Someone *threw a brick through your window*," he repeated.

"But it was addressed to you."

"This *isn't. Funny*. You—"

"Tomorrow. We can fight about it tomorrow morning over toast. For now, put some shoes on and let's clean the kitchen."

On that, they seemed to agree. He got his sneakers on while Raina took a couple of photos of the note. Then they tackled the mess, clearing away the glass, which seemed to have gotten into every corner.

"Poor Astrid," Raina said. "That must have been terrifying."

"I'll check her paws, make sure she hasn't stepped in any of it."

While he did, Raina went downstairs to find cardboard and duct tape to cover the window. She hazarded a peek out the back, but the truck, the Merc, and her bike looked unmolested. She'd sweep up any shards that had found their way to the gravel in the morning, but not now. Tough as she was playing it with Duncan, she was rattled. Rowdy drunks she could handle, but this was upsetting. Someone out there had the balls to fuck with her dad's bar—her dad's *home*—and that was so fucking far over the line . . . Perhaps worst of all, it was clearer now that the vandalism on Duncan's car was not an isolated, intoxicated impulse. This was a campaign, and that meant there were more moves to come. They were going to need a plan. Though it would have to wait until morning, when they could think rationally.

Upstairs, she found Duncan in the bathroom, dabbing at his neck with a cotton ball.

"Astrid not take kindly to your examination?" she asked.

"No. Though luckily she's not got a scratch on her." He took the cotton ball away, frowning at it. "Which is more than I can say."

"There's Band-Aids in the cabinet. Come to bed."

His reflection raised an eyebrow at her in the mirror as he blotted his wound. "I'm afraid this latest incident rather killed the mood for me."

"Not for sex. Just . . . You know." Raina could think of precisely zero words she was comfortable employing to accurately label what she wanted; she didn't *cuddle*, or *snuggle*, and unlike Duncan, she wasn't going to come out and ask to be held. "Just come to bed," she said again, and left him to head there herself.

She changed and got under the covers, and when he joined her, she wrapped her body around his. There was no absence of lust, merely a mutation of it. Just now, she wanted to feel him against her, if not inside her; she wanted the strength of his body, not the visual glory of it. It was shockingly reminiscent of the weeks she'd spent sleeping with Miah. And that scared the shit out of her, to realize if she was here, physically clinging to Duncan Welch . . .

Shit, she was more than just literally attached to him, wasn't she?

Whatever. Deal with it in the morning. She buried her face against his neck.

"I doubt we'll be seeing much of Astrid anytime soon," he murmured, stroking Raina's hair. "I kicked her once by mistake and she wouldn't come out from under the bed for almost two days."

"Did you take her to a cat therapist?"

He gave her hair a gentle tug in admonishment.

They lay in silence, and with each passing moment, Raina felt her body making demands. *Reach down. Stroke him.* While this simple contact felt so good on its own, a cagey part of her was trying to wreck that, to twist it all into a framework she felt equipped to handle, and initiate sex. She parted her lips and dragged them against his throat as her hand slid from his chest to his belly.

He caught her wrist and moved her hand back up.

She huffed her frustration. "Killjoy."

"Coward."

Easy for the guy with the hold-me kink to say. He'd told her the other day, he didn't hug. Wasn't this all just horizontal hugging, really? And if she wasn't getting laid—or falling asleep anytime soon—maybe she could at least meet his needs, if not hers. "Turn over."

He did, and she wrapped her arm and leg around him. After a tense pause, he relaxed and his broad, smooth palm closed around her hand, above his heart.

Oh shit, this feels nice. He felt *right*, like a set of clean, dry clothes after a swim in a cold creek. Comforting. And in no more than a minute, she felt his muscles soften, heard his breathing deepen.

She couldn't guess what had happened to this man, to have landed him with this surprising—and surprisingly sweet—need to be held. The why of it seemed moot just now, though. So rather than analyze it, she waited until his grip went slack and his fingers fell away from her wrist, and she kissed the back of his neck softly and said, "Good night, Mr. Welch."

Chapter 15

Raina slept poorly at the best of times, so Monday morning naturally found her wide-awake at dawn. Soothing as Duncan's body was, she'd never fallen into any restful sort of sleep, too wired, too distracted by straining for the sounds of trespassers' footsteps outside.

She had a client in the afternoon, so she'd need to take a nap at some point—she'd no sooner tattoo someone drowsy than drunk. But sleep wasn't coming now, so she slipped her arm from under Duncan's warm back, dressed quietly, and snuck away. With the coffee started, she headed downstairs to sweep and mop and stock the coolers. Might as well save Abilene the trouble.

By five thirty the bar was ready for the customers who wouldn't arrive for another eight hours, and she grabbed the broom and headed to the front to tend to the previous night's inevitable harvest of cigarette butts. As she unlocked the dead bolt, a zap of fear went through her, a twinge of misgiving to imagine the person who'd thrown that brick lurking outside, waiting for her. She held her breath, opened the inside door. Pushed the screen door out and—

Nothing. Cold air and scattered birdsong, the buzz of the neon sign overhead. Her shoulders dropped, and she tended to the lot.

It wasn't until she turned to go back inside that the blow came—and not in the form of an assault, but in words. Two-foot-tall letters, fluorescent orange, scrawled jaggedly across the bar's façade.

WE SERVE JACKALS.

"Oh, *fuck* you." She glared at those ugly words, the bulk of her fear replaced with anger. And worry that did remain was a new one, because she'd never imagined in a million years that anyone would have the balls to deface Benji's.

At least she'd gotten up early enough to prevent just about everybody from seeing it. She took a few photos with her phone, then marched back inside.

She found spare paint in the back and dug a brush and rags out of the storage closet. It'd take a couple of coats, and the fresh paint wouldn't match the faded stuff on the wall, but like Duncan's poor car, it was better than nothing. She got to work.

With barely two letters covered over, a noise rose in the distance, and her gut dropped, blood rising to her cheeks. She knew that rumble, and she didn't relish the conversation that was about to go down.

Vince rode by, as he did every morning on his way to the quarry. Raina was often out here just after dawn, and typically they just exchanged waves, but now his bike squeaked to a halt. She turned back to her painting, listening as he made a U-turn and scrabbled into the gravel lot. His engine went quiet behind her.

"The fuck?"

"Morning, Vince."

"What the shit is this?" He knocked his kickstand down and strode over. "You got vandalized?"

"Keep your voice down—I'd rather Duncan be spared this." Though there wasn't much chance he could have missed it, with the din of Vince's arrival coming through the broken window.

"'We serve jackasses'?" Vince read, the final two letters obliterated. "That's not exactly news."

"Jackals. As in Duncan—heartless corporate criminal. And I got a brick through my window last night, with a note telling him to confess or else. He got a similar love letter spray-painted on his car, the morning I convinced him to leave the motel."

"Jesus, that's what he needs a touch-up for? Why didn't you tell me this earlier?"

"We'd both hoped it was a drunken one-off. Apparently it wasn't." She waved at the orange letters.

"Apparently."

"Until Duncan gets his name cleared, we might need to arrange—"

The bar's door popped open, Duncan marching out in his

sleep clothes. He turned to the wall, eyes widening. "Oh for *fuck's* sake. This is ridiculous." He himself looked a touch ridiculous, with a yellow bruise still smudged around his eye and a bandage on his neck from Astrid's attack. Like his gleaming car's damage, Duncan's injuries were wildly conspicuous. Any one of the Desert Dogs could've rolled up with a flesh wound and not raised a single eyebrow.

Raina turned back to Vince. "Like I was saying, we might need to arrange a watch. So far, this shit bag only seems to operate under the cover of darkness. Maybe just have somebody park across the way or around the side, between closing and dawn." Thankfully that left a small window.

"Don't want to involve the sheriff's department?"

She shook her head. "They'd just scare this asshole into staying away, and I want them *caught*. And I want two minutes alone with them before the cops take over." Her boots were made for more than just walking.

Vince nodded, and Duncan looked relieved. She didn't blame him—discretion was only half the reason she didn't want the authorities involved. Duncan not winding up in protective custody was the other half—

"This is unacceptable," Duncan said, still glaring at the paint, its orange glowing incandescent in the sunrise. "I'm moving back to the motel."

She rounded on him. "The fuck you are."

"Yes, the fuck I *am*. They can threaten me all they like and I won't run and hide, but this is another matter entirely. I'm not letting you get wrapped up in it as well."

"Well, it's too late for that, isn't it?" She came closer, held his stare. "Plus, you don't need to *let* me do anything—I make my own decisions. And I'm deciding that neither of us is going anywhere, just because some angry dumb-asses managed to write a note and throw a brick and aim a can of spray paint." Twice in her life she'd been made to feel like a target, like a victim, and both times by people she'd thought she'd known. To let a coward, a faceless stranger, intimidate her now? No fucking chance. "We're both staying right where we are."

Duncan crossed his arms. "To what end? To find out the next projectile that comes flying through your window is a Molotov cocktail?"

"I don't submit to bullies any more than you do," she returned.

"We'll get a watch organized," Vince cut in, businesslike. "Two of us at a time, one around back, one on the road. One armed. Kim and I could take tonight's—Casey can watch Mom."

"You'd let Kim get anywhere near this?"

Vince's jaw clenched. "She'll want to help ... and I'll never hear the end of it if I refuse. We'll plant her down the block with her camera—thing's got a zoom like a sniper's rifle. She'll be safe. Miah and Case could take tomorrow's watch, and you two could handle the day after. Between the six of us, we got this covered. If things quiet down in the next few days, maybe we can downgrade to a security camera. Sound good?" He looked between Duncan and Raina.

Raina nodded, satisfied. Duncan's nostrils flared, but after a stubborn moment, he dipped his chin stiffly.

"Good. Better forget my fixing your paint this afternoon, though. I'll need that time to steal a nap." Vince cast the orange letters a final glance, head shaking. "The messes never fucking end around here."

"Goddamn idiots, shitting where they eat. This bar's more sacred than the church to most of the residents. There'd be a lynch mob forming if it gets out that somebody pulled this shit." Unfortunately Duncan would be in protective custody the second the authorities got wind, so going public was out.

"Few weeks ago I'd have agreed with you," Vince said, then turned to Duncan. "Sadly it looks like the pitchfork-wielding natives have already found themselves a target."

"This could be one person's work," Raina said.

"Or a dozen," Vince said grimly. "Though considering they're sneaking around in the dead of night, I think you're probably right. A whole posse of shitheads wouldn't be so shy about it. Let's just hope whoever it was is dumb enough to brag about it ... Right, I gotta get to work. But me and Kim'll be by around last call, to go on watch duty."

Raina gave his arm a grateful slap. "See you later."

Duncan offered a stony "Thank you," his attention moving back to the vandalism.

"Good luck with the bike," Vince said to Duncan, then took off.

"What bike?" Raina asked Duncan.

"I'll explain later."

And having enough mysteries on her mind already, she shrugged and got back to painting.

"Let me do that," Duncan said.

"Nah. My clothes are way cheaper than yours."

"I—"

"You can pay for the window, okay? Don't act like this is your fault."

"This wouldn't have happened if I weren't staying with you."

"You wouldn't be staying with me if I hadn't made you," she countered. "Go upstairs and make us some breakfast, okay?"

He relented, rubbing his face wearily. He looked handsome, even disheveled, annoyed, and underdressed, with messy hair. It burned away her own angst.

Blotting out the orange K, she awaited a protest, but all he said was, "I'll make a frittata."

Her mouth said, "Sounds good."

But something in her heart chanted, *He's staying, he's staying, he's staying.*

Duncan remained rattled through breakfast, dishes, his shower, and grooming. Happily, Raina went back to bed and slept through all his furious puttering.

There were layers to his anger. The thinnest was his indignation at having his own safety threatened. The thickest was his rage that Raina was being punished as well, whether it bothered her or not.

And nested between those two was a third layer, a hard and thorny one that had formed the moment he spotted those words, painted across the front of the bar. And it wasn't the words themselves, or their meaning, or even that they'd been directed at Raina. Those things all bothered him, but it was the fact that the *bar* had been defaced.

Duncan couldn't have guessed when he first walked into Benji's, nearly two months ago, that he'd ever call himself a regular. To say nothing of it growing on him, and becoming a place he looked forward to going to. He'd never have guessed he'd wind up in its owner's bed, or gazing upon the pages of her father's notebooks, outlining the man's dreams for the business. As deeply as Duncan had hated Benji's upon first glance, he felt protective of it now.

Perhaps because Raina herself would never put up with protecting. True. She'd never welcome his concern or doting . . .

But this didn't feel like a simple case of projecting. He really had grown fond of the bar.

So fond, in fact, in idle moments, he found himself fantasizing about funding its renovation. Getting Raina to accept such a gift might prove a challenge, but he could afford it. A onetime gift of fifty thousand, perhaps, a good-bye present, when the time came for him to return to his own world. Back in his clean, modern condo on the harbor, he would be pleased to know that seven hundred miles away, the dive bar that had served as his strange little sanctuary during the worst period of his adult life was doing well, and in part, because of him.

If that's what you really want, though, he thought, *you've no business going back to Sunnyside.* The biggest threat to Benji's was the casino and its attendant commercial boom. And Duncan's sole function at Sunnyside had been to help ensure its completion.

It was a case of "You're either for it or against it." If he was for the casino, he was against Benji's. If he was for Benji's, he'd better pack up and find a new job the moment his name was cleared.

Stay with your job, bask in her venom for two more years. Tell Sunnyside to fuck off, and lose your only reason to ever see her again. He had to assume that the latter was the only real option; he didn't think he could handle sticking around and risk witnessing it if Benji's got sold or shuttered or demolished, to make way for the future. The future of an entire town, as envisioned by a soulless, out-of-state conglomerate.

So keep your money, you idiot. The gift would prove about as useful as his gifting someone with a makeover seconds before pushing the poor sap in front of a speeding train. After helping lay the tracks himself.

And that thought had him striding to the kitchen, emptying the cabinets of dishes, and scouring the shelves.

It wasn't until ten—with the kitchen half-cleaned and a window replacement service scheduled for the next afternoon—that Duncan found himself able to take a deep breath again.

This still beats protective custody, he told himself, looking around the place. And even if he went back to the motel, Raina would only take it upon herself to follow. With a plan in place to keep watch at night, perhaps this was for the best. Better to be semisafe and comfortable here than considerably less safe on his own, and miserable to boot.

He allowed himself a moment's pleasure, remembering how they'd fallen asleep. He'd not spooned with anyone since his last girlfriend, and that had been over six months ago. Tall as he was, he'd always been the big spoon before. Leave it to Raina to steal the pants in any given situation . . . though this time, he had to admit it had been heavenly. He hoped it wouldn't take another scare to entice her to do that with him again. Perhaps something more akin to a date could find them there just as easily.

With that in mind, just after two, Duncan entered the kitchen with a bag of groceries cradled in one arm. A high buzzing noise came from behind the closed door. Raina had mentioned over breakfast that she had a client that afternoon, but Duncan didn't allow himself the petty indulgence of frowning. He oughtn't care.

I also oughtn't be in the center of a criminal investigation or the target of death threats, he reminded himself. *Since when did I start expecting life to be fair?*

Not caring to linger, he put the groceries away and changed for his appointment with Casey Grossier.

By the time Duncan left his room, Raina had emerged and was in the kitchen, puttering. No company in sight. She met his eyes for a beat and smiled, the gesture warm but tough to read. *She's likely just exhausted.*

"Your client's left, I take it."

"He has," she said, loading the dishwasher.

He. Duncan rankled.

"He liked your cat. And she seemed to enjoy the attention, so I guess last night didn't traumatize her too deeply. I just hope she doesn't require any shots for fraternizing with bikers."

His cat? No, Astrid could do as she pleased, and was quite capable of fending off unwanted affection. But had this man hugged Raina? Called her *sweetheart* or *honey* or *girl*? Called her *baby*, as she'd called Duncan yesterday? Hit on her? Fucked her, ever? Oh, those trespasses were another matter entirely.

Raina straightened, shutting the washer, and did a double take at Duncan. "Wow, you look . . ." She scanned him slowly, seeming to approve. "This for your riding lesson?"

He'd changed into jeans, a tee, and his toffee-colored leather jacket. The latter was fitted and designer and outrageously expensive. "I suspect this pairs better with a button-up and a six-dollar coffee than a motorcycle ride. But it's better than nothing." He'd told her about the bike that morning, but not the real mission of the exercise—to look for those bones. He wouldn't be telling anyone about that; the naïveté of the goal was too laughable. He'd said he missed driving, and with the Merc limiting him to the finite miles of pavement within Fortuity town lines, the bike seemed an interesting diversion. Whatever kept him away from the bleach, she'd said with a shrug.

Now she came close and touched the seams at his shoulders, the contact warming him like a hot gulp of tea. "How can clothes even look this good on somebody?" she asked. "Everything you wear looks like it just . . . snaps on. Like a phone case."

"It's called tailoring."

"It's freaky," she said, stepping back. "But keep it up. It's worth every penny." She glanced at his feet and let out a theatrical little gasp. "Red Wings? Are you trying to get fucked, Duncan?"

He'd found the boots at the blue-collar outfitters at the edge of town. So not his style, but he hadn't owned anything that covered his ankles. He smiled. "If only I had the time."

"Too bad about your eye," she said, ever adept at skirting an actual apology. "Let's hope that fades before the feds call you back in for another round of scrutiny."

"How did your strategizing with Kim go last night?" He'd neglected to ask, with everything that had gone on.

She shrugged. "Good. I've got to see how many of my clients I can convince to come by for a little photo shoot in the next couple weeks."

"I'm sure it'll make very interesting subject matter."

"Kim's certainly banking on it. She's got the props and shots all figured out in her head."

"Props?"

"Oh, bottles and glasses and shit. Pool cues. Bikes, out front. She wants the bar to be a character itself, or something like that." Her expression dulled.

"And you don't?"

Raina turned away, filling the kettle. "It's fine."

Liar. He knew her well enough to sense that something was *not* fine.

"What?" he asked.

"What, what?"

"It's not fine. Why?"

Another shrug. "I dunno. Everything to do with the bar just feels funny now."

"Since the vandalism?"

"No, no. Since the notebooks."

"Ah." His heart sank, and his stomach squirmed, and he had to squeeze his hands into fists to keep from blurting, *I'll give you the money! Let me give you the money!*

"That's all I feel like saying about it," she said.

And Duncan didn't have the luxury of pressing now. He pulled his fingerless driving gloves from his pockets and tugged them on.

Raina sucked a dramatic, overwrought breath at the sight and bit her lip. "Why is that so fucking sexy?"

"I couldn't begin to guess."

"Let me know when you're back so I can watch you peel them off, real slow."

He smirked at that. "Only if you slip some singles down my trousers."

She sighed a little laugh. "Trousers. You're the best."

He rolled his eyes. "I picked up groceries, and someone will be by to fix the window tomorrow between ten and noon. I hope that serves."

"Wow, busy boy. Knowing me, the cardboard would've stayed up through New Year's."

"You're welcome. What time do you go downstairs tonight?"

"It's a Monday, so Abilene'll probably be fine alone until eight, eight thirty. Why?"

His heart beat quicker. Like a bloody teenage boy, angling to spend time with a certain girl. "I'm cooking us dinner."

She smiled. "Are you? You good for more than just a frittata, then?"

"I suffice. And I've not had access to a kitchen in two months, so the urge is strong."

"Some of your urges mystify me," she said. "But other ones have an awful lot to recommend them. Count me in. What are you making?"

"You'll see."

"Guess I will."

"Seven thirty."

Her brow rose a fraction.

"What?" he asked.

"That leaves no time for sex."

Duncan felt his face flush hot and was pleased he wasn't prone to blushing. "I suppose it doesn't."

"Come down to the bar tonight." She stepped close to trace his lapels with her thumbs, gaze on his chest. "We can eye-fuck each other until last call, then head up here together for the real thing."

He swallowed. With Vince on top of security, Duncan might even be able to relax enough to enjoy such a thing. "Sounds like a plan."

"And you seem like a man who likes plans." She stepped back, just when he'd hoped they might come together at the mouth.

He tried to look blasé. "I'd better head out for my riding lesson."

She smiled, grabbing a mug off the table. "Which of you is less excited about this little playdate—you or Vince?"

"Casey's taking me, actually."

Raina snorted, dropping a filter in the cup. "Man, what I would pay to see the outtakes from that. I'll look forward to hearing how it goes, over dinner."

"I'm sure you will." And late tonight, they'd head upstairs after last call and teach each other a few different sorts of lessons. His body was crackling at the promise of it. "I'll see you at seven thirty."

Only a week ago, Duncan's car had been a gleaming, enviable manifestation of his ego, but now shit-spattered and vandalized, it hit way too close to home as a representation of how banged up he was feeling himself. He cast it an apologetic glance before skirting the side of the bar, preferring not to be seen in it.

He walked three blocks up Station Street and found the garage wide open, Casey pacing around Duncan's appointed bike, eyeballing this and that, buffing the tank and mirrors with a cloth.

Duncan entered, the shade offering a respite from the baking sun. "Good afternoon."

"What's up, motherfucker?" Casey put his hand out, inviting some sort of clutchy high-five thing. Duncan submitted to it, pleased when he was let go.

"Heard you're getting death threats."

"Yes . . . Sorry about any sleep you might lose this week, thanks to the watch Vince organized."

Casey shrugged. "Doesn't bother me. Just try to maybe not fuck Raina too loud that night so I don't have to spend my shift listening to Miah's teeth grinding."

Duncan felt his face warm. "Yes. Well. I doubt—"

"What's up with your eye?"

"No comment."

"Suit yourself. So, you ready to become a man?"

"I'm ready to learn how not to kill myself on this thing," Duncan said, studying the bike. It had changed a lot since yesterday. The dirt was gone, its enamel scuffed and a touch faded, chrome similarly savaged, but the overall effect was one of sturdiness. Capability. It did resemble Vince's quite a bit—not many frills. Responsive-looking suspension, straight bars, knobby tires fit for the rough terrain. Duncan gave it a quarter mile before the desert dusted it rusty red.

"Looks good," he said. "I hope I prove worthy."

"You'll live. Probably. Got the money?"

"I've got a personal check. Will that do?"

Casey grimaced. "Fuck no."

"Oh. I haven't got five grand in cash."

"No, but you'll get it. You're good for it."

"But I'm not trustworthy enough to accept a check from?"

Casey smiled. "Not about trust, Welch. It's about keeping things simple."

Duncan inventoried his wallet. "I've got about three hundred on me. I'll give you that as a deposit and get you the rest as ATM withdrawals allow. Deal?"

"Works for me." Casey disappeared into a back office with the bills. When he returned he said, "There's no deed, since Vince rescued her from the scrap yard."

"I've no aversion to strays." Duncan had become one himself, of late; Raina had taken him in as surely as he'd adopted Astrid. "Did I dress properly?"

Casey studied Duncan's ensemble. "Close enough. Jacket's a bit metrosexual, but it'll keep the skin on your arms. Boots look good. You got a license?"

"Not for operating a motorcycle, no."

Casey stared a moment. "You're willfully breaking the law?"

"I am, yes."

"Fucking awesome. You'll match the bike—her plates are expired. Let's find you a helmet."

There were a few strewn about the shop, and Duncan picked one that seemed to fit and didn't smell too strongly of its bygone owner's sweat and cigarettes.

"You've been edging your way into our little clique via my brother's trouble, and Raina's pants, and now the garage," Casey said, squinting at Duncan. "I think you need a nickname."

"I strongly disagree."

"Welchy. DW. Dunky. The Dunkster."

"I'd prefer if you stuck with 'Motherfucker,' thank you."

"Gimme a couple hours. I'll come up with something good. What's Raina call you?"

She called me baby, Duncan thought, the memory chased by an undeniable shiver. "Nothing special." Surely not special to her, anyway.

They wandered back to the BMW. "Had a real good time finishing this fucker up," Casey said.

"I'll treat it well, barring beginner's mistakes."

Casey snorted. "Fuck that. Ride the shit out of her. That's what machines like this were built for. Not sure what this girl's story is, but Vince's bike used to belong to this old Kerouac type—guy took it all the way down to Bolivia or some shit, in the eighties. Had almost three hundred thousand miles by the time Vince bought it. These old warhorses are indestructible."

Duncan fussed with his helmet straps and sunglasses. "Just getting around the badlands will do."

"Got you covered, then."

"I can't leave Fortuity, incidentally."

"Oh man, parole light. The feds are such bitches."

Duncan couldn't disagree.

Casey walked him through the basics—getting on, feeding it gas, stomping on the starter, then walking it out of the garage, where Casey climbed onto his own bike. It was a smelly, noisy, dirty, dangerous hobby, and they hadn't even left the lot.

"Here comes the worst part," Casey said. "Your first turn. Just give her a *little* taste of gas."

"Do I lean into the turn?"

"If you're going fast enough, yeah, but don't think too hard about that shit for now—your body'll figure it out."

If Casey said so. Duncan and his subtler senses had never been especially familiar companions.

"Off we fucking go," Casey said, and headed for the road with a roar of throttle.

Duncan followed, the bike feeling as though it must weigh ten tons as he let it shepherd him uncertainly down a shallow dip and onto the street. His heart seized up as he made the first turn, then resumed beating as he straightened out, unscathed. His acceleration was jerky and comical to start, but half a mile down the main drag, the fear drained out of him, perhaps rattled free by the relentless vibration.

They stuck to the pavement, crisscrossing all over Fortuity, Casey forcing more and more turns on the route, the longer Duncan went without toppling—almost as though willing the inevitable spill. Still none an hour in, Duncan was almost beginning to feel nearly competent. Casey pulled over along the shoulder of the road that led out into ranch land.

"Pretty good so far," he said.

"No grievous injuries, at least."

"Try a little off-road?"

Duncan nodded. "What the hell?" Had to happen sooner or later—those bones weren't buried in the asphalt.

"Shouldn't be too bad here," Casey said. "Dirt's real hard and packed. It's the soft shit you need to look out for. I'll take us into the brush as deep as I can, but my bike's built for cruising, not safari."

"Sure."

Casey paused, leaning forward to rest his forearms on his handlebars. "What's this all about, anyhow? You trying to be what you think Raina's into or something?"

Duncan had to laugh. "I suspect it'd take more than a show of ill-fitting machismo to win that woman's approval."

"Yeah, she's not really the kind you woo."

"Indeed." She was no coy creature in need of tempting. Of taming. She was a mountain lion. The best you could hope for was to avoid getting ripped to shreds.

"So why, then?"

He considered telling Casey the truth, but something about it felt too . . . personal. He was uncomfortable even recognizing himself precisely how out of character all of this was—such a fruitless, illogical pursuit. Obsession he was wired for, but not of the pointless variety.

Plus, admitting it would mean accepting that he wasn't above the mess surrounding him. On the contrary, he was neck deep in it. In this exhausting mystery, in this awful town. In his infatuation. In his own suffocating uncertainty. *Uncertain, but not helpless.* He was taking the situation in hand, surely as the bars in his gloved fists.

He told Casey, "I have my reasons."

"And they are?"

Duncan shot him a cold stare. "While we're prying, what exactly *have* you been up to the past nine years, Mr. Grossier?" He'd overheard enough conversations between Casey and his friends to know nothing shut the man up as quickly as that question.

Casey revved his bike and aimed it straight into the wilds of Fortuity. Duncan followed.

The rough red earth was peppered with rocks and ruts, and the bars juddered in Duncan's grip, the bike feeling like a half-broken horse beneath him. It was brutally sunny, oven-hot. His wrists were already sore from the civilized riding, hands all but numb from the vibration, and off-road multiplied all of that by fifty. But he didn't fall, not aside from when attempting the maneuvers Casey walked him through—how to tip over with purpose when he felt the machine going down. He seemed good at knowing how much gas to give it, too, how much speed to hazard. And he'd be lying if he said there wasn't a certain satisfaction to hearing and smelling all that dust shooting out in his wake when he coaxed the bike up a hill.

If pressed to guess the activity he'd be the least competent at, Duncan would've put motorcycle riding on the top of a very short list of candidates. But to his great surprise, he seemed to be rather a natural. His instructor agreed.

"You sure you've never done this before?" Casey asked.

"Not even in my daydreams."

"Well, I hereby grant you your diploma. I don't think you need much more help—not unless you feel like building some ramps or something."

"No, this should do." There was nowhere in Fortuity he couldn't get to, Duncan imagined. Precisely his goal.

Now if only he had the first clue where he *needed* to get to.

"Ready to head back downtown?" Casey asked.

"Yes, I'd say so."

Duncan guessed it was about five thirty by the time they reached the main road, the sun edging low toward the mountains. They neared asphalt not too far from Three C's head-quarters, its gate just visible down the quiet two-lane highway.

It was odd, but Duncan wasn't especially looking forward to hitting pavement, jarring though the dirt was. And he wasn't looking forward to the silence and peace that'd follow once he dismounted back at—

A few yards ahead, Casey's body seemed to sway, the bike following.

"All right?" Duncan called.

The man's posture righted, then went slack again just as quickly, the motions of someone jerking awake and falling asleep in turns. Duncan gave his bike more gas, trying to catch up, but not before Casey slumped a third time, motor guttering and his bike tipping over in seeming slow motion. The noise of it was horrible—metal scrabbling on gravel—but worse than that was the silence that came from its rider. No shouts, no swearing. No nothing, before or after Casey hit the ground.

Duncan squeezed his brake levers and got off too quickly—he missed the kickstand but was already tipping sideways, so he let the bike fall, hopping to keep his foot from getting crushed. He hurried to where Casey lay, relieved to see motion—the man's hand twitched and clutched, and his eyes were open and moving. The bike was pinning his leg, though, and helmet or not, he was sure to have rattled his head.

"You okay?" Duncan grabbed the Harley's bars and pulled hard, trying to shift it. It was far heavier than the BMW, and he shoved Casey in the ribs with his foot until he rolled out of the way. Duncan prayed his leg wasn't broken. He eased the bike back down, then knelt at Casey's side. He shook him by the shoulders. "Hey. Hey."

Casey's eyes were wide, bright blue, his lips moving but no sound coming out. He'd looked limp as he'd gone down, but now his muscles were rigid, fingers still twitching, gaze at once sharp and vacant.

"Are you having a seizure?" A stroke, a bad drug trip, who knew what?

Faint words answered him. "Fire. Miah. Star. Night."

Duncan gave Casey's cheek a soft slap—that always seemed to work in the movies. "What's wrong with you? Tell me this instant or I'm calling nine-one-one." Selfishly he prayed Casey would come around. The last thing Duncan needed was to be found wrapped up with a drifter in a strange accident, while riding an undeeded motorcycle without the license to do so. He was flirting with detention or house arrest, he realized in a flash. And if that came to pass, this foolish, impulsive quest to find those fucking bones was done.

"Say something," he demanded. "Are you on drugs? Are you epileptic?"

"Miah," Casey said, strength coming to his voice. "Fire. On a starless night."

"Shit." The man wasn't getting lucid anytime soon. Seeing no choice, Duncan removed his helmet and dialed his phone, but no luck—not a single signal bar out here. "Fucking Fortuity."

No way could he prop Casey on the back of either bike and get him back to town. He was about to urge the man to stand, to pray he could walk so maybe Duncan could help him hobble toward the ranch, when a vehicle appeared from the west. Duncan waved his arms, and the black pickup slowed along the shoulder. Jeremiah Church hopped out, not even bothering to slam the door. There was a dog in the truck's bed, medium-size, with pricked ears and a reddish, short coat, looking like a Rottweiler's less bloodthirsty cousin. It didn't move a muscle as Miah ran to Duncan and Casey.

"He okay?" Miah asked, dropping to his knees.

"I'm not sure. He must have hit his head—he's babbling like a drunk."

Miah tried the old cheek-slap routine as well. "Case? Casey. You awake?"

"It's you," Casey said, smiling dreamily. "Fucking shame, what's going to happen to you."

Miah shot Duncan a look.

"He's not right," Duncan said. "He's not spoken a word of sense since he went down."

"He hit a rock or something?"

"Not a rock," Casey interjected, spacey. "A fire. On a starless night."

"No," Duncan said to Miah. "He swayed, right before he went down. Like he fainted, almost. Though a head injury could explain the nonsense he's talking."

"Weird. And he hasn't been drinking?"

"Not as far as I know. And the sun's rough, but the temperature's already dropped. Drugs, maybe?"

Miah shook his head. "I doubt it. Never Casey's style, not aside from weed."

"I tried calling nine-one-one, but there's no signal."

"Let's get him to the house. We can call from there if it comes to that, though he seems more dazed than anything."

Miah backed his truck closer and lowered the tailgate, then unfurled a couple of thick, woven blankets Duncan suspected were meant for horses.

"You grab his feet," Miah said, stooping to get a hand under each of Casey's armpits. The man kept mumbling about *fire* and *starless night* as they fumbled with his limp body, carrying him over and sliding him into the bed. The dog looked on stoically.

"Fuck me, you got heavy," Miah said to Casey. "Sorry about the smell, kid. Watch your feet." He curled Casey's legs in and flipped up the tailgate.

Duncan collected the keys from both bikes, then joined Miah. The man's black Stetson sat on the passenger seat and Duncan moved it to the console between them.

Once they were moving, he said, "Good timing, Mr. Church."

"Miah's fine." His expression was cold, but his tone casual. "You're the last man I'd have expected to find out there. That the BMW Vince's been resuscitating?"

"It is. This was my inaugural lesson. I rather expected if anyone was going to wreck, it'd be me."

Miah shook his head. "Fucking weird."

They turned into Three C's big lot, passing beneath the tall timber archway. Miah backed them right up to the front porch's steps, and as the tailgate dropped, a screen door swung out.

"Good God," said a tall, slender woman—surely Miah's mother, to judge from her age and coloring. Duncan had wondered if Miah was half Hispanic, like Raina, but his mother amended the theory—she looked strikingly Native American. "What's happened?"

"He took a spill," Miah said. "Get the doors open and clear the table."

"Is he bleeding? Anything broken?" Mrs. Church asked, propping the screen door wide.

"Don't think so, but he's talking like he must've got conked on the head." To his dog, Miah said, "That'll do," and it jumped out of the bed and trotted off.

"I'll call the clinic," his mother offered.

"Not yet," Miah said as he and Duncan hauled Casey to the truck bed's edge by the ankles. "Casey's funny about doctors."

Funny about paper trails, more like, Duncan thought, and grabbed Casey's feet. Miah handled the other end. They weaved him through the two open doors and around a short hall into a large, rustic kitchen. They laid him out along the oversize trestle table and Duncan got his helmet off. Miah's mother slid a couple of folded dish towels under his head.

Casey resumed his muttering. His voice was more peaceful than manic now, though he still shook with the odd, tiny tremor. To Mrs. Church he said earnestly, "I'm so, so sorry for your loss."

She smiled at him, confused. "That's sweet of you, Casey. How many fingers am I holding up?" She showed him two.

"If there's anything I can do to help, just let me know," Casey went on.

She shook her head. "He must be concussed. I'm calling the clinic."

Duncan and Miah exchanged a glance, nodding in unison, and she grabbed a phone from its dock on the hutch, disappearing into the next room.

Miah pulled an outmoded cell phone from his back pocket. "And I'll call Vince."

"So much for his beauty sleep," Duncan murmured, circling the table, wishing he knew how to check vitals—how to do *anything* useful just now.

"Hey. Listen, it's about Casey," Miah told his phone. "He wrecked while he was riding around with Welch . . . No, he seems solid, except he definitely thumped his head—he's talking complete nonsense." A pause. "I dunno, weird bull. He just apologized to my mom for her 'loss.' She's calling the clinic, but you wanna get over here, if Kim or Nita's around to watch your mom? I can drive him back to yours later, but somebody'll need to get his bike home, or at least ride it up here. It's ditched half a mile down the road—you'll see it on the way in. Okay, great. See you."

Miah's mother returned, replacing the phone. "Ronnie Biscane's on duty. Says he'll come straightaway."

"Vince is coming, too," Miah said.

His mother looked to Duncan. "I'm Christine, by the way. You must be a friend of Casey's."

Duncan looked to Miah for a split second, realizing he was basically asking the man's permission to claim such a thing. "Sort of," he said to Christine, and shook her slender hand. "I'm Duncan Welch."

She frowned, looking thoughtful. "Your name sounds so familiar."

I'm sure you're overheard your son wishing bodily harm upon me. Or the local news calling me a conspiracy suspect. "I know Vince better than I do his brother," Duncan said. "I got wrapped up in the events that led to the late sheriff's arrest."

"Oh dear—are you the one who . . ." She touched her mouth fretfully, and Duncan's tongue reflexively sought his fake tooth.

"I am, yes. Small price to pay to help."

Behind her, Miah rolled his eyes.

"You work for the developers?" she asked.

"I did. Things are at a bit of a standstill at the moment, of course." Because of the VRC investigation, he let her infer. He was pleased her ignorance must mean that Miah wasn't petty enough to gossip gleefully with his family about how someone from Sunnyside had been accused of taking bribes and lost his job. The Churches had every right to distrust Sunnyside, of course. The casino was going to cause the ranch no end of headaches by the time it was completed. *If* it ever got completed.

"Everyone in this town owes you a debt of gratitude," Christine said to Duncan. "Vince said he doesn't know if he'd have been able to expose Tremblay without your help."

"I don't know about that." And there'd been many times when Duncan wished he'd never gotten involved at all, justice be damned. He was a capitalist, and they rarely made good humanitarians. The praise didn't fit him any better than the stiff, heavy boots on his feet.

Christine looked to each of the coherent men. "Coffee?"

Miah shook his head. "Nah, I'm good."

"No, thank you," Duncan said.

She studied Casey, who'd gone quiet, his chest rising and falling deeply. He could have been napping, if not for his half-open eyes.

"We better get him sitting up," Miah said. "Can't have him falling asleep concussed."

Duncan helped shift Casey onto the long bench seat.

"I sure hope he doesn't need to go all the way to Elko," Christine said, watching as the men balanced Casey upright, the table's edge at his back. He blinked dozily, supported by a hand on each of his shoulders.

"Okay there, Case?" Miah asked.

"Where the fuck am I?"

"At Three C. You took a spill on your bike."

"She okay?"

Miah looked to Duncan.

"I think it'll be fine." Scratched up like its owner, surely, maybe short a mirror, but the bike seemed tough to maim. And unlike Duncan's poor Merc, the Harley looked better with a bit of abuse. He supposed there were advantages to fetishizing a vehicle whose cachet was rooted in performance, not perfection.

"Welch," Casey said, seeming surprised to look up and find him standing there. "The fuck you doing here? You find that coyote yet?"

"Excuse me?"

"You gotta find the coyote, man. Step one."

Duncan glanced nervously at Miah. "I'm not looking for a coyote," he said to Casey.

"Why you here, then? You and Miah having a duel for Raina's love or some shit?"

Christine's eyebrows rose at that, and she turned to dig through drawers in the hutch.

Miah told Casey, "You were giving Welch a riding lesson. I drove by right after you went down. Ronnie's coming out, to make sure you're okay. You were talking some serious nonsense, Case. We think you concussed yourself."

Casey frowned, his gaze more focused now. "Nonsense?"

"Yeah. Vince is on his way, too."

"What exactly did I—"

"Hold still," Christine told Casey, and she set a first-aid kit on the table. Duncan stepped aside to give her room. She dabbed at the scrapes on Casey's cheek and temple, ignoring the stream of multisyllabic oaths that came pouring out of him.

Miah jerked his head to tell Duncan to follow him, and headed back out to the front porch.

Once the door swung closed, Miah sighed into the open air. "What the *fuck*?"

Duncan nodded. "Indeed. It has to be a concussion."

"You sound confident."

"I was a defense lawyer for three years before I went corporate. I specialized in fighting personal injury claims. I never saw a plaintiff present hallucinations as one of the symptoms of suffering a blow to the head, but it does happen. In very severe concussions, and traumatic brain injuries."

Miah smirked. "You were an ambulance chaser?"

"I was an ambulance deflector. I saved a lot of construction companies a lot of money over fraudulent claims."

"What a saint you are. How many legitimately injured workers did you fuck over in the process?"

Duncan kept his gaze cool. "Fucking over was never in my job description. The law, when practiced well, leaves no room for emotion, and fucking over requires an unprofessional amount of contempt."

"Or greed."

Duncan spoke evenly. "I carry out my job with the precision and detachment of a surgeon. But enough about me, Mr. Church."

"Miah."

Duncan cocked his head. "Are you really so invested in establishing familiarity with me, *Miah*?"

The man smiled. "It's not unlikely that you and me might get trashed some night, and exchange a few punches in the bar's front lot. Seems silly for us not to be on a first-name basis."

"You want to fight me for Raina's affections?" Miah would win, no doubt about that.

"No, I don't. Raina's affections are hers to misplace as she sees fit." He smiled again. "I just really want to hit you. Just once." His gaze zeroed in on Duncan's black eye. "Though it looks like somebody beat me to it."

"Perhaps one day the opportunity will arise. But getting back to Casey—you've never known him to have a history of seizures or anything like that?"

"Never. Head injury explains the babbling . . ."

"But not the reason he fell to begin with. And he was shaking, too. I represented a contracting company against a seizure claim once—the plaintiff's lawyer insisted it had been caused by heavy equipment vibration."

Miah made a curious face. "He's been riding for years, though, and I've never heard of him having one."

"And all that said, I won that case—I have no clue if the claim was legitimate."

The rumble of an engine sounded, and they turned to watch Vince cruise down the road. He looked as fitting on his bike as Duncan surely looked laughable. He turned into the lot and parked, expression grave as he strode to the porch. He nodded to each of them. "Hey."

"Hey," Miah said.

Vince stood before them and crossed his ink-covered arms. "How's Case?"

"Better. He's in the kitchen. Not shaking and shit, anyhow, and he's talking *some* sense. My mom's patching up some scrapes, and Ronnie should be here soon. I know it's a pain in the ass, but maybe he ought to go to Elko. Get an MRI or whatever. If you need to get back to your mom, I could drive him myself. Provided Dad could return a few calls for me."

Vince shook his head firmly.

Miah shot him a leveling look. "You weren't here, Vince. He didn't just fall—he had some kind of . . . spell. Like a bad trip. Maybe even a seizure or something, Welch thinks."

"Casey's no fan of hospitals," Vince said.

"Casey's no fan of paperwork," Miah corrected dryly, confirming Duncan's suspicions. "The kid's got a pay-as-you-go phone with an area code he hasn't lived in for, like, six years. But we're talking about a possible brain injury."

Vince swallowed, glancing between them. "He said stuff?"

Duncan nodded, and Miah said, "Yeah, a lot of stuff. Weird stuff. Welch said it could be from the head injury, but shit, I dunno . . . Any chance he was on something—mushrooms, or acid?"

"Or peyote," Duncan offered. "He told me to 'find the coyote.'"

"What else?" Vince demanded.

"That I was gonna die in a fire," Miah said, smirking.

Vince, however, wasn't smiling. "'Scuse me?"

"He kept talking about Miah being killed. About a fire on a starless night." Duncan couldn't help thinking back to the long minutes he'd spent in that smoke-stinking mine, listening as Casey had spouted a seeming forensics expert's knowledge on the topic. "What is it with your brother and fire?"

"Case has always been a bit of a pyro," Miah said. "But a starless night? We get maybe a handful of those a year, and the rainy season's just about the only time when I'm *not* worrying about fires . . . He came to and offered my mom his condolences," Miah added, his smile fading when Vince didn't mirror the levity. "What?"

Vince stared at his friend and his tone grew grave. "Raina ever tell you what almost happened to her, the night of the meteor shower?"

Miah's expression darkened, and Duncan's blood went cold, brain filling with question marks and fog.

"Yeah," Miah said stiffly.

"What nearly happened to Raina?" Duncan interjected. Something terrible, to judge by Vince's voice and Miah's expression. Something bad enough to make her punchy about getting held down? And what on earth was it to do with Casey's spill?

"It's none of your fucking business," Miah said, pink rising in his cheeks.

Vince seemed to concur, turning back to Miah. "I gotta talk to you, after we get the bikes sorted out."

"To do with what happened that night?" Miah asked. "To Raina?"

Vince shook his head. "Not directly, no. Just clear your schedule for the next couple hours. Actually, see if you can't get the night off—you might need a few drinks."

A white minivan turned into the ranch's lot.

Vince stood up straight. "That'll be Ronnie."

"Case'll be in good hands," Miah said. "I'll drop Welch back off with his bike, and if one of you can help me, we can get Casey's bike in my bed and drop it back at the spot."

Vince nodded. "No problem." He looked to Duncan. "You get enough of a foundation to know how to ride yourself back to Raina's?"

"I have." But Duncan wasn't going back to Raina's yet. He was rattled, and needed time to turn everything around in his head.

Vince greeted the older man from the clinic and they disappeared inside for a minute. When he returned, Vince said, "Okay, let's figure out the logistics and worry about a hospital run later. I'll meet you by the bikes."

Duncan followed Miah to the pickup.

"Fucking strange," Miah muttered, starting the truck as Duncan buckled up.

"Indeed."

Behind them came the ripping noise of Vince's throttle, then relative silence descended as Miah drove. After an eternal, awkward minute, he finally huffed, "So."

"So?"

Another pause, and Miah asked, "Have you?"

Seeing no reason to be coy, Duncan simply said, "Yes." He nearly added, "We have," but for whatever reason, the *we* didn't feel right. He and Raina weren't a *thing*, hot sex and needy spooning notwithstanding.

Miah said nothing, and his face was unreadable. The face Raina had no doubt watched who knew how many times, just as she'd watched Duncan with wonder the previous morning.

I still love Miah.

Yet she'd slept with Duncan. They were different as lovers, surely. Was Miah more tender or rough? Duncan had to wonder. Louder, slower, more or less . . . *sensual*? More or less of whatever Raina wanted? And which was better—to be the man who got to enjoy her, or to be the man who actually meant something to her? Surely the latter was a far more rare honor.

Miah interrupted Duncan's increasingly frantic—and increasingly pathetic—stream of consciousness. "Treat her good," he said gruffly. "That's all I'll say about it."

"She'd demand nothing less."

Miah nodded. "That's fucking right."

Chapter 16

They reached the abandoned bikes without another word, and once Casey's was secured in the bed of the truck, Duncan bade Vince and Miah good night. As soon as he recovered his rhythm with the BMW, his mind began wandering in earnest. He turned Casey's spacey words over, feeling like a hound who'd caught some curious, unshakable scent on the wind.

You find that coyote yet? Utter nonsense, yet it nagged at him. He was seeking something as grisly as carrion, after all. He wished he possessed the primitive scavenger's instincts necessary to catch the scent.

Off-road was tricky, to be sure, and Duncan tipped over a good half dozen times as he edged deeper into the badlands, too slow at dodging rocks, misjudging the softness of the earth. The dust was brutal at low speed, but he found that the closer he edged toward the creek, the harder the packed clay became under his tires, making for a more stable ride. The sun began its descent in earnest, the wind biting more sharply and the blue above him deepening to indigo in the east.

The scrub grass grew denser, and then stubby trees began to appear, announcing his arrival at Dead Creek. The stream was currently shirking its moniker, a thin but steady trickle snaking along the pebbled creek bed.

Everywhere Duncan looked, he saw bones. He imagined the hands capable of sifting through dirt and burying those charred remains. Or pulverizing them. Just touching those dry black sticks, maybe knowing what they'd looked like when they were still clad in flesh.

Duncan normally shied from morbid thoughts, from reminders of the frailty of the human condition—his own frailty—but they came to him unbidden now, notions and images like tugging hands. Like swarming, buzzing insects, impossible to disperse. He . . . *felt* them somehow. Nearly as if they were calling to him, the way a couple of stray notes taunt as you try to recall a forgotten song.

That was all insanity, of course. Duncan possessed no sixth sense—he operated on facts alone. And lust, it would seem, though that impulse was new. He'd followed his instincts with Raina, against his brain's better judgment, and he couldn't say he had any regrets. And it was in that spirit—or with that breed of surrender—that he let the landscape call to him, taking its direction, angling the bike without thought or expectation.

As the creek made a sharp curve, a pumpkin-colored box appeared beyond the scrubby trees—an ancient camper van. Duncan slowed.

The thing belonged in the dictionary beside the passage for *sketchy.* Straight out of the seventies, the vehicle promised to be housing a cook operation, or a load of illegal immigrants, or perhaps a pregnant runaway.

Still, if one was looking for evidence, one might be well advised to make the acquaintance of criminals. Duncan killed his engine and knocked down the kickstand. He'd hoped the motor would've made his arrival known, but the van showed no signs of life, despite the rear door hanging wide open.

"Hello?" He wandered closer. There was a warning painted neatly along the vehicle's faded orange flank, PRIVATE PROPERTY. BEWARE OF—

A sharp click at Duncan's back froze him where he stood. His heart went very still, very quiet, and he turned slowly to find himself staring into the business end of a hunting rifle.

At the other end stood a man roughly Duncan's age; long and lean, wearing a tight T-shirt and old jeans, sockless feet in sequined flip-flops. Like the van, he looked as though he'd stumbled out of the seventies—from a long stay in an opium den, all rock star snake hips, black goatee, and wild hair, the lead-lidded eyes of a hobbyist sex offender.

Oddest accessory of all, there was a large white parrot perched on his shoulder.

"Hello," Duncan said, feeling eerily calm.

The man smiled. "Greetings. What the fuck d'you want?"

Though he'd not arrived wanting anything in particular,

Duncan's mouth offered, "A quick word. Would you lower the rifle, please?"

"That's some bike." The man's gaze flicked to the BMW. "Looks like Vince Grossier's taste. But you don't look like no friend of Vince Grossier."

"Strangely, I am."

The bird bobbed its head with a little *whoop*. Its owner moved the barrel up and down, as though making an inventory of Duncan with the sight. Or perhaps choosing an organ to target.

"Am I trespassing?" Duncan asked.

"Haven't decided yet. What're you looking for?"

Unbidden, the truth fell from his mouth. "Human remains."

The man's eyebrows rose. So did the rifle, the barrel seeming to settle over Duncan's heart. Still, the fear didn't arrive.

"You don't say. And why's that led you to me?"

"It hasn't," Duncan said, then got caught on an odd thought. He stared hard at this man, this scavenger who made his home at the edges of civilization. Perplexed, upended, he muttered, "The coyote . . ."

"'Scuse me?"

"Are you . . . are you the coyote?" Duncan asked him.

"Why? Are you the Keymaster?"

He shook his head, shocked he'd even asked. "Nothing, never mind." Of course he wasn't the bloody coyote. Casey had been speaking with a head injury, not from some cryptic well of clairvoyance. "And no, I've not been led anywhere—I'm utterly lost. But I'm looking for bones. Burned ones."

The eyebrows and barrel dropped. "You part of the investigation? All that drama with the foreman and our dearly departed sheriff? Man likes to know, before he takes aim at a detective."

Duncan shook his head. "I'm no one." No one at all, not anymore. He was as displaced as those bones, stripped of their flesh, location likely known only to a dead man. He let the honesty flow. "I lost everything because of those bones. I just want to find them. I need to. To keep from going completely insane."

The man lowered the weapon, looking intrigued. He strode back to the open van and leaned his long body inside. When he turned back the rifle was gone, and he tossed something to Duncan. A fifth of rum.

"Sobriety never did sanity any favors," the stranger said.

Duncan felt inclined to agree. He unscrewed the cap and took a sip.

"Who are you?" the man asked. "And where's Kansas to you, Dorothy?"

"Duncan Welch. I was a lawyer for the company that's planning the casino. I live in San Diego, but I grew up in London. Who are you?"

"Dancer."

"Is that your surname or your profession?"

The guy smiled. "Save your singles. John Dancer. How do you know Vince Grossier?" The way he said it, Duncan had to imagine the two might not be mutual fans.

"We met when he was looking into Alex Dunn's death. I was appointed by my employers to keep an eye on him. I wouldn't quite say we're friends, but we'd both agree that he owes me."

"Join the club."

Duncan felt the rum already, reminded he'd not thought to eat lunch. "Tell me, John Dancer . . . if you were looking to get rid of a pile of burned human bones, where would you hide them?"

"Me? I'd crush 'em. Toss 'em in the creek, or let 'em blow off across the badlands on a windy day. Nice and organic. Sure as shit wouldn't bury 'em, though."

Duncan nodded and winced through another sip. "That's what I was afraid of."

"Then again, I didn't get rid of any bones," Dancer said, crossing his arms. "Tremblay did, I bet. Now, if I was the sheriff, I'd have hid that shit in plain sight. Sealed those things up in a cardboard box and tossed it on some dusty corner of an evidence shelf. Only place in town where a load of burned-up human remains wouldn't raise an eyebrow."

Duncan took another drink. "You're rather good at this."

"I'm way smarter than our late sheriff, though. I'd put decent money on him reburying that shit."

"So don't give up hope, you're saying?"

"I'm saying, gimme back my rum."

Duncan capped the bottle and tossed it to Dancer. "Cheers."

"You know much about our dear dead sheriff, Sherlock?" Dancer asked.

"A bit. What I gleaned from the news, and from a few brief

conversations I had with him myself, over legal matters pertaining to the casino construction."

"You think old Tremblay owned himself a bike like yours?" Dancer nodded at the BMW.

"I couldn't say for sure . . . Though it seems unlikely."

"He didn't." Dancer took a drink. "So that narrows your search down to the radius a panicking, middle-aged man is willing to hike himself and a bag of bones off the beaten track."

True, maybe. "That shrinks the most probable area to perhaps a mile on either side of the roads fit for civilized vehicles . . . and likely routes with no streetlights, no nearby homes, little traffic."

Dancer tapped his temple with the bottle's neck. "Now you're thinking like a murderer."

"That still leaves an awfully large area."

"Sure. But tell me this—you're the sheriff, out on your little mission to ditch some evidence. You gonna take your cruiser or your civilian wheels?"

"The latter, I suppose . . . Though actually, the cruiser might be less conspicuous, potentially. On duty, he'd look less out of place patrolling quiet roads, if someone saw him."

Dancer tossed back the bottle, making Duncan feel like a trained dolphin, thrown a fish for encouragement. He drank.

"What else?" Dancer prompted.

Duncan tried to paint the scene in his mind. "He'd take his cruiser, which would look less suspicious on the back roads . . . provided he stayed in his own jurisdiction. In Brush County."

Dancer smiled. "Go on."

"It's still a needle in a haystack—it's an evidence burier's paradise out here."

"You strike me as the kind of prick who's got loads stashed away in the stock market," Dancer said. "Am I right?"

"You are."

"Right. So think of that evidence like an investment. Think of those bones, tucked away in their grisly little dirt safe-deposit box. Tremblay's investment in covering his own ass, right?"

"And?"

"And what do people do with their investments?"

Duncan considered it, thinking of his own stocks, feeling the knee-jerk urge to whip out his phone and open his trading app. "We monitor them."

Dancer snapped his fingers approvingly, then made a grabby gesture. Duncan capped and tossed back the rum.

"The greedy and the paranoid," Dancer said, then toasted them with a drink. "How they love to keep an eye on their stashes."

Gears turning in earnest now, Duncan nodded. "The badlands are nothing if not redundant." You could drive for fifty miles in either direction and the landscape stayed identically, *relentlessly* the same. Same brush, same earth, same rocks and hills. "It'd take a landmark to find what you've buried out there. A landmark, or GPS coordinates."

"Guess you better hope he went with the former, huh?"

"A landmark," Duncan muttered, trying to imagine what such a thing might look like. "It'd have to be distinctive, but not interesting enough to invite much notice." So, nowhere as well trafficked as Big Rock or the hot springs, nor any of Fortuity's other modest wonders.

"You got the reasoning part down," Dancer said. "Your brain's taken you as far as it can. Now you turn this shit over to your gut."

"My gut?"

"You want my advice—which nobody ever does, 'cause you're all dumb-asses—you go at this like that coyote you were babbling about. All hunger."

Duncan frowned. "I'm afraid I trust logic far more than I do intuition."

"Fuck intuition. I'm talking *hunger*, man. Like you haven't eaten in a week and those bones are fucking Thanksgiving dinner. Animal hunger. That growling in your gut that leads a man to what he wants most—easy money, free pussy, or in your case, some poor bastard in a smoke-stinking sack."

Stymied, Duncan asked after a moment, "And where does your hunger lead you?"

Dancer smiled. "Opportunities." His bird shrieked, crest flaring. "Hush, Cookie."

"Well, I'll see if I can't manifest some of that hunger, then."

"Yeah, you do that. Now stay the fuck off my property."

"I rather doubt this is your property," Duncan said dryly. "You're also wearing women's sandals, if I'm not mistaken."

"Don't you make my hunger get in a mood for fighting now, son. Fuck off and good luck."

Duncan offered a nod of thanks and walked back to the bike.

My hunger...

Felt like such rubbish, when all he'd ever hungered for before was order, stability, control, security. And where had that gotten him, really? Fucked over and unemployed, that was where.

"Fine," he muttered, and stomped on the starter. He was a starving stray now. And if any pathetic, scrounging creature was fit to find itself some bones, Duncan supposed he was it.

Chapter 17

She'd waited for him.

Expected him by six thirty, to start this supposed dinner.

Gotten a touch annoyed by seven.

Nervous by seven thirty, scared by quarter of. She texted Where are you?

By eight, the alternating irritation and anxiety drove Raina downstairs to the bar to join Abilene behind the taps. At the bottom of the stairwell, she jumped when her phone buzzed against her butt.

Alive and well. Just got back into cell range.

And with the fear assuaged, she was pissed. *Fucker*. He'd stood her up—and for the date he'd planned himself. He'd had her checking her phone, for fuck's sake. When was the last time a man had driven her to that shit? Years. And she was far angrier with herself for caring than she was with Duncan for leaving her hanging. She shrugged it off. Or told herself she did. Stupid spooning, messing with her head.

"Looking quiet," she said to Abilene, stringing a towel through her belt loop. Just a dozen quiet drinkers scattered around the front room.

"Very. I had to load up the jukebox myself or it'd be crickets serenading us."

"Ouch."

"I heard the ranch hands are throwing some cookout kegger tonight."

Raina nodded. "There's two-thirds of our clientele spoken for."

"I could probably fly solo," Abilene offered.

"Nah. I need to do a stock take anyhow." And no way was Duncan getting back to find Raina sitting around upstairs, looking as though she had nothing better to do than wait on him.

She grabbed a pad and began tallying up the bottles and cans in the fridges.

"Oh," Abilene said. "Our tips just doubled, at least."

Raina straightened, heart going hot and cold at once to spy Duncan walking in from the back. Still dressed in the jeans and jacket, he met her eyes, strolled to his usual stool, and sat. A couple of patrons eyed him, and a pair of them began talking in earnest, too quietly to be overheard. Raina added their names to her mental list of potential vandals.

Duncan's hair was messy from a now absent helmet, and it seemed unthinkable that he hadn't taken the time to fix it. "Quiet night, I see," he said mildly.

She smiled, leaving any measure of charm out of the gesture. "You stood me up, Duncan."

His eyes grew wide, realization dawning. "Good God, I did. I'd forgotten completely. Apologies. Some very strange things happened since last we spoke."

"Oh?" *They better be fucking good.*

He took a breath, brow furrowing. "Can you spare a moment, away from the bar?"

She looked to where Abilene was loading the washer. "Sure. Abilene—I'll be back in five."

The girl nodded.

Raina led Duncan into the office in the rear, shutting the door on the pop-country and chatter.

She sat on the edge of her cluttered desk. "What happened?"

"I had my lesson. It went fine for two hours or more. Then Casey had a . . . an incident."

She frowned. "What kind of incident?"

"He fell off his bike, babbling and shaking. Talking as though he was hallucinating. Miah passed—we were out near the ranch—and we got Casey there in his truck."

"He okay?"

"I think so. A man from the clinic came out. Vince came, too, and he seemed rather rattled."

"That doesn't sound like Vince."

"Rattled . . . but also not especially surprised, I don't think. Casey's not epileptic, as far as you know, is he? He seemed unsteady right before he went down. And he shook quite a lot after the fall."

Her frown deepened. "Not that I've ever heard of."

"Whatever Vince might know about it, I wasn't deemed worthy of cluing in. He and Miah were going to talk, after I left."

She drew a deep breath, stymied. "Well, as long as Case is okay, I guess."

After a loaded pause, Duncan blurted, "What happened to you, the night of the meteor shower?"

Raina froze. "Excuse me?"

"Vince said something to Miah, something about a meteor shower. It sounded as though you'd been in trouble. What it had to do with Casey's issues, I couldn't say, but he looked rather grave."

As he should. It was the runner-up for the worst night of her life, second only to when her dad had passed away. It might even have taken the prize, except Vince had managed to show up, right when she fucking *needed* someone. She'd already had her skirt shoved up to her waist, her panties ripped, three sets of rough hands on her, holding her down and covering her mouth. A fly had already been lowered and repulsive, drunken promises made.

Then she'd heard it—the most glorious sound in the world. Vince's R80. His headlight had shown him everything he'd needed to see to inspire what came next. His bike had hit the dirt, and then his fists had gone to work. There'd been a nose broken, and a jaw, a thousand bruises, and maybe a few cracked ribs. And Vince had told those men—men they'd both grown up with—that if they ever showed their faces in Fortuity again, he wouldn't hesitate to get a gun involved.

He'd ridden her home without a word. Raina hadn't worn a skirt or dress since, and though she'd held Vince tight and maybe even fallen half in love with him for as long as that surreal ride lasted, they'd never talked about it aloud.

He'd given her a .22 the next day; given her shoulder a squeeze and kept his gaze on the floor. It had taken over a year for him to look at her without that loathsome softness in his eyes—that look that made her feel like a victim as surely as those pinning hands had. She *hated* that look, and every hard, honed edge already built into her personality had grown sharper, telling the world she wasn't helpless, or hurt, or traumatized, or scared. That she refused to be any of those things. No man got the right to break her like that. Not with his hands, and not with his pity.

Not with hateful words scrawled across my home, she thought, spine stiffening.

In time, Vince had gone back to treating her as he always had done. And in time, she'd gotten to a place where she could forget about that night for days at a time.

She'd never told her dad. She told Miah about it, years later, after she'd run off to Vegas and gotten herself humiliated in a far different way, and slunk back home with her tail between her legs. She'd never seen Miah's eyes go so black, but she'd told him it was the past, and he'd respected that, much as she knew it had killed him.

Though *how* Vince had managed to find her, or to even be looking for her . . . That was a mystery she'd never solved, and since asking him about it meant acknowledging the incident, it would just have to stay a mystery.

Before her, Duncan's expression was pure worry. She didn't want his worry, or horror, or sadness, or anger. She wanted his lust and his banter, and his rare, heart-stopping laughter; a flash of perfect—nearly perfect—white teeth when she coaxed a true smile out of him. No heavy things. No conversations that would change how he thought about her, recast her as someone helpless.

"What happened?" Duncan prompted.

She stood. "I have to get back to work."

He grabbed her arm, poised to stop her, but she met his stare with such fire in hers that he immediately released her. She brushed past him, and he looked subdued as he sat across the bar from her once more.

Duncan finished his drink a few minutes later, and when she took his glass to pour a refill, he shook his head. "I'm heading up."

"You going to bed?"

His gaze was even. "I don't have to."

"Good. Don't. We're not done arguing."

He nodded. "As you wish."

And they both knew what happened when they bickered— their bodies took over when their mouths grew weary of clashing. And from that thought alone, she went from cold to hot in a single heartbeat. She watched him go, then threw herself into the demands of the bar.

Business never did pick up, and Raina and Abilene closed a little early, locking up by a quarter to two. She walked Abilene out, waving good night just as Vince's bike came around the side of the bar. He switched it off and dismounted.

"Right on time," she said. "Kim drive?"

He nodded. "She's parked on the street, out front, half block away. She's got her camera all decked out with the zoom."

"And I imagine you've come armed in a slightly different fashion."

He patted his side, where his jacket hid his holster and pistol. "You got your keys on you? I was hoping to sit in your truck—it's gonna be a cold one."

"It's unlocked. Have at it."

"Thanks. We'll head home at sunrise, I figured. If that works for you."

She nodded. "Thank you, Vince."

"No need. Just get some sleep."

That remained to be seen.

She said good night and went upstairs. The lights were on in the den, and she found Duncan on the couch with his headphones on, stroking his cat like a Bond baddie. He was still dressed to seduce her, though his jacket was slung over the couch's arm. She crossed the room and picked it up, finding it dusty but generally unscathed. "Guess you did okay on your first ride, then."

"I was adequate." He hadn't showered, which surprised her, and his hair was still messy, begging for her fingers to rumple it further.

She smiled and took a seat on the arm. "Adequate? You'd settle for that?"

"In arenas I have no business setting foot in? Yes, absolutely. Was that Vince's bike I heard pulling up?"

She nodded. "And Kim's out front."

"Excellent . . . Again, I'm sorry I stood you up."

"I couldn't care less."

"Well, I could. I'm never late for an engagement, to say nothing of forgetting one entirely. And cooking you dinner is far more compelling than a work appointment."

"It's fine. Sounds like you had a distracting afternoon."

"That's no excuse."

"If it was, I'd accept it. So let's drop it. You can cook for me tomorrow."

"Good." He relaxed visibly, then leaned forward, setting the cat on the floor.

"So, what else have you've been up to?" she asked. "Just Grossier drama?"

"After Casey had his incident, Vince and Miah took charge, and I continued riding, alone, from an hour before sunset until I got back here."

"You kept riding? And it never occurred to you we'd made plans, once the craziness subsided?"

He smiled. "So you *could* care less."

She rolled her eyes.

"The incident with Casey was . . . upending. He said such strange things, as though he was dreaming."

"Nonsense stuff?"

"Yes. He seemed fixated on the notion that Miah was going to die in a fire. On a starless night, he said."

She frowned. "Creepy. A starless night? We see maybe ten of those a year, tops, during our five-minute rainy season. Anyway, you kept riding. It didn't get weirder, I trust?"

He made a face. "It didn't get any more normal."

"Uh-oh."

"I rode around the badlands. Then I came upon a man called John Dancer, out by—"

"Dancer? Christ Almighty, you *have* had a fucked-up day."

"You know him?"

"Everybody knows Dancer, whether they'd like to or not."

"Is he a patron of yours?"

"Barely. He comes into Benji's maybe twice a year. Dancer collects enemies the way other men collect conquests. He'll sidle up to the bar and ask if I've seen so-and-so lately, sidle back out after a nice long look down my shirt. I've never made a dime off him."

"Did you go to school together?"

She shook her head. "He's your age, I'd guess, or maybe early forties, and he didn't grow up here. No one knows where the fuck he came from, but he's probably been around for ten years or more. It's like a coyote who took up permanent residence by the creek."

"Indeed," Duncan murmured.

"Wild Dancer spottings are a pretty common occurrence. How was he to you?"

"He aimed a rifle at my heart. We drank rum, talked philosophy. He told me to fuck off, and I did."

She nodded. "That sounds about right." Though she couldn't help feeling he was leaving something out.

Duncan sighed and stretched his long arms above his head. "Enough about my day." He crossed his legs, met her eyes. "Are you quite sure you won't talk to me about what Vince said? About what happened to you?"

Her warmth toward him waned. "Don't push me, Duncan." The whiskey bottle still sat on the coffee table from their initial head-on crash, and she grabbed it, tugging the cork free and taking a healthy swig.

"Don't push you?" he asked. "As you pushed me straight out of my motel room and into your custody?"

"I did that for your own good," she said, knowing it'd grate on him. *Wanting* to grate on him. Wanting to push him away, as urgently as she'd wanted to draw him close by the collar and taste that gorgeous mouth. Shit, that was never a good sign. Pushing a man away only ever meant one thing—that she was in danger of wanting to keep him close.

"Let's make this fair, finally, Ms. Harper. You know my secrets. Tell me yours."

"No fucking way. Plus, I don't know your secrets—only one of them. And if a man's keeping one, he's keeping a hundred."

"Tell me."

She cracked her neck. He wasn't going to shut up about this. And if he didn't shut up, they'd never get around to fucking. And man, she could use that just now. It'd take her mind off her hurt feelings over being stood up, or indeed the danger that had Vince camped out in her truck right now, armed.

"I'll give you the broad strokes," she offered.

He nodded to say, *Go on.*

"Some bad shit went down, or nearly did, and Vince showed up and stopped it. In the wake of it all, I remember wondering, how the fuck did he get here, right when I needed him?"

"Get where?"

"Way out in the badlands, past Big Rock, if you know where that is."

"I do. And?"

She raised her eyebrows. "And what?"

"Tell me."

She shot him a look. "Tell you? About the thing I don't tell anyone about?"

"You told Miah."

She dropped from the couch's arm onto the cushion. "There was a time when I was lust-drunk enough that I told him just about everything. He's the kind of man you can do that with."

Duncan's gaze grew hard, a hint of his old self falling between them, cold and smooth as a pane of glass. "And what sort of man am I, then?"

She shrugged. "The type who's as evasive as me. What do you care, anyway? It was years ago. I'm over it. Far as I care, it never happened. That's how little it affects me." *Liar.* She'd traded skirts and all the other trappings of a softer femininity for her bitch armor, and she wasn't giving up the latter anytime soon. Never for Miah, so sure as shit not for Duncan Welch.

"I want to know," he said plainly.

"I can see that."

He sighed, gaze dropping to her knees. He looked tired when he met her stare again. "I'll trade you," he said softly, and moved to the middle cushion. Goddamn if she couldn't smell him. And not his cologne for once. Sweat. Dust. Skin. The day had peppered his jaw in blond stubble, and there was surrender in those heart-stopping eyes.

"Trade me what?" she asked.

"If you tell me what happened, I'll tell you something in return. Any single thing you wish to ask."

"What makes you think I'm not perfectly happy, taking you at face value, Duncan?" She wasn't, of course. She wanted to know everything. Everything that had formed this extraordinary imposter, everything that made him whisper those things to her the previous morning. *Hold me. Say my name.* And in the silence between those spoken words, another message. *Want me.*

And she wanted this trade. Wanted to *know* him, every dark little detail she could get her hands on—and not for leverage. Not anymore. Simply for the privilege. But she was afraid to say so.

"You've let me in your home, and your body," he said softly, and his hand rose. He laid his thumb along her throat, cool, smooth fingers slipping into her hair, spurring her pulse. "Are our secrets really such a wild intimacy to share?"

"That's just sex," she lied.

His smile was tight, a touch sad. "You don't believe that any more than I do."

She pursed her lips, heart beating quick. "No, I don't."

"So tell me."

"You first."

He nodded. "Any one thing you care to know."

"What's the deal with your parents?"

He spoke to her hands, tone flat and calm. "I don't have any parents. I grew up in the foster system."

"Oh." She couldn't say she was shocked ... but surprised, yes. "And here I'd imagined your damage must've been the work of some iceberg of a withholding mother."

"No mother, withholding or otherwise."

"So is Welch not your parents' name?"

"No. The story goes that Welch is the surname of the cab-driver who found me, outside a hospital."

"And Duncan?"

"A nurse named me that. A Leeds United supporter, and great admirer of Duncan McKenzie—a man who boasted the distinction of being able to jump over a Mini, in addition to playing football rather well."

"So we were both basically left on doorsteps," Raina mused. "Are you also named for a seventies footballer, by any chance?"

She cracked a smile.

"At least you were left with your father," Duncan said.

"But you must have had *some*one, at some point. Foster parents?"

"Yes, many, but never for long. And with precisely one exception, none that ever offered me much besides resentment. I was tolerated, in exchange for weekly checks."

"Were the bad ones really bad?"

"Others have suffered worse, I'm sure. But it wasn't pretty, no."

"That scar on your back ... ?"

"I was pushed down a flight of stairs. The corner of a stone fireplace broke my fall."

She winced, sucked a horrified breath. "Jesus. Pushed by one of your foster parents?"

"Yes. Actually, I think he merely meant to hit me, but I was standing in rather the wrong place at the wrong time."

"Fuck me."

Duncan shrugged. "It could have been far worse, had I landed an inch to the right. Plus, I was sent to a much nicer home, after I got out of hospital. For a time, at least. I've always felt the injury was a small price to pay. Now, that's quite enough about my traumas, Ms. Harper. Now your turn."

She gave it to him straight. "I was almost gang-raped, six years ago."

His eyes grew wide, and he didn't reply for a long moment. "Almost?"

"Almost. I knew them, growing up. They were drunk and high. *I* was drunk. All the folks under thirty were out partying near Big Rock real late, to watch this epic meteor shower. I ignored my instincts, followed one when he said he wanted to show me something amazing, away from the group. Two of his friends followed us. No one noticed—people were sneaking off all over the place, and it wasn't like we were strangers to each other."

"And Vince stopped it?"

She smiled. "Vince stopped it. Like the scariest avenging angel ever beamed down from heaven."

She searched Duncan's face for pity, for alarm. She didn't find those, but instead a tiny hint of heat. Of anger. He took his hand back.

"So that's my damage," she said.

He dipped his head in a coy little bow. "And mine."

She held his stare, lost in those pale eyes. She didn't feel changed, or opened up, or closer to him. A touch more naked, perhaps, but she had ammo, same as he did. And she could sense it didn't need saying that neither was sharing the secrets they'd just swapped.

Raina eyed the clock, feeling the hour, but far from sleepy. "I'm taking you to bed now," she said. "And nothing about it's going to be any different, because of what we both shared just now. It'll be dirty, and fast, and rough if you like that. You can do anything but hold me down."

Another dip of that dignified head.

She stood and put her hand out, leading him to her room. And she wondered if he knew what she did—that she'd lied. That there was no way in hell this sex *couldn't* be different. They could only pretend things hadn't just changed. They could only lie to themselves.

Thank goodness they were both masters at it.

"Lights on or off?" she asked as they crossed into her dark bedroom.

"Off. Open the blinds. And the window."

"Don't forget we've got an audience." She let his hand go, kneeling on the bed to yank the blinds up. Sure enough, she could see Kim's orange Datsun parked just up the street, its lights and windows dark. Though she wouldn't be able to make out much of anything.

The sign filled the room with red light, flickering to the rhythm of a faulty neon tube. Raina pushed the window up, letting in a crisp breeze, the buzz of the sign. Downtown was silent. Benji's last call stole the activity, as sure as Lights Out stole the sun. She turned to face Duncan, watching as he slipped off his shoes, then his socks. He'd shut the door behind him, banishing the soft glow of the den.

"Keep going," she said.

He peeled his shirt up and over his head. It messed his hair up further, and he could've passed for a different man—naked to the waist, dressed in jeans, that long, muscular body bathed in the sinful crimson light. When his pants were kicked away, she said, "Stop."

"What else do you want?"

To know how different this is going to feel. They could both have been buck naked and Raina couldn't have felt more stripped than she did now, in the wake of that talk, and in the wake of last night's *cuddling.*

The night was cool at her back, her lover glowing hot as embers before her. "I'm feeling pretty indulged just now," she said. "What would *you* like?"

He held her stare for a beat. "To taste you."

A shiver tensed her back and parted her lips—nothing to do with the open window. She'd not have guessed that offer was in Duncan's repertoire. It seemed too . . . messy somehow. Too hungry, and personal. Too *animal*. Though none of that changed her answer.

"You got it."

Chapter 18

"You've had your show," Duncan said, sitting on the end of the bed. "I wouldn't mind the same."

Raina smiled at that, slipping into seduction mode as she pulled off her boots and socks. She might not wear skirts anymore, might be cagey about presenting herself in any soft sort of way, but once sex was a foregone conclusion, Raina could tease and entice with the best of them. She left the bed and walked to where Duncan had undressed, letting the sign drape her in its red light, the sheerest negligee. Her hair was pulled back. She freed that first, then peeled her tank top up and off. Duncan's gaze was mild, almost lost to the shadows, but she felt his attention moving over her, real as fingertips, as she dropped her jeans.

Standing before him in her mismatched underwear, she asked, "Keep going?"

"Every stitch."

She reached back and freed her bra clasp, letting the item drop. She tucked her thumbs under the little strips of lace at her hips, but—

"Stop."

"You said every stitch." Granted, the thong was only made of about five of them.

"Come here."

Another shiver, and she realized she liked him this way. Bossy. Even with him stripped to his shorts, that voice alone kept him dripping in tailored luxury. Though curiosity did have her wondering yet again . . .

As she joined him on the bed and let him tug her close, she asked, "What does your real accent sound like?"

"This is my real accent."

"Your *old* accent. The one you got rid of."

"Does it matter?"

She smiled. "No, of course not. I'm just curious."

"I'm not sure I could affect it if I tried."

She didn't believe that, but let it go. "Show me what your mouth *can* do, then."

"In good time." First he cupped her jaw, kissing her lightly as their legs tangled. The contact deepened, and Raina gasped against his lips as his palm claimed her breast. His skin was rougher than before, dry and hard from a long day riding in the badlands. Would this sex be the same? Rougher and harder?

His breathing deepened, giving away his excitement. She let him roll her onto her back, and gripped his messy hair. His erection pressed along her mound, sending a thrill down her body and heat gathering between her thighs. She cocked her leg, wanting him closer, right up against her. He gave even more than that, his blunt head taunting her lips through cotton and satin—so close, so frustrating. It was the only thing in the world, this urge.

"We can skip to the good stuff," she murmured between kisses, stroking his stubbly cheeks. "I'm more than ready."

"You don't want to skip what I can do to you," he whispered, and kissed her jaw, her throat. The cockiness in his voice made her grin.

"Giving head doesn't seem your style," she said.

"Then you'll be pleasantly surprised." He moved lower, stealing away the hot pressure of his excitement, trailing kisses over her collarbone, nuzzling each breast, dragging his lips down her belly, breath steaming. His knees drove her legs wide. Two strong hands slid under her ass, palming her bare flesh as his nose flirted with her clit through her panties, setting her on fire.

Rumpled or not, his hair was soft as she raked her fingers through it—soft and fine as silk. Soft as the tongue now teasing her labia through wet fabric, surely. She shut her eyes tight, wanting him so bad it ached. His mouth, his hands, his cock— she didn't care what he gave, only that this man's body was spoiling her. Or using her, or simply needing her. Yes, needing her. She'd give him this act; then she'd show him she could be what he craved most—someone to take care of him, in the darkest ways.

The satin was soaked now, his lips and tongue so explicit she could come without him even taking the thing off. And he didn't take it off—when the time came, he merely dragged the flimsy strip aside with his thumb, and he gave her his mouth for real.

"Fuck, Duncan."

Slick—everything, slick. Her sex, his tongue. The lace of her thong was tugged taut, digging at her ass and hip, the awkward sensations contrasting with the shocking perfection of his mouth.

Duncan gave head the same way he dressed, and spoke, and moved—sumptuously. There was luxury in every stroke, elegance in the steady, precise motion of his thumb tracing her lips.

"God, you're good." She felt his stubble against her thighs and labia, that rough bristle making the slippery tease of his tongue all the more exquisite. "Deeper." He obeyed, tongue delving, and she slid her fingers to her clit. He pushed them aside, taking over the motions himself.

She moaned, lost in it. In being so spoiled. Catered to. Mastered. She'd fantasized about this man dozens of times before they'd ever touched, but she'd never imagined this. Every time they talked seriously or came together sexually, a few more of her assumptions fell away. That man from those dirty daydreams wasn't the one who was tasting her now. He was cardboard. Two-dimensional, soulless. This man pleasing her, this man whose breaths and lips and teeth and tongue were driving her insane . . . he was a mess. A beautiful, vibrant, broken, perfect mess. And good God, could he eat pussy.

"Keep doing that," she panted, flexing her hips, curling her toes, every little taste of added tension ratcheting her tighter. His tongue lapped deeply, thumb rubbing her clit with just the right intensity and speed, friction mounting. "Keep doing exactly that."

She cupped his head in her damp palms, and remembered what this man wanted most from sex. She could wind him up as he pleased her, watch him fall apart when his turn came. She stroked his hair, everything about the gesture speaking of affection and fondness. "You feel good, Duncan."

His touch sped, tongue losing some grace.

She cradled his head, stroked the curves of his ears. "I want you so bad . . . You want to hear what I wish we could do?"

A pained "Yes" warmed her lips.

"I wish you could fuck me bare, Duncan." She gave his hair a soft tug with her fist. "We'd do exactly that right now."

He moaned against her, and the hand holding her panties aside began to tremble.

"You'd fuck me until I came," she went on, smoothing his hair. "Then I'd taste exactly what you do to me, when I take your cock in my mouth."

He stumbled, fingers and mouth losing their rhythm. She even wished he'd give her exactly those things, foolish though it was. His bare, slick excitement coursing in and out of hers . . . Such a cautious man, such a reckless idea.

She was close. So fucking close.

"Look at me," she said, and when those eyes met hers across the rose-tinted planes of her naked body, she was done. The pleasure crested in a bright, hot rush, curling her back up off the covers, digging her nails into his shoulders. His fluttering tongue mimicked her most intimate muscles in the strike of the climax, and in a breath, two, the world was Duncan. This man, now whispering lazy kisses along her fevered seam, thumb barely grazing her pulsing clit. He made a sound she imagined he might reserve for a first bite of lobster, or the moment he shrugged into a new, tailored suit jacket. A sound of ultimate satisfaction and opulence.

"Christ . . . You're full of surprises, Duncan Welch."

He knelt between her legs, seeming to study whatever intimate changes he'd brought to her sex, whatever dark flush or plumpness he could make out in the low light.

"Come here," she said, curling her finger.

For long minutes they lay kissing, until Raina's satisfaction burned away and her excitement bloomed anew. He'd spoiled her; now she'd do the same to him. She urged him to lie back, then straddled his leg. He was beautiful this way, stripped and excited, on her bed. Aside from that arresting face, he was nothing like the man she'd first taken him for. Clothes gone, hair a mess, due for a shave, and with that trademark cologne swapped for the warm scents of sweat and sex.

She reached for his shorts, toyed with the waistband before easing it low and exposing him—every inch of hard flesh telling her he wanted her as badly as she did him. She loved the *smell* of him. Animal. Human. He smelled of heat and need, and she couldn't wait to taste those same things when she took him between her—

"No." He halted her as she planted her knees and brought her face close, clasping his cock.

She shrugged his hand from her shoulder. "Oh yes."

"I'm telling you no," he said more firmly, grip closing tightly around her upper arm. "Consider this my equivalent of an elbow to the eye. I don't want that."

A man who didn't want his dick sucked? Did such a thing actually exist? "Why not?"

He swallowed, distracted by her stroking hand and clearly struggling for composure. "It doesn't matter why."

"It always matters why. No question ever matters more than *why*."

"I prefer to be . . . doing," he said carefully.

She frowned, all at once worried where this trigger had come from. "Were you—"

"No. Just chalk it up to my control issues. I find few things less rousing than passivity."

She relented, though the frustration nagged. It wasn't a favor she'd have been doing him—it would have turned her on as surely as feeling his mouth between her legs had.

"What *would* you like, then?"

He answered with his body, urging her onto her back, bracing himself with his erection hovering above her mound. She opened a condom, then watched him roll it on with those beautiful hands.

He said, "Let me feel what I did to you." And no doubt he felt just that as his cock sank deep with a single, slow, slick push. She locked her thighs to his hips and closed her eyes.

"Whatever you want," she whispered. "Take it."

What he wanted was slow as honey, punctuated by a moan each time he slid home. Little by little, minute by minute, the thrusts came faster, until finally he was embodying that word that had taunted her from the moment he'd uttered it. *Vigorous.* He was rocking into her body, setting her breasts bouncing, recalibrating her breathing to the rhythm of his demands. He had to be close—his control was gone, the pace so clearly his cock's dictation.

"Duncan." She stroked his back and arms, his bunched shoulders, touched his face with wonder. *Say it,* she willed him.

Those tender pleas that felt more explicit than the nastiest pillow talk . . .

He moaned against her throat, his cock driving quick and steady.

"Say it," she whispered, holding his head.

His breath warmed her skin. "Hold me."

She wrapped her arms around his shoulders, palms flat, fingers splayed—every bit of the contact saying, *Mine*. And in every motion of his needy body, he seemed to tell her, *I'm yours*.

Finally, those words she craved. "Say my name."

She kissed his ear. "Duncan."

His hips sped and another low moan hummed against her neck. A minute later he panted, "Say what . . . ," then trailed off.

She stroked his hair. "Say what, what?"

"Say what you've called me before. Not my name."

It took her a moment to make sense of the mumbled, shy request, but then she put her mouth just below his ear and murmured, "Baby."

He groaned.

Kneading his back, she said, "Come on, baby. Come for me." She kissed his ear again, nuzzled it with her nose. "Like I did for you."

He was panting now, fucking hard and quick—almost too rough, yet so helpless.

"Come on, Duncan. I want you."

Another groan, so fierce he could've been in pain.

"I want you so much."

He lost it, hips racing gracelessly, pleasure calling all the shots. "Oh. Fuck."

"Good," she whispered, stroking his hair. "Show me."

"Hold me."

She pulled him to her, arms around his shoulders, so close they were chest to chest, his thrusts reduced to short, desperate little motions. But it did the job—brought him home. He went rigid against her, burying himself deep for three long, clenching thrusts. Then he stilled.

He propped himself up on his forearms, the rest of him going slack, his back bowing and his belly moving with needy gulps of air. He rested his forehead on hers, their collective skin damp and hot. She moved her nose against his, and wondered if he could sense her smiling.

Smiling, after everything he'd leveraged out of her tonight. Smiling, after he'd stood her up to chase after ... what, precisely? Distraction, or peace of mind? Fixation, more likely. His mind was faulty in some ways—wired not quite right. Was the sudden interest in riding just a different manifestation of his obsessiveness, some new facet of his disorder that bore no resemblance to her now gleaming bathroom?

They rolled onto their backs, and Duncan's fingers closed loosely around her wrist, the gesture equally possessive and tender.

"You cooking for me tomorrow night?" she asked.

"Tonight, technically."

True. It was easily past three a.m. "What are you making?"

"Nothing fancy."

"Something involving vegetables, to judge by the contents of my fridge."

"Is that okay?"

"Asparagus has some logistical issues ... But we can fuck first."

He laughed softly, the noise packing her heart with daisies. Christ, how did he *do* that?

"Must have cost you an arm and a leg, all that stuff," she said, forcing her attention off the squishier feelings. "All the stickers said organic, and even regular produce is overpriced way up here. Unless you dig alfalfa hay."

"Do I seem like a man who skimps on quality to save a dollar?"

"Never for a moment."

"Don't tell Agent Flores," he said, "but I had to cross the town border to get it all."

"Naughty you."

He turned and she did the same, letting him hold her stare.

His irises looked dark in the red glow, as did his hair. Cologne gone, crisp cotton traded for bare skin. A stranger, nearly, yet she could touch this version of Duncan in ways his well-dressed, calculating persona would never allow.

"What happened to that law-abiding man who first strolled into my bar all those weeks ago?" she asked.

"He's been getting dismantled from the second he met you."

"And he's adapting well."

He smiled and she felt another welling in her chest.

"It'll be weird when your name's cleared," she said. "And Sunnyside takes you back, and we're on opposite sides of the casino again . . . *If* you'd even take your old job back, of course. You can't be impressed with how they've treated you."

He turned to stare up at the ceiling once more. "For the amount they pay me—and the raise I'd likely negotiate in light of everything I've gone through—I could be convinced to muster forgiveness. Maybe."

And that means you'll stick around. At least until the Eclipse is built. Why should she even care? Why care if a man would still be warming her bed in a week, let alone in two years?

Raina's lovers kept about as long as Duncan's precious organic vegetables; history promised their affair would spoil in a matter of days. Hell, she and Miah had grown up together, known each other inside and out, shared affection and trust and respect before they'd ever hooked up, burned like wildfire after dark . . . yet they'd still only managed a couple of months. So Raina and Duncan? No fucking chance, sadly. Even if she searched her soul and caught some voice whispering that maybe, just maybe she'd like this to be something real . . . well, she had no guarantee Duncan felt the same. It was more likely than not that this fling could only last as long as his professional exile. And while that was a touch sad, it was also infinitely understandable. He'd shelve her along with those Red Wings the second his normal life resumed, tuck them neatly into a dusty box labeled *Fortuity*, and the most she could hope was that he'd think of her fondly. If he thought of her at all.

Still, she couldn't help wondering, had he grown attached as well?

"I feel like I ought to warn you," she said, grazing his collarbone with her fingertip, "this town's very hard to escape from."

"Oh?"

"It's the Fortuity bungee effect. My dad used to say it was the dust—you get the red dust in your lungs, and it always calls you back."

"It's certainly difficult to get out of one's floor mats."

"Casey almost escaped," she said. "Maybe his bungee was just really long. But even he's finally snapped back."

"Do nonnatives stand any better chance?"

She made a curious face, stroking his stubbly jaw. "Time will tell. We'll have to make a case study of you." *Unless of course you decided to stay.* She could laugh at herself for even thinking such a ridiculous thing. Duncan Welch, settling in Fortuity?

"Have *you* ever tried moving away?" he asked.

She held her breath, and nodded. She rarely told this story, but she was kind of enjoying the naked feelings tonight. With this man as her witness, anyhow, and facilitated by the judgment-clouding sex.

"When?" he asked. "And to where?"

"To Vegas, when I was twenty-six. It lasted less than a year."

"What made you go?"

She shrugged one shoulder, cringing inside. "To run away from that horrible night, partly. And partly just to get away from Fortuity." Away from too many familiar faces, too many ugly thoughts about what the people you thought you knew might be capable of.

"Why Vegas?"

"I thought I wanted glamour and excitement." She laughed. "Can you tell I'm from the sticks, that I thought Vegas was the epicenter of urbane sophistication?"

He smiled. "Second only to Paris."

"Anyhow, I ran down there thinking I'd get some dream apprenticeship at a cool tattoo studio, build a reputation for myself. Escape the town where nobody thought of me as anything other than Benji Harper's daughter. But I barely had any experience, and nobody'd hire me, and I wound up bartending at a couple casinos. I made good tips, but at least back here, there's no dress code dictating how much cleavage I have to show."

"Is that why you came back? Professional frustration?"

"I wish. But no, I fell in love."

"Oh."

She rolled her eyes. "Like, head-over-heels, brain-out-the-window in love. He was a real slick number—not like you, though," she said, tracing his ear. "Real flashy. Web entrepreneur. This guy was waving so many red flags, but I totally thought he was, like, the one. My ticket to some luxurious, awesome new life."

"And?"

"And after about three months, he tells me to meet him in his hotel room that night after I get off work. He said we'd order room service, a bottle of champagne, and that he had something to ask me. Idiot that I was, I was hoping he'd guessed my ring size right."

Duncan winced, his anticipatory horror well founded.

"So I got my boss to let me off early, and I spent the afternoon making myself beautiful—and sick with nerves. And I head up there. He makes a toast to the future or some vague crap like that. Then he pops the big question—did I know what camming was?"

"Camming? Like web-camming?"

She nodded, stomach flipping even now, more than four years later. "He wanted to be my digital pimp, basically. I've never felt so slapped in my life."

"Understandably."

She spoke to Duncan's throat. "I didn't say anything, at first. He opened his laptop and showed me the site he ran, the different feeds. I remember him saying the words 'Real classy stuff' while I watched some clip of a girl sucking on the end of her pigtail, dressed like a cheerleader."

"And?"

She had to smile, both proud and embarrassed of what came next. "And I threw his computer through the window."

"Oh my."

"Slapped it shut and flung it like a Frisbee. It *just* missed the pool, probably fifteen flights down."

"Did you get in trouble?"

She laughed. "Oh, hell no. I told security he got pissed because I wouldn't fuck him, and threw it himself."

"And that was the end of your Vegas period."

"Pretty much. I stayed for another month or so, but the shine had totally worn off. The next time my dad told me he missed me on the phone, I burst into tears and caught a bus headed north in the morning. He got diagnosed the next month, but even if he hadn't, I doubt I would've left again. Not anytime soon. And I'll be happy if I never set foot in Vegas again."

"Is that why there are no gaming machines in the bar? Bad associations with your casino days?"

She shook her head. "Nah, there never have been."

"Did your father not approve of gambling?"

"Oh no, he had nothing against the gambling. He never missed a poker night, not even during chemo. Those machines bring in good money, and just about anyplace can get a license, but my dad found that stuff depressing—video poker and slots. He said if you're going to throw your hard-earned money away, at least have the dignity to lose it to your friends. Or a blackjack dealer, or because of a slow horse—something with a pulse."

"Interesting."

The once-refreshing breeze was cold now, rousing goose bumps down Raina's arms and legs.

She froze where she lay, her gaze locked on Duncan's chin. *Shit. I just told him all that, didn't I? Totally sober. And it felt good.*

With the sex haze burned away, fear crept in. She'd told him about the assault—before tonight, Vince and Miah had been the sole audience to that secret. Now he knew about Vegas, and she'd only ever given Miah the vaguest summary. Miah knew her better—there was no doubt about that—but she couldn't help realizing that Duncan knew more of the things that mattered. The things she *chose* to share. The things she almost always chose *not* to share, not even with her dad.

Duncan would never understand her the way a childhood friend could, but she'd handed him her secrets—the only two events she was truly shamed by. The one that had left her feeling helpless, and the one that had left her feeling used. The two times she'd ever doubted herself in her thirty-two years, ugly bookends bracketing a phase of her life she'd give most anything to erase.

It had taken two decades' shared history to let her open up to Miah this way. She'd known Duncan seven weeks . . .

What the fuck have I done?

And why on earth did it feel so nice?

She got to her knees, relishing the ache in her hips and the faint sting between her thighs as she shut the window on the night and dropped the blinds. Dropped them into darkness.

She held her breath as she wrestled her way under the covers, sure Duncan would excuse himself to his own room, but curious to see if he'd kiss her good night.

He left the bed without a word, and she bit her lip, hating how disappointed she felt.

But to her surprise, he returned a moment later after opening the door, his bare legs finding hers under the sheets.

"You sleeping over, then?" she asked.

"I see no reason to rumple two beds. This is far more efficient, don't you think?" he asked, and pulled her close, kissed her neck.

A happy shiver crept through her, though this didn't explain why he'd bothered to open the door—

With a soft *prrrup*, the cat was on the end of the bed, settling in the well the blankets made between their two pairs of ankles.

Duncan laid the reassuring weight of his arm along Raina's waist, and said to them, "Good night, ladies."

Chapter 19

Duncan was gone by the time Raina rose the next morning. Eight fifty-five, a bleary squint at the alarm clock told her. Crazy. The sex seemed to be curing her insomnia. It was better than a prescription, getting well and truly laid. Now all she needed to do was fuck Duncan so good he'd never have to buy another jug of bleach.

Her phone buzzed on the side table, telling her she had a text waiting—sent by Vince around five thirty, to her, Duncan, and Kim. Didn't see a thing all night. Heard a few disturbing noises, but that's a different matter entirely.

Raina rolled her eyes and texted him back privately. Guess we're even for the time you banged that chick in the back room while I was trying to close.

Brrrzzzz. Don't know what you're talking about.

She wrote You broke my office chair.

Brrrzzzz. I have to get back to work.

Dick. She pocketed her phone.

She didn't hear Duncan when she emerged from the shower, didn't spot him. But on the kitchen table she found a note propped against the pepper mill, bearing his tidy handwriting.

> *Out riding. See you later if I don't break my neck or get shot by a drifter. If I fail to return, I hereby charge you with the care of my cat.*

Astrid brushed against Raina's shin, and she cast the tabby a dry look. "You much harder to keep alive than a jade plant? Because that's the extent of my nurturing skills."

The cat didn't reply, sauntering to its new favorite corner by the pantry to commence mouse patrol.

Probably best that Duncan was out, Raina decided, starting a pot of coffee. Yesterday's client was coming by in a bit so she could finish the shading that had been cut short by his work schedule. Like Vince, he worked at Petroch Gravel, and he'd agreed eagerly when she mentioned she was going to organize a big portfolio shoot at the bar. He'd even asked for Raina's card, to give to his cousin. She underestimated shit like that— word of mouth and self-promotion. She'd never taken her side job seriously enough, always putting the bar first. That was her *real* job, she'd told herself. Her duty. Her real role here in Fortuity. But this town was going to change if the casino went through. Not for the better, not in most ways. Sure, there'd be fewer potholes, more public services. But far more strangers passing through, and many of the locals would likely only be sticking around long enough to see what the boom did for their property values before they sold up and shipped out.

Fortuity wasn't much, but it had always been home, for better or worse. Now Raina felt her loyalty waning, knowing this town might not be recognizable two years from now.

Kim was right, and so was Vince: Raina owed it to herself to treat tattooing as a serious pursuit. They meant it as a validation of her talent, probably, but for Raina, it was just as much about survival, and adaptability. An escape route.

The window guy turned up shortly, and though she tried to pay, Duncan had beaten her to it. In no time the kitchen looked as though nothing had happened . . . Well, no, it looked better than before the brick, actually, as her guest appeared to have taken his anxiety out on her cupboards.

Her client arrived at noon, and he tipped outrageously once the piece was complete, beaming like a man who'd just been handed his newborn baby. He said he could come by Benji's anytime for the photo stuff, and that he'd bring friends.

In no time it was pushing two, and she headed down to open the bar, humbled to register how satisfying her tattooing work was. Handing a drink to a patron was a nice enough transaction, but being extended the honor—and the trust— inherent in etching permanent art onto their skin . . . ? Nothing touched that.

Abilene was off until the evening, and Raina was looking forward to spending the afternoon slump diving headfirst into the small-business book she'd rush-ordered, making notes that might help her turn her hobby into something substantial enough to support her. Selling the bar would give her a beautiful hunk of savings, but she wasn't stupid—that sale would supply her with a retirement fund, but with no plans to ever marry, her working days were far from over. If she did decide to sell up, she wouldn't touch a dime of the money it brought her, not until she was sixty-five. The windfall would offer some security, but no leisure. She had to go into this next phase of her life the smart way.

She opened the bar and welcomed the old-timers, and had gotten two hours into the workday and fifty pages into the book when her mood suddenly took a nosedive.

An early drinker arrived—that fed, the one she'd ripped a new one in at the diner.

"Well, well," she said, leaning on the bar. "To what do I owe this pleasure, Agent Flores?"

"Ramon's fine." He stopped on the other side of the counter, scanning the area and his gaze seeming to halt dead center along the bottle-lined shelf behind her. Dead center, on her dad's urn. He quickly looked back to her. "Do you have a moment to chat?"

"What about? Duncan?"

"Yes."

"What about him?"

"I understand you two are . . . involved."

She smiled. "Wow, well done. Maybe we ought to make that *Detective* Flores."

"So you two are a couple . . . ?"

"We're fucking. And we're friends." What more did a person need?

"But you've never been professionally affiliated?"

She blinked. "A bar owner and a PR sniper? No, not remotely."

"And Duncan has never asked you to do anything inappropriate on his behalf?"

"Oh, we've done all sorts of inappropriate things together, Ramon."

Flores rolled his eyes. "I'll be blunt. Have you laundered money for Duncan Welch?"

That one threw her. "Have I what, now?"

"Have you, say, accepted large sums of money from him

and held it for him? Filtered it through the bar's cash transactions?"

"Where is this even—" *Oh, wait.* "He gave me some cash, for room and board. Three hundred dollars. It's upstairs." All wadded up from having been forgotten in the midst of the sex, and run through the laundry, in fact. She'd been meaning to give it back to him.

"I understand that's not the first sum you've accepted from him."

She had to think a long moment before she caught on. "You mean last month? He did give me cash then, too, you're right. A donation to a party we threw here. Three hundred bucks, maybe four. I can't remember."

"Off the books?"

"Kind of. Some friends covered the cost of the beers that night, and Duncan's little gift paid for the open-bar expenses and then some. Everything went into the deposit bag at the end of the night, and I didn't ring up drink orders. It'd just look like a really profitable day, if you checked the records. I probably made a couple hundred bucks off him in the end."

"Right."

"I don't bother getting picky about the accounting for things like that—it was a friend's welcome-home party. People chip in, I provide the drinks." She shrugged.

"Yet it was held in your place of business."

She put her hands on her hips. "My place of business is pretty casual, as you may have noticed." She cast a pointed gaze around the no-frills barroom.

"Let's hope your accounting's a touch more organized, then."

She froze. "Wait. Are you *auditing* me?"

"In a sense. I'll need your accounting and tax records from the past three years—"

Her arms dropped. "Three *years*? You're investigating Duncan, aren't you? He's been in Fortuity for less than three months."

"Yes, but we need multiple years of records, in order to establish that no unusual patterns have emerged since his arrival. Now, have you *ever* accepted any other large sums of money from Mr. Welch, since you two became acquainted?"

"Aside from ten-dollar tips? No. This is ridiculous."

"This is all in aid of clearing your friend's name, I promise. Provided everything's been aboveboard, of course."

"Of *course*. Jesus, you're a pain in my asshole." She sighed, knowing there was no way out of this. And also that yes, it could theoretically help Duncan's case. "Fine. When do you need this stuff by?"

"Tomorrow morning."

There went her date night, once again. She'd be stuck in the office until all hours, trying to get her shit together. Thank goodness three years covered only her tenure, though—she'd be fucked if she had to make sense of her dad's so-called book-keeping. "Fine. Tax shit, inventory, bank statements . . . What else?"

"Anything with dollar signs printed on it, basically."

"I'm gonna kick myself for even offering this, but I'm also a licensed tattooist. You need to check those records for signs of money laundering, too?"

Flores smiled. "That was my next bit of business. Please."

She shook her head, annoyed as fuck. But her records on that front were already in good order, computerized.

Christ, her entire life would be so much simpler if that was her sole gig. What was the bar these days, really, other than a ten-ton weight slung around her neck?

"Anything else?" she asked. "You need to pry my walls apart, check for stacks of bills? Rip my mattress open?"

"One step at a time." Flores checked his watch. "And one more thing."

"What?"

"An Amstel, please. Provided that little threat about spitting in my drink was an idle one."

She grabbed a bottle from the fridge and opened it, set it on a napkin before him. "Four bucks."

He left her a five and took his beer to a table by the front, dropping off the empty ten minutes later. He nodded politely. "Raina."

"That's Ms. Harper to you."

He smiled. "As you like it, Ms. Harper."

She glared at his back until he was gone, then pulled out her cell. She cued up Casey's number and listened to the tone for four rings. She was poised to hang up and text him instead when—

"Yeah?" He sounded breathless.

"This a bad time?"

"No, this is fine—unless you care that I'm naked. Just ran in from the shower—"

"Yeah, fine. Visual established. Moving on. I need your help tonight at the bar."

"Fucking shit. You realize I'm on stakeout tonight, don't you? From what—two till dawn? Is a man not allowed to sleep?"

"I just found out I'm getting audited by the feds, Case. I can't dig through my filing cabinets and mix drinks at the same time, and I don't want Abilene getting stressed-out, manning the taps on her own."

A noisy sigh crackled the line. "When?"

"Seven till close?"

"Goddamn . . . Okay, fine. It's my night off Mom duty. Probably would've wound up there anyhow."

"Thanks, Case. I owe you."

"Fucking right you do."

They hung up, and Raina wiped her phone's screen with her thumb, heart suddenly beating quickly for no good reason. Duncan's number was listed under *Welch*, which felt funny now. She hit CALL and he answered after a ring.

"Hello, Ms. Harper." Damn, that voice. "To what do I owe the pleasure?"

"What are you up to?"

"Aside from dwelling on the memory of your sex against my mouth?"

Raina flushed hot from her heels to her hair, his phantom tongue and lips whispering between her legs. "Aside from that."

"I just got back. I'm due to have a long call with my accountant in just a couple minutes."

"Wow, I can sympathize there . . . I'm afraid I need to cancel our dinner party, darling. Just had a visit from your little fed buddy. I have to spend the evening digging up my financial records from the past three years, to prove I'm not laundering your bribe money."

"Oh, for *fuck's* sake."

"I know. Anyhow, guess we'll be even now—you stand me up, I stand you up."

"Nonsense. We'll eat in the office."

She pictured it, the two of them camped at the desk in mismatched chairs, papers piled everywhere, bar din drifting through the door. A weird sort of date, but more charming than the ones she normally got taken on. "Okay, then. You're on."

Late that afternoon, Duncan hung up after a marathon of a phone call with his accountant. He sank back on the couch and registered the morning's ride. He had blisters from the stiff new boots, sunburn warming his neck, aching wrists, a twinge in his lower back. He must've covered a hundred square miles with nothing to show for it, and the urgency of yesterday's pursuit had bled out of him, leaving little more than weariness and frustration. He dragged himself to the bathroom to shower away the dust.

At least he and Raina would have their date, he thought as he soaped up. He was looking forward to helping her with her accounting tasks—he was good at paperwork. And he desperately needed to feel useful after the waste he'd made of his day.

And the other task set before him—cooking—he was good at that as well.

Not quite an hour later, he was kicking at the bar's office door, hands busy with steaming plates.

Raina opened it and smiled. "Guess you didn't decide to stand me up again, then."

"Perish the thought." He slipped past her to set the plates on the cluttered desk. Not caring to dwell on his shortcomings as a biker, he'd dressed like a gentleman. And he'd made his specialty, minus a few components not stocked by the small supermarket in the next town—no saffron for the chicken, and olive oil in place of grape-seed. Asparagus, red bell peppers, baby potatoes, plenty of rosemary. It seemed he was a failure as a detective, but at least he still did civility well. "Dinner is served."

"Wow." She accepted the utensils and napkin he procured from his pocket. "Not bad for a bachelor."

"I have a strong domestic streak."

"You do windows?" she teased, sitting.

"I do indeed, as well you know." He locked the office door—this date wasn't what he'd first envisioned, but he'd at least get her to himself, uninterrupted and undistracted, for twenty minutes. Taking a seat across from her, he watched as she took her first bite. Satisfaction moved through him like lust to see the way her lids fluttered.

"Wow," she said again. "I'm not a terrible cook, but you put my best efforts to shame."

"Thank you."

He barely tasted his own dinner, even though he'd not eaten this well since he arrived in Fortuity. Her pleasure felt far more nourishing somehow, particularly in the wake of everything they'd told each other last night.

Duncan had thought before, if he ever found himself in possession of such deeply personal information about Raina, he might wield it as she had done with his OCD — exploit it as a weapon to get himself released from her custody. It had seemed only fair. But he knew now he wouldn't. She wasn't his adversary, not anymore.

They spoke little before their plates were clean, and Raina wadded her napkin with a happy sigh, sinking back in her chair.

He smiled. "Oh good."

"Better than good. I needed that, to get through this crap." Her eyes took in the heaps of records before moving to Duncan's chest, then his face.

"Yes?"

"Just admiring you."

His pulse quickened.

"Your eye looks way better."

"Tell me, have you been as distracted as I have today, remembering last night?"

She seemed to stifle a smirk. "About getting stood up, you mean?"

"No, that isn't what I mean. Do you need reminding?"

"I might."

He stood, rounding the desk. She got to her feet, then sat on its edge, smiling expectantly. Her thighs spread to welcome his hips as he stood before her. She stroked his chest through his dress shirt, fingers toying with his buttons but not undoing them.

"I never would have guessed," she murmured, "how hot it is to get cooked for."

He smiled, pressing his forehead to hers, loving how it felt when their noses touched. The subtle, innocent intimacy of that contact roused him as truly as a probing kiss might. "You're welcome."

He kissed her — lightly, but that was all it took to get his cock growing heavy and warm, pulse restless. Though now wasn't the time to take things too far . . .

Her hand curved around his neck as her lips parted, inviting more. *Well, perhaps a minute wouldn't hurt.*

There was heat in the kissing—that was inevitable, when the two of them came together—but underneath that, something more. Something unmistakably solid and reassuring and *right*, just as he'd felt last night, falling asleep beside her. It stood to reason he'd grown this besotted. This affair was the one pleasant aspect of his life at the moment, a port in the storm of the accusations and threats and uncertainty. So he'd been wrong about that first encounter being the last, and wrong to think a second one wouldn't burn as hot. Deeply, laughably wrong. So, fine, let this unlikely flower bloom for as long as Duncan was trapped here—in this awful town, in this professional nightmare. After all, if he couldn't work, he might as well get laid.

Between fond, lazy, savoring kisses, Raina asked, "How far is this going?"

"As far as we'll both take it—but not until we've sorted your books out."

Her fingers toyed with his collar, a wicked smile curving her lips. "You sure?"

"Quite."

"Can we at least keep kissing for a bit, Herr Taskmaster?"

He took out his phone to mark the time. "Five minutes, starting now."

And as if on cue, the doorknob rattled. Knocking followed.

After an annoyed sigh, Raina called, "What is it?"

Casey's muffled voice answered, "Need your help a sec. The register's jammed and hitting it isn't helping."

"Give me five minutes."

A pause. "Jesus, are you *fucking* in there?"

She snorted against Duncan's collar, then called back, "Five minutes."

"More like two," Duncan shouted, caught up in the ridiculousness of it.

Raina dissolved into silent fits.

"Fucking unbelievable," Casey said, any following words trailing off with his footsteps.

Duncan stepped out from between Raina's legs, mustering dignity. "I think that rather dampened the seduction, don't you?"

She nodded grudgingly. "I think you're right."

He gathered the dishes and napkins. "I'll take these up and make you a coffee, and me a tea. You figure out where on earth we left off."

"Fine." She twisted her hair into a bun and surveyed the heaps of papers. "That was delicious, though. And the food wasn't half-bad, either."

"I aim to please."

She gathered a stack of receipts. "Would you swing through the front and make sure Casey's got the register working?"

"Sure."

He dropped the dishes in the sink upstairs, then headed back down to the bar. The evening was growing busy, and Duncan wended his way between the boisterous drinkers to approach the counter, catching Casey's eye. "Is the register fixed?"

"Yeah, no thanks to you two," Casey said, setting a cocktail before a waiting customer. Duncan had come to appreciate that the man had two settings—gregarious and annoyed. But Casey seemed to relish both equally, and there was no real anger behind the jab.

"Glad to hear it."

"You need drinks?" Casey asked.

"No, merely checking that—"

"Hey," came a voice from just behind Duncan, in tandem with a hard poke in the spine. He whipped around, adrenaline electrifying his body, and found his eyes level with the balding pate of a sweaty, thickset man with a laborer's ruddy tan.

"Yes?"

"You work for the casino, right?" the man demanded, a slur in his voice.

"I did."

"Yeah, I thought it was you. You're that shit who took bribes from Levins."

Duncan frowned. "I'm that shit who was framed by David Levins, yes."

"Them contractors not paying you enough already? You gotta skim off the top, too?"

"Calm your shit down, Bobby," Casey cut in. "Like you know what the fuck you're even talking about. This motherfucker helped get Tremblay and Levins arrested."

Duncan told Bobby, "I'm going to go out on a limb and,

based on your grammar and demeanor, conclude that you're not the county judge. Therefore I could give half a fuck what you think of me. Thanks for your interest all the same."

The man turned to some nearby buddies, pointing back at Duncan. "This here's that fancy faggot who took them bribes off Levins. He ain't even American."

Now Duncan was pissed. But nervous as well. He hadn't been in a fistfight in half a lifetime, and he'd never been much good at the sport. He was built like a runner, and he'd exploited that fact, escaping the schoolyard at a dead sprint more often than not, racing away from whatever antagonism his appearance had inspired. He probably could've been a track star, had he stayed at any school long enough to pursue it.

His running days were long over, though, and he never could seem to keep his snarky mouth shut in the face of bullish dickery.

"My nationality and sexual orientation are neither here nor there," he told the assorted, attentive thugs, adrenaline pulsing. "But I didn't take any bribes. And considering how much I've spent in this bar, I'll not be made to feel unwelcome." On the contrary, this place had begun to feel distinctly like *his*.

"Yeah, we seen your car around town," said one of Bobby's cohorts. "Somebody said those things go for a hundred grand."

Duncan strained at the mob's mingled, muttered comments for keywords—for *jackal*, chiefly, for any clue whether his more calculating accusers might be present—but the rabble was pure static. One thing was clear, however. He was about as popular as a foul smell.

He straightened his spine and slid inside his armor. "Being paid a disgusting amount of money for being excellent at one's job isn't a crime, thank you very much."

Someone countered, "Asshole." His neighbor added, "This bar's for locals. Your foreign ass isn't welcome here."

"Is that so?" Duncan asked coolly. "Is this bar only for ignorant twats? Because I hadn't noticed a sign—"

"Fucking Christ." Casey whapped his shoulder from behind. "You trying to get lynched?"

"It's all over the news, what you did," an older woman shouted. "It's just a matter of time before you get yours."

Duncan cocked his head. "Is that a threat?"

"You called my kid trailer trash," cut in a short tank of a man.

Duncan had to think a moment. "Ah. Now, technically, I believe I called your son a redneck little shit."

Casey groaned. "You just can't fucking help yourself, can you?"

The redneck little shit's father took a step forward, and Duncan braced himself. Then he heard a couple of thumps to his right, and the sound of glass breaking. For a beat he feared someone had just smashed the neck off a bottle, but now Casey was standing beside him—he'd vaulted the bar, knocking an empty to the floor.

"Everybody back the fuck off," he told Bobby and associates. "You don't get to come in here and start shit without knowing what the fuck you're even talking about. Chill the fuck out."

"He called my kid a redneck—"

"And he's fucking right, Ducky. Your kid was shooting dogs with a pellet gun when he was still in Pull-Ups. He's a dick—buy yourself a bumper sticker and tell the world."

Another guy nodded. "That's true, Ducky."

"Boys'll be boys," Ducky said, sounding defensive.

Duncan muttered, "Spoken like the proud father of a future date rapist."

"Would you *fucking shut your face*?" Casey hissed, though the others hadn't caught it.

Ducky cooled off a little, but Bobby wasn't done yet. "None of that changes the fact that this asshole's in cahoots with Levins." He got close, close enough for Duncan to smell the liquor on his breath and tense his jaw, praying he wasn't about to get any more teeth broken. But Casey pushed in between them. He had to be maybe five-eleven to Duncan's six-two, but anyone would've given Casey the odds in a fight—it was like choosing between a junkyard scrapper and a greyhound. Too bad they were facing down a pit bull; Casey really wasn't the ideal Grossier for the job.

"You chill your shit out or we take this outside," Casey told Bobby.

"Not your fight, Grossier."

"You accuse my friend of taking bribes off a man who helped murder Alex Dunn, this sure as shit *is* my fight, cocksucker. So you calm down, or else we head outside. Even if you kick my ass, you're never drinking here again."

Aside from the music and the din of muttered wagers, the

bar had grown quite quiet—quiet enough for every last person to turn at the sound of Raina's boots stamping across the wooden floor.

"What's this about?" she demanded, glaring around at everyone.

"We was just talking shit out," Bobby said, glancing between her and Casey and Duncan.

"Who broke the bottle?"

Casey raised his hand.

"Clean it up and get the fuck back behind the bar. Duncan, get in the office and help me."

Bobby blanched. "I didn't know you and him was friendly—"

"Go home, Bobby," Raina said, eyes blazing. "You're barred for three nights."

"We heard he was—"

"Shut up now or I'll make it a week. The rest of you," she said, rounding on the entire barroom, as though it were filled with her misbehaving children, "show's over."

Abilene passed Casey a dustpan and a bar towel to clean up the glass, and Bobby headed for the door without much drama, one of his pals following, but most of them getting back to drinking.

"Christ Almighty." Raina glared at Casey and Duncan in turn. Then to Abilene. "Pass me a longneck?"

"Sure." The girl handed Raina a beer and a napkin, and Raina stalked into the office, slamming the door. So much for coffee and tea.

Casey went back behind the bar, and Duncan watched him mix a vodka and tonic, unbidden.

"Thank you for that," Duncan said quietly, and it had to be clear that he wasn't talking about the drink. He took out his wallet, but Casey waved it away.

"You got some big-ass balls on you, Death Wish."

"And a rather large mouth, unfortunately. Thank you for being my second just now, or whatever that was."

"You're a beautiful man, Welch. Shame if you got your pretty face all busted open, now that it's all you got left to your name."

"Shame if you get blowback yourself, for coming to my defense."

Casey shrugged. "Fuck those assholes."

Duncan raised his drink to that. After a minute he said, "I won't hold you to what you said, about us being friends."

Another shrug. "Why not? You screwed your comfortable life up to help my brother. You're fucking my friend. You hauled my concussed ass into a truck—whether I'm happy about the fuss that got made or not. What the fuck else does a person need, to qualify?"

Duncan considered that, and raised his glass in appreciation.

"Don't get me wrong—I still think you're a dick. But that never disqualified anybody from earning my friendship before."

Why on earth did that tainted honor hum so warmly in Duncan's chest? Why should he care what a wayward con man thought of him, as a man, or a peer? God help him if that meant he desired Casey's friendship in return.

Still, that didn't much help the fact that this little informal opinion poll had Duncan's popularity rating looking grim. And his potential enemies list looking extensive.

"I'd better go and face Raina," he said. "I'll see you later."

"Probably. Maybe we could take another ride tomorrow," Casey said.

"Perhaps."

Duncan smirked as he aimed himself back toward the office, head held high. No one said anything to him. No one intentionally bumped his arm to make him spill his drink, or even shot him any dirty looks. Even if they had, he couldn't really care.

For the first time in his adult life, Duncan Welch had made himself a friend.

Chapter 20

With the barroom brawl averted and its attendant adrenaline waning, Duncan's evening shifted back to far less thrilling pursuits, and by one thirty, they had Raina's finances in good order.

She'd mellowed in the past few hours, and as she straightened the final stack of invoices and closed them in a folder, she proclaimed, "Done. And how about that? I'm even getting off early for a change."

Duncan stood and stretched. "Our dinner date was rather overshadowed by the demands of accounting ... and by my brush with bodily harm. Would you care to supplement it with a nightcap, or dessert?"

"I actually want to hang around out front until Miah shows up for his watch. I haven't had a chance to talk to him about what's going on. Plus, I owe him some thanks—no doubt he's going back to start another fourteen-hour workday after he's finished playing security guard."

"Right."

So she felt she owed Miah her appreciation, and Duncan had heard her tender the same to Vince, the previous morning. Had she ever once told Duncan thank-you? He had to wonder. For cooking tonight's dinner, or yesterday's breakfast; for buying groceries, or for making sure the window got taken care of? What was different about him, that she seemed so incapable of gifting him with her gratitude?

He'd been through enough therapy to know it must make her feel vulnerable. And yet that only made it sting worse, when last night he'd thought there were no walls left standing between them. He'd told her, *Hold me*, naked and hurting with need, yet she couldn't tell him thank you for something as banal as supper?

He wheeled his chair back to its corner. "I daresay Miah wouldn't be pleased to watch us go upstairs together."

She shrugged. "That'd be Miah's problem."

"Yes, in all fairness, though, it would feel rather rude all the same. Especially as he's exhausting himself for my benefit, and I'm sleeping with an ex he doesn't seem all that over. So I think I'll head up now."

"Suit yourself."

"Should I wait up?"

That brought her eyes to his, and he was surprised to detect a moment's hesitance in her gaze. Then she nodded. "Sure."

His body warmed straight through. "Good."

He went upstairs and opened the kitchen window to let in the cool night air. Astrid kept him company while he loaded the dinner dishes in the washer and cleaned the pans. Chores tackled, he poured himself a vodka and tonic and sat at the table, scanning the day's news on his phone. Comforting to see there remained larger problems in the world than the ones he was mired in.

Just after two, the sound of a vehicle pulling into the back lot drew his attention off his phone. He shooed the cat from his lap and moved to the open window. The motion sensor lights had come on, illuminating Miah as he got out of his truck and slammed its door. A moment later, light was spilling out of the building and Raina appeared through the back door. Duncan tried to leave the window to go back to his time-wasting, but his feet were rooted, stuck fast as suction cups to the linoleum.

Don't hug, he willed them.

They didn't. They spoke, Miah nodded. Raina gestured to the defaced side of Duncan's car, Miah ran an agitated-looking hand through his long hair. Duncan hated to admit it, but the two of them looked terribly *right* together.

But looks are deceiving. And she's not with him, she's with me. For now, anyhow.

But she loved him. She said she still does. And he'll likely remain a part of her life decades after she's forgotten my name.

Miah's dog was in the bed of the truck. As they continued to talk, Raina turned her attention to it, rubbing its ears and setting its tail wagging. Miah gestured to the west; Raina nodded. He pulled out his phone again, spoke to it briefly. A thermos was procured from the truck's cab; then Miah lowered his tailgate and hopped his butt onto it, settling in with the dog at his side. Raina pointed to something behind him, and he reached back and then held out a rifle. She perched it on her shoulder, looking through the sight, then passed it back. Then, freezing Duncan's heart, she put her hand between Miah's shoulder blades, rubbing. He shook his head, flicked his hand as though telling her to go inside.

Duncan ducked away from the window, feeling like an insecure ass.

The lights out back went dark; then steps sounded in the stairwell. Duncan hoped he looked casual when she came through the door a minute later, phone aglow with some news article he'd not absorbed a word of.

"Neighborhood watch in place?" he asked.

"Yup. Now with added guard dog."

"Care for a drink?"

"Sure. Mix me a Duncan Welch special."

He did, and they moved to the den to sit on the couch. She took a taste of the cocktail and smiled. Duncan held his breath until she set it on the coffee table and propped her feet beside it. Then he couldn't bite his tongue any longer. "May I ask you something?"

"Sure."

"Why is it you seem incapable of telling me thank-you?"

She stared at him, glanced at the tumbler, back to him. "It's good. Thank you."

"Not for the drink. For *anything*. For dinner. Groceries. You've never thanked me for a single tip I've ever left you, nor for getting the window mended . . ."

"I never asked you to pay for that."

He sighed, exasperated. "I'm not saying you did, I— Christ. Never mind."

She frowned. "What's brought this on?"

"I don't know. It's been a long day."

"Well, I'm not good at thank-yous. Or apologies. Or saying please, for that matter. I'm kind of a cagey bitch, in case you hadn't noticed. It's bad manners, but don't take it personally."

"You waited for Miah to arrive, specifically so you could thank him. And did you?"

"Yes, I did." She sat up a little straighter. "You know why?"

"No. I don't."

"Because I feel bad for him. He's not sleeping tonight, and he still has feelings for me, but he knows I'm up here with you. I thanked him because I feel shitty that *he's* bound to be feeling shitty. If there's some deep reason I don't thank you, it's because I'm not worried about hurting you."

But you could. And so easily. "I see."

"If you hide a thin skin underneath those suits of yours, I'd never have guessed it." She paused, then picked up her drink and resettled on the couch, kneeling, facing him. She held the glass in both hands, studying it before she spoke. "Do you know what the sexiest thing about you is, Duncan?"

Confused, he frowned. "My pocket squares?"

She cracked a smile. "No. It's the fact that you couldn't give less of a shit about what anyone thinks of you."

"I care very much what people think of me. If I didn't I'd drive a Hyundai and shop at Sears."

"You *don't*, though. You care how you look, and how you advertise, but you honestly don't give a flying fuck if anybody likes that man or not, do you? You do it for *you*. Whatever Bobby and Ducky and those guys called you, I know for a fact it didn't hurt your feelings."

"Well, no. But I don't respect them. And I . . . I rather respect you."

She sat back, looking surprised.

"So I'd like it if you'd say thank-you now and again," Duncan went on, "when I've done something to warrant it."

She looked down at her drink.

"I trust that's not such a hardship . . . ?"

She was on her feet a breath later, setting her half-drunk glass on the table. Duncan started, thinking she was about to stomp out of the room.

"What did I—"

"Come with me," she ordered, putting out her hand to demand his. He gave it, and she drew him to standing, led him to her room. She kept the blinds closed this time, though the neon sign painted them pink. She sat on the end of her bed and pulled off her boots. Unsure what to expect, Duncan followed suit, pushing off his shoes where he stood.

He looked up when he felt twin tugs at his hips, and let her draw him close by his belt loops, into the V of her spread thighs. He was hard in a beat, dizzy when his erection pressed between her legs. He'd quit lamenting how much easier this would be if she'd simply wear a skirt. Since they had their little soul-bearing session, he'd begun to worry there was a reason for her self-imposed dress code. One he didn't care to hypothesize about.

Her hands roamed low, stroking his trapped erection, freeing his belt buckle. She got his pants open and his cock bared, the dry air greeting his flushed skin.

"What's all this?" he murmured.

"This is me," she said slowly, "thanking you."

"I see."

"Believe me when I tell you, Duncan, I'm a great liar—and a coward, just like you called it. You want to know how I feel, you listen when my body's talking, and quit worrying about what comes out of my mouth. You understand?" She clasped his cock, gaze burning up into his.

All he could do was nod, struck dumb by the long, tight strokes of her fist. He held her hair and nailed his gaze to her spoiling hand.

Boiling alive, he peeled away his shirt. He could come in no time, just from this. But then she was tugging at his arms, coaxing him onto the bed, stripping his jeans and shorts and socks. He held her head as she trailed kisses down his neck, his chest, his belly, tickling the hair that led from his navel to his cock. There was no mistaking what came next.

"Stop," he said, but limply. He wanted this as badly as he didn't, confusion and lust and worry tugging him in a dozen directions.

"Not on your life."

"I haven't showered."

"I don't care."

"No, stop. I don't like having things … done to me," he panted.

She shushed him softly.

"Stop. I mean it."

She did, but only to look up into his eyes, lips barely an inch from his beading crown. Christ, she looked good. Tempting.

"Is getting head really so hard-core to you?" she asked. *"Really?"*

His eyes darted, panic seeming to flatten the room. "I don't know. It feels that way. I'm rather uptight."

She smiled at that. "But you've done it before, right? At some point?"

Duncan swallowed.

Her eyes grew round and she sat up straight, hands moving to his hips. "What, never?"

"No. Never." And not because of a trauma—not because he'd ever had this forced on him, or been forced to perform it himself. He'd suffered more than any child's fair share of abuse, but none of it had been sexual.

"I won't ask you why," she said. "But jeez ... Have you ever fantasized about it, at least? *Wondered* about it?"

He nodded. Yes, he had thought about it, and been turned on by the idea, but to actually do it struck him as somehow ... Not *disgusting*. Tacky, perhaps. Too tacky an act for the sort of women he used to fancy as his type. And too aggressive, coming from Raina. It demanded too much from him, even as he'd ostensibly be spoiled by the deed. It demanded receptivity. Demanded that he surrender control and simply take pleasure, and Duncan didn't know how to take pleasure without simultaneously being the one giving it. He didn't know how to be ... tended to. He'd had so very, very little practice at feeling cared for.

"You're going to let me do this," she said, her gaze steady, "and I'm going to love every second of it. And maybe you'll love it, too. And all this is is my mouth on your cock—a woman wanting to make a man feel good. I don't care if it's unladylike, or unattractive, or unhygienic. Or if it makes you feel like the sort of man who likes getting his dick sucked, or how you feel about that. It's what I want, and you're going to give it to me. Okay?"

He blinked, uncertain. Swallowed. Nodded.

Raina smiled. "Thank you."

He flushed. She knelt between his legs, easing them wider. Duncan's eyes shut and he swallowed again, the anticipation looming large and dark and heavy.

She stroked his legs first, palms gliding up and down in lazy trails from his ankles to his hips. In time she grew bolder, and he shivered as her thumbs traced the creases of his uppermost thighs. He was getting hard again. He stole a glance at the evidence confirming that, yes, he wanted this. His cock felt hot and heavy, foreskin drawing back, head flushed—and she'd not so much as grazed him there yet.

All at once, he needed this. Needed to know if her mouth

was warmer than her sex. What the suction would feel like. What her tongue might do, and how tight she'd make her lips. Would she use her hand as well? Would she take him deep, in her throat? Did he even want her to? Christ, he could've been a teenager, for all the certainty he felt.

Her cool hand closed around him, and he groaned from the quenching pleasure of her slow strokes. "Yes."

"You don't have to just lie there," she said.

He realized he was doing just that—surely as erotic as a man bracing himself for a medical exam. One of her hands was on his hip, and he covered it with his own. When she lowered her face, he gathered her hair in the other, wanting the view unobstructed. She blew a soft breath across his aching skin, and his cock twitched in reply. She smiled. Then she kissed him—a whisper of her lower lip along his crown. Another. The softest lap of her tongue.

He gulped a breath. Good as it felt, the anxiety still hounded him. His muscles were taut, eager to be *doing*. He tuned them out as best he could, focusing on the pleasure. And the pleasure was exquisite. She tasted and teased him with the relish of a woman sampling a fine wine or a delicious bite of food. She didn't serve him—she consumed him.

He shuddered as her mouth took him deeper, grunted as she eased back, tongue taunting. He bucked when her hand slid low to cup his balls, and his back arched up off the covers. "Yes."

Cool air enveloped his fevered cock, and she spoke. "Say my name. My actual name."

Surely she'd noticed that he'd never managed to speak those two syllables in simple conversation with her. *She can't say thanks, yet you can't even call her by her own name?* Was she really the cagey one on this bed? *Really?*

She took him back inside. He sat up, gathering her hair in his hand. Her eyes met his, the contact shooting sharp pleasure down the length of him.

"Raina." The name made him feel naked, but the sensation was apt. He dressed her up when he called her Ms. Harper, same as he'd dressed himself, to paper over the vulnerability. But everything was different, since last night. He said it again, craving that exposure. "Raina."

Her mouth was perfection. Hot, slick, hungry. He'd never

felt so big, never felt half so *wanted*. Nor half so naked, or owned. He had to wonder, if he came, would . . . Yes, she would. She'd taste him. Drink him down like whiskey. Fuck, why was that so exciting?

This was so much more than he'd ever guessed . . . and he'd theorized about it plenty in his thirty-eight years. But this was so . . . so intimate. So *fucking* intimate. Dirty, personal; pure and utter spoiling. It made his blood hotter than he'd imagined it could, made the pleasure surge in such exquisite, perfect time with her actions. She was controlling him, and Christ, it felt fucking magical. "Suck me. Please."

I'm not a man who begs, he'd told her once. He hadn't been then, but he'd changed in the past few days—hell, he'd been changing since the second he set foot in her bar. He'd beg for this, and happily.

"Please, Raina. Don't stop."

He felt her moans as surely as he did her lips or tongue or breath.

"I'm close."

And cruel creature that she was, she backed off. He moaned his frustration at her lighter touches and suction, the slower pace, but she seemed determined to draw this out. No—to draw *him* out, he realized at once. He held her hair a little tighter, and gave a gentle, shallow thrust, slipping deeper. Another, and what she offered intensified, rewarding his motions. In time they were moving and meeting as one, her mouth mirroring his curt thrusts, deeper and deeper until her lips teased the hair at the very base of his cock. Fucking mesmerizing.

"Yes. Suck me."

So much more welcoming than any embrace he might crave, any utterance of his name he could request. With every motion she told him, *I want this. I want you.* And it was with those unspoken words ringing through him that he came apart. Her moans joined his as the orgasm crested, and she drank him down.

He knew in that blinding, brazen instant, he'd be fantasizing about this moment for the rest of his life. And just as surely, he knew something else, something that paled this act, utterly.

Good God, I'm in love with you.

Dazed, rattled, and spent, he sank back against the covers, muscles so limp the bed could've been a hot tub.

Raina stretched her body along his and cupped his jaw in

her palm. She held his stare as she spoke. "You got any more doubts how grateful—how *thankful*—I am to be with you?"

He shook his head limply against the pillow, unraveled. Totaled. Obliterated.

"Good." She smiled, leaned in, and kissed his forehead. "You're welcome."

Chapter 21

Duncan woke up well after the sun had risen, finding himself alone—Raina and Astrid were nowhere to be seen, and the clock told him it was nearly eleven. "Dear God."

He gave himself a minute to lie there and remember the things she'd done to him, but stopped before he got too heated. It took an icy shower to finally scare his erection away.

He skipped a shave and dressed for another day of riding, then found Raina and Astrid both in the kitchen, perched on adjacent chairs.

"Morning," Raina said. She was drinking coffee, a book open before her on the table.

"Good morning. What's that you're reading?"

"Small business stuff. In case I ever make something of my side gig. I'd have had a cup of tea waiting for you, lazybones, but I wasn't sure when you might be joining us."

"I can make it myself," he said, and got the kettle heating. "I didn't mean to sleep in."

"I wouldn't even say you did—I don't think I put you to sleep before three."

"Yes, about that . . ." About the most mind-blowing sexual experience of his entire life. "It was rather unchivalrous of me to fall asleep right after."

"Not unchivalrous—merely male."

"In either case, I owe you some reciprocity." Even thinking about it, he was ready to drop to his knees and deliver.

She smiled. "And if I had a spare minute today, I'd totally take you up on that. But I'll be camped out with Flores till God knows when. Then tonight the bar should be packed—Kim's going to do the shoot, with some of my clients."

"Tonight? That's awfully soon."

Raina shut her book and set it aside. "I left a message for one of my clients yesterday—this girl I did an amazing back piece for. I heard back early this morning; she's in town just until tomorrow, visiting her parents. It's probably in the top five of my favorite pieces I've ever done. So I called Kim, then a bunch of other clients, and suddenly it's happening. Here's hoping Flores is done with me early enough that I get to enjoy it."

"How many clients, all told?"

"Five for sure, and I left messages for another dozen. Free drinks can't hurt. And I told everyone to bring friends. It's a start, anyhow."

"An excellent start. Would you like me to draw up a release for them to sign so you'll have permission to use the photos as you wish?"

"Kim's got that covered. You gonna come down and watch?"

Duncan made a face, torn between curiosity and distaste. This woman might have fucked off the great, fussy bulk of his armor, but he still rankled to imagine her hands engaged in such strange intimacies with other men's bodies. Though perhaps the evening might demystify it all.

"We'll see." He rose when the kettle sounded and got his tea steeping.

"You riding today?" she asked.

"I am."

"Not alone, I trust?"

"Casey sounded interested last night. Do you have his number, by any chance?"

Raina laughed. "Now, that is one weird bromance." She pulled out her own phone and Duncan copied down Casey's number.

"Bromance? Perish the thought. Merely a mutual tolerance. When does Flores descend?"

She craned her neck to check the microwave clock. "In about an hour."

"I think it's probably best if we don't mention to him that I helped you sort things out, if he thinks we're somehow in cahoots."

"He already knows we're fucking."

"True." And she was in good shape, either way. The authorities would be hard-pressed to infer any money laundering into the business; the bookkeeping had been chaos before they sorted through the piles, but nothing important was missing. "You should be fine today. Most everything's in order."

"More your doing than mine, but yeah. Man, I've got to keep better records downstairs. My dad's method was always just to shove everything important-looking into the filing cabinet. I really shouldn't have carried on that tradition."

"The feds are grasping at straws—I suspect this is all a formality, and they'll leave you be when nothing obvious presents itself." Duncan bobbed his tea bag and glanced at where she sat. He felt compelled to walk up behind her chair, to lean down and kiss her cheek or temple or the crown of her head, but didn't. He didn't think he was the sort of man who did such a thing, nor that she was the sort of woman who'd welcome it. Ridiculous that it should seem too intimate, considering everything they'd done in the name of sex, everything they'd spoken about. But in a way, that delineation so perfectly encapsulated their . . . courtship? No, not courtship. Their *crossing of paths.* Yes—a brief intersection of two incompatible lives. A fleeting, *glorious*, perpendicular encounter, but not a merging.

Though it was becoming more and more difficult to see it that way. If he didn't know himself so well, he might worry he was growing attached.

Just a by-product of the identity crisis.

He texted Casey and was about to sit, just as Raina stood.

"Need to hole up and get my crap in order with the tattooing stuff." She nodded to the door to her little studio.

"Right. If I don't see you, good luck with Flores." Wait— could he kiss her good-bye, or . . . ? "And good luck with the shoot, if I don't attend."

She leveled him with a look.

"What?"

She curled a finger and he stepped close. She hooked that same finger under his tee's collar and bade him to bend close, until their faces were level. "Come," she said. "Come to the shoot."

And could he really say no to that mouth? After everything it had done for him? "Fine."

"Good. See you there." She kissed his chin and let him go. Astrid followed her to the door to the tattooing room. "Bipeds only, beyond this point," Raina told the cat, and shut herself inside. Astrid's tail twitched irritably; then she sat, glanced morosely back at Duncan, and sighed.

"Chopped liver, am I now? Don't forget who changes your litter," he warned, just as his phone buzzed.

He hadn't expected Casey to be awake, given his security shift, but the text read its a date mf. meet at garage. 12:30.

That gave Duncan time to finish his tea, eat some toast, and put Band-Aids on his blistered toes. He gave Astrid a parting stroke on his way to the stairs, and something odd happened when he stepped into the back lot—his gaze passed easily over the Merc, settling instead on the old bike. Surely an avoidance instinct, since the car's injuries pained him. Surely *not* an affection for this death machine, he decided as he mounted the BMW.

When he pulled the helmet on, a wolf whistle from above drew his gaze to the open kitchen window. Raina grinned and made a cheesy feline growling noise and clawing gesture at him, Astrid in her arms.

"Drop my cat and I'll murder you."

"Go on. Lemme see you start it."

He rolled his eyes and pulled his driving gloves out of his jacket pocket.

"Yes, good," she called as he tugged one on. "Now the other."

"Pervert."

He was relieved when a single, smart stomp had the bike rumbling happily—nothing cooled him quite so readily as feeling incompetent. And he hoped she watched until he'd ridden out of sight.

Down the street, Casey was waiting in the front lot of the garage, astride his bike—or rather, no. Astride Vince's. He was glowering at his phone, and waved a lazy greeting without looking up.

"Afternoon," Duncan called over the growl of the BMW. "Thank you for keeping watch last night. On top of your little show of chivalry in the bar."

"Whatever keeps your neck unbroken, Dunky."

"I see you've borrowed your brother's bike."

"Yeah. You're Mr. Off-Road Warrior, and I can't keep up on my Harley."

"Where are we headed?"

"You tell me. I got no agenda." With a final frown, Casey pocketed the phone.

"That expression suggests romantic troubles," Duncan said.

"I wish—I could stand to get laid, let me fucking tell you. Client troubles, sadly."

Client? "I think I know better than to bother asking."

"That you do," Casey said. "Speaking of agendas. 'Fore we get going, you gotta answer me one question, man."

"That strikes me as hypocritical, but fine."

"What's this all about—you and the bike?" Casey nodded to it. "I'm not complaining, but I know you didn't just watch a Steve McQueen movie last week and get a hard-on for it. And I know it's not some ploy to impress Raina, proving you're one of us or something."

"No?"

Casey shook his head. "Trying's not your style, and Raina's not impressed by anybody. Period. You got some other reason."

Duncan shrugged, a touch unnerved to feel so easily—and accurately—analyzed by this man. Casey Grossier might present as blunt and simple, but more than once he'd shown he was savvier than the good ol' boy he imitated.

"You sound awfully sure of yourself."

"I've seen the way you scan every last inch of the ground," Casey said. "Just tell me you're not trying to find those fucking bones, man."

Duncan smiled, his face growing hot.

Casey's arms dropped to his sides, expression pure incredulity. "You're shitting me. You don't seriously think, what? Tremblay buried them, in Fortuity someplace? When he could've destroyed them, or hid them God knows where, way the fuck away from town? That's beyond needle-in-a-haystack, man. That's a fucking dust mote in the Mojave."

Duncan fished his sunglasses from his jacket pocket and donned them, feeling far too transparent. "It's merely a curiosity that distracts me when I'm out riding, surrounded by all that dirt."

"You couldn't be easier to read if you were a billboard, Welch. But fine. Sure. Let's go take a lovely little scenic cruise through the badlands."

"Yes, let's."

Duncan aimed them east, in the general direction of the

ranch. To the north and south of Fortuity proper stretched long miles of dry desolation, seemingly endless expanses of scrubby high desert, fading into the hills in the distance. He searched the horizon for landmarks—for boulders, lone trees, anything distinctive that a man could hike to from the road. He searched for any sign that this endeavor was anything aside from hopeless. But all that came back was an echoing nothing. The urgency of that strange day must have been some contact high—the doing of Casey's accident and John Dancer's rum. Adrenaline. Klonopin withdrawal, perhaps. Even his reasons for wanting to find those bones had grown hazy ... To clear his name, salvage his reputation, get his job back. To get his *identity* back.

But why?

Did he really miss it all that much? All that grasping at perfection, clutching at a sense of control but never feeling truly possessed of it for more than the odd moment. All that artifice and isolation. He'd shed those things this past week, given up so much control, and to what end? He'd caught only whispers from his compulsions, and not a Klonopin had been swallowed in days. He was drinking less. He was sleeping far better, and having the best sex of his life. Sex like a sizzling, oversize slab of prime rib after years of rice cakes. And he doubted Raina would have taken his perfect self to bed. It had taken his dismantling to earn that invitation.

But it was hard to simply turn his back on twenty years' effort. As ambivalent as he might feel about returning to Sunnyside, neither did he much relish waking up next year with a license to practice bottom-feeder law in Nevada, his face plastered on billboards up and down I-80, bleaching in the sun. WORKPLACE INJURY? GAMBLING DEBTS? MEDICAL MALPRACTICE? CALL WELCH AND ASSOCIATES—THEY DUN-CAN GET YOU THE SETTLEMENT YOU DESERVE!

Shudder. He'd sooner go all in on his urges to fund the bar's improvements, and offer to buy the place outright. Fix it up and run it to Raina's and her father's specifications, free her up to pursue the work that matched her talents, fed her passion. Sure, Duncan had no business running a bar. But he also had no business on this bike, and his adolescent self had had no business thinking he was bound for university ...

No. Silly, idle thoughts.

And the future could wait. Bones aside, all he'd truly cared about of late was getting invited into Raina's bed, and waking up there come dawn. Sitting across the bar from her. Cooking her dinner in the evening and drinking the tea she made him each morning. Watching her pet his cat. Watching his hands moving over her naked body.

Goddamn treacherous infatuation. But it was more than that, wasn't it? He'd never been in love before, but he'd imagined if he ever found himself capable of it, it would've looked far more dignified than all this. More civilized, and elegant.

Not so much. Elegant, no. Fraught and a touch frenzied? Absolutely.

And was that really so surprising? This clinging, addictive persuasion of lust-love had waited thirty-eight years to manifest, after all. Figured the strain that finally laid him low would prove both rare and incurable.

Before long, they turned off the sleepy paved route and onto a dirt road, heading north. The sun warmed Duncan's back through the leather, and Casey sped up to ride alongside him—the only way, given how much dust the bikes kicked up.

Like Raina, the landscape had been growing on Duncan, sneakily, steadily. He couldn't say precisely when it had gone from depressing and stark to raw and wild . . . Since he'd begun getting taken to bed by a raw and wild woman? Or since he'd quit caring what that dust might do to his car and shoes? All those changes, converging as one.

Perhaps it's none of those external things, Duncan realized. *Perhaps it's me.*

They rode for two hours or more, picking their own slow paths through the brush and boulders. Duncan was scanning, always scanning, but Casey rode more like a kid on a dirt bike, flirting with spills simply for the fun of it. Duncan tipped over on a sharp turn himself once, but so did Casey, so he didn't feel too badly about his overall performance. With the sun still high and punishing, Casey slowed to a stop and signaled for Duncan to do the same.

"I need gas," he said, and a glance at his own gauge told Duncan he did as well. They made their way to the Sinclair station on Railroad Ave, parking at adjacent pumps. Casey went inside to pay cash while Duncan swiped his card.

"Couldn't help but notice," Casey said a minute later, eyes on his pump's meter, "you haven't asked me about what happened. When I fell."

Duncan shrugged. "Your brother gave me the distinct impression it was none of my business. Though if you've got a medical condition I ought to know about, I'm all ears, Mr. Grossier."

"Call me Casey, asshat."

"Casey, then. So, do you know what made you fall? Did you get an MRI?"

"No, I was fine. Just the heat, probably, on top of a hangover."

"You were shaking, and talking complete bollocks—"

"I'm not crazy, man. Lay off."

Duncan blinked, taken aback. "I didn't say you were."

"You're the one out here looking for those fucking bones. If anybody's crazy, it's you."

"Apologies."

Casey's chest rose and fell with a deep sigh—perhaps annoyance, perhaps uncertainty. Duncan didn't relish further offending his only platonic human friend, so he offered, "*I'm* half-crazy, you know. So I don't take it too personally."

Those red eyebrows rose. "Oh yeah? How so? Whatever you take those meds for?"

"I've struggled with compulsions and control issues for twenty years or more." Ever since he'd papered over his old identity with his new one, and had grown so obsessively attached to the precarious perfection of the latter. So much of that grasping desperation had left him of late, though. His mental breakdown had offered a peace of mind he'd never gotten from a prescription.

"Compulsions and shit," Casey said. "Like what?"

"I become rather obsessive when I don't have enough work to keep me occupied," Duncan said. "I can clean my bathroom for three hours at a time. Daily. And I need my possessions arranged in a certain way, or else I find it nearly impossible to leave the house. Or I did until a few days ago. Until I swapped all that for a new preoccupation." He nodded demonstrably down at his bike.

"Huh. That stuff doesn't sound *too* bad, though. At least there's meds for it. You met my mom yet?"

Duncan shook his head.

"She's off her rocker—so far off she landed in the next county. She . . . she talks some real spooky bullshit, when she's lucid."

Duncan's body cooled. "Oh? Did Miah tell you what you said, after you fell?"

Casey nodded. "And I remembered some of it, eventually."

"Have you done that before? Had that sort of . . . episode?"

The reply was barely more than a mumble. "Couple times, yeah."

"Oh dear."

Casey snorted. "Yeah. Oh fucking dear. My mom went crazy in her forties, so if it's genetic, I got maybe ten years before I'm wandering around in my bathrobe full-time, muttering like a nutcase."

"Has she been screened for anything? Dementia?"

"I think so, but Vince hates talking about that shit. I never asked what her official diagnosis is, if she's got one."

"If it's hereditary, the two of you could have your DNA mapped. Find out if you share the same indicators."

"Maybe . . ." Casey trailed off, looking thoughtful.

"What?"

"Nothing. I better call it a day out here—I'm opening the bar so Raina can get her shit together for tonight's photo shoot thing."

Duncan nodded, disappointed. He'd rather enjoyed having such a personal conversation. As actual friends might do. "You aren't taking part, are you?" Casey had at least one tattoo— he'd noticed the edges of it on his upper arm, when he wore short sleeves.

"Raina didn't do any of my work, but I'm gonna tell her to get some shots of the bar, too. Benji's'll need a Web page for when the tourists descend."

If there is *a Benji's still,* Duncan thought grimly, resolving to have a little talk with Raina, regarding his wish to help on that front.

"Nobody just wanders into places anymore," Casey went on. "Not without photos and reviews and crap. And I'd totally pose for that shit. I qualify as a hot bartender, right?"

"I can't say you're my type, personally."

He frowned. "Yeah, maybe Raina'd look better. But I could be a patron. 'Still Life with Beard and Bourbon,'" Casey said, framing the imaginary portrait with his hands.

"Arguably more inviting than having your brother play the part." Though Vince would surely be there—the crow's wing on his neck was Raina's work. Duncan wondered which she thought back on more fondly—ex-lovers or former clients. Then he wondered if she'd ever slept with Vince, and his guts flipped inside out. He told his brain to shut the fuck up. He might not be sure of where he and Raina stood, but Vince and Kim had a palpable current strung between their bodies, a confident, mutual magnetism that was at once easy and electric. If there'd ever been anything between Vince and Raina, it was well and truly over.

"You gonna be there?" Casey asked.

"I said I'd stop by."

"I'm sure you'd rather be amputated than tattooed, but it'll be fun to watch. Anyhow, see you later. And don't tell anybody what I said about my going crazy, you got it?"

"Crystal clear."

"Later, Welch."

Duncan nodded. "Grossier." He watched until Casey disappeared around the corner onto Station Street, then looked to the foothills to the west, to the brush and the dry red earth, the mountains beyond.

Follow your hunger. Easier said than done, with the urgency of that first ride bled away, all those eerie words reduced to empty echoes. *Starless night. Hunger. Coyote.* John Dancer fit the bill for the latter, but to what end? To this advice he was finding it harder and harder to follow. His so-called hunger was running dry. Perhaps he needed a rifle leveled at his chest again—that might jump-start his stalled instincts.

"To the coyote himself," Duncan muttered, and aimed himself south.

Chapter 22

AWAY ON BUSINESS, read the poster board nailed to a twisted tree beside the river, yards from where John Dancer's van had been parked on Monday. Duncan slumped. "Shit."

There went his coyote—the last little scrap of his shapeless excuse for a plan. He gave the town one final, long lap, all the way east and along one of Three C's private access roads. All that awaited him there on the open range were scattered cattle, the odd antelope, and a thick assembly of crows gathered on the headstones of an old family cemetery, looking like a bad cliché. Some poor animal must have died amid the stones, to have garnered such an audience, its remains an oasis of blood and flesh. Stark and strange, the way death and life seemed to feed each other out here.

He studied the weathered iron fence that framed the little graveyard. The fence was barely two feet high, with CHURCH worked into its lattice design on one side. *Plenty of bones here,* he thought. Just not the ones he was looking for. He slumped, officially defeated.

Perhaps this was for the best. He had to make good on his promise and show his face at Raina's gathering, after all, much as he'd prefer not to. Feeling tired, and sunburned, and grumpy, and not at all in the mood for mingling with tattoo enthusiasts, Duncan headed downtown.

Though the sun was only just beginning to flirt with the point of Lights Out, the bar's lot was nearly maxed. There were normally half a dozen motorcycles lined up out front, but tonight he counted twenty or more. Duncan added his to the line and took off his helmet, making a half-assed attempt to smooth his hair as he walked to the entrance.

The front room was as noisy as he'd ever known it, music and chatter elbowing each other for dominance. Everywhere Duncan glanced—tattoos. It was like a mini convention, with everyone dressed to show off their trophies, men and woman alike. He couldn't even take in the designs, too overwhelmed by the . . . realness of it. Of her clients. They were all ages and sizes, all ranges of attractiveness. It took him a long moment to even spot Raina in the crush.

She was way across the room, talking intently with Kim and a ropy woman with a rainbow's worth of color splashed from her wrists to her jaw. Duncan didn't relish intruding. Or if he was being honest with himself, he didn't relish walking over and discovering precisely how Raina might greet him. Would she be pleased to see him? Would she kiss him, in front of these witnesses, introduce him to people with whom she shared personal histories? Or would she toss him a passing glance of acknowledgment and then turn back to more pressing matters? Would he discover she was proud to be linked with him in front of this crowd, or not? After such a long, fruitless, discouraging day, he wasn't sure he had it in him to find out. He eyed the bar, thinking he'd nurse a drink and let her discover him there herself. *Coward.*

Could he really not bear to walk up to his lover, of all people? He wasn't a child, and these weren't the popular kids, poised to mock him. He summoned his nerve and crossed the room.

Kim spotted him first. Her hands were busy with her camera and a shade, so she smiled her greeting while Raina talked with the colorful woman and a couple of other such specimens. Duncan did his best imitation of blasé patience, but as the moments wore on, he felt his anxiety rising.

Kim moved to stand next to him. "Do you feel like as big of a square as I do?"

"Never more so in my entire life. How's it going?"

"It's awesome, actually. The most fun I've ever had on a paid shoot. Beats the pants off engagement photos—that's for sure."

Duncan replied without even taking in what he said— Raina's eyes had met his. Only for a beat, and then she was back to chatting with her friends.

He wished he had a drink, something to occupy his hands. Kim excused herself to get the next shot set up, leaving him to hover awkwardly at the edge of the crowd. Raina was too absorbed to take the slightest notice of him, and he couldn't suffer this invisibility another moment. He headed for the bar, unable to recall the last time he'd felt so alienated.

She had to know how he felt about her. Had to see it on his face when their bodies came together, feel it when they held each other. They weren't a couple, weren't anything official or explicit, but surely she *felt* this.

To judge by that reception? He rubbed at his heart and throat, anxiety rising.

But Raina wasn't the kind to tolerate bullshit, nor to define the bounds of a relationship with unspoken words, vague signals. She was the least coy woman Duncan had ever met, so maybe he needed to spell it out. Not *I love you*, not just yet. Too soon. But a gift. A gift lavish enough to tell her, unmistakably, *This means something to me. You and I mean something.* And thankfully gifts were an arena Duncan excelled in.

It was seven, and Duncan's favorite jeweler back in San Diego would be closed. No matter, though—for the amount of money he intended to spend, he felt no qualms slipping outside and making use of the owner's private number. He explained what he wanted, and she said she had just the thing.

He felt a touch calmer as he went back inside, if not completely. He was out of place in Fortuity at the best of times, but tonight he'd felt downright discarded. It was the amorphousness of everything, just now. His professional issues were beyond his control, but at least he could put to rest any ambiguity regarding where he stood with Raina. Her gift would arrive by Friday morning, and he'd tell her how he felt. If not "I love you," at least "This is real to me." And he'd have her answer, whether it made his heart soar or sent it crashing to the ground in flames.

He realized now why he'd never dated anyone he stood a chance at feeling deeply for—caring this much felt like a crushing amount of power to surrender to another person.

He looked down to find his hands shaking, and felt the beginnings of an attack brewing. Could feel himself catching on invisible brambles, the edges of him fraying. His pills were upstairs, but he didn't fancy having to pass right by Raina to go and get them. A drink would have to suffice.

On his way to the bar, amid the sea of hard-bitten strangers, he spotted a familiar face—Vince. The man was sitting at the counter with a beer before him, chatting with Casey, who was pouring drinks. Casey skirted the bar with a pitcher in each fist, leaving Abilene manning the register.

Duncan neared, staring at Vince long and hard, all at once overcome. *He saved her,* was all he could think. He'd not laid eyes on the man since Raina told him what had nearly happened to her.

Vince noticed Duncan and raised a wary eyebrow, seeming to misinterpret the scrutiny. "Welch."

Duncan stood by the empty stool at Vince's side. "Evening."

"We got a problem I don't know about?"

"Not at all. I want to buy you a drink."

Now his entire brow furrowed. "Do you, then? How come?"

"I had rather a long talk with Raina," he said, taking out his wallet. "About certain events."

Vince looked puzzled for a breath, and then his expression went pitch-black with recognition.

"What spirits do you drink? Bourbon?"

Vince shook his head. "I'm not drinking to that night. Not ever."

"I'm not asking you to. It's just a token—" He was cut off by Vince's broad palm rising between their faces.

"Don't want it. Just treat her good and don't ever fucking bring it up with me again."

Duncan sat, feeling more foolish than ever. Fuming. He might as well have been slapped by that hand for the way his face was blazing. "Fine."

What did it fucking take, to find oneself on par with these people?

Only a couple of weeks ago, Duncan had considered himself so above them all. Enlightened, successful, on an enviable trajectory in every way. But he was coming to realize he was dead broke in all the currencies that mattered to Raina and her friends. Loyalty, history, trust—even among thieves. He felt diminished, barely better than the child he'd worked so hard to erase from his identity.

The only thing he felt rich in, just now, was sex. Passion. He had that in abundance, though at Raina's behest. He stole a glance, finding her laughing, across the room. Laughing at someone else's joke, someone she'd not felt moved to introduce him to. Laughing as he'd rarely caused her to do himself. She could grow bored of him tomorrow, and then he really would have nothing aside from a stock portfolio, a condo, a cat.

And only one of those things had ever seemed to love him back.

When Abilene caught his eye, holding up the Absolut bottle questioningly, he nodded. "Double." Again, he wished he had a pill handy. He could feel himself shaking, feel his hold on his emotions growing slicker by the moment.

"How's the bike treating you?" Vince asked, not looking at him.

"Better than expected."

"Case and I want to get everybody out for a group ride this weekend. Morning, because of Raina's schedule. Probably Sunday, because of Miah's."

"In lieu of church?" Duncan asked, then thanked and paid Abilene when she set his glass before him.

Vince smirked. "You could say that. You're welcome to come. Case said you've pretty much mastered the off-road stuff, and this would only be pavement."

"'Mastered' is far too generous a word. And I'm not allowed outside town lines at the moment."

"Shame."

Duncan smiled, feeling cold and apart. An outsider. "I'm surprised to have garnered an invitation. I can only imagine you still feel beholden to me."

"Not about feelings, Welch. I don't hate you, don't love you, either. But you're with Raina, and she's one of my best friends. Raina'd invite Kim along, whether they were friendly or not."

"So I'm some kind of Desert-Dog-in-law, for as long as Raina and I are sharing a bed?"

He'd meant it as a joke, but Vince nodded. "Pretty much."

Duncan couldn't hide his exasperation—it rattled out of him in a weary sigh.

"Spill your guts, Welch."

"What precisely would it take for me to actually earn your respect, Vince? I've lost a tooth for you, lost my *job* over you. Learned to ride a worthy vehicle, came to your brother's aid." He'd taken up this man's obsession, for Christ's sake, lost days of his life now, looking for those wretched bones. "Does one of you need a kidney, perhaps? Do I need to die for one of you fuckers?"

"Since when does a man like you care about the respect of a man like me?" Vince countered.

Since I fell in love with your friend. Because this man had saved her from something too heinous to imagine, something that could have broken the spirit he'd so come to admire. "Since I realized I respect *you*, Vince," he said simply. "And I can't stand feeling like the lesser man. So tell me what it would take so I can bloody get on with it."

Vince's smile was mild and a touch uncertain. "You're gettin' kind of emotional on me, Welch."

"Don't I know it . . . ?" He sighed, rubbed his face. Sipped his drink. Tried to surrender to the swirling clouds of discomfort gathered all around him. He studied the tattoo on Vince's neck—the crow's wing Raina had drawn there. More dark feathers all down the man's arms. Rendered shiny and black, just like those malingerers Duncan had seen out by the ranch that afternoon, in the cemetery. A perfect match, he thought, those birds and Vince Grossier. Brash, shameless scavengers, born in this town and surely planning to die here—

"You in love with her?" Vince asked.

Duncan blinked, upended. "Why do you say that?"

"Because dead pets and new love are the only things I know of that make men lose their shit like you seem to be doing."

"Well, my cat is alive and well, so make of that what you will." He drained his glass with a wince. "Good night, Mr. Grossier."

"I was Vince a minute ago. You regressing?"

Duncan ignored that. "Enjoy your evening."

"Enjoy your identity crisis."

"Indeed." And with that, Duncan headed for the back stairs. Raina had wandered elsewhere, so there was no need to discover if his presence would go ignored a second time. But then he found his feet carrying him past the stairwell, through the hall to the rear door. Found his hand on the knob, then had the indigo sky above his head once more. He let his feet lead him past his sad car and around the building, right back to his bike. Right back to fixation, always his dearest friend when he felt lost in his own skin.

And something was growling in his belly. Something was tugging, but he couldn't figure out what. He shut off the need for a *why*, and instead he let the hunger lead him.

What would John Dancer say? He conjured the man in his mind's eye.

How would one man bury those bones?

With a shovel, obviously.

You've been to the building site. You think they dug those foundations with a fucking shovel?

No, not even with backhoes—with dynamite. But that was in the foothills. Elsewhere the ground was soft enough for one man to dig up, surely.

He rode down Station Street, then east. He passed the little clapboard church that marked the end of downtown, its steeple a fang stained yellow by the beam of a sallow spotlight.

Church. He frowned, feeling snagged on that word. Beside the building was a dead tree, the silhouette of its twisted branch looking like talons clawing the sky. *Fangs and talons.* Duncan had scavengers on the brain—coyotes and crows. Those crows that had shat on his car. The ones etched all over Vince's skin. *Church.* Those crows that had loitered in the Churches' lonely little cemetery way out in the ranch land that afternoon. Loitering . . . but with no obvious purpose. No evident prize, yet so much intent. Just like Duncan. All intent, no payoff.

Dancer's voice cut through his jumbled thoughts. *You think Jeremiah Church's great-great-granddaddy dug graves with TNT?*

Of course not. Some spots must be soft enough for shovels.

Soft enough for shovels. Designed for burying the dead.

Duncan frowned.

Quiet, remote spot, the voice taunted. *But not too far from the road. All partitioned off with a pretty little fence and everything. Just needs a neon sign and a flashing arrow.* BONES GO HERE.

Nonsense.

But even nonsense seemed worth pursuing, when the alternative was to give up entirely.

Duncan was beyond racing the sunset—the dark had already swallowed all but the white buildings and lit windows. No matter. No matter that the bike's headlamp was completely inadequate, because once he left the town proper, the roads were deserted. Past Three C's arch, and he began to question what he'd even seen, the rutted dirt access road appearing miles later than he'd expected. He took a right, the world becoming deep blue above, black below the horizon. He stopped long enough to pull out the powerful LED flashlight Vince had left in the bike's cargo box. He gripped it and the handlebar in one hand, making an already awkward ride all the worse. In three days, he'd tipped over or fallen perhaps ten times. In the next three miles, he wrecked an additional four. Slowly, harmlessly, but still. If he couldn't find that bloody graveyard, he'd be—

In the glare of the beam, four glowing discs. *Eyes.*

Coyotes, but more important, the bright gray glow of limestone slabs. He skidded into yet another graceless dismount, his surely already black-and-blue leg earning fresh bruises.

No matter. He felt no pain, only purpose. He was on his feet, beam illuminating the two scrappy scavengers. Tucking his flashlight in his armpit, he stole a trick he'd seen Vince use once, clapping and bellowing until the animals slunk off into the blackness beyond the artificial aura.

He walked to the cemetery, no more than fifty paces from the road ... but five miles or more from the nearest streetlight. Discreet, but distinct. And first the crows had made a curiosity of it, now the coyotes.

And me.

What did they smell that he couldn't? he wondered. The cemetery wasn't suspicious, though, merely eerie. He stepped over the low fence, mentally apologizing to Miah's dead relatives. No X marks the spot, just coyote tracks in the dirt. He followed them to where the earth turned powdery, churned up by coyotes. A large, thick headstone lay flat on the ground— intentionally or because it had been overturned, Duncan couldn't guess. Eugene E. Church was carved into it, the letters softened in the decades since it had been carved—died 1932. And there was a gutter framing the fallen marker, a rut carved in the dirt by scrabbling paws. A deep one.

Suddenly the headstones all shifted in unison, approaching headlights washing the scene in added dimension, the shadows of the stones and fence and grass blades sliding across the ground. Duncan squinted to the road, but it was impossible to see who'd arrived with their high beams trained in his direction.

He heard a door slam, and shouted, "Hello," as he got to his feet.

Not Miah. Please not Miah. The man had never trusted Duncan, so finding him on his property, poking around the graves of his dead relatives ... ? Yeah, if ever he was going to earn that fistfight, now would be it.

"Welch?" Shit, he knew that voice, and that body as Miah's

long silhouette started toward him, rifle in hand. He said, "To me," and in a breath his dog was trotting at his side. And that dog had never looked quite so intimidating.

"I realize this doesn't look very good," Duncan said.

Cowboy boots crunched over the dry earth. "You know this is private property?"

"I suspected as much. Apologies. My ride took me rather far off the beaten track."

Miah stepped over the fence, stopping mere feet from Duncan. He rested the rifle on his shoulder, posture taut and leering. His black hair had grown long of late and his beard was nearly full, and Duncan had to remind himself he had about four years and three inches on him. Miah moved and spoke with the inherent, egoless confidence of a man who broke horses and roped cattle, and had probably shed stoic, manly tears over the bodies of animals he was forced to euthanize. With his rifle. At sundown.

Trimming Astrid's claws is no trip to the malt shop, either, Duncan assured himself.

"You wanna tell me what the *fuck* you think you're doing on my land? In my family's fucking *cemetery*?"

"It won't happen again." Though if Duncan's intuition did indeed work, before the night was over, there could be quite a party out here in the middle of nowhere. He glanced to the side, to that overturned headstone.

"No, it goddamn will *not* happen again. But you tell me why right now or God help me, I will *fuck* you up before I even bother getting your ass arrested."

"I thought I saw something strange here this afternoon, when I was out riding."

Miah's chin cocked with the force of a shotgun. "Saw what?"

"There's a large headstone just there, lying on its back. Eugene Church."

He frowned. "What do you mean, on its back? Show me."

Duncan aimed the beam on it. Miah snatched the flashlight from him. "Son of a bitch."

"I take it it's not usually like that."

"And what's with all the tracks? Did the coyotes dig it loose, or some drunk asshole?"

"I'm not certain it was either," Duncan said, then eyed Miah's dog. "Does he have a keen sense of smell?" he asked, pointing.

"She's a dog, so yeah."

"Would you indulge me for two minutes?"

"Why in the fuck would I do that?"

"Please. Just let your dog sniff around, just there. I was riding earlier today and I saw a load of crows gathered here. And when I first came tonight, two coyotes."

Miah frowned. "They're probably smelling blood from a dead animal."

"A dead animal, tucked beneath a fifty-pound slab of limestone? Please, Mr. Church. Two minutes of your time."

Miah shook his head, but his sigh was limp with surrender. To the dog he said, "That'll do, King." It relaxed visibly—posture softening, tongue appearing—then left them momentarily, its main concern seeming to be its bladder.

"So your female dog is named King?" Duncan asked.

"You can go fuck your small talk, Welch."

"As you wish."

The second the dog was done with its business, it returned to the cemetery at a trot. Then it changed course abruptly, snuffling around the fallen stone.

"Because of the coyotes," Miah said. "King."

The dog ignored its master, now sniffing madly at the ground all around the stone. Its tail was frantic, paws scrabbling at the rock's edge, then pacing, digging, pacing, digging, whining.

"Whoa— Hey! King, here to me."

The dog abandoned its frenzy to stand by Miah's side. "Jesus, she never cries. Load up," he ordered, and the dog took off toward the truck.

"There's something under there," Duncan said.

"No lie. And dead animals don't bury themselves, tucked up all cozy under gravestones." Miah eyed him. "If you know what the fuck this is about, tell me now, Welch."

Duncan swallowed. "I've a strong suspicion I do."

"And?"

Duncan looked to the ground, lit up like an alien landscape before them. "And I think this is where Tremblay hid them. The bones your friend was murdered over."

Chapter 23

For half a minute, Miah just stared back at Duncan, black eyes wide.

"Bones?" he finally asked.

Duncan nodded.

"Like the ones from whoever got burned up in that mine?"

"I don't know for sure. I don't *know* anything. It's just what I suspect."

"Based on?"

"Three days' exhaustive riding, a few scavengers, a gut feeling. Some logic." Though not nearly enough for his comfort.

Miah looked to the stone, and took a deep breath. "If it's nothing, and we move this thing, no harm done. If you're fucking right, we could be contaminating a crime scene."

"We'd sound like idiots if we called the feds to do it for us and then found nothing, so I vote we move it."

"All right, then." Miah leaned the rifle against the fence and got in position, and Duncan set the flashlight down and did the same.

"On three. One. Two. Three." Fifty pounds? Try a hundred. Duncan pulled so hard his bad elbow screamed, but nothing.

"Again," Miah said. "One, two, three."

And after a moment, the stone lifted. Just an inch or two, but with the next heave they managed to tip it up onto its edge, then eased it onto its face, exposing the ground it had been covering.

Miah murmured, "Sorry, Great-great-grandpa."

Duncan grabbed the light. The earth he shone it on didn't look like anything special—more pebbles, more dried grass. He got to his knees and began drawing dirt aside, flashlight clamped between his cheek and shoulder. Miah followed suit. Duncan's already thumping heart raced, as clods of dry roots came away too easily, as though they'd been wrenched from the dirt already. *Someone buried something here,* was all he could think, the realization of it a frenzied mantra after all this blind speculation. *Someone buried* someone *here.*

"Whoa." Miah froze, and Duncan could see why. A black stone as big as a plum, amid the rusty red and sandy brown.

Not a stone.

"Your sleeve," he said to Miah.

Miah had a long thermal shirt on, and he understood. He wrapped his hand in his cuff and began clearing the dirt from around the unmoving black shape. Not a stone, no. A knob of bone, the tip of a femur.

"Fuck—fuck—fuck—fuck—fuck." Miah was on his feet in a blink, slapping his dirty sleeve against his jeans as though it were on fire. "Fuck. Jesus. This is fucked. Call the fucking feds."

Duncan stood, heart pounding with fear and triumph at once, adrenaline coursing like a narcotic. He pulled out his phone and found Flores's number, hit CALL, but nothing—zero signal. "Goddamn it. My carrier's useless out here."

Miah offered his own phone, hand shaking visibly. Duncan cued up the digits, and after four rings—

"Flores."

"It's Duncan Welch. If you're not dressed, I suggest you remedy that."

"What is it, Welch?"

He took a single rattling, intoxicated breath and said, "I've found the bones."

A pause, miles long. "You found the bones."

"Correct. I'm just going to wait until you and your people show up."

"Where are you?"

"If you head east past the Three C ranch's main gate and take the dirt access road about four miles farther, you'll see my motorcycle and Jeremiah Church's pickup perhaps another two miles down the road."

"Don't move, you hear me?" The sounds of a frantic man were layered behind his stern voice—keys jingling, clothes rustling. "And don't fucking touch anything. What phone are you calling from?"

"Church's cell. Do you need the number?"

"It's in my call log. Just stay right where you fucking are," Flores ordered, and the line went dead.

Duncan handed the phone back. "Now we wait, I suppose." The chemicals were already bleeding out of him, manic energy giving way to a softer persuasion of shock. And a tidal wave of uncertainty—it wasn't as though Duncan's achievement didn't reek of wild coincidence. Of *outrageous* convenience.

Miah shook his head and stared skyward, into an ever-expanding sea of stars.

Miah blew out a mighty breath. "Goddamn, I could use a drink just about now. This is so completely fucked." He sat on the ground, forearms on his knees.

"Agreed." And Duncan was humble enough to be grateful he wasn't alone in it all. "I appreciate your—"

Miah waved his words away like a nasty smell. "I'm not here for you. And I'm not here because it's what Raina would want me to do, or Vince. I'm here for Alex, you got that?"

Duncan nodded.

"Good. So don't waste your breath thanking me."

"Noted."

Miah called his dog to where he sat.

After a pause, Duncan said, "You're working awfully late."

"We've found evidence of some drug dealing happening out here lately. I've taken to making the odd sweep after dark, see if I can't catch the fuckers."

Casey's addled words echoed in Duncan's memory. *A fire on a starless night.* The rarest of conditions out here, no doubt. And a fire, set by whom? By a drug dealer? Duncan wondered for a split second. He set the ridiculous thought aside. He was reading mysteries into everything in this state.

Miah kept his attention on his dog, scratching its neck. "I heard Raina's got a thing tonight. How come you're not there?"

Duncan shrugged, mood souring. "I stopped by."

Miah smiled, neither cruel nor kind. "Lemme guess—not a big fan of her hanging out with a load of men she's seen half-naked, right?"

"Something not unlike that."

Miah nodded. "Been there. I used to tell her it was don't ask, don't tell, with me."

"It's a bit more complicated when you can hear the buzzing coming from the next room. At any rate, I'm sorry for ruining your night. I couldn't have blamed you for calling the authorities. Or beating me senseless."

Miah just shrugged.

Silence descended for ten minutes or more, until vehicles appeared down the road.

"King, load up." At once, the dog ran and leaped into the bed of the truck and Miah stood.

Flores's silver SUV and a BCSD cruiser approached and parked. Two male deputies appeared, and Flores and his sometimes partner exited the SUV, and the four of them came marching across the dirt toward Duncan and Miah with duffels and bins in tow—crime scene accoutrements, presumably.

"Where?" Flores demanded.

Duncan pointed and kept his mouth shut and his feet planted, watching as spotlights were assembled and switched on, illuminating the cemetery.

Flores crouched, not speaking for nearly a minute. Then, "No way. No fucking way."

And the authorities got busy. Duncan and Miah were ordered to stay put, and in time another cruiser appeared, then another. A wide area was cordoned off with tape, all the way from the graves to the road.

It was easily forty minutes before Flores broke from the group to approach Duncan and Miah. By then they'd already told their story to two other agents. Flores dusted his shins with latex-gloved hands, a limp halting his gait after all that time kneeling.

"It's them, isn't it?" Miah asked him. "Those goddamn bones Alex got killed over."

"They're bones, yes."

"Burned?" Miah asked, but Flores ignored him.

He stopped before Duncan and stared him dead in the eye. "You got any idea how bad this looks? How fucking suspicious *you* look?"

Duncan's stomach turned. "That's not lost on me."

"You just . . . *found* these. Out here, miles from any place."

"That's accurate. 'Miles from any place' seemed a good place to start looking, considering what I was after."

"How, Welch? If you didn't know how they wound up here to begin with, how? On private land? Based on *what*?"

Based on that fucking hunger bullshit. Instinct had muted logic . . . or perhaps enhanced it. But intuition wasn't proof, and Duncan needed very badly to sound as rational as possible just now.

He forced a calm breath, tired deep down in his own bones. "I tried to imagine what Tremblay would have done with them. Put them somewhere hastily, somewhere he stood a chance at finding them again, when he had the luxury of destroying them properly, perhaps. Trust me, it's no coincidence I wound up out here. I've ridden every mile of passable road in this town, looking for a place that screamed both discretion and distinction. I saw the crows here, this morning, and thought little of it. Then coyotes tonight, and that toppled headstone . . ."

Miah nodded. "That's true—he didn't *just* find them. He's been riding around since Monday."

Flores raised a snarky eyebrow. "I'd love that statement from a character witness who's not also a part of your little motorcycle gang. What do you all call yourselves? The Dirt Dogs or something?" Duncan knew Flores's style well enough to guess the gaffe was intentional.

Miah made a gruff sound at that, like a rankled bull. "Look, this pompous dick is sleeping with my ex. Trust me, I wouldn't lie to protect him."

"Three days of looking," Flores said, turning to Duncan, "against the sheer square acreage of Fortuity's badlands, with the help of some woodland friends. Fuck of a lucky break, Welch, that's all I'm saying."

Duncan's temper was fraying. He needed a Klonopin. With the blind drive of his mission suddenly gone, all the anxiety and uncertainty he'd been ignoring was exposed, bright and raw as an open wound. He wanted to go home to Raina. He wanted her arms around him, his face tucked against her throat. He wanted her warm sheets and body, and her voice telling him everything was going to turn out okay. Wanted warm recognition in her eyes, not the passing, indifferent glance he'd been offered at the bar.

He didn't know anymore if this past week's insanity was a good or bad thing. Only that it had changed him, that he'd never been laid so bare before—never been *laid* so intensely in his life. He only knew he really didn't care what anyone thought of his car anymore, or his clothes, or even his innocence. He only cared that he got to see that fire in a woman's eyes when she took him to bed. Only cared that he got to feel wanted for a few hot moments at a time, wanted on a level he'd never felt before—not as a lover or a man or a human being.

Christ, he was so fucking fed up.

"I called you, you know," he said to Flores. "*I* called *you*. If I had anything to do with Tremblay and Levins's cover-ups, why the fuck would I produce these bones and help your investigation?"

"Plenty of reasons."

"I'm innocent." Duncan nodded toward the crime scene, lit up like a tiny stadium. Press had begun to show up, kept at bay by BCSD officers. "Dental records or missing persons leads are going to identify this body," Duncan said, "and Levins's lie is going to unravel—you know as well as I do that he's full of shit. Fingers are going to get pointed, and none of them will be aimed at me."

"Don't tell me what I know, Welch."

"I assumed I was merely giving your intellect due credit," Duncan said sharply, fevery from anger. Behind them, camera flashes strobed as the exhumation continued. "The bottom line is, it doesn't matter how suspicious I look. I won't be disbarred, because I won't be found guilty of anything. But if Sunnyside rescinds my termination tomorrow, fuck them. Not even an *obscenely* generous bonus is going to keep me in this terrible town a single day longer than need be." He pictured Raina then, and wondered how true that statement might actually be. "I can be found innocent tonight, and I'm still basically ruined."

"You already planning your defamation case?"

Duncan took a deep, ragged breath, struggling to muster some semblance of calm. "I don't even bloody know. I just want this to be over, Mr. Flores. I want permission to get on with my life. I want answers. That's why I found these bones for you. And I'm not even asking for a thank-you card."

"The both of you are going downtown," Flores said to Duncan and Miah.

"For fuck's sake," Miah said. "He just did your goddamn job for you."

Flores whistled and called a couple of patrol officers over. "These two need to be detained and questioned. Somebody get them into separate cars. Church can go to a holding cell, Welch in my office."

Miah tossed his hands up, exasperated. "Wow. You're welcome." As he was escorted to the road, Duncan heard him say, "I gotta drop my dog off."

Before Duncan could be led away, he turned to Flores. "Wait. One phone call first. One fucking minute."

"Later. At the station."

"Now, please. No privacy required—I just want to tell Raina why I'm not coming home tonight, all right? One minuscule little favor, after the tremendous break I've just given you. *Please.*"

Flores eyed him, expression hard.

"One minute," Duncan repeated. "Even criminals get a phone call."

"Later."

"It's far more modest a prize than the posted reward for leads to do with those godforsaken bones."

"*Later,*" Flores repeated.

Godforsaken. That word echoed, and Duncan cast his gaze on the crime scene. *But not completely forsaken.* Whoever those bones had once been, whatever they'd done to inspire another person to murder, those things would be known. It could be shocking how easy it was for people to be forgotten. Discarded. Deemed inconvenient and shut away in a hole or a box or an institution and left to rot. But this man or woman or child wasn't slipping so quietly out of public consciousness.

No. He or she would be front-page news by the time the sun rose.

Chapter 24

Hooded bulbs illuminated the pool table—and the gigantic biker sitting on its felt in a sleeveless vest, gripping a bottle of beer between his legs. His leather-clad wife, Juliette, was standing a few feet away, angling a white reflector thing that looked to Raina like a miniature trampoline.

"That's great, Bill," Kim said from behind her camera. "No need to be a statue—feel free to take a drink or whatever, talk to people." The camera clicked madly on its tripod, the lens focused on Bill's spectacular half sleeve—a shoulder-to-elbow full-color of the Virgin Mary. Raina's specialty wasn't portraiture; she much preferred text and line work. But Bill's piece—like the imitation Tiffany billiard lamp—had a stained glass look, and she was damn proud of how it had come out, and how it had held up.

"That's a wrap," Kim announced, standing up straight and freeing her camera. "Want to see?"

Bill eased himself off the table, and Raina joined him and Juliette, gathering at Kim's shoulders. She cycled through the dozens of photos she'd taken, and they were stunning. The green of the table and the bright primary colors of the pool balls under that bright light, the colors of the tattoo and of the lamp . . .

"Fuck me," Raina said. "You are *good*."

"No doubt," came Vince's voice, and he snuck up from behind to wrap his arms around his girlfriend's waist and admire the shots. She'd taken ones of Vince before anyone else—to warm up, she'd said. They were gorgeous, too. Striking. They'd look amazing in black and white, especially next to vivid shots like these ones of Bill. Raina hadn't cared about a Web site last week, but now she couldn't wait to display these pictures. They made her feel undeniably proud, and legitimate. The real deal. A real *artist*. So much more than a beer dispenser.

And as she glanced around the bar, she reveled in what was the most enjoyable night she'd spent down here in recent history . . . It was enjoyable because she finally felt recognized, for what she wanted to be. In a breath it became clear; the time had come. Time to give herself permission to put her own hopes ahead of her dead father's.

She knew in that moment, she'd be selling this place in the next year.

Raina hit PAUSE on that bittersweet thought, turning back to Kim.

"I know you haven't billed me yet, but based on your quote, I'm not paying you enough."

"I'm surprised she didn't pay *you*," Vince teased, letting Kim go. "She's been peeing her pants all day, waiting for tonight."

Kim smacked his arm. "Gross. But guilty," she admitted, gaze lingering on her screen. "Who's next?"

"Melissa. Long black hair," Raina said, pointing across the barroom. "Halter top. She's got a huge back piece."

"And a fascinating profile," Kim said, eyeing her subject and thinking aloud. "Think I'll get her from behind, sitting at the bar, head turned to take a drink . . ." And she walked off with the tripod and shade to get the next shot strategized. Vince watched her go, predictably.

Casey wandered over with spent longnecks speared on his fingers, looking like Edward Bottlehands. "Happy so far?" he asked Raina.

"That's a ridiculous understatement."

"I'm feeling kinda left out."

"Only yourself to blame, Case. You never gave me the chance."

"I left, like, three years before you even got licensed."

Raina sighed, faking sorrow. "You didn't call, you didn't write . . ."

"Yeah, yeah. Gimme a few weeks, maybe I'll think up something worthy of gracing my dewy porcelain complexion."

"Porcelain doesn't break out in freckles by mid-May." Though yeah, it was a shame none of his tattoos were Raina's doing. She'd begun seeing everyone through Kim's lens, reduced to colors and shadows. The red hair and beard and the blue eyes would've looked great.

Miah hadn't come tonight—he was always busy with work, but more to the point, he didn't have a speck of ink on his body, not by Raina's hand or anybody else's. She'd tried to talk him into one countless times over the years, and though he didn't have anything against tattoos, he'd never once seemed tempted. It'd take a wife or a child or the passing of a parent to inspire such a commitment, she'd bet. Always family first, with that man. The only person less likely to get one was Duncan.

Duncan. She scanned the crowd, not spotting him. She hadn't seen him in a couple of hours, and apparently he'd lingered just long enough for her to see he'd made good on his promise to show. And of course he hadn't stuck around—no doubt he hated tattoos. Probably wasn't too fond of the sorts of people who commissioned them, either. Still, she wanted him here. Wanted him to see who she was, what she did, whether he liked it or not. Her pride had never hinged on others' approval; she just wanted him here, to be present for it, whether he fit in or not. And she wanted a photo of him. Duncan, in the bar . . . while those two entities were still a part of her life.

She remembered the first time he'd walked through that door, the night of Casey's welcome-home party. Her initial impression? *Fucking gorgeous.* Followed swiftly by *Holy Christ, what a smarmy dick.*

She smiled at the memory, wishing she could go back in time a couple of months, take herself aside, and tell that woman, "Just wait till you meet him for real."

At nine, impatience got the better of her. With Kim well in control of the shoot, she snuck out back and up to the apartment, ready to tug Duncan physically downstairs by the hand, if need be. But the only soul she found was Astrid—a very, very annoyed Astrid, meowing loudly and pacing back and forth in front of her bowls.

"Sorry, kid. Where'd your wrangler get to?" She gave Astrid half a can of her gourmet food, then opened the window and leaned out, and saw no bike in the back lot. "Weird." Very unlike Mr. Safety to go out well after dark.

She tried calling, but it went to voice mail after five rings. He might simply be out of range. . . . Or maybe Flores had called him in for questioning again? It seemed late for that.

Her stomach dropped into her shoes, her gut not buying the excuses.

Images flashed—of Duncan hurt or unconscious, crashed way out in the middle of nowhere, or struck by a car, or confronted by belligerent rednecks over the bribery scandal. And the kicker was, even if he strolled in ten minutes from now, every hair in place . . . Even then, she didn't get to scold him. That was a right reserved for girlfriends. For a woman with the balls to admit she cared for a man, to his face. She hadn't earned that privilege. Not yet.

"Fuck." There was nothing she could do for now. The badlands were massive—impossible to search until daylight, and even then it'd be daunting. She knew you couldn't file a missing person report for something like twenty-four hours, and in fairness, Duncan wasn't even technically *late*. He'd not told her where he'd gone or when he planned to be back.

With nothing to be done, she went back downstairs. But now her smiles felt forced, small talk grating. Kim showed her the latest photos on the camera's screen, but she couldn't manage to focus. She made empty noises of approval, hoping they passed for enthusiasm.

"Just one model left to shoot," Kim said, sliding a fresh memory-stick-thing into her camera.

"Who?"

Kim shot her a goofy look, and Casey said, "You, genius."

"Oh. Right." Damn. She'd look like a dazed deer in the photos if she couldn't pull herself together. "Just tell me where you want me."

Kim wound up taking hundreds of pictures, sticking Raina behind the bar, in front of the bar, *on* the bar; framed in the front door, lit by Vince's headlight; back inside, standing before the jukebox . . . Raina didn't have to fake a smile, at least—Kim told her to smirk instead. "Look unimpressed," she directed.

"Is that my brand?"

"Pretty much," Casey said, chiming in. "Look at the camera like you think it's a complete douche. That's your default look."

"Yeah, just pretend you're looking at Case," Vince said.

"Fuck you."

Raina tuned them out, just wanting to get through this. Wanting to rush out back and check for Duncan's bike, try his phone again. Hell—climb onto her own bike and go out looking for him. Totally futile, no doubt, but fruitless searching beat passive waiting any day of the week. Horrible thoughts tugged at her, thoughts of Duncan crashed, or jumped, of a brick finding his skull instead of a window. God, that last one . . .

"I'd say that's a wrap," Kim said at long last.

Raina eyed the clock. A minute to eleven. "That must've been six hours."

"Went by fast, didn't it?"

Raina nodded. The first few hours, sure. Since she'd realized Duncan was missing? Molasses on the moon. Had anyone seen him leave? Had anyone followed him—someone drunk and pissed and spotting an opportunity to rough up Public Enemy Number One? Or someone not drunk at all . . . Someone calculating and dangerous, their late-night vandalism MO thwarted by the watch and replaced by a more direct strategy?

"Case," she called, drawing him over.

"Change your mind?" he asked. "Need me in makeup?"

"When you quit riding this afternoon, did Duncan say what his plans were?"

"No. Just that he was coming by here tonight."

"He did, for about a minute."

"Must've gone upstairs—this probably isn't his scene."

"He's not upstairs. And his bike's gone."

Casey frowned at that. "You check in front?"

They went outside, but nothing.

"Weird," Casey said as they went back in. "I don't think he's ridden in the dark before."

"See if Abilene needs any help. I'll look upstairs again. Maybe he wrecked and had to walk back or—"

"Whoa!" somebody shouted, whipping everyone's heads around. "Turn up the TV. Looks like somebody found 'em. Somebody finally found the bones!"

Raina started. "What?"

"Son of a bitch," Casey said in wonder, and leaned over the bar for the remote. "That motherfucker actually did it."

Chapter 25

People shuffled out of Benji's close to three, well after their final glasses were empty, and still wide-awake and talking about the news. About the bones that had been found, and about how it had been that Welch guy who'd apparently found them . . .

And didn't that seem awfully suspicious? Awfully coincidental? It had been bad enough that he'd taken those bribes off Levins, but to think he'd actually been a part of the murders . . .

Raina had squeezed her fists and let her nails bite her palms, the pain the only thing that had kept her from screaming at everyone to shut their ignorant mouths. With the door finally locked, she marched to the bar and downed a shot of whiskey, gave her head a sharp shake.

Casey slid a second tumbler over for her to fill. "That was some fucking weird night, huh?"

She beamed him an annoyed look as she poured. "I can't *believe* he told you and not me."

"He didn't—I guessed. I can't believe *you* thought he was out there joyriding all this time. Like that guy even knows how to do anything just for fun." He knocked back his shot.

"Still. I never expected that." And she was pissed he hadn't told her, considering every other secret he'd deemed her worthy of hearing. Though in fairness, she'd likely have told him he was wasting his time.

She shut off the TV, buzzwords and sound bites cycling through her head relentlessly. The press hadn't known much, but what few facts they did seem to possess, they'd repeated ad nauseum these past four hours.

Who was the second man who'd been with Duncan? everyone was asking—the one also reportedly taken away by the feds. And had people noticed just how *black* the bones had looked, how disturbing, in those little glimpses caught by the first news crew on the scene?

And who on earth had they *belonged to*?

And what about Welch? Always *what about Welch?* He'd seemed like an asshole, but a *murderer* to boot? You just couldn't trust foreigners, could you?

Raina rolled her eyes at the thought.

Kim, who back in August had gotten far too close to the danger for anybody's comfort, had become visibly upset after the news broke. Vince had taken her home around midnight. Raina had sent Abilene off around that same time and had asked Casey to stay on until last-call orders were filled. It was her and Duncan's appointed night to stay up, peering into the shadows, but seeing as how his detainment had made the news, a fresh wave of vandalism wasn't top of her list of worries just now. The belligerent locals who'd been harassing him were probably throwing themselves a big-ass party right now, to think he was in custody . . .

In custody for questioning, or detention? she had to wonder.

She looked to Casey, who was loading the last of the glasses into the washer.

"You think Duncan's done himself any favors," she asked, "finding those things?"

He shut the washer and shrugged. "In the long run? I hope so. I mean, we all believe he's innocent."

"Of course."

"No doubt the feds'll be fucking with Levins's head over this shit, too. Let's hope he cracks under the pressure, spills whatever it is he knows. Him or that so-called witness."

She nodded, feeling deeply uneasy.

Casey's expression grew worried and he came close, wrapping his arm around her shoulder.

She shrugged him away, alarmed. "Ew, what are you doing?"

"I'm being brotherly and comforting. Is it working?"

"No, it's weird. Knock it off."

He crossed his arms and dropped the concerned shtick. "Sorry. Usually chicks like getting hugged when they're stressed-out. Forgot you've got a bigger dick than most of the dudes in this town."

She rolled her eyes.

"If you need me to stick around and talk, or drink, I can."

"I appreciate that, but no. I'll be fine. Go home, Case."

He slumped in relief. "Thank fuck for that—I've been up for, like, thirty hours. See you tomorrow?"

"Yeah. Place'll be busy all week, thanks to the news. Come in around four?"

"You got it." He whipped his bar towel off his shoulder and onto her head, enclosing her in the damp, sour-smelling shroud before she snatched it off.

"Shithead."

Casey smiled. "It was that or the hug. I choose wisely?"

"Probably."

"See you tomorrow, boss."

She kicked him in the butt on his way out, then locked up behind him. Silence descended when his bike's rumble faded, and she sighed, tired. And yeah, maybe she half wished Casey had stuck around.

She shut off the main lights and wiped down the tables. It felt odd to be the only one left, in the wake of all that energy and noise. Odd to recall what a great night she'd been having, only a few hours ago, and how hopeful she'd felt. Odd to know that Duncan was less than a mile away, in federal custody—

She jumped at the sound of knuckles rapping glass and whipped around. Her brain was already preoccupied with the shotgun under the bar, but the instinct was misplaced.

It was Miah, of all people. She crossed the floor to let him in. "Hey. You're a little late to the festivities. But I'm guessing you've heard the news."

"Actually, no. I just got released from the sheriff's department, half hour ago."

"Whoa, what? That was you, with Duncan tonight?"

He strode to pick two stools up off the nearest high top and set them on the floor, taking a seat. "That was me."

"How the heck did that come about? I know he found them way out on the range, but how'd you get involved? He ask your permission?"

He patted the other cushion and she sat.

"No, he didn't. I was half a heartbeat from fucking him up when he told me he thought he'd found them."

"The bones."

Miah nodded, and told her what had gone on after. "After

they questioned me, a deputy gave me a ride home. Then I got in my truck and came here."

"Well, you just missed the party—the shoot *and* the breaking news."

"I came to see you, actually."

She tightened at that. "Oh yeah?" *You're going to tell me to stay away from Duncan.*

His palms rubbed together between his knees, always a sign of emotional constipation.

"Something you need to say to me, Miah?"

A sigh, and he met her eyes, hands going still. "I'm not over you."

Her stomach dropped. "Right . . ."

"I need to be, trust me. I *want* to be. But I'm not, and I think the only way I'm gonna get there is to straight-up avoid you for a while. It sucked bad enough before, when we were both single, but I won't lie—this past week's been fucking torture."

Raina wasn't one to apologize for other people's feelings, but she wasn't sure what else to offer. "Sorry. That sounds real shitty."

He nodded.

"I wondered if maybe you'd come to tell me to stay away from him. Duncan."

"I got no clue what to make of him, to be honest. I don't approve of him, but I also know you've never held your breath for a second, waiting on anybody's blessing."

She smiled.

"I'd never really talked to him before tonight," Miah added. "Not like a human being. He always came off so . . ."

"Stiff?"

"Or fake. Or just mean. The way he spoke to people, it always felt like he was . . . toying with them."

"He probably was, before he lost his job."

"It's not like we bonded or anything—not remotely—but I guess maybe he became more human or something, watching him, like, digging through the dirt on his knees. Caring about something. I think before . . . I didn't believe he was capable of that. Of caring about anything."

"Of caring about *me*," she supplied.

"Something like that. I'm still not a fan, but he's a person now, instead of some . . . I dunno."

"Snake?"

"Just about." He paused, attention on his hands. "I wasn't ready to let you go before."

"Well, I shouldn't have kept going to bed with you."

"Not because of that . . . Not quite. Now I really just fucking *need* to let go. I can't spend another week — or month, or *year* — feeling like this." He shook his head, drew and released a long breath, and met her eyes. "I think I always assumed that the only reason we weren't together was that you were afraid. Because you couldn't stay with *anyone*, so it wasn't personal. It wasn't *me*. I had it in my head that we were so right — like an irrefutable fact. And that someday you were going to grow up and finally get sick of running, and realize what we had, and we'd wind up together again."

"We should've been right. You were my friend — I already loved and respected you. And the sex was fucking . . ." She rolled her eyes. The sex had been ridiculous. Different than with Duncan — not better or worse, no more or less intense, but as different as the men themselves. And yeah, ridiculous.

He nodded, smiled sadly. "It was."

"I thought, if you can have stupid-hot sex with your good friend, that's got to be it, right? That's, like, the recipe for something that'll last. I thought we were right, too. But I was never going to give you kids. A wedding day, maybe, if you'd pushed, but never a family. And I know you want that. And I knew if I gave you the chance, you'd talk yourself out of wanting it, to keep me."

He sighed a long breath through his nose. "I don't know about that . . . But maybe. It doesn't matter anymore, though. You like somebody, and I'm man enough to admit he's not as awful as I'd thought. Sort of fucked-up — "

"You have no idea."

"But you like him, genuinely?"

"Yeah, I do."

"I can tell." He went quiet for a long moment, then frowned, looking puzzled. "So, if it's not as simple as friends having stupid-hot sex, what is it? What do you two offer each other?"

She considered it. "He needs me, I think. And I need to feel like I'm the strong one."

Miah smiled at that. "You never needed me. Not for a second."

"I don't need Duncan, either. That's why you and I never worked — you wanted to feel needed in return. I can't fall for a man if I feel like I depend on him. That'd turn me off, that kind of dynamic."

"If Welch can handle that imbalance, more power to him," Miah said. "You and I . . . You saw things about us I refused to. Like how I'd probably have come to resent you, a few years down the road, feeling like I was giving so much, when you can seem so . . ."

"Cold."

"Not quite. But indifferent."

She nodded. "Maybe it's telling, that I fell for a cat owner. Duncan's used to settling for scraps of withholding, cagey female attention."

Miah laughed. "I've always hated cats."

"That's *so* my style—stingy little morsels of affection. Give a man a taste, then wander off and do my own thing. Dogs are . . ."

"Dog love is like a hose you can't turn off," Miah offered.

"Yeah, one that never runs dry. Too much. All you can do is try to dodge the spray. Ugh. Sloppy."

He grinned—that broad, genuine smile she hadn't seen him wear in two years, not since they'd still been together. "Bring it on."

His hands were splayed on his thighs, and she thumped the back of one softly with her fist. "I'm gonna toss out one of those rare little morsels, Miah, and tell you this: you're going to make a great father someday."

"Someday."

Predictably, this little heart-to-heart left her feeling drained and vulnerable. But also proud for having said what she had. What he deserved to hear.

"Anyhow," Miah said, standing—he was an old hand at reading when Raina's sincerity well was tapped out. "It's late."

"Yeah. And with the investigation suddenly cranked back up, it's going to be a crazy few days here in Gossip Central. I better turn in."

"Ditto. I just want you to know why I won't be around much, for a while. I'll see you at club meetings, for important stuff, but otherwise . . ."

"It's fine. Whatever you need. Whatever gets us back to how we were before we fucked everything up with the stupid-hot sex."

"Exactly."

She walked him to the door. "Thanks for filling me in."

"Sure. I'll see you sometime."

She nodded. "Whenever you decide to." She'd nearly said, *You know where to find me,* but in all honesty, who knew which would come first—her selling the bar or Miah moving on? But she had enough questions dogging her for one night.

She drew him into a hug. Though she felt none of their old heat—not in her own body, at least—there was warmth. She stepped away and flipped the bolt. "Take care of yourself."

"And you get some sleep."

She closed the door, listened to his truck start up and drive off. As the night went silent once more, she slumped.

Slumped, wondering if Duncan was stuck sleeping on some hard cot or bunk tonight, and how he was being treated. Like a criminal, likely.

And underneath that, she felt slumped and weary and up-ended for more shapeless reasons, ones she couldn't quite get a hold on. But something scary, to judge by the hollow feeling in her stomach.

Something Miah had said hounded her. *I'd probably have come to resent you. You can seem so indifferent.*

Totally true, totally fair.

But when she thought about those things Duncan had said—whispered in the most intimate, needy moments, with his words and with his body . . . *Hold me. Want me.* During sex, no problem. But that *wanting.* Would that need bleed her dry, in time? Would she wind up running from yet another man who required more than she was willing to give? More than she was brave enough to offer, or perhaps more than she simply had in her. She'd given her dad so much, lost such a big chunk of her-self when he died . . .

Then she straightened, registering how egotistical it was, get-ting spun up over how crummy it'd feel if she had to break that man's heart. He hadn't even offered his heart yet. Hadn't asked her for exclusivity, hadn't asked if they were a couple. *Certainly* hadn't told her he loved her. It was foolish to be telling herself she understood what he needed and expected, telling herself she understood him, had him all figured out, when all this really was so far was hot sex and a growing mutual fondness and cu-riosity.

"My God, you really *do* think highly of yourself, don't you?"

she muttered, echoing Miah's sentiments from last week's not-quite breakup.

What she did know for sure, what she trusted, was that Duncan got her. Or if not got her, he accepted her. Unlike every guy she'd ever dated, he took her as she was, instead of projecting some idea onto her. As good as Miah had been to her, he'd wanted to tame her. Soften her with his steady brand of love, domesticate her, turn her into the marrying kind, change her mind about kids. With that douche bag she'd fallen for in Vegas, she'd been taken for an easy mark. She'd dated a dozen guys and had had a dozen sets of two-dimensional expectations projected onto her. She'd been one man's wayward fixer-upper, another's brush with the wild side, another's rebellious rebound, another's sex goddess. Duncan Welch might have fantasized about dressing her up, but she knew that by the time they'd kissed, he'd realized she wasn't the kind of girl you molded and modified.

He didn't want to change her.

And she couldn't say that about any other lover she'd let herself get close to.

She had to wonder, though, now that she could admit she was becoming attached . . . would he even be here in a week or two?

God willing, Duncan would be found innocent before long. He could tell Sunnyside to go fuck themselves the day he got released, leave for San Diego feeling only relief, seeing Raina as nothing more than some unlikely fling from a surreal, regrettable episode of his life. The fling to end all flings, maybe, but shit—he could leave without ever considering her his girlfriend.

And she was worried about breaking *his* heart?

"Narcissist," she scolded herself, flipping off the last of the lights. And she marched her chastised butt up the back steps, praying exhaustion might just let her sleep and forget these worries for a few hours.

Chapter 26

Since the initial story broke, Raina had been bracing herself for another round of questioning. She hadn't been put through one, not yet, anyhow. A couple of feds rang her bell early the next morning, with a warrant to search Duncan's things. She tried to get some sense of his situation out of them, but nothing. They were efficient and polite, and after twenty minutes, they left with only his computer and briefcase. By eight o'clock she was alone again, left to her cold coffee and worrying.

At least I know he's safe, for a change.

Astrid was no comfort—she'd planted herself on top of the fridge and seemed unlikely to come down. Her only contribution to the household was an occasional, mournful wail from on high.

"I hear you, kid. I miss him, too."

People would no doubt want to assemble early, so Raina headed downstairs at one. As she flipped on the lights and AC, she realized she'd got it wrong—people were already standing around in the front lot, gossiping. She let them file in without bothering to sweep or mop, barely able to keep on top of orders until Abilene arrived at three.

The jukebox stayed dark, all ears trained on the news, and when Casey turned up she had him lug her heavy television down from the den, just to spread the crowd out so people could reach the bar to order drinks.

The story began to unravel, one tiny knot at a time.

The next tangle to come loose was the preliminary forensics report. After having the same old nonupdates regurgitated at them again and again, people fell dead silent when the breaking news bulletin came on.

Ramon Flores himself appeared on-screen, standing before a cinder block wall whose pale blue paint turned white with every camera flash. A massive bouquet of microphones was set up before him, and Raina could feel the room leaning in, collectively, everyone starved for the details Flores held in his hands on a thin stack of papers. He took his glasses off, and read.

"The victim was male, aged roughly twenty-five to thirty-five, standing approximately five foot six. One of the victim's legs appears to have been crushed before the time of the body's incineration. The victim's dental records do not appear to match any files in the national missing persons database" — murmurs rose at that — *"leading us to believe he may have been an immigrant. If anyone has any information about a male fitting this description, who may have gone missing sometime in July or early August of this year, we urge you to please come forward. Your identity will remain confidential. Thank you."* A phone number came on the screen, and that was that.

The bar erupted with speculation, theories growing wilder by the hour.

At the top of the eleven o'clock report, everyone went mute once again, now conditioned to shut up at the chime of the *KCBN News* jingle.

"Coming to you live from the Brush County Sheriff's Department," said a local reporter, standing outside the building in question, *"where it appears there may have been a break in the ongoing federal murder investigation in Fortuity. While dental records found on Wednesday evening from that now infamous skull failed to match any known missing persons, authorities say they've received a tip, and that it's being looked into, though no details are currently being made public. Wes Wheeler, KBCN News."*

The anchor appeared and began recapping the now-stale updates from earlier in the day, all but drowned out by a collective groan.

"Fucking tease," someone shouted, summing it up nicely.

Raina went back behind the bar, to where Casey was mixing drinks. "You think it's a good thing that Duncan's not getting mentioned as much today?"

"Dunno . . . All people care about are the bones right now. Seems like an improvement."

She nodded. She was dying for some clue to how he was

doing, but getting nothing but crickets might be a good thing. It beat phrases like "Duncan Welch, former representative of the casino developers, currently under investigation for conspiracy." Those had peppered last night's news, but today it was all about forensics.

Casey made change and turned to Abilene. "You still got that article up?"

She handed him her smartphone, and Casey tapped at the screen. "You seen this, Raina?" He handed it over.

She squinted at the tiny text. It was a short, fact-starved, hateful piece on Brush County's online newspaper, a profile titled "Sleuth or Sleaze: Did Duncan Welch find the missing bones because he buried them himself??"

"I'm not reading that. It's designed to inflame the same sorts of assholes who threw a brick through my kitchen window."

"I dunno," Casey said. "Double question marks are always a sure sign of credible journalism."

Raina wished it had been a real paper, so she could have burned the thing.

Though it could have been way worse. And as the afternoon wore on, the frenzied speculation had definitively shifted to the identity of the victim. Thank goodness for short attention spans, Raina thought. At least nobody seemed to be talking much about Duncan anymore.

Though that didn't stop Raina from thinking about him. Not for a minute.

Though he was offered a ride, Duncan left on foot when he was released on Friday morning.

He'd been afforded a shower the day before, but not a shave, not a change of clothes, and his jeans and tee had been dirty even before he was brought in. Flores had interrogated him for hours, confronted him with a text message Tremblay had sent to Levins the morning Duncan and Vince had visited one of the building sites back in August, asking after those bones. *Keep him sweet,* Tremblay had told Levins, and Duncan insisted a hundred times, Flores had it all wrong. Tremblay had probably wanted Levins merely to kiss Duncan's ass, should he come around to Levins's site, asking uncomfortable questions. Nothing to do with bribes. Duncan had talked himself hoarse, and seemingly for nothing.

He'd begun to despair, when all at once Flores's partner appeared, and Duncan was moved from a private holding cell back to the old makeshift interrogation room. Jaskowski plied him with weak, store-brand tea and asked if he'd like a change of clothes. Duncan had declined. He waited for Flores to appear with an apology. He needn't have held his breath. After twenty minutes or so, Jaskowski got a call, told his phone, "Okay," and hung up.

"You're free to go," he'd told Duncan. "Don't leave town until you hear from us."

"What's happened?"

"Can't say—investigation's still well under way. Hang on and I'll find somebody to give you a lift."

"I don't want a lift—I want to know what's going on."

But Jaskowski had simply left the room, leaving Duncan with little choice but to follow, and no energy to protest.

Jaskowski, at least, had had the courtesy to thank him. "You did good," he said to Duncan, standing just outside the station.

"And was treated like shit for it." Duncan had felt as if the morning sun was going to fry his eyes.

"You did good," Jaskowski had repeated, and handed Duncan his phone and briefcase, the latter heat-sealed in an oversize plastic bag. "And you made yourself look remarkably suspicious in the process. I think Flores wanted to believe you were innocent all along, if that's any consolation."

"It's not."

"Fair enough. Your laptop's in your briefcase. The boys in evidence said it was the dullest computer they've ever searched."

No doubt. Duncan was probably the only man on the planet with a folder full of video clips labeled "Opera" that *was* in fact stocked with arias, not pornography.

"This has all been terribly anticlimactic," he'd said to Jaskowski.

"You complaining?"

"Not passionately."

"I hope we won't need to call you in again," Jaskowski had said. "Sure you don't want a ride?"

"Positive."

And with that, Duncan once again found himself walking toward Fortuity's gritty little heart.

The man he'd been a couple of weeks ago would've been

mortified to be spotted strolling through the town center in dirty clothes, scruffy from two days spent being treated like a criminal.

But the man he was now didn't much care. He'd prefer to look half-decent when he walked up Raina's steps and through her door, hopefully to be greeted by the woman he'd thought of, every moment when his mind wasn't preoccupied with his predicament. But she'd cared for him when he was shaking and drunk and losing his mind. A bit of dirt and sweat seemed unlikely to dampen her affections.

It was after ten and Fortuity was awake, but by some miracle of mercy, no one confronted Duncan on his short journey—perhaps they didn't recognize him without a suit and a clean shave.

His phone was stuffed with messages. None from any Sunnyside numbers, so his exoneration probably hadn't made the news yet. He looked forward to when it did, and not just because his innocence might spell an end to the harassment; he was looking forward to telling his old bosses to go fuck themselves.

A few days ago he might've considered taking his job back, if only for an excuse to stay in Fortuity another two years. To stay with Raina, if she'd have him. But there was more than just a reunion awaiting him at her place. There should be a package as well. Her gift. He'd tell her how he felt, and let her reaction dictate whether he stayed or went.

His name should be cleared soon, danger abated, but his reason for living with her gone. If his feelings were reciprocated, he'd make noises about moving out, then wait with bated breath to hear her reply. An apathetic "If that's what you want," perhaps? He hoped not. Maybe fists on hips instead, and a demand of "And where exactly do you think you're going to find a better deal around here?"

Yes, let it be that.

He checked the news, relieved to see the remains had likely been identified. There was little else to be gleaned. It would be a strange but memorable way to kick off his and Raina's official courtship, he thought, camped out on her couch or down in the bar, glued to the news.

He didn't have the energy to listen to all those voice mails, but he read his texts as he walked. There were dozens from journalists who'd finagled his number, wanting interviews. One from Casey: they letting you use your phone? whats going on mf? dont get waterboarded.

Duncan sighed. "You're pure class, Grossier."

Vince had left one as well: Got your bike out of impound. It's at the garage when you want it. Duncan couldn't say if he'd ever get on that thing again—its original purpose had been served, after all. Plus, just now the pavement under his feet felt essential.

No messages from Raina ... but several missed calls from her, he noted, somewhat cheered.

You tried to destroy me, he told Fortuity as he walked down Station Street. *But you'll need to try harder than that.*

Benji's appeared down the block, growing closer with every step. He'd felt nothing but contempt when he first walked through those doors, but now it looked ... not quite like *home*, but the closest thing he had to one. He imagined driving the Mercedes into the garage of his slick glass high-rise by the harbor, taking the elevator up to the thirty-eighth floor to his condo, after a long day at work. He'd be eager to see Astrid, eager to push his shoes off and loosen his tie, but the place itself ... it had only ever been a picture frame, fit to contain the image he'd called his life.

He walked quicker, the bar getting closer, closer.

The bar where he'd found a strange breed of salvation, amid the storm of these past few weeks. The bar where the woman he loved had grown up. The bar built by a man whose dreams had been watered down and abandoned in the worthy name of raising his daughter, by himself, helping her become the strong, stubborn, bullshit-proof woman she was now. Duncan had given that man a lot of thought these last couple of days, and had wished more than once he could shake his hand, tell him what a fine job he'd done, tell him how central his business remained to this town. He couldn't, of course. But there was plenty Duncan *could* do. Or that his money could do, at any rate. A gift that would make the one he'd ordered look like the token it was, if only Raina would accept it.

He'd first set foot in that bar knowing the progress he represented was going to wind up dismantling it, and feeling not an ounce of remorse about that. He'd felt *pride*, in fact, to imagine he played a key role in the betterment of this town.

But it was Fortuity that had dismantled Duncan, in the end, and put him back together again, worse for wear yet more whole than he'd ever felt. This place had rewritten his plans, just as Raina had rewritten her father's. And now—with her blessing—he'd take a load of the money he'd once been paid in the service of endangering that bar, and he'd implement every last goddamn plan sketched and listed in Benji Harper's notebooks.

Those thugs had called it—Duncan had trotted into town as a jackal. He couldn't stop the casino, couldn't say for sure whether it was even good for Fortuity or not, but he could save Benji's. Take the place he'd once wished to euthanize and do everything in his power to help it thrive, come what may.

The woman who'd been raised there had saved his soul.

The least he could do was save her goddamn bar.

Chapter 27

Duncan strode through the front lot and around the side of the bar, hand trembling to the stutter of his heart as he took out his key. When he was halfway up the steps, he heard it—footsteps overhead, running. Raina yanked the stairwell door open just as his fingers were about to clasp the knob.

"Oh my gosh." She sounded breathless, gaze traveling the length of his body, then back up. "Hi."

"Hi."

She stepped back, and Duncan entered, shutting the door. For a moment they merely stared at each other as Astrid dropped from the fridge to the counter to the floor, mewling her alarm. The both of them were surely surprised to see him, after nearly two days' radio silence. He was struck by the familiarity of this woman standing before him. That face and body and voice; her clothes, her smell. Her home. It all felt so strikingly like *his*; he was lost in the shock of it.

She snapped out of it first, laughing. "Jesus, come here." She drew him close, clutching his shirt tight, burying her face against his neck. "Call a woman, why don't you?"

"I had my phone confiscated until this morning." His heart rose and his throat ached and he doubted heroin felt half this good. Not to be left out, Astrid drove her body into his calves, again and again.

Say you missed me, he willed Raina. *Say you love me, that I'm all you've thought about.*

But all he got when she stepped back was "Congratulations." She rubbed his arms. "You're officially innocent, huh? A hero, even. And a free man."

"I don't know about hero, and I'm only half-free for now. I

have to stay in town until I'm told otherwise." Soon he *would* be free, though—free to leave, yet incapable of doing so for as long as this woman made him welcome in her life. Nerves crept in to temper Duncan's pleasure.

He hefted his turbo-purring cat and kissed her head. "Yes, your primary food dispenser's returned. How about that?" To Raina he added, "Thank you for feeding her."

"I don't think she's even looked at her bowl, since that night you didn't come home."

Home? Is that where I am? Dear God, he hoped so.

"I can't fucking believe you found those bones," she said, laughing. "Or that you didn't bother telling me that's what you were up to."

"I felt foolish that I was looking at all."

"Paid off in the end, though. Has Sunnyside come groveling yet?"

"No, not yet. I imagine they'll wait until my exoneration's a bit more official."

"Maybe you could score yourself a raise."

"That would come with negotiation . . . but I'm not certain I'd pursue it, either way."

"No?" Her expression was impossible to read. Was that surprise? Relief? Disappointment?

"They've rather injured my feelings," he said simply, setting Astrid down. She rushed to her dishes, not looking likely to resurface soon.

"What would you do instead," Raina asked, "if you didn't go back to them?"

He shrugged. "I've not decided yet." *Ask me to stay, and I'll do anything. I'll chase ambulances, flip burgers, break rocks. Anything. Just ask me to stay.*

"Well, one step at a time." She looked around, seeming awkward somehow. "A courier came with an envelope for you this morning—a big fat one. I signed for it and left it on your bed."

My bed. The guest room bed, more like. If he couldn't count Raina's bed as his own, none would do.

"I'm guessing it must be legal stuff," she went on. "But sounds like you won't be needing it, huh?"

How could she so easily be chatting with him, this way? All Duncan wanted was to wrap his body around hers and stay that way for a week.

How? Because she's cautious, same as you. Neither of us can seem to bare our hearts without first cracking each and every one of our ribs open. Why expect that of her, when you've been too cowardly to offer it, yourself? He would, though, and soon.

"I need a shower," he said, "and a change of clothes. Badly."

"I'll bet."

"And a shave."

She frowned at that one.

"Or perhaps not . . . ?"

"I like you scruffy, but whatever makes you feel like a free man, go for it."

"Would you set aside an hour for an early drink with me?"

"Up here?" she asked.

He nodded. "Give me until one, to reacquaint myself with hygiene and grooming. Just a small drink—I feel I deserve a toast."

"That you do. I'll grill you about your detention once you're all freshened up. And how you even found those things to begin with."

"And I'll grill you about the news—I've somehow been left out of the loop, even though I was wrapped up in the middle of the case."

"It's a date."

He waited for more—for *Christ, I missed you.* For a kiss so deep she'd taste the way he'd ached for her these past few hellish days, in his chest and skin and bones and blood.

"I'll get something thrown together for lunch," she said. "You're probably starved."

"That would be nice. The feds seemed to think I deserved mainly untoasted bagels and packets of light cream cheese."

"Our tax dollars hard at work."

I missed you so much. Say you missed me.

She turned her attention to the fridge.

Under the hot spray of the shower, Duncan assured himself, *That's simply how she is.* And he liked her as she was—*loved* her as she was. So he'd just have to take the rose with the thorns, as they said. It wasn't as though he was much better with these things.

Duncan lathered and scrubbed and rinsed, toweled himself, dressed in a button-up and fresh jeans—a sort of hybrid of his old and new selves. He styled his hair but left his nascent beard alone. He didn't feel like himself anymore, so there was little urgency to look the part. He pulled on socks, then sat on the edge of the bed, holding his breath as he ripped the courier service's plastic envelope open.

Inside, between sheets of bubble wrap, was a velvet box, long and slender as a remote control. He popped it open, turned it this way and that, watched the sun catch on innumerable, exquisite facets. *Yes,* he thought. This was right. Exactly right.

When he found Raina in the kitchen, there were easily ten bottles of champagne lined up on the table. She gestured at the selection like a spokesmodel.

"Goodness. I'm spoiled for choice."

"I get sent samples all the time by distributors, but I don't really like wine, so they just sit in the cupboard, waiting for something worth celebrating. And I'd say your exoneration more than qualifies."

He picked a bottle and Raina washed a pair of dusty flutes while he opened it.

"I hope it pairs with grilled cheese," she said, watching him pour. "That's about all I've got the ingredients for."

"Cheers." He handed her a glass.

"To your freedom, Inspector Welch."

They clinked, and he said, "Sit."

He dragged the other chair around the table, close enough for their knees to brush. Astrid claimed his lap, but he dropped her back on the floor. After a deep drink that he barely tasted, he set his glass aside, then Raina's, and took her hands in his.

She looked a fraction as nervous as Duncan felt. He cleared his throat.

"Being detained left me with quite a lot of time to think."

"I'll bet. Especially if you might have a job search ahead of you."

"About that, but other things as well. More pressing things. Things I've had on my mind since before I even found those bones."

"I'm sensing some sort of revelation."

"Yes, as a matter of fact." He reached into his breast pocket and drew out her present. It was a heavy thing—a bracelet of quarter-carat round diamonds, three dense rows, set in platinum.

Her eyes were gigantic, pinned to the dangling cuff. "Whoa. What the fuck?" Her chin jerked up. "Duncan?"

He'd pictured this exact item in his mind, as he'd sat in those depressing cinder block rooms at the BCSD, pictured giving it to her. He'd felt his throat ache and his heart race as he'd rehearsed words in his mind. And this was the least of the gestures he intended to make this morning.

"It's a gift. Open your hand." He had to do it for her, uncurling her fingers and laying the bracelet across her palm.

"A gift?"

"Yes, a gift. I want to spoil you." *I love you.* He could think those words, but not quite seem to push them through his lips. He imagined if the bracelet had been better received, the words would've followed more easily.

"Spoil me?" she echoed.

He nodded.

A long, long pause. "You want to dress me up," she corrected slowly.

Duncan's heart went from pinwheel to boulder in a single beat. "No—"

"You still want to *Pretty Woman* me, don't you?"

And he couldn't help blanching, because once upon a time . . . yes, he had. Badly. He'd wanted to strip away what he'd seen as her cheap packaging and remake her as someone more . . . worthy. Worthy of him, he'd thought, as though he'd been anything special. He'd wanted to fix her exterior as he'd spent years doing with himself. He'd wanted her tattoos gone. Her clothes replaced. Yes, he'd wanted all that. And it shamed him to think it now.

He shook his head. "I like you just as you are. All I want is to treat you."

She frowned but held her tongue.

"Tell me you like it."

Raina studied it, draped along her palm like a snake, glimmering.

"Tell me."

"What would I ever wear this with? I don't own a single dress. Not even a skirt. I'd get mugged if I—"

"Stop. Tell me."

She closed her hand with a sigh. "It's beautiful. It's the most beautiful, exquisite, *expensive* thing anyone's ever tried to give me."

"Tried to?"

She took his wrist, turned his hand over, and let the stones pool in his cupped palm. She closed his fingers gently. "I'm not a girl who takes diamonds from a man."

He laughed, flustered. "It's not a ring. It's not a leash, either, or a promise of any sort, or some brand to mark you as mine. I'm not after your freedom, Raina. I'm just a man who wants to give a woman an extravagant, ridiculous gift. Because I spent two nights away from her and missed her. Because I want to delight her."

Her fingertips rubbed his knuckles, but she wouldn't meet his eyes. She let his hands go. "I appreciate the thought. But I don't *delight*. I'd have thought you knew me well enough to realize that."

Desperation fell over him, suffocating. "Take it, please."

Finally those brown eyes met his. She shook her head, looking sad. "No."

"I told you once, I'm not a man who begs, but again, I'll demean myself for you. *Please.* All I want is to take your breath away, and this was the only way I could think to."

She smiled, the gesture weak. "It's very you, Duncan. But it's not me."

"Okay, then . . . I'm sorry it seems to have offended you."

"I'm not offended. *I'm* sorry if I led you to believe that I'm something I'm not. Like the kind of woman who expects gifts like that one."

"Not expects them, no. Forget the bracelet—it was only a preamble anyway."

"A preamble? To what?"

He took a breath, let it out slowly. "I want to fund the improvements your father wanted to make to the bar."

Silence. Dead silence.

Nervous, Duncan went on. "I don't know how much it might cost. To add a kitchen, quite a lot, but perhaps that could come later. But to start, I thought fifty thousand could go quite a way to—"

"Stop." She shook her head, eyes shut. "What on earth are you talking about?"

"All the things your father had wanted but hadn't had the chance to do. I want to make those things a reality. To help the bar stay viable once the competition arrives."

"Those were my father's plans, not mine."

"I assumed—"

"Yeah, I can tell you assumed. A lot. Listen, Duncan. That's insanely generous—*insanely*. But you don't know what I want. I don't think you even know *me*, not like you think you do."

"I don't *know* you?" In a breath his desperation sharpened to something far more aggressive.

"I thought you did . . . I've never been with a guy before, and thought, 'He gets me. He knows me, and there's nothing he'd change about me.'"

"And there isn't. And I *do* know you."

"How can you, if that's what you think I want—"

"I don't know how to touch you," he demanded, "to make you come in three minutes flat? I don't know what your skin smells like, and how your voice sounds, first thing in the morning?"

She looked taken aback, as though he'd threatened or insulted her.

"I don't know what the sadness in your eyes looks like," he asked, "when you think of your father, and touch his things, and listen to his music?"

"You've never met my father."

"And I'm not speaking as though I do. I'm speaking about you. And your feelings—lust and satisfaction and amusement."

"What the fuck is this about?"

He considered it. "This is about you, and me. Perhaps I chose the wrong gift, perhaps I overstepped my bounds, but I *do* know you. I've memorized you. I've seen things in you I *ache* to experience, written all over your face. Longing. Attachment. Grief."

"You want my grief? You're more than welcome to it. Have at it."

He glared at her tone. "I've grieved for one person in my entire pathetic, empty life. *One* person, whom I knew for a *year*. Your father cared for you for twenty times longer, and surely a thousand times deeper, than *anyone's* ever cared for me. So yes, I want your *fucking* grief. That's a pain you earn, and a pain you get gifted with. I want that pain."

Her head was shaking, eyes hot. "No, you don't. You have no fucking idea how bad this shit hurts."

"No, I don't. I *want* to. I'm asking you to let me close enough to risk feeling all that one day." He stared at her hard, diamonds biting as his fist squeezed, anger tensing the whole of him. "What is this? What are we?"

Though she didn't shrug, he saw apathy in her eyes. "Lovers," she offered. "Friends?"

"Do you even like me?"

"Of course I do."

Not enough to introduce me to your friends. "If I took my job back, if I were slated to stay here another two years . . . Would this continue? What precisely is the expiration date on your attentions?"

"There's no way to know to how long these things last—why bother trying to guess?"

"These things?" he echoed.

"Yeah. These things. Our thing."

Our thing. Again, his brain caught on the encapsulation inherent in the notion. Of them sharing some unique attachment, just between the two of them. Christ help him, he wanted to belong to someone. "Have I really misread this so badly, that I care this much, and you could be so ambivalent?"

"I'm not ambivalent—I'm freaked-out. You're trying to buy yourself some spot in my life, when all you ever needed to do was ask if you could stay."

"I'm not trying to do that at all." Duncan paused. Frowned. All at once shame overcame him, because yes, that was precisely what he was trying to do.

Much as he'd changed in the past week, he still didn't believe he was enough, on his own. He didn't trust he was enough, just as he was. He didn't trust what they had was enough. And yes, he'd tried to buy his place in her life; he just hadn't realized it.

"It was meant to be a gesture," he said softly, sadly. "It felt safer to hide behind it, rather than to simply tell you I'm in love with you."

"Duncan . . ." She took his hand, gaze on their fingers. "This week has been . . ."

"No, it's nothing to do with this week. Not the way you're thinking."

She met his eyes. "Everything's been amplified—by the threats, and the case, by the lack of sleep. By too much adrenaline, and by the fucking *sex*. Hell, by you going off your meds, for all I know."

His anger flashed. "I've never felt so lucid."

"I believe that whatever you're feeling for me, it's intense. You love somebody, but she's not me. You've never even seen me cry—how can you possibly think you love me?"

"You won't talk me out of how I feel. Or out of the fact that I do know you, no matter how much that scares you."

She let his hand go, heaving a silent sigh. "You think I'm afraid to be known?"

"I do."

She shook her head. "I've been waiting my whole adult life to meet a man who saw me the way my dad did, and who wants me just as I am. I thought maybe you *were* that guy. The last man I'd have expected to take me at face value, but I really did think you got me."

He was lost. Because he'd thought the same. Part of him still did . . . Only could he, really, if he'd misjudged this all so terribly?

"I can't take your money, Duncan. And I can't be the reason you stay in a town you hate. You keep your job, you stick around because of that? Great. But I can't pursue this with all that pressure weighing on it. All that expectation. All I've ever wanted was independence. I can't love somebody if I feel beholden to them."

Duncan studied her mouth, scared of her eyes. "All I've ever wanted was to belong somewhere. To someone who wants me."

"You know I want you. But not like this." She nodded at his hand, and the bracelet it hid. "That's a deposit, Duncan. Whether you want to admit it is or not."

"I'm trying to treat you, not . . . not reserve you. Don't project your tiresome baggage onto my intentions—I've enough of my own already."

She sighed, twisting her hair into a chaotic bunch. "Listen. Even if you're staying for another two years, I don't know for sure that I am."

His heart stopped. "What?"

"I'm selling the bar."

"Since when?"

"Since I spent Thursday night feeling like I was good at something more than pouring beer and making change. You know, I thought with my dad's things moved out, it'd feel like mine, this place. But it still doesn't. It was always ours—his and mine, but without him, *mine* feels as good as empty, most days."

"Your entire life is in this building," Duncan said, not sure why he felt so hurt by her plans. Because he'd not been consulted about them? *No, because I had no right to have been consulted about them. Because we were never anything that serious, not outside of my delusions.* And because she was planning to throw away the thing he'd ached for so badly, for so many years—a home.

She took a deep breath. "You said it yourself, you don't know what it's like, missing someone this badly. *Hurting* this hard from the absence of a person. From memories of them."

Anger simmered in him, and he dropped the bracelet back in his pocket. "Of course I don't. You've lost more than I've ever even been offered. You've *run* from things I've never dared dream of having within my grasp."

"What Miah wanted to give me, you mean."

Not quite. "Loyalty, affection, acceptance. Does it even matter who gives it—a lover or a parent or a friend? Do you know what *I* have?"

"It's not a contest—"

"I have a cat, Raina. A cat and maybe my tailor, my old dry cleaner, my shrink. *That's* who'd mourn me if I disappeared tomorrow. Unless perhaps you'd like to admit that maybe you'd miss me, and for more than sustenance or income. For something human . . . ?"

A long pause. "Of course I'd miss you."

"Would you *mourn* me? Would the lack of me ache in your bones, and echo in your bed? Would losing me take a part of you away for good, one you could never replace?"

She held his stare, though her eyes flicked uneasily between his.

When the pause grew sharp enough to cut, Duncan turned away. "That's my answer, then."

"Duncan—"

He shrugged her hand from his shoulder and headed for the guest room.

"You know I want you," she called, her steps trailing his.

"As a fuck and a fencing partner," Duncan clarified, hauling his suitcase from the closet. He began filling it, scooping his clothes from the dresser in armfuls. "And that money wasn't a deposit, I want you to know. It was a thank-you, for all the ways you've changed me. I thought you'd be pleased, but I guess you're right—I don't know you after all. Because apparently you could give a shit about your father's precious plans—"

She marched across the room and slapped him. Hard and neat, making fire bloom in his cheek. He blinked, eyes welling from the sting.

"I give *way* too big a shit about my father's precious plans," she hissed. "That bar *is me*. I'm Raina Harper. I own Benji's. The place with my dead father's name in neon over the front door, and his *ashes on a shelf above my fucking head*. And maybe I'll get to breathe again if I finally put this place in my rearview. You want a piece of my grief? You buy it and run it your own goddamn self. Because I'm done with it."

"And done with me, apparently."

"That's your shit, not mine. Don't bother billing me for your therapy."

He went still, so hurt and angry and lost he was petrified for a breath. *Fuck you.* That was what he wanted to say, but he'd lost control of himself so many times already over this woman. He calmed his breath. Turned, walked to the kitchen, and set his suitcase by the door. Raina didn't move as he laced his shoes, collected his suits, his plastic-wrapped briefcase, Astrid's bowls. Raina was standing in the kitchen when he came back up from a final trip to his car, not speaking as he wrestled his squirming cat into her carrier.

"Enjoy your life," he said, not looking back. "I was an idiot to hope I'd ever have a place in it."

She didn't reply. And as he shut the door quietly behind him, all he could think was *So much for that.*

Duncan loaded Astrid into the passenger seat foot well and aimed the car at the mountains. To the south was the motel, where he'd be stuck until the feds gave him the green light to go. But in a few days, he hoped, he'd be free to turn north, toward the highway that would get him back to San Diego. He'd text Vince later, tell him, *Keep the bike.* It had only ever been a loan, anyhow. With that settled, his business with the lot of them would be done, officially.

But he hadn't gotten two blocks, not even to Railroad Avenue, when the Merc gave a sudden jerk as the dash lit up, telling Duncan the front right tire's pressure was low.

"Really? Fucking *really*?"

Astrid hissed in time with the deflating tire, the right side of the car dipping morosely.

Duncan exited, slamming the door. Apropos of his entire time here, he found a broken beer bottle had ripped up his tire—no doubt jettisoned by someone stumbling home from Benji's.

It could have only been more poetic if he'd come to rest on the tracks, been made to watch as a freight train did his car in for good, dragged it screaming into the badlands until it burst into flames, all his worldly possessions vaporized.

He called a garage, arranged a tow, and waited twenty minutes until a stocky man disappeared down the road, hauling the erstwhile physical manifestation of Duncan's ego off to get fixed. He'd gathered his luggage and Astrid's carrier but left his suit bags in the car, along with his shoes. His old costume. He imagined them getting stolen in the middle of the night— of the entire *car* getting stolen—and he felt nothing.

As he walked back to the Gold Nugget, he realized his feet didn't hurt anymore. He'd broken the boots in . . . or perhaps the other way around. And he couldn't for the life of him decide what to make of that.

Chapter 28

Raina sat on the guest room bed, for an hour or more, turning a key over and over in her fingers. It was Duncan's apartment key, left behind on the covers.

"Don't bother billing me for your therapy," she muttered, then shut her eyes and flopped over backward. Last thing she says to him, and it's a potshot. "Good one, Harper, you fucking asshole."

She tried to guess what her dad would've said, if he'd seen that exchange.

If that's how you react when a man gives you diamonds, I'd hate to see what happens to the one who insults you.

She rolled her eyes.

Outside, the protracted crunching of tires on gravel told her Abilene had arrived to help open the bar. Raina peeled her pathetic ass off the bed and found her boots. She didn't let herself look at the bottle and flutes still sitting on the kitchen table, though avoiding the scene only drew her eyes to the now empty spot where Astrid's bowls ought to be.

"Goddamn it."

For better or worse, it was another hectic day downstairs. The natives were getting restless, waiting for news updates that simply refused to arrive. Whatever the feds had gleaned, they'd managed to keep it to themselves for the time being. Nobody craved an update more than Raina today. Without one, she had no distraction strong enough to keep replays of the morning's drama from cycling through her brain.

She'd fucked that up. Maybe not outrageously, but at least moderately. She had no doubt in her mind that Duncan had meant well. But you just didn't descend on a woman with diamonds and I-love-yous and huge sums of money after one week of sex, no matter how insane said sex had been. He'd come at her too hard, and she'd pushed him back, probably too hard as well. Too hard to expect him to show at the bar tonight, too, which left her with only one question: go after him tonight, or give them both a day to calm down?

He tried to make my dreams come true, she thought. He'd gotten her dreams wrong, but it wasn't as if he'd done something psycho. Considering that she'd kicked off their courtship by extorting him, those weren't *such* terrible crimes.

And worse even than the regret, she missed him. After a few short hours, she missed that man. He ought to be sitting across from her now, V and T in his manicured hand ... His previously manicured hand. Harder and rougher now, thanks to Fortuity.

So she'd go tonight after last call, find him at the motel. She'd own her part in the ugliness and apologize. A week or so ago, she hadn't been the sort of woman who issued apologies ... but Duncan deserved one. And she was woman enough to tender it. If he accepted, and they seemed good again, maybe some make-up sex—the second-hottest kind there was, trumped only by angry sex—and that would shift what was undeniably *right* about them back to center stage. Future-talk could wait.

"You all right?" Abilene asked, returning with empty pitchers.

"Yeah, I'm fine. Thanks." *Just fine, just fucking shit up left and right.* "It's been a long week."

"No kidding. Least the tips have been great."

Raina smiled. "At least there's that." And she settled in for the longest night of her life.

Duncan had been lying in his dark motel room for he couldn't guess how long. He'd been too beat, too defeated to even succumb to any of his typical urges. Fuck the state of the bathroom. Fuck unpacking. Fuck order. Fuck bothering or caring or trying. All he wanted was to fall asleep and stay unconscious for a week, wake up in San Diego to discover the past couple of months had been some sick dream brought on by bleach-fume poisoning.

No such luck. He lay atop the covers still dressed, flat on his back with Astrid warming his middle, until insomnia was a foregone conclusion.

Time passed, divorced from any frame of reference. Ten minutes? An hour, six hours? With the drapes drawn, it could have been morning, and Duncan wouldn't have known . . . Except no, it was quiet, still. The kind of quiet that never came over a city. An endangered quiet that Fortuity might not know two years from now, if and when the casino finally arrived.

Whatever. It won't be my fault if it does. And for now, quiet.

Quiet—save for the faint scuff of approaching footsteps.

Duncan froze where he lay, heart beating fast; hope rousing, if not rising.

Closer, came the steps. Slower. Hesitant.

She's come for me. To apologize, or to salt the wound further? He couldn't care. Kind or callous, he wanted her words, her voice. Wanted her hands, should they draw him close or brand his face with another slap. He wanted her, no matter the nature of this visit. Wanted precisely what was happening—those footsteps growing sharper, louder, nearer, bringing her to him, the reason inconsequential.

He held his breath, heart beating loud enough to rival the footfalls.

And he realized too late, no engine had preceded those steps.

The crash of breaking glass snapped him upright; he tossed Astrid to the floor between the bed and wall. The heavy curtain kept the shards from flying, but something blunt was smashing in the window, shoving the folds aside. The butt end of a baseball bat. It was gone before Duncan could edge near enough to grasp it or get a look at its owner, silhouetted by the parking lot lights.

He lunged for his phone, but something blunt and brutal struck his calf—blunt, and blazing. Fire licked at his foot and the bedspread, a rag-wrapped brick painting the room yellow and stinking of gasoline. He rushed for the nearest water—Astrid's bowl—and dampened the blaze. With a dash to the bathroom to refill, he doused the fire for good, snuffed a couple of flames guttering on the rug with his bare foot. He grabbed his phone and bolted for the door, jerked it open so hard he was struck in the chin by the chain bolt's catch as it ripped free of the jamb. He barely felt it. What he did feel, however, was the push of Astrid brushing past his calf and running off into the night.

"Fuck." Chase the cat or the criminal? Had to be the latter. He took off, barefoot, in the direction past where the baseball bat had been dropped. He felt no pebbles, no glass he might have trod in, not the burn he'd just incurred; nothing but rage and hate and violence screaming to be let out. If his fellow motel guests were awake and emerging, he didn't register it. He reached the end of the long building, and voices drew his attention to the side. Two bodies, tangled as one on the asphalt beside a parked camper. A man in a ski mask and gloves, on his hands and knees, and on top of him—

"Raina."

She had her knee jammed into the small of the man's back, and a gleaming black object pinned to his neck—the barrel of a gun.

"Don't move. Don't you give me a fucking reason to shoot you."

The man did move, but not voluntarily. He was shaking—trembling. Weeping, chanting something again and again, quavering words Duncan couldn't pick out.

The man was in hysterics, clutching the back of his head, wailing. Raina straddled his back and used her free hand to yank the mask from his head.

Duncan stared at the man. He'd almost expected to recognize him, but he'd never seen this face in his life. And he realized what the man was saying, then. *"No me lástimes—por favor, no me lástimes."*

Don't hurt me—please, don't hurt me, over and over and over. Confusion descended. Duncan looked to Raina. "This is no angry local."

The man was small, and looked fairly young—twenty-five, perhaps—but he was dressed like a laborer, not a street thug.

Raina looked thrown; she sat up straighter, the weapon dropping to her side.

Duncan got to his knees and in a slow, clear voice demanded, *"Habla inglés?"*

If the man did, he was too busy sobbing his fearful mantra to make it known.

"He can *write* in English," Raina said, "if he's the same brick-thrower who vandalized your car and my building . . . Though I wondered once if the notes had looked so stiff because someone wanted to disguise their writing. But maybe they were stiff because someone had been copying them in a language they didn't know."

Duncan nodded. He had never taken Spanish, but having

lived in San Diego for over a decade, he could cobble together enough to be understood. "Who are you?" he demanded.

More sobs answered him.

"Who told you to do this?"

An answer came back, one Duncan translated to "Can't say. Can't say."

"Did they pay you, or ..." He didn't know the word for "threatened," but it didn't matter—the man began chanting a lament, something about family.

"They hurt ...," Duncan relayed to Raina. "They said they'd hurt my family."

"Goddamn."

"Who?" Duncan asked in Spanish. "Who was going to hurt your family?"

The reply was complex, but Duncan gleaned something to the effect of "They'll send everyone home." He told this to Raina.

"Send everyone home? Does he mean the construction workers?"

"Do you work for Virgin River?" Duncan demanded. Nothing intelligible came back. "We'd better call—"

Sirens cut Duncan off then, telling him another motel guest had beaten him to it. He stood as the first beige cruiser arrived. It skidded to a halt with a screech of brakes, and it was Deputy Ritchey, the female officer who'd helped Flores search Duncan's motel room. She jogged over, Taser drawn.

"That man threw a flaming brick through my window," Duncan told her, then pointed to Raina. "She caught him."

"Stay where you are," Ritchey warned the man as Raina slowly got to her feet and backed away.

"I think he's been coerced," Duncan told the deputy, but she was preoccupied with cuffing him and speaking far stronger Spanish than Duncan did.

"Call Flores," Duncan said. He would himself, but his phone was trapped in his room-turned-crime scene, beyond a minefield of broken glass. "This man was sent to intimidate me." Intimidate, or perhaps hurt, or even kill?

Ritchey told her radio, "I need Flores at the motel," then got back to whatever protocol she was going through with Duncan's terrified assailant.

Raina came to stand by Duncan's side as more officers arrived, crowding them away as the man was led to a patrol car.

He called behind him, *"Perdóneme,"* over and over, the message meant for Duncan. *Forgive me, forgive me.* It gave him chills. He nearly wanted to call out in kind, shamed to have ever been a part of the project that had brought so much violence and death to this once-sleepy town.

"I can't decide whether this is better or worse than angry locals," Raina said, watching the scene.

"It's worse." Both motivations—ignorant anger and cold calculation—were unsettling, but there was something sharply disturbing about the impersonal nature of the truth. Something cowardly to boot, to realize the person sent to scare him had been frightened as well. They were both victims, both disposable in the eyes of the people playing this game. That man had been their pawn, and Duncan their target, obstacles in the way of, what? Progress?

No, money. Always money, when you dug deep enough. The rotten root from which all progress sprang.

"I guess I can stop suspecting my customers, at least," Raina said.

"Yes. That's something."

A silver SUV arrived, and a moment later Flores was marching over, eyes narrowed at the cuffed man now sitting in the back of the cruiser. The door was open and a flashlight-wielding officer was talking to him. As he drew closer, Flores looked startled. "The fuck?"

"He threw a brick through my window," Duncan said.

"And it's not the first time," Raina added. "I have photos."

"He doesn't speak English," Duncan said, "but he's terrified. I think he's been coerced. Same as my so-called witness."

"That *is* your witness," Flores muttered, brushing gruffly past him.

Duncan spun around. "What?"

"You two stay put," Flores barked over his shoulder.

"Jesus," Raina said.

Duncan nodded. "Well put. I suspect we've a long night ahead of us. And my room's a crime scene, so I doubt I'll be sleeping soon . . . Astrid ran off as well."

"Shit."

"There's no way they'll let me go after her now . . . I can only hope she's holed up somewhere safe and stays put."

An officer came by and took statements, photographed Duncan's various injuries, then asked them to wait. Duncan could feel his feet now—cut up and dirty, tender where he'd stomped out those flames. He shifted from one foot to the other, and wished he had a sweater.

Raina's hands were in her jacket pockets, and Duncan eyed her. "Why on earth did you come armed?" he asked. "You weren't camped out here on security detail, were you?"

"Armed? Oh no." She pulled a hand from her pocket, revealing not a pistol, but Duncan's cologne, of all things. He'd mistaken its round black cap in the shadows.

"I was just bluffing." She handed him the bottle. "And I wasn't on watch duty—I came to see you. You left that in my bathroom."

He cracked a weak smile, turning the bottle over in his hands.

"For five hundred bucks," she said, "it better goddamn double for a weapon, huh?"

"True. Who needs Samuel Colt when you've got Tom Ford . . . ?" He set the bottle on the concrete walkway and took a seat beside it. "Why did you come, exactly? Had you failed to tell me off in all the ways you'd meant to?"

She winced. "You know, you weren't much nicer during that fight."

"No, perhaps not."

She spoke to his hands. "But I came to apologize. To tell you that I was too harsh." She met his gaze. "And I realized I missed you. I didn't want you leaving for good, without hearing me admit that."

"Oh."

"It just hurt, because before that bracelet move, I really thought you *got* me, you know? I know that wasn't you trying to buy me or dress me up, not really. But in the moment I just . . . I dunno. And then what you said, about the bar . . . I'd *just* given myself permission to let it go. I couldn't handle somebody telling me their plans to keep me chained to it. As generous as your idea was."

He nodded. "I could see how that might be a touch overwhelming."

She gathered her hair in both hands, twisting it into a knot. "I've been with too many guys who had plans about how they wanted to change me—whether that meant convincing me I was the marrying kind, or talking me into stripping on a fucking webcam. I've been told too many times that I swear too much, that I dress too cheap, hang out with the wrong people, that I've fucked too many guys to be taken seriously as 'girl-friend material.' Like I'd even asked, you know? Like I could even give a shit."

"I made you feel that way? Like I wanted to change you?"

"I dunno . . . Maybe a little, when you gave me that gift. That's why I flipped out on you. I'd really, *really* thought you liked me exactly the way I was."

"And I did. I do."

"Yeah, I know you do. You just wanted to give me a fucking bracelet." She smiled at him, looking sheepish and weary. "Like I said, I'm sorry. I don't usually let anybody get close enough to stand a chance at hurting my feelings. It stings way worse when you're out of practice at it."

"You hurt my feelings as well. The night of the photo shoot, when you snubbed me."

She blinked. "Snubbed you?"

"I must have stood there like an idiot for five minutes or more, waiting for you to introduce me to people. Acknowledge me."

"When did— Oh. Who was I talking to?"

"Tall woman, thin. Colorful."

"That's my friend Angie. Her husband just started radiation—lung cancer, same as my dad. It wasn't the kind of conversation you just hit Pause on, I guess."

"Oh."

"I'm sorry, though."

"Well, thank you. Even if that does make me feel rather petty."

Her gaze dropped. "You've got blood on your chin."

Duncan touched the spot, feeling a small gash. "That'd be my chain lock."

"Here." She wadded her hand in the cuff of her jacket and spat on it, dabbing at his wound. It would have been gross, if it hadn't so perfectly encapsulated their affair.

"This is giving me déjà vu," he said.

"At least you get to keep all your teeth this time." She finished fussing and stretched, then leaned forward to wrap her arms around her knees. Resting her cheek there, she blinked up at him. "I assumed you left the photo shoot because it wasn't your scene. And I wanted you there, trust me. I was really looking forward to telling everybody I was sleeping with the Nordic sex god in the dusty jeans."

He smiled at that. For a time they were quiet; then Duncan asked, "So you really want to close the bar? Really?"

"I don't *want* to close it, no. But I can't run it anymore, not when I know selling it would give me the time and the capital to try doing what I really want to. And I know that's what my dad would want, more than all the stuff in his old notebooks put together."

Duncan nodded. "And would you leave Fortuity?"

"I don't want to. If I can make a place for myself here, if the casino comes and there's a market for my work, great. But I'll move on if I have to. That might be a relief, actually, if Benji's gets turned into some awful chain."

"That would be a shame—"

"Harper," someone called. Flores. He walked over, offering Duncan a curt nod of acknowledgment. "You're needed for further questioning. Welch, you're free to go. You got someplace to stay aside from that busted-up room?"

Raina stood, fished in her pocket, and handed Duncan her keys. "Stay at mine. You can take my truck, too. I'll get somebody to drop me off." She shot Flores a look.

The man nodded. "Sure."

Duncan got to his feet, wishing they had one more minute to talk before she was taken away. He needed to know what would happen when she got home. Needed to know which bed to climb into. Whether they were over, or just about to start up again. But she just smiled, then turned to follow Flores toward the clustered cruisers.

In an instant, Duncan was beat—exhausted to the edge of oblivion. With some effort, he talked one of the officers documenting the motel room into fetching his boots and socks and phone, though only after they'd been thoroughly photographed.

He found Raina's truck parked haphazardly just inside the entrance to the lot, and climbed behind the wheel. When the engine woke, so did the ancient tape deck, and Jim Croce was singing about saving time in a bottle. Duncan hummed along, the lyrics long forgotten, and parked behind the bar just as the song came to an end.

The motion sensor lights were still switched off, and with the truck locked, he squinted in the darkness, searching Raina's loaded ring for the back-door key.

Prrrowwwp.

Duncan started, fumbled for his phone, and illuminated its screen. And there, in the corner beside the Dumpster, was Astrid, amber eyes wide and glowing.

"Fucking hell, you treacherous thing. Come here this instant." He got the door unlocked and enticed her close enough to catch, then carried her, writhing, up the stairs. He crouched to set her on the kitchen floor, petting her with such aggressive relief he was shocked she didn't run away. "I could throttle you, if you weren't so beautiful."

He filled a cereal bowl with water for her, then texted Raina. Found Astrid in the back lot. I guess we know where her true loyalties lie.

Duncan patched up his various injuries, and two replies chimed as he was stripping to his shorts in the guest room. She's always had good taste.

Doesn't seem like they'll be done with me for a while.
Don't wait up, just leave it unlocked, if you're okay
with that.

He wrote back See you for breakfast and climbed under the covers.

Good God, this bed felt all wrong.

Yet he was asleep the moment his head found the pillow.

Chapter 29

Raina was stuck at the BCSD until nearly sunrise, recounting her role in the night's events over and over, until it was decided her arrival at the Nugget really had been a stroke of fortuitous timing, and not a hint at some nefarious, deeper plot.

"Three a.m.'s a strange hour to be attempting a reconciliation," Flores had mused, tapping a yellow pad with the butt of his pen.

"I got off work at two thirty."

"And it couldn't wait until the morning?"

"If you'd ever had sex with Duncan, you'd understand my urgency."

He'd rubbed his face at that, sighing. "You're free to go, Ms. Harper."

"Call me Raina."

A patrol deputy had given her a lift home just as the sun slipped out from behind the horizon, and she found the back door unlocked.

Upstairs, she stooped to stroke Astrid, then tiptoed to the open guest room door, finding Duncan asleep. She was strung between wired and exhausted herself, and decided to start a pot of coffee. She didn't want to fall asleep before they had a chance to talk.

Astrid followed when Raina carried a steaming mug and her small business book into the den, and they sat in companionable silence until just after ten, when the guest bed creaked. After some rustling, Duncan appeared in yesterday's clothes, both feet wrapped in cotton gauze.

"Ouch," she said, eyeing them, then the bandage on his chin. "This town just really loves to scar you, doesn't it?"

He smiled, looking bleary, and dropped into the easy chair. The cat was on him a moment later. "Good morning, Jailbreak. And speaking of jailbreaking," he said to Raina, "I gather they released you."

She nodded. "Not till after five, but yeah. Flores says hello."

"Have you been to sleep?"

"No. Later. You left your cologne—again. They wound up seizing it as an accessory to the crime scene."

"Perhaps I just wasn't meant to keep it."

"Shame. It smells fucking amazing."

He smiled, eyes crinkling, then asked quietly, "Are we all right again?"

Raina paused, then nodded. "I think so. Do you?"

"Yes, I do."

"Let's try to keep from getting too intense, for now. Since you don't even know if you'll be sticking around or not. Is that okay? Maybe you could stay here while you figure it out—"

"Of my own free will?" he teased.

She nodded. "No more blackmail, I promise. Just stay here, decide what you want, and you and I can get back to sleeping in the same bed. If you want that."

"I think you know I do."

"Okay. Good." And with that settled, she yawned widely into her palm. 'Scuse me. I haven't slept much, even before last night."

Duncan nodded, gesturing toward her bedroom. "Go rest. Properly. I don't want to see you until sunset."

"Maybe not, but my patrons will."

"I have Casey's number; I'll get him to open the bar."

"It'll be too busy for just one, and Abilene's not in until seven."

"I'll help him," Duncan offered.

Raina laughed. "You?"

"Have you any idea how rigorous the California bar is? I'm sure I've the mental capacity to make change and fill pitchers."

"All right, then, if you insist. It's probably good public relations, you getting seen behind that counter. Even your detractors will be forced to forgive you, if they want to get served. Just be prepared to have your ear talked off about the case."

"I'm sure I'm the worst-informed person in town on the matter. Perhaps I can finally catch up. Now go to bed." They owed each other a proper reunion, later. Rested, showered, free to get lost in each other's bodies with no other obligations nagging. Duncan rounded the table and kissed the top of her head. "I'll see you tonight."

"That you will." Her chair scooted back with a squeak, and she headed for her room.

Duncan texted Casey, and was surprised to be met with no resistance. The reason for his cooperation became clear once he and Duncan were downstairs, readying the bar.

"So, what the fuck went down last light?" Casey asked. "Raina shot that guy who accused you of taking bribes?"

Duncan laughed. "Not quite, no. Where do you get your news from?"

"What happened?"

"My harasser paid me another visit, late, just when Raina was coming to the motel. We'd had a spat."

Casey snorted.

"Anyway, she tackled him. She wasn't armed, she just got him to believe she was. It was all very dramatic for a few minutes. Then we spent the rest of the night giving statements."

"Guess you made up, then, if she's got you working."

"This was my idea. Though yes, I think we'll be okay." *For as long as I'm meant to stay here, anyway.* With Sunnyside off the table, he was left with few options. He could take the Nevada bar . . . though the thought didn't rouse anything in him besides apathy. Still, he had plenty of money. He could afford to be idle for a time, to see where things went.

Though of course, Duncan plus idleness never added up to superior mental health.

It was a Saturday, and a busy week, and twenty minutes after they unlocked the door, Duncan had mastered filling pints and pitchers, opening longnecks, and navigating the medieval cash register, as well as deflecting questions—curious and hostile alike—about his role in the investigation. Casey helped with the more aggressive approaches, having no qualms about telling trumped-up customers to "Shut your face and tip your fucking server."

Duncan smiled at the latest such exchange, eyeing Casey as he carried four dripping pints to the other end of the bar. When he returned, Duncan said, "You seem rather at home in this setting."

Casey shrugged. "I worked here ages ago. The drill hasn't changed."

The bar may, though. Benji's might be unrecognizable in a year, or nonexistent. Though that certainly wasn't Duncan's news to spread.

"Would you ever consider managing this place?" he asked. "If Raina wanted to pursue her tattooing full-time?"

Casey laughed. "Yeah, because she can totally afford to pay a manager."

Duncan mixed what he hoped was a potable whiskey and Coke, then turned back to Casey. "But if she could. Would you consider it?"

"I dunno. I'd—" Casey stopped, turning at the sound of twenty people all shushing each other. "News," he murmured, and Duncan went still, straining along with everyone else to hear the TV. He could see one of the sets from where they stood.

"There were two big breaks overnight in the ongoing murder and conspiracy investigation here in Fortuity," said Michelle Pastor, the stern-yet-perky Latina weekend anchor. *"KBCN has just been told that the identity of those human remains at the center of this stunning case have been made public."*

Murmurs moved through the room like a brush fire, chased by an eerie hush.

"The victim, we now know, was an undocumented migrant— twenty-six-year-old Luis Alvez, of Mazatlán, Mexico."

From somewhere in the crowd, "Goddamn illegals—"

"Shut your shit, dumb-ass," Casey shouted.

"Alvez's remains were identified by his older sister, Cecilia Alvez, who lives in Reno on a student visa. She says she'd been worried about her brother, having not heard from Luis in weeks. Cecilia Alvez has declined all interviews, but was quoted as saying, 'I knew something wasn't right—my brother always called on Sundays. I was afraid to report him missing. I knew he was here illegally, and I didn't want him to get deported over nothing. But when I heard about the bones, that the person had been his age, his height, I just knew. I knew it was Luis.'

"Ms. Alvez was apparently shown a scrap of fabric, collected from the disused mine where the victim's dead body was believed to have been burned last month. She confirmed for authorities that it had been her brother's—a distinctive handkerchief that could have only been given to him by their mother.

"Luis Alvez had been employed by Virgin River Contracting as a manual laborer, and stunning police interviews with his

former coworkers reveal that a cover-up has been in effect for weeks. KCBN was able to speak with one of those men."

The screen switched to previously recorded footage of a dark-skinned, nervous young man standing before a trailer in the bright noontime sunshine, clutching a baseball cap in both hands. He spoke in rapid Spanish, and a voiceover translated. *"Luis just disappeared one day. Another guy, he said Luis ran off with this woman he met a couple towns over."* Another guy—Duncan couldn't help wondering if that man might be the very same one who'd been coerced into harassing him. *"A foreman said the same. Luis was young, girl-crazy. He hated this job, so we all assumed it was true. Now we hear the truth? I can't believe he was murdered. I can't believe it."*

The anchor reappeared. *"Except it appears that Alvez wasn't murdered. Late last night, another worker was apprehended in Fortuity, and his confession broke this case wide open."* Duncan's assailant, no doubt, though it seemed the man's identity was being kept confidential.

Luis Alvez had been the victim of a negligent industrial accident, his left leg crushed when a piece of heavy machinery fell into a ditch he was clearing. Forensics experts believed that he'd died of shock, or massive internal bleeding.

The man who'd corroborated Levins's accusation against Duncan might've been a false witness on that count, but apparently he'd seen Alvez's accident. Levins had told him not to speak of it, on threat of deportation.

"Fuck of an effort, just to hide an accident," Casey muttered.

"Not if it was negligence, on the contractors' part. If it came under investigation, Virgin River could have lost the entire project. It's a huge contract. Big enough to ruin a company."

"Levins allegedly also ordered that worker to tell others that Alvez had run off with a girlfriend. After Levins was apprehended last week, the worker was approached by another employee of VRC, a man whose identity has not yet been made public. That man allegedly threatened the worker and his family with bodily harm unless he agreed to testify that he'd seen Duncan Welch, an employee of the casino's development company, accepting bribes from Levins."

Duncan glanced around, all eyes now riveted to him. He waved awkwardly.

"Welch, who made headlines Wednesday night by locating

Alvez's remains, is now believed to have been framed by Levins and his coconspirators, as retribution for his involvement in exposing Levins's part in the August murder of Alex Dunn. The unnamed worker was apprehended after throwing a flaming rock through Welch's motel room window, one of an escalating number of intimidation tactics orchestrated by the man's extortionists. Michelle Pastor, KCBN News."

If people had been curious before, they were positively hypnotized by Duncan now.

"It was a brick," he offered the still-quiet barroom. "Not a rock."

And in the next five minutes, no less than twenty people tried to buy Duncan a drink.

That bulletin and others steadily filled in the blanks over the course of the afternoon. Alvez's body had been burned, his bones buried by the foothills, but hastily. Another worker discovered them, and Alex Dunn had been dispatched to the scene. Sheriff Tremblay, who'd been receiving kickbacks from Levins, was already aware of the accident, told Alex he'd been taking over the investigation. Of course then Alex had been murdered, to keep the secret buried. Tremblay's own murder was still under investigation.

It seemed the laborer who'd discovered the bones had been informed that they belonged to some anonymous victim of the narcotics trade, and that had been that. Until now. With Luis Alvez identified as the casualty, workers had come forward by the dozen. They accused Levins and other managers at VRC of routinely hiring undocumented migrants, paying them less than minimum wage, and threatening them with deportation to keep them quiet.

So, in the end, it seemed Luis Alvez had died in an accident, caused by carelessness, fueled by pressure on foremen like Levins to meet outlandish construction deadlines, in the pursuit of early completion bonuses. He and Alex Dunn had both died so their bosses could keep getting paid. So a construction outfit wouldn't lose a lucrative contract. Nothing more than greed, in the end.

The saddest fucking truth in the world.

Chapter 30

Fresh details grew rare as the day wore on, and by the time Abilene arrived, the din of fevered gossip had dulled to a simmer. Casey wiped the bar down, relieved to feel a lull coming on.

"So," he said to Duncan, who was tidying the garnish bins. "When do you get back to work, do you think?"

"On the casino? I suspect that's all on hold for the time being, until and if Sunnyside can find a new contracting company. It could be months before construction starts up again. And when and if it does, I won't be a part of it."

"No?" Damn, that was disappointing. Casey had come to like having Duncan around. "Can't blame you, I guess. Fortuity hasn't exactly treated you good."

"Oh, I don't know that I'll leave."

Casey gave his head a shake. "You'd stay here, willingly?"

"I'm considering it ... Do *you* see yourself sticking around?"

"For a while, maybe," Casey said. "Provided my living arrangements improve."

"Are things not all rainbows and rose petals in the Grossier homestead?"

"Dude, I share a bedroom wall with my brother—it's a fucking nightmare. If Kim doesn't find a place soon, I'm gonna make a break for it myself."

Casey filled a few orders, and found Duncan still studying him with that curious look on his face.

"I know what you're thinking, Welch. It's not gonna happen."

Duncan's eyebrows rose. "You know what I'm thinking?"

"It's so fucking obvious. You and Raina want to recruit me for a three-way. Sorry, man, but I couldn't bear to show you up like that. I'm a lot of things, but a home wrecker ain't one of 'em."

Duncan laughed, looking as disgusted as he was amused. "And for a second I thought you were a mind reader."

Nope, not quite. Not far off, but not quite. "So, what is it, really?"

Duncan took a deep breath, then surprised the hell out of him. "I want to buy the bar."

Casey squinted at him, way confused. "This dump?"

Duncan nodded.

"*You* want to buy Benji's?"

"I believe I do."

"Is Raina even looking to sell?"

"She is. Though do keep that between us—no reason to worry people." He nodded subtly in Abilene's direction.

"Well, that's a kick in the balls . . . But you gotta tell me why you want it, Dunky. I'm fucking dying to hear."

"I came here with the casino. Fortuity was nothing more than a weedy lot to me then, a blank bit of land for building on, its residents no more than loitering pests."

Casey's hackles rose a fraction, but he held his tongue for once, curious where this was headed. Plus, he couldn't really be too annoyed—he'd been over the fucking moon to escape his podunk hometown nine-plus years ago.

"Those opinions changed, obviously," Duncan said.

"Raina sure must be psycho in bed."

Duncan ignored that, tending to a customer. When he returned, he went on. "I came here thinking it was my job to paper over the rougher parts of this place, to better it. I thought Fortuity was standing in its own way, and that I was part of a greater vision for it."

"My brother would pop you for that one. But me, I'm inclined to agree."

"I rather hated this bar, in fact, when I first arrived, but since then it's changed me, for the better. Raina's father had a lot of hopes for it, ones that he wasn't able to implement in his lifetime, which seems a shame. Now Raina may be ready to move on and leave it behind, but I can't help feeling I'm not."

"Town's got its creepy-ass vines on you, huh?"

"Its what?"

"Nothing. It's just fucked, how hard it is to leave this place. Thought I'd managed it myself, but just look at this shit." He gave his bar towel a flick. "Back working the same job I had before I left. Swear to God this town's built on quicksand."

"So you're staying?"

Casey shrugged. "I promised my brother I'd stay through all this shit with the investigation, and that's far from over. We still don't know for sure who arranged to fuck with you. Or who killed Tremblay, for that matter."

"One would hope the conspirators are among the VRC managers who've been indicted."

"Yeah, you would hope that, but considering how the fucking county sheriff was involved, don't hold your breath that this rot doesn't go deeper." Plus, there was the little matter of waiting for the rainy season to arrive with its so-called starless nights, to make sure that scary shit he'd seen didn't actually come to pass.

And beyond the dangers, Casey had to admit there was a certain satisfaction to doing the right thing by his mom, depressing though it was.

"So yeah, I'm here for a while, anyhow," he told Duncan. "Maybe when you take over Benji's you could give me a raise. Raina barely pays me more than her dad did when I was twenty-three."

"I was actually wondering if you might like to go into business *with* me. As partners."

Casey laughed, incredulous. Lost. He delivered the shots and dried his hands on his towel, turning to face Duncan properly. "Okay, hold up. First, you want to run a bar. That's fucking weird. On top of that you want my help, which is just *fucked*. I can mix a few drinks, but my expertise ends there. Plus, who the fuck would take me for a businessman?"

"I would," Duncan said. "Because I suspect your simpleton shtick is as put-on as your Southern accent . . . What do you *do*, Mr. Grossier?"

"Something that pays real good," Casey said carefully. "With shit benefits."

"I believe that. You don't reek of desperation, the way so many of your fellow natives do. You've the confidence of a man who doesn't need to check his bank balance before writing his rent check."

Casey shrugged, deflecting. "I live with my mom."

"You know what I'm implying, Mr. Grossier."

"You've got more money than I do, I bet. Why not go all in?"

"I could. But part of me thinks Benji's deserves to be owned, at least in part, by a native son. I buy it outright—if Raina would even let me—and I can make it as true to her father's vision as humanly possible, but it'll still be an outsider's makeover. Plus, I can't help thinking you rather like being back here. Back in your spawning grounds."

"You suspect a lot of shit about me, Welch." And too much of it was true.

"I'm a very presumptuous man."

"You're a confusing bastard is what you are . . ."

"What do you think?"

What did Casey think? He thought precisely zero things that were respectable enough to share. He thought, first and foremost, that this bar was a cash-based business, and that he could launder a fuck-load of sketchy income through it. Except this wasn't any old convenient storefront. He loved this shit hole. He didn't trust himself not to piss all over that with the opportunity to exploit it right there in front of him. He was a man who considered every situation, every invitation and relationship, first and foremost with the question *What's in this for me?* It had taken him thirty-three years to notice that about himself, but since he had, it had begun to unsettle him. After all, his father had looked at their house, this town, at his wife and young sons, and asked himself that same question, twenty-some years ago. And the conclusion he'd come to was *Not enough.*

Casey shook his head. "You don't want me for a business partner. Trust me on that one."

"You'd have to keep it separate from whatever endeavors you've been calling your career these past few years, that's true. Fortuity's made me lax, but I still respect the sanctity of accounting."

"That settles it, then. We're not built to be partners."

"You're not twenty-five anymore, Mr. Grossier. And in a blink you'll be fifty."

Casey frowned. He also couldn't keep reporting that his assets were gambling windfalls forever.

"In a blink you'll find yourself attached to a place, or a woman, or a child," Duncan went on. "Like Raina, you may want to quit mistaking roots for anchors, and realize setting them down has its benefits."

"That's real deep, Dad. Thanks." But he couldn't help picturing Abilene. Sure, there was no future there, but the shit she'd made him feel when they first met . . . That could happen again, with some girl who wasn't such a train wreck. There was a bigger snag, though—miles bigger. "I could be fucking incompetent in five, ten years," he reminded Duncan. "Camped out on the couch in my slippers next to my mom, waiting for the *Family Feud* to come on."

"That all remains to be seen. Just give me two years," Duncan said. "I'll buy you out after that. I'll put as much in writing."

"Why not ask Vince? He's not going anyplace."

"Your brother's rich in loyalty, not capital."

Casey slumped. "True enough."

"He also lacks the disposition this job demands. But you—you're as charming as you are offensive."

"Thanks?"

"Two years," Duncan repeated. "Long enough to renovate, to install a kitchen, to set Benji's up to be the last authentically local venue in this town. The last place that truly belongs to Fortuity. Be my manager, if not my coowner. Help me get it set up, and whatever shape it takes, I'll keep it that way."

"You settling down here for the rest of your life?"

"I couldn't guess," Duncan said. "But I'd like to leave this town feeling I've helped preserve something. A penance for the man who arrived thinking Fortuity was fit for a wrecking ball."

"I dunno, man. Neither of us knows jack about running a restaurant."

"But I guarantee we're smarter than the vast majority of the people who manage to pull it off."

Goddamn if this prick didn't know just the right angle to do the old reach-around and stroke Casey's ego.

And he could picture it a little now. As the sole heir to the ranch, Miah was surely the crown prince of this town. But the owner of Benji's commanded a certain level of respect, too. If Fortuity had a heart, the bar was it. Plus, two years . . . He'd promised Vince he'd stick around through this casino drama. Light had been shed on Alex's death, but there was still plenty of upheaval likely to come in the couple of years before the Eclipse would open. Probably longer than that, now that Sunnyside had to find a new contracting outfit to finish the fucking thing. Casey could commit himself to the club long enough to be here through the changes destined to come to town.

And yeah, it really was a bit pathetic that he worked, like, fifteen hours a week and lived with his mom.

Plus, if he ran Benji's, he could give Abilene a big-ass raise. Get his Robin Hood on, just as he'd been wishing he could.

"I'm not saying yes," he said to Duncan, but the man's smile said it all. Yeah, Casey had cracked. Just a little.

But cracks never got smaller with time or pressure, did they?

"You're not saying no," Duncan countered.

"Not yet. But I prefer my assets liquid. And my commitments flimsy. Manager, sure. Owner? I dunno yet. And this is all *if* Raina will even agree to it."

"Naturally. So, shall we shake?"

"No fucking way. Gimme a chance to sleep on it."

Duncan was pleased Raina had obeyed his orders and taken the night off—the night off work, and since her TV was downstairs, a night off the news as well. She'd called the bar's number to check in around eight, saying she'd slept plenty and was ready to relieve someone, but he'd been insistent.

"Abilene and I got this," Casey said later, when things quieted. "Go up and tell Raina your crazy-ass plan. Lemme know how it goes."

So Duncan surrendered his towel and checked his phone. Missed calls, many of them, most probably from the press, and one from his boss at Sunnyside. And one from the auto shop. He'd forgotten about the car.

How very unlike me. The old me. A few weeks ago, he could no sooner have forgotten about his car than he might have misplaced his spleen. It had been very much a part of him, and yet now . . .

He actually missed the *bike*, if anything. It was an accepting sort of machine, whereas Duncan had always made sure to dress well enough to look worthy of the Merc. Like a trophy wife.

How utterly fucked that made him, he thought as he headed up the back steps, that he'd so prized a vehicle he felt judged by. How fucked that he'd spent so long *craving* judgment, living in a constant state of approval-seeking, all the while presenting as the epitome of self-satisfaction.

Upstairs he was greeted by the cat, and was surprised to see her steel bowls back in their place. To the lit den he called, "You collected my things, I see."

Raina wandered over to the threshold, looking as alluringly disheveled as always in her shorts and tank top, hair messy from a marathon of well-deserved sleep. "I didn't, actually — Flores had somebody bring all your stuff over."

"Finally that man decides to do me a favor . . . Just as well. I could certainly stand a change of clothes."

She smiled, looking just a touch shy. "Hello, Duncan."

"Hello, Ms. Harper."

"Come hang out," she said, a curling finger inviting him to join her. And not in the den — she led him to her room. Duncan found his suitcase on the floor and changed into lounge pants and a clean T-shirt. As he sat cross-legged with her on her bed, everything about this room felt right, smelled right.

"You do okay, downstairs?" she asked.

"Surprisingly well. I'm not much use with a shaker, but there's hope for me."

"Thank you. For that. I really, really needed a night off. Not as much as you, I bet, but thank you all the same."

Nervous and a touch needy, he reached out to take her hands. "I did a lot of thinking down there." He swallowed, took a deep breath, all at once awake and fretful. Idle chat with Casey was one thing, but as he braced himself to tell her his wishes, he realized with a fearful pang exactly how badly he wanted this.

"Thinking," she prompted. "What about?"

"Do you remember how you told me, if I wanted the bar to stay, I should buy it my own goddamn self?"

She laughed. "Oh Lord — stop now, please."

He plowed onward. "I want to buy the bar from you. Casey and I would run it."

"Casey? Casey Grossier?"

"Yes. We want to take over Benji's from you, and do our best to respect your father's plans, without turning it into a memorial to him."

She was shaking her head, more incredulous than angry, he hoped.

"That bar changed my life," he went on, "and I want to see it thriving beside the competition the casino might bring. I want to preserve something from the town I came here planning to renovate. I want the people who live here to have a place to drink that still belongs to them."

A pause. "Any other reasons?"

"No, none like those you worried about, when I said I wanted to give you that money yesterday. It's not a shackle to keep the two of us attached. Whatever may happen with you and me, whether you decide to stay here or not, I want this. For myself. You'll get any say you want, of course—you want to hang on to the building and just sell me the bar, that's fine. You want to move away one day . . . ? Your choice. The property or just the business—whichever entity you might wish to part with. Whichever would give you the freedom you're after, that's what I'll buy."

"And how on earth did Casey get sucked into this madness?"

"I want a local involved, for authenticity. And because I have no clue how to run a bar."

"And Casey's going to sit still long enough to make this all happen?"

"He says he will. If he runs off after something shiny next week, I'll find a way to make it work. Tell me, would this make you feel better or worse—knowing the bar's staying?"

"Run by you and Casey? Better. Bought and bastardized by some cheesy chain outfit . . . ? I'd rather see it burned to the ground. Though I know that's who most of the potential buyers are likely to be."

He rubbed her knuckles with his thumbs. "That settles it, then. I want to buy your father's bar. Your bar. I'll buy it and run it to the best of my abilities. And I'll change the name. I'd never claim I know your father's wants enough to make it what he imagined—"

"You'll change the name over my dead body."

Duncan smiled at that, just as Astrid arrived to head-butt his thigh. "All right. Benji's it stays."

Raina sighed softly, dropping her head, smiling when she raised her chin and met his eyes again. "When he was dying, my dad told me that bar's the best tombstone a man could ask for. His name up there, lit for everyone to see, dozens of well-wishers visiting him every night. You want to keep it going, you have at it. But don't you dare change the name over that door."

"I won't. So, do we have a deal?"

"Not yet. I haven't decided what I want to do, aside from make tattooing my full-time focus. Maybe I *would* like to hang on to the building. Maybe . . . maybe I'd like to keep a little stake in this place myself. Like a silent partner."

Duncan felt light as air. "Anything you like. I merely want it to stay open, and to succeed."

"On that we agree."

"I've a fair bit of savings, and I'll have more soon enough, once I sell my place in San Diego. I doubt I've purchased the last three-thousand-dollar suit of my life, but I'm ready to start investing in things more substantive than my self-image. Plus, I'll be saving quite a lot on therapy."

She laughed softly, squeezed his hands. "You're so goddamn weird."

"And goddamn exhausted." Though there was one thing he still needed to say tonight. He toyed with her fingers. "I'm worried you'll write this off again, because it's impulsive, or because I'm falling asleep, or any other reason. But I need to tell you again, I'm in love with you."

She didn't say a word, just held his stare.

"I'm *so* in love with you," he said. "So deeply it hurts. More deeply than I've ever felt anything . . . Any nice emotion, anyhow. As intensely as I've ever suffered panic, or anxiety—I want and need and love you."

She laughed, looking shy. "Thank you, I think."

"I want to be with you. For as long as this is supposed to last."

"I want that, too. It'll take me longer to say those words, but I want those things. I want *you*."

He smiled, feeling the best kind of drunk. "Come here." He urged her to come close, to scissor her legs with his. He took her face in his hands. He studied her eyes, lips, skin, fascinated by this woman he loved. By the vulnerable, frightening, dizzying height of these feelings . . . and by the view they afforded, so worth the risk of falling.

"You've seen the worst of me," he murmured, thoughts breaking free, rushing out as though a dam inside his heart had burst. "I never thought I'd let anyone see that. I never believed anyone would like that man."

"Smile," she said softly, and he did. He let her trace the lines beside his mouth and eyes, the contact warming him more than any sexual touch could. She took pleasure in these details, or perhaps in the gesture, to judge by the way her thumbs stroked his rounded cheeks.

"What do you see?" he asked.

"A happy man. With a face that gives away every last thing he feels."

"I used to fancy myself as having quite the poker face."

"Nope." She rubbed the spot between his eyebrows. "This pinches together when you're annoyed."

He put on his best irritated expression, and she laughed.

"And these here— You get crow's-feet when you smile, and a little roll under each eye. You've got three lines across your forehead from that judgy face you're always making at commoners. And when you laugh, it shows all your perfect top teeth."

"Not all perfect," he said.

"Perfect to anyone who didn't know. And I *do* know." When she ran her thumb over that tooth, he remembered her crouching before him, pressing the bottom of her shirt to his bleeding mouth. She'd held his head that day. And though the moment had been nothing but confusion and bright scarlet pain, he remembered being struck by the contact. Soothed. Maybe his body had known all along that this woman was essential to him.

For a long time they sat in silence, studying each other's faces, fingers flirting. Finally Duncan sighed and said, "I'm going to get ready for bed. I'm exhausted."

She held his hands tight, not letting him go just yet. "How exhausted?"

"Quite," he said carefully, studying the glint in her eyes. "But perhaps not completely . . . ?"

"I hope not."

"Why? Whatever do you want with me, Raina?"

"That's Ms. Harper," she teased. "Now go get cleaned up, and I'll show you."

Chapter 31

Three weeks later found October looming, the air as dry as ever but the bite in the midmorning breeze markedly sharper. Duncan squinted against the sun as he fumbled with the bar's mailbox key, then smiled at the sight of manila amid the assorted catalogs and bills.

Back upstairs, he called, "Mail's here," pulling the stairwell door shut behind him.

Raina rushed in from the den, grinning. "Did it come?"

He frowned, holding out a stack of junk mail.

"Aw man. I thought today was—"

He whipped the fat envelope out from behind his back.

She snatched it and whapped his arm. "Shithead." He watched with pleasure as she tore at the closure and pulled out the papers—the documents officially outlining the joint ownership of Benji's. She scanned the pages, then read the bit pertaining to her own role aloud: "'... limited partnership, functioning in a consulting capacity, with no involvement in the daily operations and management of the business ...'" She sighed, head dropping back.

"How about that?" Duncan teased. "All of the power, nearly none of the responsibility. And you deny being a savvy businesswoman?"

She looked back to the page, smiling as she scanned the words one more time.

"You're free," Duncan said, and took the papers from her. "How does it feel?"

"Kinda fucking amazing. And with none of the guilt I'd imagined I'd feel when I assumed I'd have to shut that place down. Or the dread, thinking I'd have to move out of my home."

Duncan glanced at the microwave clock. "I'd suggest a toast, but it's barely ten a.m."

"We have to wait for Case, anyway," she said. Casey's interest in the bar had evolved and grown since he had first agreed to act as manager, and ultimately he and Duncan had gone in equally, with Raina retaining a token stake.

"We'll have our toast downstairs, tonight," Duncan agreed. "I can't think of a more appropriate setting."

"Speaking of propriety . . ." Raina crossed her arms, leaning against the counter. "Casey is officially Abilene's boss now."

He laughed. "Yes, we may need to have a discussion regarding our sexual harassment policy . . . Though if I'm not mistaken, his flirtation's been mellowing, the closer her due date looms."

"True. Nothing like impending birth to scare a man out of his infatuation. Plus, Casey's basically harmless. It's actually Abilene you'll probably want to have a serious talk with. And soon."

"What about? Maternity leave?" he asked.

"No. Do you know who that baby's father is?"

"I hadn't wanted to ask, since she's never once mentioned him."

"And normally I'd say you're smart to butt out, but not in this case. He's incarcerated."

"Oh my. What for?"

"Gunrunning," she said. "Vince knows him, from one of his stints downstate."

"Is he dangerous?"

"To Abilene? I couldn't say. But he doesn't sound like the most levelheaded, gentle guy, and he's up for parole this winter. And apparently he doesn't know about the baby."

Duncan frowned.

"I don't know what kind of terms they broke up on," Raina continued, "but I think you better find out. Vince has been trying to get Abilene's permission to talk to the guy for her, which only makes me worry she's afraid to do it herself. If he's about to get out, and there's any chance he's going to show up downstairs with an ax to grind . . ."

Duncan nodded. "I'll talk to Vince. Maybe he and Casey and I can meet with her together. Get a plan in place, if we need one." Duncan had once asked Vince if he'd slept his way into in-law status with their little club. But now that he was so deeply, and legally, enmeshed with the bar, his membership was beginning to feel rather official, whether he liked it or not. Then again, he hadn't driven his car in two weeks or more. The bike was his now—paid in full, plated, and his new license would be arriving any day now, complete with Class M designation.

He'd been claimed by this town, as surely as he had been by Raina, and he wouldn't have it any other way. To think how much he'd been missing his condo, before everything had fallen apart . . . He'd gone back to San Diego last week to collect a few things, and had been shocked by how suffocating his former sanctuary had felt. Stifling, and cold, and lonely in its perfection. It had been with relief, not uncertainty, that he'd signed the papers giving a real estate agency permission to list it. God knew it didn't need staging—it was in showroom condition, looking as though no human being had ever made a real home of it. And that was true, sadly.

The man he was now was different. Scarred and callused. Imperfect in many, many ways, but also more accessible than he'd ever imagined he could be. Vulnerable. Known. A mess, but a whole one. And he liked this man. He could breathe again, with his old costume finally shed for good. He felt exposed, and he wanted more of that scary sensation. Wanted to follow it to the next level of surrender.

Raina eyed him. He'd fallen silent, pensive. She came close, and her nail traced a line from his collar to his belly. "You look sad."

He kissed her forehead. "Quite the opposite. Merely thoughtful."

"What about?"

After a long moment's hesitation, Duncan finally mustered the courage to say, "I've a special request . . . if you've got the time. When is your client due?"

"Not until four."

He swallowed, and she laughed at how scared he surely looked.

"What? We survived both death threats and Braceletgate, so I bet I can take it."

"Would you . . . Would you tattoo me?"

She stared. "For real?"

He nodded.

"Like, today? Right now?"

"Preferably."

He'd been fixated on the idea for three weeks—from nearly the exact moment he and Raina had gone back to sharing a bed. The notion had come to him in the wake of the make-up sex, in fact, and the urgency of the impulse had never faded.

Impulse had never held much sway over Duncan, not until he'd met this woman. And now that he had, he wanted to keep making the acquaintance of his more reckless instincts. Impulse had gotten him on a bike, and it had made him a bar owner. Impulse had awakened him, freed him . . . Let it brand him as well.

"Well, of course I would," she said. "Nothing would make me happier. What do you want? And where?"

"You choose. Whatever suits me. And anywhere that won't show with a dress shirt on."

"I choose? Wow, no pressure."

He took her hands in his, lacing their fingers. "You said something to me last night," he murmured, lost in those brown eyes, just as he had been when she spoke the words. Words he'd never been gifted with before, not by a guardian or friend or lover, ever in his life. They'd been standing in the empty bar just after close, the world feeling dark and calm and quiet. Raina had taken his hands, just as they stood now.

She nodded. Swallowed. Smiled, and said it again. "I love you."

"Perhaps a hundredth as deeply as I love you."

"I beg to differ."

"I want a souvenir of this moment in my life," he said. "Of the woman who tore me completely apart, only so I could put myself back together, better. More human. More . . ."

"Lovable?"

His face warmed. "Perhaps."

She took a mighty breath, looking daunted but determined. "Guess I should get sketching. More human, you say . . . ?"

He nodded.

Inspiration seemed to strike her. "A heart," she said.

"A heart?"

"An anatomical one, like in an old medical illustration. Here, give me your phone."

He did, watching over her shoulder as she looked up antique engravings and illustrations. The more he thought about the idea, the more he liked it. It really did feel as though it had taken her eyes to see the humanity in him; only fitting it be her hands that drew such proof across his skin.

"Yes, I like those. A lot. Just black?" he asked.

"Yeah."

"Where?"

She set his phone aside and laid her palm on his chest, above the actual flesh-and-blood heart she'd excavated from his stony façade. "Here, of course."

He nodded. Apt, and private. A valentine he needn't share with the entire world. "Do it."

"I won't tattoo anyone who's drunk or high," she teased. "You sure you're in your right mind?"

"Not at all. I'm in love for the first time in my life. No man's ever felt half so intoxicated as this."

"Oh, very smooth."

He smiled. "Very true. And yes, I'm sure."

"Make us an early lunch while I draw, and in an hour we'll get you all shaved and vandalized."

"I don't have the highest pain threshold. Will it hurt badly?"

"On the chest? No, not too bad. This," she said, tapping the lace design draped along her clavicle and shoulder, "was an unholy bitch. Anything right over a bone is rough, but you should be fine. It feels nothing like a needle, incidentally. More like a hot, scraping sensation. Should take two hours, probably."

She stood, pressing a kiss to the top of his head before excusing herself to collect her sketching supplies. Duncan went to the kitchen, feeling giddy and exhilarated. He made toast and poached eggs, and after they ate she perfected the design, showing him a version outlined precisely in pen. No color, no gray—all black, the heart's contours shaded with hatch marks. An antiquated look, yet there was something modern in the precision of her style.

"I love it."

She smiled. "Me, too. And I can't wait to put you on my Web site . . . You know how some of those old anatomic illustrations have different parts numbered or lettered? Like with foot-notes?"

"Yes."

"How would you feel if I added that, but with my initials? Like a secret signature?"

His chest felt hot and funny and . . . nice. "I'd like that very much."

She added the letters in, a discreet little R, C, and H scattered across the organ, posing as labels. She handed him the sketchbook for a closer look.

He'd always assumed she was talented, but to witness the process brought it to a new level. "I love it," he said again.

She bade him to follow her, and in no time she'd scanned the drawing, finessed the size, and printed it on transfer paper.

"Shirt off and get comfortable," she said. Astrid wandered in and Raina ushered her back out, shutting the door, closing Duncan in the one room in his new home he'd never actually been in before.

He took a seat in the black upholstered chair—not unlike a dentist's. Raina washed her hands in a little sink and prepped a variety of equipment, the smells of sterilization nostalgic to him, rousing memories of old, outgrown rituals and compulsions—hopefully outgrown forever, now that he'd loosened his death grip on perfection. Deep down, he'd thought perfection was the ticket to being lovable . . . to being worthy of love. But perfection could never have brought him to where he was now—it had only ever kept love at bay.

He eyed her legs as she puttered, their skin bare between her boots and the hem of the skirt, which landed just above her knees. Exactly what had triggered this sudden diversification of her wardrobe, he wasn't certain. He'd gawked two nights ago when she debuted the item, but she'd blushed and told him, "Don't make a big thing about it." So he wouldn't. Instead he merely enjoyed the view, and hoped perhaps he might have had something to do with the change.

His body went oddly calm as Raina slowly, gently shaved the hair from his left pectoral with a disposable razor and toweled him dry. He winced as she swabbed the spot with an alcohol wipe.

"That size looks just about spot-on," she murmured, eyeing the transfer. She wet his skin with a washcloth and pressed the paper in place. Once she'd peeled it away she handed Duncan a large hand mirror. "Look good to you? Size, placement?"

He studied himself. Familiar skin, but stained with alien purple lines . . . perhaps to mimic the alien sensations she roused in him. "Perfect." He laughed softly, a touch hysterical.

She smiled. "What?"

"You're about to change me forever."

The smile deepened. "Tell me I already have."

He sat up and kissed her, humming his happiness, then said, "You have." Again he eyed her bare legs, hoping the sentiment was mutual.

"Last chance to abort," she said.

He shook his head. "Do it."

"It'll be nice to tattoo somebody I'm sleeping with," she said, organizing her tools. "I can straddle you for a better angle without it being a breach of decency."

"Oh, I suspect it would still be that."

"A welcome one, anyhow." She donned gloves and arranged pots of ink and the tattooing device itself.

"What's that called?" he asked. "A gun?"

"A machine." She unwrapped a gleaming new needle from a sterile sleeve.

"It looks positively medieval." Industrial, at any rate—as unapologetically mechanical as the guts of an old typewriter, Duncan thought, watching her prep it.

She rubbed a blob of ointment over his skin. "Almost magic time."

"Do you take pleasure from this?"

She grinned. "Oh, loads."

And did her clients ever take pleasure from it? Sexual pleasure? Duncan could imagine it. He wasn't sure he'd get there himself, as his pleasure never normally accompanied a physical surrender—his growing, newfound fondness for receiving oral sex aside—but surely any man with decent pain tolerance and who relished being at a woman's mercy could find some intrigue in this situation.

All at once she was at his side, machine buzzing. "Just hold still, breathe nice and slow and deep, and tell me when you need a break."

He nodded once, and shut his eyes.

But a moment later he opened them, wanting to see. Wanting to see purple lines filled in with pure black, wanting to watch those hands—hands that had spoiled him with so much contact, be it sweet or dark or hungry or kind—as they made a canvas of him.

It felt precisely as she'd described—a hot, scraping, tugging sensation. Uncomfortable, but not painful. It eased as the minutes wore on, until Duncan felt all but disembodied—numb and content. Now and then she wiped away the excess ink, revealing crisp black lines. The overall outline was thickest, and he watched, transfixed, as she moved on to the finer ones that shaped the valves, the cleft between the two lobes. The shading marks came next, giving it depth. Last of all, she traced those three letters, her own initials.

"Oh yes," she said, smiling at her busy hands. "Now, this is it. *This* is my gift."

"Better than a diamond bracelet?"

"To me it is."

He'd returned that outlandish token during his trip to San Diego. The money would be far better spent downstairs.

"Done?" he asked when she set the machine aside.

"Nearly." She ran a hand towel under the tap, and when she returned to him, she straddled his hips, skirt gathering between their middles.

"Why, hello."

"Hello." The cloth was warm, cleaning away the last of the extra ink. In a bright, physical rush, Duncan wanted her. His entire body was flushed, cock warming, muscles tensing, mouth dry. He grabbed her waist, pulling her against him.

"Is this my tip?" she asked, grinning.

"I'm not stingy." He moved against her, letting her feel his excitement. She answered with her own motions, and he was panting in seconds.

"This is wildly unprofessional," she whispered, even as her hips stroked their centers together, friction burning bright.

"Tell that to the old Duncan. He might be idiot enough to care."

"Hang on. Let's get the boring stuff out of the way." She escaped his groping, swabbed the tattoo, rubbed it with ointment, and dressed it with a neat gauze square framed in medical tape.

She snapped her gloves off, jacking Duncan's pulse. "Now, where were we?"

"Somewhere rather unethical."

She rinsed her hands, then twined his fingers with her damp ones. "Come."

And as she led him through the apartment, it was strange to think this bedroom had ever been anything but *theirs*.

Yours and mine. Ours. Her covers, and now his overpriced

sheets, full of scents and memories belonging solely to the two of them.

He pulled her down onto the bed, let her straddle him.

"Say it again," he murmured, holding her waist.

She lowered herself to her forearms, smile growing wicked. When their noses touched, she whispered, "I love you, Duncan Welch."

He shut his eyes and let those words warm him. Her breast glanced his bandage, and the tenderness it triggered felt so precisely, startlingly right. He held her tight, stroked her hair.

"Say it back," she whispered.

"I love you."

She sat up, smiling, and traced the tape framing the gauze with her fingertip. "Good. Now show me."

And he rolled her onto her back, showed her with his body every thrilling thing she made him feel, with the window open and the sun burning bright, for that entire, endless blue desert sky to see.

See how it all began for Raina and Miah in
Cara McKenna's next scorching-hot read,

DRIVE IT DEEP
A Desert Dogs Novella

Coming soon in May 2015 from InterMix in e-book.

Two summers back in Fortuity, Nevada

It was a lazy Tuesday in Benji's. The drone of the dozen patrons chatting in the big barroom melded with the hum of the AC and the crooning of Merle Haggard from the jukebox, all of it blending into a comforting, timeless hum that Jeremiah Church knew well. The only bar he'd ever really known, the warm and worn-out heart of the only town he'd ever called home . . .

The underlit place fit like an old leather jacket, smelled of wood and whiskey, and felt like an oasis from the baking July sun still blazing outside, even now at suppertime. Everything a bar ought to be, Miah thought, glancing around. He'd had a beer already and a fresh one sat before him, and the sentimentality that alcohol always soaked him in with was ripening, filling him with memories and an easy feeling of belonging. There were angry drunks, sloppy drunks, weepy drunks. Miah rarely ever got drunk, but when he did, it made him softhearted and nostalgic, emotions he normally didn't have the time for. Which was how alcohol ought to work, he felt. Like saddle oil for your soul.

There was just one thing missing from this scene . . . as elemental to this place as the wooden eaves or the sound of clinking glasses, and it had been missing since late January.

He turned to the front door as it swung in, and a grin split wide across his face.

"About goddamn time," Miah called. He sat up straight and swiveled his stool around, watching his best friend stride in. His best friend, whom he hadn't seen in his street clothes—or outside the penitentiary visitation room—in over five months. Vince Grossier, a free man once more.

A couple of the older drinkers in the corner shouted their greetings or waved, and Vince nodded their way.

Miah abandoned his untouched bottle on the counter and crossed the room. The two men's chests collided in a violent hug set to the sound of hands whapping backs.

Miah stepped away, holding Vince by the arms. "Goddamn, they really let your ass out, huh?"

"Not a minute sooner than they could, but here I am." Prison might diminish some men, but Vince looked just as he should in his jeans and boots and old leather bomber, his expression pure, eager mischief.

"Prison suit you or something?" Miah teased, leading Vince to the bar. "Aren't you supposed to be all regretful and haunted-looking? Or at least skinnier?" If anything Vince looked bigger. Miah supposed that could happen when all you had to pass the hours were chin-ups and crunches.

"I regret nothing," Vince declared, then slapped the bar. "Raina! Where are you, girl? Escaped convict in need of bourbon, here."

"She's changing a keg. Here." Miah offered Vince his own beer. "Haven't even tasted it yet."

"Nah, we need to toast." Vince slid the bottle back over. "I can wait."

"Yeah, you would know something about patience by now, huh? Five goddamn months . . ."

"Don't I fucking know it? And over an innocent little bar fight."

"Well, for about six fights in, like, two months."

Vince waved the semantics aside. "Whatever. Not a single one of them wasn't asking for it."

Miah took a drink of his neglected beer. "Sorry I couldn't have picked your ass up, Vince. My dad's hip surgery means I'm really on my own with all the stock duties." The demands of the cattle business eased for no man, and Miah was now the foreman of his family's Three C ranch, in charge of more than a couple dozen employees and the oversight of the stock and all manner of maintenance. He was lucky to have gotten off by seven this evening, but he still needed to be up and ready to start again by five.

"No worries," Vince said. "I know how bad that place has you whipped."

"And then some. So who brought you home?"

"Alex."

Miah laughed. "Police escort, huh? That fits." Their friend was a deputy with the Brush County sheriff's department. It was his boss, Sheriff Tremblay, who'd arrested Vince, and not for the first time. "Where's he now?"

"He went to drop his car back home. You know Alex."

Miah nodded, mood darkening. "Yeah, I do." And he knew if Alex Dunn was off duty and drinking tonight, he wouldn't be driving home. He'd barely be able to walk, in fact. Alex was an excellent deputy and a good man, and he'd never touch a drop until his workday was done, but it seemed lately that more often than not, if he had a sip, he wouldn't stop until he passed out.

It bothered Miah. A lot. He hoped his friend could get his shit together, but it seemed like the only time they saw each other nowadays was here in Benji's, and a bar was a fuck of a setting to tell your friend to get his drinking under control.

But tonight wasn't the time to be getting gloomy.

Tonight was a celebration. Miah had his best friend back again.

"Raina!" Vince shouted again.

"She'd better not hear you—" The sound of stomping boots cut Miah off, as the woman in question came marching in from the back room, door slamming shut behind her.

"Just who the fuck do you think you are," she demanded, "shouting at me like I'm some servant in my own fucking bar?"

Vince stood roughly, stool tottering. "'Scuse me, bitch?"

She made a beeline for him, dark hair bouncing with every livid step. "I've got half a mind to call the sheriff and get you shipped back downstate." But she dropped the angry shtick the second she reached Vince, grinning. "How you been, motherfucker?"

He hugged her hard, picking her up off the ground and swinging her around. She smacked his arm when he let her go. "Goddamn, it's good to see you."

"You too."

"What are you drinking?" she asked as she circled around to go behind the U-shaped bar.

"Beer and a shot."

"You got it." She cracked open a longneck, then grabbed a bottle from the highest shelf.

"Whoa now, don't break the bank," Vince said. "I got fines to pay off still, and no job yet."

"On the house." She poured three shots of the best bourbon and slid two of them across the wood. "Welcome home."

Miah lifted his. "Welcome home."

"Good to be back in this shit hole," Vince said, and they all drank, glasses clacking the wood in unison.

"Goddamn." Vince thumped the counter with his fist, his mouth surely stinging from that shot just as Miah's was. "Now *that* tastes like Fortuity."

Raina leaned on the bar, low enough to flash a deep shadow of cleavage between her breasts in that snug tank top. That was like her personal uniform—black tank and tight jeans, cowboy boots—and her wavy hair fell wild around her shoulders. Like Miah, she was half white, but her dark hair and eyes came from a Mexican mother, whereas Miah's came from his own mom's roots, Shoshone and Paiute.

He could remember the first fight he ever got in, and it had been because of Raina. He'd been in maybe fourth grade, Raina in second, and some boy whose name Miah had long forgotten had called her a mutt. The boy had been older, but Miah had busted him one in the nose and made him cry. He'd also nearly gotten grounded, until he'd reluctantly confessed to his mom what the fight had been about. Then her face had gone all funny, like she couldn't choose between a frown and a smile, and she'd sent him to his room with a half-assed order to go think about what he'd done.

The lesson he'd taken away from that had been if you're going to punch someone, don't punch a tattletale. But the real takeaway had been Raina—they became friends a few years later, and had remained close ever since.

She'd always been sexy to him, though he'd never fixated on her too much—it was more of an objective fact, her sexiness. She was a little too wild for his taste, or had been, back in their teens and early twenties. He'd disqualified her then as potential relationship material on the grounds that she'd slept with more people than he had. Now that they'd both entered their thirties, it was hard to care. Part of what made Raina so magnetic was her no-shits-given attitude, and that allure trumped his outgrown insecurities. After all, Miah had dated steady girl-friend after steady girlfriend, never had so much as a one-night stand in his life, and where had that gotten him? He'd been single for six months now, and he could feel the lack of sex nagging at him. He liked to imagine he was more evolved than Vince about that shit, but every man had his limits.

And lately, he couldn't seem to quit thinking about the woman currently standing just on the other side of this bar, smiling, laughing at a story Vince was telling. Single, like him. With no qualms about getting with someone for just one night, if that's all an affair was destined to be. Miah couldn't say if he wanted more than that, only that he wanted *her*. Badly. And the shot was wasn't helping. Made his morals feel all fuzzy and his body warm.

Ultimately, what he wanted was a wife and children: an inti-mate, reliable family unit like the one he'd been raised in. A soft place to land at the end of a long day—and all of his days were long. But before all of that materialized, maybe just once he ought to find out what it was like to be with a woman like Raina. Try a taste of that—a taste or a feast or whatever she might be into—for as long as it was meant to go on.

Vince started beside him, rocked by a hard clap on the back. He and Miah turned as one to find Alex behind them, and both got to their feet.

"Started without me, I see," Alex said, and accepted a half-hug from Miah.

"Making up for lost time," Vince said.

"What can I get you, Deputy?" Raina asked, though Alex was dressed down in jeans and tee shirt, his badge retired for the evening. His brown hair was freshly buzzed, reminding Miah of how he'd planned to joined the marines, back in high school. See the world and all that. But a motorcycle wreck when he was seventeen had fucked up his knee and those grand plans.

Raina slid him the requested double shot of whiskey, her smile tight, if Miah wasn't mistaken. Alex's drinking bothered her, he bet, as did her role as his bartender. Couldn't be much fun, having to cut your childhood friend off when he got messy.

"You know who ought to be here?" Vince asked, glancing at each of them. "My goddamn brother."

"Good luck," Raina said, smirking. Vince's little brother had left Fortuity seven years ago and hadn't been back since. Without that dumbass around, there was something missing. A certain foulmouthed levity. The five of them had been tight all through junior high, high school, and after. They'd named their little gang the Desert Dogs way back when Miah, Vince, and Alex had been in, what? Sixth grade, maybe. Raina and Casey had been a couple years behind, but tenacious in their tagging along.

"You tell Case you were getting out?" Miah asked Vince.

"Left him a message last week, but I was never gonna hold my breath."

"Where's he at? Not Vegas, still?" Alex asked.

"No, he's been bouncing around, it sounds like. Same number though. Last I knew he'd moved to Texas," Vince said. "Hang on—I need a smoke."

Miah rolled his eyes.

"What? You think I'm gonna magically quit while I'm in *prison*? Everybody gets a vice, Church. Wish you'd find yourself one."

Miah was glad Raina was busy with a customer. Her dad had died of lung cancer barely a year ago, and it felt insensitive, somehow. Then again, Vince had never been one to tone himself down out of consideration for others' sore spots.

"I'll make you a deal someday," Miah said. "You quit smoking, and I'll do most anything you could name, in exchange."

"How about," Vince said, smiling, "I *keep* smoking, and you go and get yourself laid and loosen the fuck up?"

"Ohhh," Alex groaned, wincing, then laughing. "Fucking mean, Grossier."

"Fucking true," he said, standing. "How long's it been, Church?"

Six long-ass months. "No comment."

"I rest my case," Vince said, and headed for the door.

Miah eyed Raina, struck anew by how everything about her body so perfectly matched her personality. She could be hard and stubborn, and you saw that in her shoulders and the bold shape of her collarbone, the set of her jaw. She was sexual, too, and that aggressive femininity was reflected in the way her hips and her backside flared out from her long waist. She moved like she spoke, with confidence and self-possession and no apology, like she had every right to be moving through this world and you might just want to keep out of her way. She'd always been like that. Known exactly who she was for as long as Miah could remember.

They'd never dated or really hooked up, though they had seen each other naked back in their days of group skinny-dipping in the creek—hardly a coup. The youth of Fortuity were not a modest crowd. Miah and Raina had made out once, too, in their early twenties, at a big barbecue at the ranch, but Miah barely remembered it. They'd both been wasted, and it had felt more like a dare than a romantic impulse. All he could recall about it was the taste of pepper and whiskey on her lips, and the sounds of their friends catcalling them in the background.

He remembered watching her at her dad's funeral, last summer. He'd never seen her cry before, and she'd looked absolutely pissed off, like her own eyes had betrayed her. Her hug had been stiff as a statue that day, her hands cold as stone. He'd felt them through his shirt. He might have even begun falling for her a little, way back in that moment. She hadn't gone to pieces sobbing, but in the rigidness of her body and in the tight, shallow pitch of her breathing, he'd felt something he'd not ever sensed from her before. Vulnerability. Softness hiding behind that hard, willful shell. She hadn't clung to him; quite the opposite. But in that closed-up, cagey hug, she'd been as frail as he'd ever felt her. As *real* as she'd ever felt to him.

They'd known each other for ages, but until that hug, he'd never been in danger of losing track of his head with Raina Harper. Sure, he'd noticed her body plenty of times, but he'd never really imagined what it'd be like to kiss her for real, or touch her hair, or feel the weight of her in his lap or those muscles moving against him. It had almost been as though he'd never noticed what color her eyes were. A revelation, discovering that feelings hid behind that attitude, that cool self-possession, that aggressive breed of femininity.

They had a past, too, countless shared memories. Twenty years or more of friendship, and that counted for a lot with Miah. History. She'd always been fun and a touch intimidating, but that day at the funeral, she'd become more. He hadn't seen her the same way since.

Unlike his best friend, Miah couldn't get hot over just any attractive woman. He had to feel something first. Attachment turned him on, and possession lit him on fire. Familiarity and affection got him as hot as a beautiful pair of breasts or a stunning face. As a result, Vince had called him a pussy a thousand times in the past fifteen years, but Miah didn't care. If you were going to sleep with someone you didn't feel something for, what was the point? Why not just jack off, if it was as impersonal as scratching some biological itch? Save everybody involved an awkward morning after.

Miah didn't want sex to be convenient, or opportunistic. Sex should be memorable and meaningful, and hopefully kick off the start of something real and intense and maybe even for keeps. Not some in-and-out transaction of necessity, like pulling into a goddamn gas station.

He studied Raina, standing barely three feet from him, talking to Alex. Her smile made his body flash hot, and when her gaze met his, his breath was gone. Just as quick, she turned away.

These past two evenings, there'd been a little *something*, hadn't there? He'd come by last night and the one before, needing a drink to dull his frustration toward a problem employee, and a little time away from the ranch. Her gaze had lingered on his longer than usual, he'd thought, and his own gaze had been lingering more and more, lately, as his celibacy wore on. Could she tell that something had shifted in him this past year? That his attraction was no longer a moment of curiosity now and then, but nearly an infatuation? Probably. She could probably smell it like a shark detecting a drop of blood through a mile of ocean.

Vince returned from his smoke break.

"Another?" Raina asked him.

He looked to Miah. "Pitcher?"

Miah shook his head. "Pacing myself." Unlike Alex or Vince, he couldn't get tanked and walk home later—the ranch was way out at the eastern edge of Fortuity.

Raina handed Vince a fresh bottle. "So what are you going to do, now you're finally out?"

Vince took a deep gulp. "I'm going to get drunk, and I'm going to get laid. Probably in that order."

"I meant for work," Raina said, "but okay, those sound good, too. And I can help you with the first one." She grabbed his shot glass and the bottle of bourbon.

"Help me with both, if you want," Vince said, leaning on the bar and flashing her one of his shameless smiles.

Miah rankled but kept his temper in check. He had no claims on Raina, these past couple nights' new heat notwithstanding. Plus he doubted there was much behind Vince's pass aside from five months' pent-up testosterone. Vince and Raina had had their whole lives to turn into something, but never had. Miah knew that for a fact—his best friend wasn't exactly discreet about his conquests.

She set the shot before Vince. "No, thanks."

Vince craned his big body to scan the barroom, but only a few new faces had arrived, and none were female. "When do your hands get off work?" he asked Miah.

"Leave my poor employees alone. Most of those girls are ten years younger than you."

"And some of the biggest flirts I've ever seen," Raina added, grinning. "I really don't think they need any protecting, Miah. If they can handle themselves with all those steer, they can handle Vince."

"I'm not choosy who handles me tonight," Vince said, and downed his shot. "Most any willing party will do."

Miah shook his head. "Know what's sexier than consent, Vince? Enthusiasm."

Raina smiled, and Alex laughed.

"You spend a few months in jail," Vince cut back, "and see how high your standards are when you get out. Hey, now—here we go."

A group not short on women had arrived along with the dusk. From there the evening took a sharp turn, as more young folks arrived and the jukebox got in the mood for dancing. They moved tables aside, and the grumpy old men shuffled out into the night. Raina shut the windows and switched off the AC as the sky outside went black and the din of chatter and laughter rose.

Vince was on the hunt in due time, and Raina grew busy with orders. Miah talked with Alex for two hours or more, until a whiskey glaze dulled his friend's eyes and the conversation grew stilted and a touch slurred. It cooled Miah's own interest in drinking, and he let his beer grow warm.

A good dozen ranch hands had arrived, and after a few rounds they lost their inhibitions about Miah being their boss, and tried to get him to dance, one of the girls tugging on his wrist.

"No fucking way. You kids'll never respect me again."

Raina watched with a smirk on her lips as he continued to deflect. "Go on, cowboy. Let's see your moves."

"You ever seen me dance, ever, in our entire lives?" he asked, just as the hands all rushed to the dance floor at the opening notes of some popular song.

"Junior high semiformal," Raina said.

"That doesn't count as dancing—that's just shuffling around in a circle."

"You never shuffled with me," she countered, affecting a pout she'd never actually wear in earnest.

"You were twelve when I was fourteen. I have some dignity, you know."

"'Nother, please," Alex said, sliding his empty tumbler across the bar.

"You are cut off, Deputy," Raina told him cheerfully. Her tone was light and chiding, but Miah could see tension hiding behind it in the set of her jaw.

"Oh, come on."

"I've got water, ginger ale, Coke, Sprite . . ."

"Fine, fine. Water."

She poured him a big glass, but Alex drank only half before declaring he was tired and heading home.

"Need a lift?" Miah asked him.

"Nah, I'm good." As he got to his feet, a sway in Alex's step contradicted this statement. Miah considered insisting, but then made the fateful mistake of glancing at Raina. If he dropped Alex off, he might as well just go home himself. It was after one, and Vince had already disappeared, presumably with a woman. Miah was done drinking and had no good reason to come back . . . yet he wasn't ready to go. He felt like tonight was the night. He needed to make a move on her, take the temperature of the situation and find out if he had it wrong or not. If Raina wasn't feeling anything, no problem. Better that way, even, as he could snap out of this spell and quit fixating on her.

And if she did feel something? His blood pumped quicker, just imagining it. Imagining leaning in, kissing her, pulling her against him.

And so he bade Alex a good night and told him to walk safe, because he wasn't going anywhere until last call. Not until he knew, once and for all, whether this strange new energy between them was all in his imagination, or as real as electricity.

Last call arrived in a blink. Raina clanged the bell, drink orders were placed and filled, and still Miah sat there losing his nerve, utterly unsure how or even whether to make a move. His employees shouted their good-nights, and the crowd dwindled, and dwindled, until it was just him and Raina and a handful of others.

In time, voices at his back called out parting words to Raina, who smiled and saluted from the register she was counting out. The door creaked shut behind Miah and he craned his neck.

Just him, now. Him and her. Alone together, for the first time in who could guess how long.

Raina came by, wiping down the counter. "Another?"

He shook his head, and she smiled.

"Don't tell me you're here for the charming company," she said, looking around demonstrably at the deserted barroom. "Because that's way too much pressure on me."

He shrugged. "So what if I am? It's been a while since we had a chance to chat, you and me."

"I saw you last night, and the night before. That's more than usual."

"I suppose."

"Does that mean I'm extra interesting all of a sudden, or that life isn't all peaches and cream back at Three C?"

His turn to smile. "Little of both."

"Do me a favor," she said, and pulled two shot glasses out of the steaming glass washer. "Lock that door for me."

Miah rose and did as she asked, flipping the dead bolt. The parking lot was empty, save for his truck.

He returned to the bar to find Raina tilting the bourbon bottle to the glasses. She instructed, "Now drink this."

"I need to drive home."

"One little shot won't hurt you. It's been two hours since I handed you a beer."

"Tell me why, first."

She bit her lip, that coy little gesture from this normally brazen woman making Miah's head spin. He didn't need the goddamn shot.

"Because I want to ask you something," she said.

His heart beat quicker as he spoke, a spark of hope flickering in his chest, itching to catch fire. "Something you can't ask me sober?"

She nodded to his shot and he lifted it. They downed them together.

She set hers aside, staring at the empty glass as she let the sting of the liquor cool, tongue tracing her front teeth. Miah felt that same fire on his own lips, and the fever spread through his neck and chest as her gaze snapped to his.

"There's been something different lately, hasn't there?"

Miah froze, unsure if she meant what he hoped she did. What he *prayed* she did. "How do you mean?"

She smiled and leaned on the bar. "You've been looking at me different. And I noticed because I've always looked at you."

His face flushed hot and all his charm abandoned him. "Have you?" He felt lucky he hadn't stammered those words.

"Of course I have. You're the most handsome man in Fortuity."

"I don't remember being given a tiara."

She laughed. "You, though—you've never really looked at me, like that. Not aside from the occasional glance down my shirt."

Now he was definitely blushing. Though he couldn't deny it. "Sorry."

"Don't be. Why do you think I wear these?" she asked, plucking at the lace straps of her tank top.

He took a breath, and said, "I guess I have noticed you, lately. Different from before."

She smiled and stood a little straighter. "Better late than never, I guess."

Was that some kind of confession? A green light? And shit, if it was, what did he want to do about it? What did *she* want to do about it? Should he ask her on a date, or—

Her dark eyes narrowed. "You want to kiss or something?"

Miah paused; then the truth shoved rational thought aside. That shot could have been half the bottle for how woozy he felt. He nodded. "I think I would."

Her smile deepened. "Help me close up, then."

He did, accepting a damp towel, wiping down the tables in a hot haze, putting up the stools and chairs in a weird, disembodied rush.

He was going to kiss Raina Harper.

For real, this time, and sober. His friend of twenty years or more.

Christ, was this a terrible idea? Or completely natural?

"Looks good," she said from behind him.

He turned, finding her drying her hands on her bar towel, approaching with slow, lazy steps. There was something in her eyes . . . something hot. Something hot and playful he didn't think he'd ever seen there before. Miah swallowed and set the final chair upside down on its high top.

"So do you," he said, probably too late for it to even make sense, let alone sound smooth or clever. Raina just smiled, stepping closer, until there were perhaps two paces between the toes of their boots. Without thought, he gave voice to his worries, barely louder than a whisper.

"We about to wreck a good friendship?"

She blinked. "Since when did kissing have that kind of power?"

Since when does it not?

Miah had never dated a friend before, and never stayed close with an ex. Too awkward, too . . . too something. Something that made him uncomfortable. Whether you got hurt or did the hurting, how could you get back on equal footing? Perhaps with good friends, as he and Raina were, no kiss could undo all those years already invested. He hoped, he hoped. And something inside him—something taut and fiery and ready to snap—told him to quit with the worrying and take the chance, find the fuck out.

He reached out, and he touched her. Put his fingertips to her neck, and slowly, softly, curled his palm to cup her jaw. Her cheek was soft where his thumb stroked, and he got lost in that tiny touch for long seconds, feeling high. Hypnotized. She clasped his wrist—not stopping him, not urging him, only holding. He freed his fingers to lace them with hers, studying their two hands. He sensed her gaze on his face, but he was lost in the feel of his bare skin against hers.

"I always imagined if this happened," she murmured, "that we'd be completely shitfaced."

He laughed, the spell broken, but this new moment was just as fascinating. He met her eyes. "You always imagined this would happen?"

She shrugged. "I wondered, when we were younger. Then I figured you just didn't feel anything like that for me. But I was always curious about you. About us, and what it would be like if we ever went there, together. But by the time I was twenty-five, I knew how to tell if a guy was into me. And with you, I just never felt it. Not until this week."

"I didn't really let myself feel it, until recently."

She touched his hair, toying with an overgrown lock and tucking it behind his ear. "What changed?"

He didn't want to bring up her dad's funeral and the slow,

steady evolution of his feelings, so he fibbed. "Maybe your being away in Vegas made me notice you more once you got back. Plus now's the first time we've both been single in a long time. And I'm not the sort of man who gets designs on other guys' girlfriends."

"No, you're not. And here we are. Both single, like you said. Both here." She tilted her face up and her nose brushed his. He felt his brain dissolve and the room fall away. Her lips were there, right there.

He whispered, "You remember the last time we kissed?"

"The only time we ever kissed. At that cookout. You were completely plastered."

"Weren't you?"

She smiled, their noses glancing again when she shook her head. "Not really. And I guess maybe you weren't too drunk to remember."

"It's a little hazy," he admitted. "How were we?"

That smile deepened to a grin and she touched his chest, traced his collar. "We were pretty fucking hot together."

"Even drunk?"

"Oh yes. You can kiss, cowboy."

He swallowed, his pride so inflated it was filling his heart up tight like a balloon. "Good to know."

"It's probably been ten years, though. So feel free to refresh my memory."

And he did. Dove right in. He cradled her head, fingers tangling in her wavy hair, and pressed his lips to hers. He felt that kiss like a lightning strike, like a heat wave, like a million perfect clichés converging between their bodies.

Her mouth was hungry and he took her cues, tasting her deeply. No place for slow and steady with this fast, wild woman.

They kissed like they'd practiced this for hours, days, years. Like a dance their lips and tongues had mastered and made their own. He felt crazy from it, and let her hear it, moaning as she tugged him closer by the belt. Raina was tall, though he felt every one of the four or so inches he had on her. Felt big in the best way, aggressive like he had to get on top of her, push his body into hers. Unleash these feelings like a caged and angry animal.

Goddamn, no woman had ever done this to Miah before. Not like this. Not from sex, let alone *kissing*. All those things that got him so hot in a new relationship were gathering deep and low in his body. Possession and familiarity. He knew her, better than any other woman he'd done this with. And he wanted her all to himself. Wanted to be hers and to call her his in return. Wanted to make her feel all these things with his body.

He held her head, slid his other palm down her back and pulled her close—close enough to register exactly how hard he was when her flat belly pressed along his fly. He groaned against her lips as her pawing hands stroked his arms, his chest, his face.

Suddenly, big as it was, the barroom was too tight. Not intimate—just crowded, even in its emptiness, the high ceiling looming much too close. Miah's claustrophobia always got worse the hotter his body was. Normally that meant he was frustrated or overheated from physical labor, but just now it was from pure lust. He needed the open air and the black sky and a million stars above them, night chill be damned.

"Come outside," he murmured, gathering her wavy hair in his hands, aching to bury his nose behind her ear and breathe her in, get drunk off her. Feel her skin against his palm and her nails on his back, hear her voice saying his name as he drove his body into hers, again and again. Fucking crazy.

"What for?" she asked, but her sharp smile said she knew exactly what for.

"For whatever's supposed to happen between us next."

She stroked his cheek, dragged her thumb across his lower lip. He caught it in his mouth and drew it deep. That parted her own lips, and dropped her lids low. Low, like the blood flowing south to leave Miah's cock heavy and hot and hurting.

"Outside?" she echoed.

"Outside. Now." And if he didn't goddamn get *inside* her tonight, he was going to lose his ever-loving mind.

LOVE
ROMANCE
NOVELS?

For news on all your favorite romance authors,
sneak peeks into the newest releases, book
giveaways, and much more—

"Like" Love Always on Facebook!
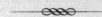 **LoveAlwaysBooks**